A NEW DAWN FOR THE MILL GIRLS

PART 1 OF THE LOCKWOOD INHERITANCE

CHRISSIE WALSH

Boldwood

First published in Great Britain in 2025 by Boldwood Books Ltd.

Copyright © Chrissie Walsh, 2025

Cover Design by Colin Thomas

Cover Images: Colin Thomas

The moral right of Chrissie Walsh to be identified as the author of this work has been asserted in accordance with the Copyright, Designs and Patents Act 1988.

All rights reserved. No part of this book may be reproduced in any form or by any electronic or mechanical means, including information storage and retrieval systems, without written permission from the author, except for the use of brief quotations in a book review. This book is a work of fiction and, except in the case of historical fact, any resemblance to actual persons, living or dead, is purely coincidental.

Every effort has been made to obtain the necessary permissions with reference to copyright material, both illustrative and quoted. We apologise for any omissions in this respect and will be pleased to make the appropriate acknowledgements in any future edition.

A CIP catalogue record for this book is available from the British Library.

Paperback ISBN 978-1-83633-402-6

Large Print ISBN 978-1-83633-403-3

Hardback ISBN 978-1-83633-401-9

Ebook ISBN 978-1-83633-404-0

Kindle ISBN 978-1-83633-405-7

Audio CD ISBN 978-1-83633-396-8

MP3 CD ISBN 978-1-83633-397-5

Digital audio download ISBN 978-1-83633-400-2

This book is printed on certified sustainable paper. Boldwood Books is dedicated to putting sustainability at the heart of our business. For more information please visit https://www.boldwoodbooks.com/about-us/sustainability/

Boldwood Books Ltd, 23 Bowerdean Street, London, SW6 3TN

www.boldwoodbooks.com

For my family

1

ALMONDBURY, WEST YORKSHIRE, APRIL 1897

Crash! The sound of breaking glass echoed in the stillness of the night.

Startled, Verity Lockwood let the book she was reading fall from her hands, and swinging her long, slender legs over the side of the bed, she perched on the edge, uncertain as to what she should do. The sound had come from below, and with her breathing pent and her ears pricked, she waited and listened, flinching when she heard the dull thuds of heavy objects hitting hard surfaces.

A glance at the clock on the mantelpiece told her it was a quarter after midnight. Had the house been broken into by robbers?

Her limbs trembling, Verity crossed the bedroom floor, her feet making no sound on the thick carpet and her palm moist against the doorknob as she turned it. Inching the door ajar, she peered cautiously into the gloom on the landing then, widening the gap, she crept out to the head of the stairs and, leaning against the balustrade, she listened. The noises had ceased, the silence thickening round her.

Earlier in the week, she had returned to live with her father at Far View House in Almondbury, the house where she had been born twenty-one years ago and that had intermittently been her home in between boarding school and the homes of different relatives. For the past five years, she had been residing with her aunt in Leeds, and now, feeling like a stranger in the known yet unfamiliar surroundings, she waited and listened, deliberating on what to do next.

The single oil lamp in the hallway glowed eerily and Verity's shadow performed a grotesque dance as she slowly descended the wide, sweeping staircase.

In front of her, the solid oak front door was fast shut: no sign of a forced entry.

Breathing a sigh of relief and wondering if she had imagined the noises, she stepped forward, the flagstones cold against her bare feet.

Then, from behind the drawing-room door, she heard the sound of someone moving and almost leapt out of her skin as a strangled roar split the night. No longer afraid of robbers, she still had to steel herself before finding enough courage to open the door.

'Father! What are you doing?'

Verity stared, shocked at the disarray. Scattered about the overturned side tables were the remains of a porcelain salver and a carved wooden cigar box, its lid askew and its contents littering the rug. Next to it, its head parted from its body, was a bronze figurine of Queen Victoria. In the hearth were the shattered remains of a large, crystal decanter.

Jebediah Lockwood swayed on his feet, brandy slopping from the glass in his hand. Blearily, his eyes focused on his daughter, his expression a mixture of puzzlement and surprise as though he was trying to register who she was. His lips curled into a sneer and his florid face rutted into a malevolent glare.

'What be thee doin' here, tha grett, gawky witch?' he snarled. 'Bugger off back to bed an' leave me in peace.'

Smarting at the insult, Verity stood her ground. 'You've had too much to drink, Father. It's you who needs to go to your bed.'

Verity's sharp retort took Jeb by surprise. He hadn't expected her to defy him.

'Sez who? Since when did I need thee to tell me what to do?' he blustered, and shambling across to the sideboard, he grabbed the nearest carafe and poured until it was empty. Amber liquid sloshed into the glass, spilling out over the brim and puddling on the polished wood before trickling onto the rug.

'You've had enough to drink already,' Verity cried, and rushing over to the sideboard, she placed herself squarely in front of it and the overflowing glass.

'When I need thee to tell me what to do, I'll bloody ask,' Jeb roared, slamming down the empty carafe then lunging for the glass behind Verity's back. When she deflected him at every move, his outstretched hand curled into a fist.

Verity ducked, but not quick enough to avoid the sharp blow that caught her cheekbone. She reeled sideways, her cheek throbbing and her eyes watering.

Smirking at her pain, her father shook his fist in her face.

Verity, too proud to rub where it smarted, stood her ground and Jeb, goaded by her defiant glare, lashed out to strike again, and would have done so had not the toe of his boot caught on the edge of the rug. He staggered and fell.

She gazed at the heavily set figure sprawled on the floor, a feeling of deep sadness and disgust enveloping her as she watched him flounder.

'Don't just stand there tha grett, gormless bugger. Help me up.'

Verity placed her hands under his armpits, and screwing her face as though she was handling something distasteful, she heaved him to his feet.

When he was upright, their faces were on a level and the foul mix of strong tobacco and brandy on Jeb's breath wafted up her nose. She pulled away from him, leaving him swaying and in danger of falling again. Then, assailed by an unexpected urge to prevent this, she put her arms round his thick waist and chivvied him across the room, Jeb protesting loudly.

Seething with anger, Verity pushed him on the couch. He lay back, snuffling and snorting, his sparse, grey hair on end and a stream of spittle snaking its way down his whiskered chin. He looked her up and down and sneered.

'It's a good job for me thas as tall as many a lad an' as strappin' as a bloody ox,' he slurred, sarcasm like treacle on his tongue. 'But then, tha allus wa' a grett, ugly lump. Pity tha didn't tek after thi mother. She wa'...' His bloodshot eyes drooped and his head lolled to one side as he lost consciousness.

Hurt by his cruel remarks, and shocked by his drunken rampaging, Verity dowsed the lamps and went back up to her bedroom. Her father hadn't welcomed her arrival, and now five days later, days in which she had seen little of him, he had let her know just what he thought of her. Laid back on her pillows, her eyes closed, she viewed the future with despair.

* * *

The next morning, Friday, on her way to the dining room for breakfast, Verity peeped into the drawing room. The couch was empty, the wreckage cleared. Clara Medley must have made an early start. Maybe the housekeeper was well used to her master's violent, drunken outbursts and took them in her stride. Verity didn't think she herself could tolerate such dreadful behaviour, but what could she do? It wasn't as if she had any options. She had very little money of her own and nowhere else to live. Shrouded in despondence, she went and sat down at the dining-room table.

Her father didn't appear for breakfast. When Mrs Medley served up a boiled egg and toast, she made no mention of the havoc in the drawing room, and neither did Verity.

'Thi Aunt Martha will be joining thi for dinner tonight. She allus comes on Fridays,' Clara announced as she set down the teapot. 'Is there owt else I can get thi?'

Verity told her no, and after she had finished eating, she went upstairs to her bedroom. It was a large room, furnished with dated pieces of dark furniture: a walnut wardrobe big enough to house a family in which her few garments hung – a blue dress and another in brown, both past their best, and two skirts and blouses also well worn. Only her fine, woollen, mauve suit seemed to be worthy of hanging in such a space. The dressing table with six deep drawers – most of them empty – housed her underwear, and her hairbrushes, ribbons and pins. Her sewing box sat on top. The half-canopied double bed with tables either side dominated the room, and at its foot, a rattan chest held her best button boots and a pair of grey kid shoes. She had yet to stamp her personality on the room and as she crossed to the wardrobe and then the dressing table, she was conscious of the air of disuse that the room exuded.

Sitting on a low chair by the partially opened window that overlooked the front gardens and driveway, she mended the hem of her brown dress then read her book. At midday, Mrs Medley brought up a sandwich of cold beef and a cup of tea, and although the weather outside looked inviting, Verity kept to her room until early evening when she heard the sound of cart wheels on the gravel. Aunt Martha had arrived. Verity went down to greet her.

In the hallway, she dropped a kiss on her aunt's plump cheek. It smelled of chocolate; Aunt Martha had a voracious appetite for sweet treats. Verity had called on her the day after she had arrived back from her lengthy stay with Aunt Flora in Leeds and Martha had welcomed her fulsomely, plying her with tea and Madeira sponge cake and telling her how much she had missed her company. Unlike her father, who seemed to be avoiding her.

Verity helped her aunt out of her cape and hung up her bonnet before ushering her into the dining room.

'Is your father home from the mill, Verity?'

'I couldn't say. I've barely seen him since I came home.'

She thought it wise not to mention the debacle of the previous night.

Martha gave a disapproving sniff and sat down at the table. She seemed lost in thought. Verity took her seat, and in the ensuing silence, she wondered how her father would greet her when next she saw him. Would he remember what he had said and done last night?

She didn't have to wait long to find out.

Wheels on the gravel then the slam of the front door signalled Jeb's arrival. He barged into the dining room, his ravaged face bloated with the excesses of alcohol.

'Martha,' he barked by way of a greeting as he slumped into his chair at the head of the table. Ignoring Verity, he filled a cut-crystal glass to the brim from the decanter on the table then emptied it in one huge gulp.

'You're drinking far more than is good for thi, Jebediah. It'll be the death of ye.'

Martha Boothroyd's sharp rebuke had little effect on her brother. Jeb refilled his glass, his shaky hand slopping dark brown spots of brandy on the white, damask cloth. He rubbed at them with his meaty paw.

'Mayhap that's why thy business is going down the drain,' Martha continued, her sour expression deepening the creases in her fleshy face until her gimlet eyes all but disappeared.

'Thee mind thy business an' I'll mind mine,' Jeb Lockwood growled, his whiskered jowls wobbling with suppressed rage as he slammed his empty glass on the table and reached for the decanter again.

In the basement kitchen, Clara was loading a large wooden tray when her husband came in. 'Master's back,' he grunted. Clara lifted the tray and plodded up the backstairs. In the dining room, she ungraciously plonked platters, tureens and a jug on the table then asked, 'Will that do thi?'

'Tell Medley we need more brandy.' Jeb poked a finger at the depleted decanter.

Clara mumbled something unintelligible and trudged back downstairs.

Martha glared at her brother, and sniffing her contempt, she helped herself to two succulent lamb chops from the platter then scooped a more than generous amount of mashed potato from one of the porcelain tureens. Next, she spooned up a liberal pile of greens and a large slice of Yorkshire pudding. 'Pass me the gravy boat, Verity,' she ordered.

Her niece did as she asked, at the same time silently telling herself, *And whilst you, dear aunt, eat yourself to death and my father hastens his demise with strong drink, I will wither away in Far View*

House, and neither of you will notice when I am no longer here. She let her gaze roam the drab room with its faded wallpaper and dusty wood panelling, her eyes settling on her father's face, square-jawed and framed with untidy, whiskery sideburns under sparse straggles of greasy hair raked across his balding scalp. Not a handsome man by any means, but then, she thought fleetingly, I'm no beauty.

They continued eating, Jeb alternatively sloshing and slurping as he shovelled in food and washed it down with swigs of brandy. Martha sucked noisily at the meat and fat on her chop bones and Verity, feeling faintly nauseous, picked at her plate, her appetite waning as the tension in the room swelled.

'An' any roads, who told thee my business wa' in trouble?' Jeb loudly demanded, the purple veins in his florid cheeks darkening as he clattered his knife and fork on his plate.

'It's common knowledge in the valley, Jeb. Tha spends so much time carousing in the watering holes in Huddersfield tha's no idea what's going on. Tis on'y the decency of Oliver Hardcastle that keeps Lockwood Mill running, that an' him not wanting it to go belly-up an' leave goodness knows how many men, women and children without earnings.' Martha spoke with conviction and Verity was surprised by her grasp of a situation she herself knew nothing about but that Jeb certainly did, judging by the venomous look that he gave Martha.

'Is the mill in difficulty, Father?' Verity turned her clear, grey eyes on her father and looked searchingly at him.

'Nowt to do wi' thee,' Jeb roared, glaring malevolently at her. 'Bloody interferin' women. Tha knows nowt abaht runnin' a mill an' mekkin' cloth an' I'll be damned if I'm going to listen to thee pratin' on.' He thrust back his chair with such force that it crashed to the floor, and on unsteady feet, he stamped from the room.

Verity and Martha exchanged despairing glances.

'Medley, bring t'trap round to t'front door,' they heard Jeb bellow from the hallway.

In the basement kitchen, Albert Medley pulled a sour face and pushed his half-eaten dinner aside. 'Bloody hell. T'master must want tekkin back into town.' He stood and put on his cape and then his cap, his expression that of a man going to the gallows. 'I'll be back late; don't wait up, Clara.'

His wife looked up from the pot she was scouring at the sink and shrugged.

'Another night's boozing an' we not paid us wages for the last two months. Remind him o' that, if you dare,' she scoffed, banging the pot down hard on the draining board.

Cursing under his breath, Albert scooted out of the back door.

In the front hall, Jeb paced impatiently until he heard the rattle of the trap's wheels on the gravel sweep. He blundered out, slamming the door behind him. The sound reverberated through the house, Verity flinching and her aunt tutting her annoyance.

'He'll be for the Pack Horse or the Fleece. Tha'll not see him till tomorrow,' Martha dourly predicted. 'He's not welcome in the inns in Almondbury wi' out he has any brass to settle what he already owes. He has to go traipsing into Huddersfield running up more debts to quench his thirst.' She scraped the last spoonful of treacle tart from her plate and chewed on it before addressing her niece authoritatively. 'Tha needs to mek him see sense, Verity, or tha'll be out on t'street afore the year's over.'

Startled by the remark, Verity clattered her spoon on her plate. 'And how might I do that, Aunt? I barely know him, and he's made it quite plain he has no regard for me.'

The hurtful names he had called her the previous night still stung. Her fingers strayed to her bruised cheek, still sore from where her father had hit her.

'Aye, well, tha mun find a way. It's up to thee, lass,' Martha wheezed. Then pressing the flat of her hands on the table, she eased her rotund body out of her chair. 'I'll be off now, back to a bit o' peace in me own home though goodness knows I'll not enjoy the walk,' she groused as she waddled to the door into the hallway.

Verity got up and followed her.

Martha had arrived at Far View House in a trap driven by the local carter and had expected to be driven back home by Medley, but now that Jeb had dragged him off to Huddersfield, she felt extremely disgruntled. 'That brother o' mine is thoughtless beyond words,' she grumbled as she donned her black cape and bonnet, widow's weeds she had worn since the passing of her husband, Joseph Boothroyd, some five years before.

'I'll walk with you, Aunt,' Verity offered. 'The evening air will be refreshing, and I wouldn't want you to have to take the slope unaccompanied.' The steep incline that led from her own home to that of her aunt's at the foot of the hill could be taxing enough for an obese woman of Martha's age.

'That's kind of you, child,' Martha said as she tied her bonnet strings.

Verity put on her coat and together they walked down the short, gravelled drive edged with overgrown rhododendrons and straggling daffodils that pushed their golden heads through a tangle of weeds and grasses. Albert had left the rusted, wrought-iron gates open and the two women passed between the tall sandstone pillars topped with eagles – one of them missing its head – and out into the road ready to make the descent.

Far View House stood at the top of a hill of the same name in the village of Almondbury some two miles from Huddersfield town. It had been built in the 1790s by Jeb's grandfather, Ezra, about the same time as he had founded Lockwood Mill, a cloth manufactory at Aspley Wharfe on the banks of the fast-flowing River Colne. A substantial mansion with four reception rooms and bedrooms above, and a basement kitchen and stores below, it dominated the landscape just as Ezra had intended it should do, but now the paintwork on the doors and windows was peeling and the gardens a wilderness.

Verity proffered Martha her arm, her aunt leaning heavily on it as they descended the steep slope at a steady plod. Short of stature, the top of Martha's head barely reached her niece's shoulder. Below them, the lights of the village gleamed softly in the twilight, and in the distance, wisps of black smoke spiralled up into the darkening sky from the mill chimneys, their fires damped for the night.

'Tha'll need to get a grip on thi dad's spending else he'll end up in the debtor's court,' Martha panted as yet again, she attempted to make Verity share her concern. 'Tis a pity tha doesn't have a rich husband lined up to bail him out.'

Verity snorted at the idea. 'I've no intentions of marrying simply to help Father out of the hole he's dug for himself. He's done little for me in the past.'

'Aye, that be true.' Martha's voice was heavy with regret.

'How long is it that he's been neglecting the mill?'

'Too long. But then he never did care for it. Nor his father afore him. They're not cut from the same cloth as thy great-grandfather, Ezra. He worked his fingers to the bone to make a profit but your grandfather, Amos, expected to live off it wi'out doin' a hand's turn, and your father's no different. It can't go on forever, an' soon there'll be nowt left to be had.'

'What do *you* think *I* should do, Aunt?' Anxiety coloured Verity's words.

Martha sighed heavily. 'I've no idea, child. Short o' stitching his lips together or getting him to sign the pledge, I don't think there's owt you can do about your father, but it 'ud be a shame to see Lockwood Mill go out o' business.'

They were now at the foot of the incline, and a few more paces brought them to Martha's house. Not as grand as Far View, it was larger than its neighbours and had been in Martha's late husband's family for three generations. She lived alone, and with the help of a woman who came in to cook and clean each day, she was content to spend her days sitting with her feet up, nibbling biscuits and drinking tea. Every Friday evening, she ventured out to take dinner with her brother, and now that her niece was back home, she had been looking forward to the occasion. Sadly, it had turned out to be less than pleasant. And Jeb was to blame for that. He had always been a boozer, but of late, his desire for strong drink had got out of hand, and now the rumour about the mill being in difficulties had her fearing for his and Verity's future if the gossip turned out to be true.

'Will tha come in, lass?' Martha asked as she turned the key in her front door.

'Just for a minute, Aunt. I'll see you settled then I'll be off.' Verity had no desire to listen to her aunt denigrating her father, not that he didn't deserve it. He did, and more. It saddened her to think that she felt no affection for him, or he for her for that matter. But to stay and listen to her aunt would only make her feel more miserable than she already did.

The lamps lit and a cup of tea made, Verity set out a plate of cake and biscuits and with her aunt sitting comfortably in her own parlour, she bade her goodnight and began to make her way back to Far View House. Halfway up the hill, she paused and leaned against a low stone wall as she gazed into the distance musing on her Aunt Martha's words.

Verity knew nothing about Lockwood Mill and Jeb's business affairs. However, she did know that if she were to make anything of her future, she had to get her life in order because it seemed as though for the past twenty-one years, it had been far too haphazard and she simply a pawn in a game.

She was Jeb and Leila's first child, born in 1876, and in the five years that followed Verity's birth Leila had borne three sons – two stillborn and one that had lived but a few months – each one taking its toll on her declining health. A lengthy bout of consumption had eventually caused her death when Verity was fourteen.

It had been Clara Medley who had nursed and raised the very young Verity, and Verity had never been given the opportunity to properly get to know her mother. Shortly after her seventh birthday, Jeb had sent Verity off to a boarding school in Headingly, a village on the far side of Leeds. She had liked the Misses Dowling and enjoyed her lessons – she was a quick learner – but Dowling's Academy for Girls being some twenty and more miles away from Almondbury, she only came home during the school holidays, and sometimes not even then, Jeb having notified the Misses Dowling that it was inconvenient.

She had accepted these unusual arrangements as only a child can, and if Leila was in residence at Far View House, and often she was not, for on her doctor's advice she spent the greater part of each year in Cornwall, the air being cleaner there, it was left to young Verity and Clara Medley to nurse her the best they could. Clara attended to her daily needs and Verity attempted to form a relationship with her mother. She sat reading to her or listening to snippets about her mother's life before she had married Jeb. Hearing her mother's brief reminiscences – Leila had neither the strength nor inclination to indulge in lengthy conversations – a more mature Verity became aware that her mother regretted the marriage.

It seemed to her that her parents' marriage had been an unhappy one to say the least.

Verity couldn't help but notice how unconcerned Jeb had seemed with regards to his sick wife. He rarely spent any time with her or showed her any sympathy. This did not surprise Verity; she had been no age at all when she formed the opinion that her father was only concerned about himself. And if he showed little thought for his wife, he most certainly cared nothing for his daughter.

Verity's mother hadn't been a conventional beauty and for much of the time, she was often too ill to care about her appearance. Her straight brown hair was lank, and her unhealthy pallor and shrivelled skin failed to enhance her luminous grey eyes and high cheekbones in a finely sculpted face: features that Verity had inherited. More than once, Leila had intimated that she had brought a considerable amount of money into the marriage, and Verity wondered if that was what had attracted her father.

One afternoon, not long before her mother died, she learned that Leila had been reared in Leeds, the eldest daughter of a wealthy confectioner, and that Leila's father, Samuel Foxton, had objected to the marriage. He had dubbed Jebediah Lockwood a fortune hunter, and considered him a highly unsuitable husband for his daughter. Leila had always been a sickly child in need of gentle care. However, defying her parents' wishes, Leila had married Jeb.

The more Verity heard, the more she understood why she had never met her maternal grandparents, and why their own visits to Leeds were few and far between and always to Leila's younger sister's house. Flora Foxton had made a fortuitous marriage to Arthur Elgin who'd made his fortune in the new and thriving railway business, and they had three daughters. Flora had always made her ailing sister welcome, but she never reciprocated the visits and Verity's acquaintance with her aunt, uncle and cousins had been limited.

In the summer of 1890, shortly after Leila's death, fourteen-year-old Verity had been taken from Dowling's Academy and brought home to Almondbury and Far View House. However, her stay there had been short-lived. After Leila's funeral, Jeb had immediately sent Verity to live with Aunt Martha, who lived close by. Verity had gone willingly, it being preferable to living with her irascible father, even though her aunt was strict and rather fussy. Whenever one of Aunt Martha's visitors had patted Verity's head and asked, 'Do you miss your poor dear mother?' Verity answered that she did. In truth, she did not. Time spent with her had been so infrequent that it was a case of what you never had, you never miss.

Her stay with Aunt Martha had lasted less than a year, Joseph Boothroyd's objections to Verity's presence forcing Martha to reluctantly send her back to Jeb. Little did she know that Joseph had wanted Verity out of the house because he didn't trust his urges where young girls were concerned. He had no qualms about finding satisfaction with young girls in the town, away from his overweight, bossy spouse, but to have one living under his roof was far too tempting. Using the excuse that he didn't like sharing his dear wife with anyone, Martha had been flattered and let Verity go.

A few miserable weeks later, Jeb had then shunted her off to live with Aunt Flora in Leeds, his reasoning being that a young girl would be better cared for in a house full of women. Flora had grudgingly agreed to keep Verity out of love for her poor, dead sister. Her own three daughters, two of them older by three and two years respectively and the other of a similar age to Verity, had been even less welcoming. She had soon discovered that she had little in common with them and they, finding her bookish and boring, had made the next six years tedious and unpleasant.

Magda, Ivy and Pamela were spoiled, frivolous girls who talked of little else other than the latest fashions and who they should invite to the tea parties that their mother regularly hosted. On such occasions, Verity would slip away at the first opportunity and read the books she borrowed from the library. This caused them to make fun of her scholarliness. As the girls matured, the talk turned to the young men they met at the social gatherings they frequently attended. Flora's daughters were considered pretty with their blonde, bouncing curls and diminutive figures whereas Verity's straight, dark chestnut hair and her height – she was a good six inches taller than Magda who at five feet two inches was the tallest of the sisters – made her a butt for their cruel teasing. 'What will the bean pole wear?' they sniggered as they got ready for yet another outing. 'Will it be the blue or the brown?' And when they walked along beside her, they sneered, 'What's the weather like up there?'

Verity had detested the 'at homes' her aunt insisted they attend in order to meet the right sort of people, but her cousins revelled in these gatherings. Before each event, the house rang with excited squeals as they decided on which dresses to wear and how to style their hair. Then in a froth of muslin and taffeta, they would sally forth, their flaxen, beribboned ringlets framing flushed, pretty faces. Meanwhile, Verity would brush her hair and coil it into a neat chignon at the nape of her neck then deliberate between choosing her blue muslin dress with a pin-tucked bodice or the brown wool with the white lace collar; it all depended on the weather. That she had such little choice was

Jeb's fault. He saw no reason to reimburse her aunt for housing his daughter, and her aunt in turn felt no compunction to lavish her money on Verity's wardrobe; her own girls came first. Coupled with that was the annoyance Flora felt at her niece's appearance. 'It's a pity you resemble our brother, Henry, rather than your mother,' she had remarked on the day Verity had her nineteenth birthday. Flora had then lifted a heavy silver frame from a drawer in the sideboard in the drawing room and handed it to her niece. Verity had studied the photograph of her late uncle with dismay. A tall, strapping young man in a cavalry uniform stared back at her, and to her horror, she recognised her own physique in his, but whereas his face was broad, her own was much finer and more like her mother's and her aunt's.

'At least I don't have a moustache,' she'd testily retorted.

However, much to her embarrassment, she was rarely invited to dance. Not that she wanted to, but being a wallflower or sitting with the older women whilst her cousins and the other young girls in attendance waltzed around the floor or stood chatting and giggling with young men made her feel foolish and out of place.

By the time Verity was twenty-one, Flora had given up the idea of finding her a suitable husband and had told her firmly that it was time she returned home to run her father's house. Verity had been relieved, but her relief had soon turned to disappointment. Far View House did not feel like home, and it seemed that nobody, not even her father, wanted her.

'Rather like a parcel passed from one depot to another with no one to claim it,' she mused as she began walking up the hill again.

The gravel crunched under her boots as she approached the house, the sound disturbing the stillness of the late spring evening. A solitary lamp burned in the hallway behind the heavy oak door framed in thick sandstone lintels that matched those around the windows, four on the upper floor and two on either side of the door. *How unwelcoming it looks*, Verity thought, reflecting on the houses at the bottom of the hill. Lights had gleamed from their windows to welcome home the workers from the mills. And no doubt they would be met with love and affection on their return.

She opened the door, and after hanging her coat on a peg on the hallstand that had drawers for brushes and gloves and umbrella stands with metal trays to catch the drips, she looked into the diamond-shaped mirror at her reflection. A pair of solemn, grey eyes stared back at her above high cheekbones, a straight nose and full-lipped mouth. The walk had brought colour to her cheeks and the gentle breeze had blown tendrils of hair about her forehead and ears. For a moment, she thought she looked quite pretty, then dismissing the idea as nonsense, she went in search of Clara Medley.

Clara was sitting by the fire in the kitchen knitting a brightly coloured blanket from scraps of wool. She looked up as Verity entered and smiled warmly. 'You got your aunt off home all right then? Do you fancy a cup of tea, or would you like cocoa?'

Verity opted for tea, and sat down by the hearth in a chair facing Clara's. She was fond of the plump, motherly housekeeper. She had come to work in Far View House alongside her husband after rearing her own five children until they were of an age to leave them with their grandmother, and as Verity watched her set cups, a milk jug, slices of sponge cake and the large, flowered teapot on the table, it occurred to her that she had possibly spent more hours in Clara's care than had Clara's own children. In fact, she reflected, her early childhood would have been very different had it not been for the housekeeper's tender ministrations. Clara had washed and dressed her, played with her, shown her how to bake fairy cakes and comforted her whenever Jeb had chastised her – something he'd often done when his mood was foul. Verity silently acknowledged that she owed Clara Medley a good deal of gratitude.

The kettle hissed, and Clara mashed the tea. As she waited for it to brew, she commented on the fine weather, and asked had Verity enjoyed the chops that they had eaten for dinner. Verity agreed that the weather was pleasant and that the chops had been delicious, holding back the questions that were burning her tongue until the tea was poured and Clara sat down.

'Mrs Medley, have you heard any gossip about Lockwood Mill lately?'

Clara set down her cup and pursed her lips as she deliberated on how to respond.

'Why would thi be asking such a thing?' she queried.

'Over dinner, Aunt Martha made mention of the mill being in trouble. Father bawled her out, but my aunt really did seem concerned.'

Clara frowned. If Martha Boothroyd had already discussed it then she saw no harm in telling Verity what she knew. The girl had a right to know. She was no longer a child.

'Well, Miss Verity, there's them that say the master's laid off so many workers that production is down, an' that Oliver Hardcastle has his work cut out to keep the mill runnin'. He's a good lad is Oliver, but there's on'y so much he can do... and thi dad...' Clara shrugged and fell silent.

'But why is my father letting this happen?' Verity was truly puzzled. 'Surely, he must see that he needs a full workforce if the mill is to produce the cloth he sells, else he'll go out of business.'

Clara gave a nervous little cough. 'It's summat to do wi'

payin' the workers, Miss. The more folks that work in the mill, the bigger the wage bill.'

'You mean he's cutting corners by reducing the number of people he employs to save on his expenditure? And does he expect them to produce the same amount of cloth?'

'Somethin' like that, Miss.' Clara's face creased in consternation. She didn't like the way this conversation was going, and if any word of it got back to Jeb Lockwood, she and her husband would be for the high road. 'Would you like more tea and another piece of cake?' she asked by way of a diversion.

But Verity wasn't prepared to let the matter drop.

'And is he doing this because his funds are low?' she persisted.

Clara caved in. *Oh, to hell wi' it*, she thought, *the lass'll find out soon enough.*

'That could be the way of it, Miss. Me an' Medley haven't been paid for this last couple o' months. Not that I'm complaining 'cos we get us keep an' I'm sure he'll settle wi' us as soon as he can,' she hastened to add, afraid that her tongue had got the better of her.

'That's shocking!'

Verity's angry retort made Clara even more anxious.

'Please, Miss Verity. Don't be mentioning any o' this to t'master. I wa' speakin' out o' turn an' it's nothing for thee to worry thi head about.' She made a show of looking at the clock on the mantel. It showed a quarter to nine. 'Eeh, is it that time already? An' me wi' all sorts o' things to do afore Bert gets back.' Looking flustered, she got to her feet. Verity took this as a sign for her to go and, thanking Clara for the tea and cake, she climbed the backstairs then the main staircase up to her bedroom at the front of the house.

She undressed, and climbed into bed with a copy of *Mrs*

Gaskell's North and South that she had borrowed from the Lending Library and Reading Room in Huddersfield. She began to read, but her thoughts soon strayed to her father and the mill. Clearly, Jeb was in financial trouble yet he was still squandering money on strong drink, and more than likely gambling at cards in the inns he frequented. If he were allowed to continue in this manner then her aunt's prediction could soon become reality and he would end up bankrupt. Then where would they be?

Verity had no control over his behaviour yet she was loath to stand by and watch it happen, not so much for her own sake and his, but for the hard-working people he employed. Laid back on her pillows. she mulled over their predicament and her own, and not finding a solution, she lost herself in the lives of Mrs Gaskell's characters until the book slipped from her hands onto the eiderdown.

She fell into a restless sleep, her muddled dreams fusing with what she had just read. At one moment, she was the compassionate Margaret Hale ministering to the poor. Later, she was in Mr Thornton's passionate embrace as he swore undying love. At this she had broken out in a sweat, her lips still tingling from his kiss as she was startled into wakefulness by shouts and curses coming from below her bedroom window. She waited until her thumping heart steadied then slipped out of bed. Over at the window, she drew back the curtain. Bert Medley's short, wiry body was bent almost double under Jeb's bulk as he struggled to get her father out of the trap.

Dismayed, Verity watched and listened.

'Come on now, master, 'old still while I get thee down,' Bert implored.

'I don't need thy bloody help,' Jeb slurred, rearing back into the trap and sprawling on its floor, his feet dangling over the tailgate. Bert took hold of his ankles and dragged him forward until

Jeb's feet touched the ground then he heaved him up into his arms and trailed him to the front door, Jeb swaying precariously and cursing at the top of his lungs.

'Get thy bloody hands off me. I can see meself in,' he slobbered as Bert opened the door and pushed him inside. The slamming of the door was swiftly followed by a loud crash.

Poor Bert. Verity pulled on her robe and, running to the head of the stairs, she surveyed the scene below. Jeb must have grabbed at the hallstand to support himself then fallen face down on the flagstones, the hallstand toppling with him. Bert was in the act of striding over her father's body then making his way to the top of the backstairs. 'Clara, come an' give us a hand, love; I can't manage him on me own,' Verity heard him shout.

She reached the bottom of the stairs just as Clara appeared from below. The three of them looked at the prone figure and exchanged looks of exasperation. Jeb was snuffling and snorting and trying to get to his feet. Between them, they brought him upright and, pulling and stumbling and stopping for breath every third step, they got him up to his bedroom and onto the bed. Then they stood puffing and panting and looking disgusted.

'He can stay like that,' Clara snapped. 'I'll be damned if I'll let thee undress him, the drunken sot.'

Jeb began snoring, the guttural sound making Verity feel sick.

'How often do you have to do this?' she asked as they left the room and made their way back to the kitchen.

'Too often of late, Miss Verity,' Bert replied sourly. 'There's allus been times when he's come home sozzled but this past twelve months, things have worsened to such a noit that he'd not be fit to mek it home if it wasn't for me.'

'You shouldn't have to contend with such dreadful behaviour,' Verity said as Clara boiled a pan of milk and made three cups of cocoa. 'And Mrs Medley tells me that it's two months since you last received your wages.'

Bert glowered at Clara. She raised her shoulders and the corners of her mouth turned down as she looked for his forgiveness. 'Thee an' thi loose tongue,' he muttered, and to Verity, he said, 'That be right, but Mrs Medley had no business tellin' thi.'

'But I need to know these things, Bert. I shouldn't be kept in ignorance of what's going on around me. I must take some responsibility for the running of the house, and if my father's too negligent to do it then it's up to me to put things right.' She set down her empty cup. 'I'll have words with him tomorrow.'

'Thas beating a sticky wicket, Miss. He'll not listen to nub'dy.' Bert sounded at the end of his tether.

On that sad note, Verity bade the Medleys goodnight.

2

The next day, Jeb still in bed, Verity breakfasted alone then feeling rather guilty that the Medleys were not being paid for their labour, she went to ask Clara if there was anything she might do to be of help.

Clara gave it some thought before answering. 'There's the matter of the butcher, Miss Verity. He'll not deliver to the house until his bill's settled so he told me when he brought them lamb chops you had last night, an' there's nowt but a bit o' breakfast bacon left in the meat safe. Maybe tha could go into the town an' get summat for tonight's dinner, but mind, don't go to Lionel Berry's, go to Mitchell's; they don't know us there.'

'Are you suggesting I go and buy the meat on credit, Mrs Medley?'

'I am, lass. That's if we're to have owt decent to eat. Your father'll a cause a right stink if there's no meat wi' his dinner.'

'Then I'll go to Mitchell's and pay for it out of my own money. I have a little put by that Aunt Flora gave me when I turned twenty-one. What should I buy?'

Clara seemed taken aback by Verity's offer. 'Eeh, Miss, tha

shouldn't have to spend thi birthday money on a parcel o' meat but...' she tapped her fingertips against her lips, 'a pound of stewing steak'll do. I can mek a meat an' tatie pie. Mind you, that'll empty the flour crock an' use up the last o' the lard. Still, it'll keep the master happy.'

Verity sniggered. 'Yes, we must keep him happy at all costs, even if he doesn't give a jot about our happiness, or anyone else's for that matter,' she said, thinking of the mill hands who had lost their wages when he'd laid them off. 'Is there anything else I should get?'

'No, we've plenty taties left from the last crop Bert planted, an' I've a jar of pickled red cabbage I put down at the end o' last season, so that should do nicely.'

'Then I'll be off, Mrs Medley. I have to call at the library to exchange my books.'

Dressed in her one good coat made from light-grey flannel, Verity began her descent down Far View Hill, her books in the wicker basket swinging on her arm. The day was clear, the sky a blue sheet and a pleasant warmth in the air. To her right, in the distance, she could see Castle Hill, a high hill that dominated the landscape and looked down on lush, green fields bounded by low stone walls, and clusters of cottages in hamlets, some with a church or large haybarns on small farms. Over to her left and further afield was a panoramic view of Huddersfield town, its mill chimneys towering over huge, blackened buildings, factories, houses and shops. Beyond them rose the hills that were part of the Pennine chain.

The hedgerows on either side of the slope down which she walked were in full bloom with coltsfoot, celandine and yellow gorse – pauper's gold, Clara had called it when she had taken a young Verity to the shops in the village. They were a pretty sight and did much to raise Verity's spirits. At the foot of Far View Hill, she came to Aunt Martha's house and continuing on along the tree-lined lanes, she came to Westgate and All Hallow's Church, its tall clock tower and medieval architecture serene amongst a backdrop of tall trees. Across the road was Wormald Hall, its ancient Tudor boarding stark black and white, and next to it, the Woolpack Inn – the public house where her father had worn out his welcome, so Aunt Martha had said. Now, he had to resort to going into Huddersfield to wet his throat. Verity wondered if he was already in debt to some of the inns there.

At the end of Westgate, she turned left into Northgate and on through the village centre, taking the road that skirted the enormous wooded estate of Longley Hall, owned by the Ramsden family. Somerset Road, so Clara had told her, was named in honour of the Duke of Somerset's daughter, Guendolen, who was the wife of Sir John Ramsden, the Lord of the Manor of Almondbury. It was also the better route into the town, the alternative being the exceedingly steep incline called Almondbury Bank, and Verity walked easily down its gently sloping descent.

The nearer she came to Huddersfield, the more aware she became of the smells that the thriving woollen and worsted industry emitted: a greasy stench of wet wool sharpened by the stink of chemical dyes and overladen with the reek of soot that spewed from the towering chimneys. The soil in the Colne Valley being thin and infertile and no good for crop farming had forced the inhabitants to seek other means of making a living, and so for the past eight hundred years, the people had taken to grazing sheep on the land. The water that snaked its way through the surrounding hills and moorland then into the rivers was free from limestone and 'soft', and as water was a necessity in the cleaning and finishing processes involved in making woollen cloth, it was ideal for production, and the industry had thrived.

At the end of Somerset Road, Verity walked along Storthes to Shore Foot where a massive weir on the River Colne provided a head of water that fed the mills along its banks; their prosperity relied on the river. Stopping to watch the rushing cascade, Verity reflected on her feckless father and the problems at Lockwood Mill then she crossed the bridge, passing by Aspley Basin with its wharves and warehouses on the canal banks.

Now she could see her father's mill, small in comparison to the huge edifice of Brierley's Mill that dwarfed many of the others in its proximity. She wondered how Lockwood Mill was faring today while her father lay in his bed. Was Oliver Hardcastle – a man she had never met but whom Aunt Martha had given credit to in her tirade at the dinner table – doing the job her father should be doing? Was he struggling to keep the mill afloat? She was sorely tempted to cross over the road and pay it a visit, see for herself what state the business was in, but dismissed it as foolish. She had never set foot in the place and she had no knowledge of the mill's workings. Thinking that Mr Hardcastle might think her a silly snoop, a witless girl wasting his time, Verity pressed on into the town.

When she reached Kirkgate, she had to slow her pace. Outside St Peter's Parish Church, the pavements were crowded with people. A funeral carriage drawn by two black horses was being unloaded. The glossy pair stood patiently, the plumed, black feathers attached to their noble heads gently fluttering in the breeze. The undertakers in high top hats and black frockcoats eased the coffin onto the shoulders of the pallbearers who also wore top hats, and suits fashioned from the finest worsted. Verity idly wondered who the deceased was. Some wealthy manufacturer, judging by the grand procession. The chief mourners trooping behind the coffin into the church were expensively and fashionably dressed, but a large number of poor, shabby people were also there to pay their respects, the men pulling off their flat caps and the women lowering their eyes and drawing their shawls closer round their shoulders as the coffin was carried into the depths of the church.

They must work in the deceased's mill, thought Verity, and wondered if her father's employees would attend his funeral to honour him in the same way – a funeral that might come sooner rather than later if he kept on drinking to excess.

Loath to take the pleasure from the day by dwelling on her father's vile habits, she pushed her way carefully through the crowd. Up ahead, she saw the sign for the Pack Horse Tap. Was that where her father had taken his surfeit of drink the night before? She turned the corner into Cross Church Street, surprised to find that the pavement on one side of the street was blocked with debris. Next to the Sun Inn, another ancient building had been demolished to make way for a newer establishment and had resulted in part of the Sun Inn collapsing. A chaotic jumble of curtains, pictures, carpets and clothing, iron bedsteads, furniture and broken floorboards lay in the street. Verity's heart went out to the owners whose possessions now littered the street. They had suffered the loss of all their belongings and she paused to stare at them. Would she and her father soon lose all that they had? It didn't bear thinking about, so she moved on, stopping now and then to window-shop the wide variety of goods on sale: ironmongery, tobacco, clothing, chemist's supplies and boots and shoes. Near the end of the street, she spied Lionel Berry's butchery. Clara had said they owed him money. She wondered how much, and before she could stop herself, she crossed the street and went inside. If she was to take responsibility for the running of Far View House, it was imperative that she find out.

The rotund, red-faced butcher smiled ingratiatingly. 'How

may I be of service, Miss?' he boomed, rubbing his big, fleshy hands across his bloodstained apron.

Verity took a deep breath. 'I'm Verity Lockwood, Jebediah Lockwood's daughter. I have recently returned home to run his house. I'm here to enquire how much is owing on Far View House's account with you.' Her cheeks had flushed as she spoke, and although the butcher thought she was overly tall for a woman, he considered her rather handsome. Furthermore, she was about to settle the outstanding bill. He rubbed his palms together and widened his smile.

'Pleased to make your acquaintance, Miss Lockwood. I'll just go an' get my invoice.'

He shambled into the back of the shop, returning with a greasy piece of paper. He handed it to Verity. Her heart sank when she read the outstanding amount.

'You'll find it all correct an' proper, Miss Lockwood,' the butcher said. 'Three pounds, nine shillings and eightpence ha'penny as of last week.' He coughed discreetly. 'Outstanding some three months, Miss Lockwood.'

'I... I... will settle the account first thing Monday morning,' she said, saddened that the money in her purse would not cover the bill and leave her with enough left over to buy the goods Mrs Medley had requested.

Lionel Berry's smile slipped. 'If tha sez so, Monday morning it is then. I'll look forward to it,' he growled, and not looking at all convinced, he bade Verity good day and turned to serve a customer whose coins already clinked in her hand.

Cloaked in shame, Verity left the shop and hurried into the street, almost running until she came to King Street. A tram came clanking down the middle of the thoroughfare, sparks flying from the iron rails, and Verity waited for it to pass before crossing to the other side. The pavements were busy, it being a

Saturday, and housewives in shawls and clogs with baskets on their arms and children hanging on to their skirts hurried up King Street then into a lane leading off it. Verity, reckoning that they would know where meat was sold at an affordable price, followed them.

The Shambles was packed with people looking for bargains and stallholders calling out their wares. 'Fresh spring onions, juicy parsnips an' leeks,' a burly chap in a red neckerchief sang out, vying with another across the crowded street, who bawled, 'Apples a farthing,' and both of them out-shouted by the cry of, 'Rhooobarb, get your rhooobarb here.'

Spying a stall further down the street with chickens and rabbits suspended by their legs from its awning, she picked her way through the throng. Ducking under the carcasses of the poor dead creatures, and wrinkling her nose at their animal stink, she entered the shop. Sawdust shifted under her boots. The butcher, who was hacking into an enormous cage of meaty ribs, set aside his cleaver on the gory chopping block and, wiping his hands on his bloodstained blue and white striped apron, asked, 'What can I do for thee, madam?'

Several minutes later, Verity left the butcher's shop with one pound of stewing steak, a string of fat, pink sausages and a block of lard, her purse two shillings and threepence lighter. Flushed with the success, she went into a nearby grocery and bought a bag of sugar for tenpence, a half-pound packet of tea at a shilling and butter for the same amount. Finally, she purchased a large bag of flour costing two shillings and, toting her overladen basket, she made her way to the library in Somerset Buildings on Byram Street to change her books. She roved between the book stacks looking for something new to read, and after some deliberation, she chose a copy of *The Cloister and the Hearth*. She would have preferred to borrow more than one book but her basket weighed heavily enough already so, balancing the book on top of her goods, she began the long walk back the way she had come.

By the time she was halfway up Somerset Road, she regretted buying the bag of flour for it was the heaviest of her purchases, and as she plodded past Longley Hall, her shoulders ached and the basket's wicker handle bit into the palms of her hands. The euphoria of stocking Clara's larder fading, she consoled herself with the knowledge that the housekeeper could now make bread and Yorkshire puddings; maybe she'd make toad-in-the-hole. The thought made Verity aware that she was hungry and she quickened her pace.

Before long, Castle Hill came into view. It could be seen for miles around. History had it that settlers had existed on the hill some four thousand years ago and that Cartimandua, queen of the Brigantes, had ruled there. In amongst the ruins of ancient ramparts, an ale house had been built and in the 1850s, this had been developed to house the Castle Hill Hotel. The Chartists had held their rallies there, and nowadays, local sportsmen met at weekends to compete in running races and football matches.

Now, as she trudged homeward, Verity recalled how she had sometimes accompanied the Medleys and their children to these events on their Sunday afternoons off duty. She vaguely remembered one bitterly cold day in October 1883 when they had taken her to Castle Hill to show their support for more than three thousand weavers who were striking in protest against the mill manufacturers. They had been demanding more pay and safer working conditions. Chaos had erupted, and the Medleys had fled in fear of their lives, Bert carrying a screaming Verity in his arms as they scrambled down the hillside. Afterwards, safely back in the kitchen at Far View House, Clara had impressed on her that she must say nothing about it to her father. Seven-year-old Verity had been wise enough to hold her peace.

Today, the hill basked in the midday sunshine, the gorse on the hillside shining like scattered gold coins, and Verity decided that should the warm dry weather hold, she would take a walk to the ruins the next day. Swapping the heavy basket from hand to hand and taking Far View Hill in her stride, she arrived back at the house shortly after midday.

Clara, delighted with the provisions, clapped her hands. 'Eeh, Miss Verity, I never expected thee to bring all this, but I'm mighty glad tha did. It'll keep the wolf from the door for a week or more.' She carefully opened the bag of flour and filled the crock, laughing as a cloud of white dust powdered her apron and plump cheeks. 'Sithee, I'm that excited, I'm all of a piece,' she cried, brushing at her face and her apron. 'I'll put these in the meat safe,' she said, lifting the sausages and stewing steak, and with her back to Verity, she added, 'By the way, did tha happen to see the master when tha wa' on thi way home? He's tekken t'trap an' gone into town, mayhap to the mill.' Clara's final words sounded as though she doubted them.

'No, I didn't see him,' Verity replied, her heart sinking at the thought of her father spending yet more money that they couldn't afford in the public houses in Huddersfield.

Clara backed out of the small larder, rubbing her hands on her apron. 'Now, I'll mek thee a nice spot o' lunch. I'm sure tha ready for it.'

'That will be much appreciated,' Verity said, her empty tummy rumbling and her arms and feet aching. She sat down at the table. *I'm not used to hard work*, she thought. *I never had to do any when I lived with Aunt Flora. In fact, up until today, I've been a rather useless creature who did nothing for anyone other than myself.* Looking at Clara's happy face and thinking of the food she had purchased, Verity felt highly pleased with her achievements and resolved that from now on, she would not just sit back and let things happen. *I'm quite capable of learning how to run this house, and matters concerning the mill if needs be. I have a mind of my own that's equal to or better than that of many people I've come across and it's about time I made use of it.*

'I'm going to make some changes round here,' Verity told Clara in a firm voice.

Clara beamed and rewarded her with a tasty cheese and pickle sandwich.

3

At the same time as Verity was tucking into her cheese and pickle sandwich, Dolly Armitage was hurrying across the mill yard at Lockwood Mill. Her Saturday-morning half-day shift had ended but a good ten minutes had passed since the blare from the mill hooter had faded into silence. Out on the canal bank, she ran to catch up with her friends.

'Thanks for waiting for me,' she panted as she drew level with Nellie Haigh and Lily Cockhill, who worked alongside her in the weaving shed.

'What did he want thi for, Dolly?' Nellie's lip curled. None of the girls liked Sam Firth, the overseer.

'He said my piece was too slack at the heddle. I told him my loom needed tuning and it wasn't my fault if the warp was slack.'

'Aye, you can't weave a decent piece o' worsted if thi loom's not tuned. That drunken bugger Jeb Lockwood should be shot,' Lily groused.

Jeb had sacked two tuners in the last few weeks, leaving only one man to maintain more than one hundred looms.

'Is your piece really bad, Dolly?' Nellie's voice was filled with concern because she knew as did the others that it would affect Dolly's wages.

'No, the mucky old beggar was just making an excuse to get me on my own. When he took his Tommy Todger out, I told him my piece wasn't the only thing that was slack.'

Lily laughed at Dolly's witty response 'The dirty old sod!'

'He is that! He's bloody awful.' Nellie turned to Dolly, her eyes wide. 'What else did he do?'

'Nothing. I told him our George was right and handy with the cropping shears, and that if I ever saw Sam's todger again, he'd be paying him a visit,' said Dolly, laughing at her own temerity as she pulled off her turban. Fiery red curls sprang free and fell about her shoulders.

'Aye, your George 'ud soon sort him out,' Nellie gushed admiringly. She had a soft spot for Dolly's brother.

'Sam Firth 'ud not like that. He'll get his own back,' Lily warned her.

Dolly grimaced. 'He already has. He docked me sixpence off me wages.'

'The miserly old bugger! What is it to him to keep you short. It's not his bloody mill.' Nellie's eyes blazed.

'Aye, but he's that well-in wi' Jeb Lockwood, it might well as be,' Lily reminded them.

Nodding their agreement, the girls walked along the canal bank denigrating the overseer whose sexual proclivities made working in Lockwood Mill a regular hazard.

When they reached the King's Bridge, the girls parted company, Nellie and Lily to the yards at the bottom of King Street and Dolly along Storthes to Silver Street. Tinker's Yard and Laycock's Yard, where Nellie and Lily lived respectively, were accessed by narrow passages that led into cobbled courtyards where the inhabitants of the shabby dwelling houses shared the noisy, overcrowded space with workshops that carried out a variety of trades: carpenters, hosiers and tea dealers to name but a few. They also had to share the wash-house and the privies. Whenever Dolly visited Nellie's home, she was always thankful for her own.

On reaching Silver Street, Dolly walked briskly between the rows of small two-up and two-down terraced houses that lined either side of the street until she came to the last house on the left. This was where she lived with her mother, father and her older brother, George. Beyond the gable-end of the house was an open expanse of wasteland and the River Colne, a pleasant enough spot that lent the house an air of freedom not afforded to its neighbours.

'Is that you, Dolly?' her mother called out from the kitchen at the rear of the house as Dolly opened the door from the street. 'What kept you?'

Dolly hung her shawl on one of the pegs near the door and walked through the parlour into the kitchen. 'I stayed talking too long with Nellie and Lily,' she lied, rather than disclose the real reason for her lateness. Her mother wouldn't want to hear about Sam Firth's mucky advances.

'You and your tongue. It'll run away with you one day.' Florence Armitage's rebuke was accompanied by raised eyebrows as she put a dish of mutton stew on the table. 'Sit down and get this whilst it's still hot.'

Her father, Clem, smiled wryly and shook his head. Dolly slid into the chair opposite George's. George gave her a naughty wink.

'Amy and me are going up Castle Hill this aft, Dolly. Do you want to come?'

'Thanks for asking, George. It's a lovely day for it but I plan to go to Penny Spring woods with my new sketchbook and the pastels you gave me for my birthday. The bluebells are out and I fancy seeing if I can do them justice.'

Dolly gave her brother a winning smile to show that the invitation had pleased her even though she had refused it. At twenty-one and nineteen respectively, George and Dolly were very close, and although he was courting Amy Dickenson with a view to marrying her, he still enjoyed his younger sister's company.

'Aye, they'll be grand at this time of year and Penny Springs a lovely spot but I feel like stretching me legs and letting God's good air blow the stink from me nose,' George said, pushing back his chair, his tall, muscular frame crowding the little kitchen as he stood. He worked in the dyehouse at Lockwood Mill and the putrid smell of the dyes and the hot, steamy atmosphere in the enclosed space were unpleasant to say the least. He couldn't wait to escape at weekends to exert his energy in a cleaner environment and Castle Hill was just the place for a good walk or maybe a game of football.

George walked over to the sink and filled a bowl from the kettle on the hob then, stripping off his shirt, he lathered his face and arms with hot, soapy water. Rinsed and dried, he announced that he was off to put on a clean shirt.

'It's hanging up in your room,' his mother called after him as he mounted the narrow flight of stairs leading to the two upper rooms.

Dolly stood. 'I'm off to the privy,' she said, going to the rear door to use the lavatory in the small brick building in the backyard. When she returned, she lifted the kettle that was permanently on the boil and filled a jug. 'I'll go up and get changed.' She climbed the stairs.

'Are you decent?' she sang out as she arrived at the door leading into the room that overlooked the backyard.

'I am,' George called back.

Dolly entered the room that Clem had partitioned down the middle when his son and daughter had grown too old to share. Now each part had half of the window to let in light. A door in the stud wall led into Dolly's bedroom, and as she passed through George's room, he flicked her behind with the leather belt he was about to loop into his good trousers.

'Hey, watch it! You'll have me spilling water all over the floor.'

In her bedroom, she emptied the jug into a large porcelain bowl decorated with yellow daisies. It had belonged to her maternal grandmother, as had the matching tray and powder bowls on the dressing table. Stripping off her overall, she washed then put on a green cotton dress and a white cardigan and, after brushing her hair, tied it back with a green ribbon. Over at her chest of drawers, she lifted her sketchbook and box of pastels. When she passed through George's room, he had already gone back downstairs.

In the kitchen, Clem and Florence Armitage looked with pride at their son and daughter: a handsome, strapping man with auburn hair like his father's, and a beautiful young woman with an alabaster complexion and a mane of red-gold hair. George and Dolly were just two of the five children that Florence had given birth to, their two sisters and a brother having died in infancy – two from scarlet fever and one from diphtheria – and now buried along with Clem's parents in the graveyard in Almondbury.

'Well, Flo, that leaves you an' me on our own.' Clem's eyes twinkled as he addressed his wife. 'What'll it be? Does tha fancy a walk up to Dalton Fold to watch the cricket?'

'Aye, that'll be fine,' Florence agreed. 'Just let me wash these pots and I'll get ready.'

'Will I give you a hand?' Dolly clattered the dishes on the table one into another then took them over to the sink.

'No, love, you get off. And don't be sitting too long in the damp grass,' her mother said.

'I'll be off then,' said George, putting his one good jacket over his clean white shirt.

'Wait for me,' Dolly cried. 'I'll walk part of the way with you. Just let me get a bag for my things.' She scooted to a cupboard under the stairs and, pulling out a canvas bag, she slipped her sketchbook and pastels inside. 'There, I'm ready.'

The brother and sister walked down Silver Street and across into Maple Street to Amy's house. She was ready and waiting. A small girl with fair hair and sharp features, her pale-grey eyes were too close together. Amy tilted her head so that George could peck her cheek.

'You look lovely,' he said, admiring Amy's blue and white checked dress then placing his arms akimbo for the girls to link. 'I'll be the envy of every fellow who sees me with the two best-looking lasses in Huddersfield,' he boasted as they began walking down the street.

Amy pouted. 'Are you coming wi' us, Dolly?' Her disgruntled tone suggested that she didn't approve. She didn't like sharing George with Dolly, and neither did she care for being outshone; Dolly Armitage attracted the attention of all the young men.

'No, I'm going to Penny Spring woods.'

'Well, off you go then,' Amy snapped, for by now, they had reached the end of the street where they would go their separate ways.

Dolly walked on alone up to the Rookery musing on Amy's churlishness. Unlike Dolly and most of the girls they had attended school with, Amy didn't work in the mill. She served in the small bakery shop her grandmother owned in Storthes, and was inclined to give herself airs and graces that Dolly found extremely irritating. She thought her spiteful and rather sly. But George seemed smitten by her and Dolly kept her opinions to herself. All she wanted was her brother's happiness.

When she reached the Rookery, she crossed the road into Penny Spring woods. Just as she had predicted, the ground was a dense, blue carpet of flowers dappled by the sun's rays. Slipping off her shoes, she trod softly through a little glade, her bare feet feeling the bluebells' coolness and her nose breathing in the rich scent of sap. Here and there, her feet pressed on clumps of wild garlic, their crushed stems giving off a pungent aroma that, to Dolly, spoke of witchcraft. Under the branches of beech and oak that were thick with fat buds and the first green leaflets, she danced in a magical dream. Then retrieving her shoes and her bag, she walked further into the wood until she came to where a tree stump looked like an inviting seat. Sitting on it, she opened her sketchbook and her box of pastels. They too looked inviting in their serried rows of colour, and selecting a dark green, she began making swift strokes on the creamy paper. A paler green then a dark blue was followed by a lighter blue, and smudging the pastels with her thumb, she created the background she had hoped for. Satisfied with the effect, she next concentrated on delineating the bluebells, her tongue sticking out of the corner of her mouth as she peered at their delicate form. Dolly was so engrossed that she did not hear the approaching footsteps until the sharp crack of a twig startled her into looking round. The sketchbook fell from her lap.

'Please, I do apologise. My curiosity got the better of me.' The young man gave Dolly a contrite smile. 'I should not have crept up on you in that manner. Allow me to introduce myself.

I'm Theodore Beaumont, son of Joshua Beaumont, agent for Sir Arnold Thornton at Thornton Hall.'

Dolly looked up into a clean-cut face topped with a shock of bright, fair hair, and below it, a pair of twinkling blue eyes – the same shade as the bluebells, she noted. Then lowering her gaze, she took in his fine, lovat tweed jacket and polished riding boots: a young gentleman if ever there was one.

'No need for apologies,' she said, surprised by how calm she sounded as she stooped to pick up her sketchbook.

'May I look?' Theodore gave her another placatory smile.

'I was drawing the bluebells,' she said, handing him the sketchbook. 'They're such a wonderful colour against the green of the forest floor.'

'My, but you've captured them perfectly. Are you an artist?' He held on to the sketchbook.

Dolly blushed. 'I'd like to be, but I have to be content with drawing whenever I get the chance, which isn't too often,' she said regretfully.

'Why is that? What keeps you from drawing all day every day?' Theo gazed into eyes that were a greenish-gold and at the sprinkling of golden freckles above a neat nose and rosy lips, all framed in curling tendrils of fiery red hair. He was entranced.

'Work,' Dolly replied, her tone stating the obvious. 'I'm a weaver in Lockwood's mill. Toiling six-and-a-half days a week over a loom leaves little time for such pleasures.'

'Ah, I see.' Theo nodded thoughtfully. 'And may I ask your name?'

'Dorothy Armitage, but my family and friends call me Dolly.'

'Mine call me Theo.'

'That's nice,' Dolly said, finding nothing better to say.

'And may I call you Dolly?'

'You may,' she said, thinking that it mattered little what he called her. She was never likely meet him again. With that in mind, she asked, 'Do you often come walking in Penny Spring woods?'

'No, this is my first time. I've only recently arrived at Thornton Hall. I was away at school in York and then when I finished there, I went to live with my mother in Harrogate. She and my father are divorced and since she now has a new husband, I have chosen to live with Father at Thornton Hall.'

Dolly was somewhat taken aback by the airy manner in which Theo divulged such personal information to a stranger, for after all, that's what she was. And as for divorce, she had heard of it and knew what it meant, but the people who lived in Silver Street and the surrounding district didn't entertain such notions no matter how unsatisfying their marriages were. They simply made the best of a bad match.

'And what do you do at Thornton Hall?'

'Nothing much, as yet. Father seems set on training me to follow in his footsteps.'

'And would you like that?' Dolly couldn't picture him as a land agent. The only one she knew of was the agent at Longley Hall, and gossip had it that he was a tyrant feared by all who worked under him. His master's tenants dubbed him a conniving money-grabber.

'I'm not sure. I think I might like to join the Bays.' He lunged forward, one knee bent and his arm raised as if he was brandishing a sword.

'You mean be a soldier?' Dolly had seen the Queen's Dragoon Guards parading in Greenhead Park when the entire country had celebrated Queen Victoria's Jubilee.

'Yes, I do,' Theo replied as he stood to attention.

'You'd look splendid in one of those scarlet jackets with the blue velvet facings and all that gold braid,' she quipped, her green eyes dancing as she delivered the playful comment.

'Now you're making fun of me.' Theo pretended to look hurt, and Dolly wondered how it was that they could talk so easily on such a short acquaintance.

'Truly, I think you'd look rather handsome. I suppose you already know how to ride a horse but when it comes to fighting for queen and country, would you have the heart for it?' She looked searchingly into his face.

'I don't think I would. I'd hate to have to kill someone.'

'Then it looks as though you'll have to be satisfied with being a land agent.'

Dolly's flippant remark made Theo roar with laughter.

'You're not only pretty; you're highly amusing,' he said, his eyes bright with admiration. 'I like a girl with spirit.'

For some reason she couldn't quite explain, Dolly felt suddenly uncomfortable, and reaching for her sketchbook, she snatched it from his hand. 'I'd better be off,' she said, stooping to pick up her box pf pastels then stuffing both items into her bag.

Theo made no attempt to detain her. 'We may meet again one day,' he said cheerily. Turning on his heels, he strode out of the coppice and almost as an afterthought, he called out, 'I enjoyed your company, Dorothy Armitage.'

Enjoyed my company indeed, Dolly fumed as she headed back towards the Rookery. He was just a posh, rich boy with too much time on his hands. He'd no doubt relate the incident as a means of entertaining his friends. He'd make jest of how he'd met a poor mill girl who thought she could draw, and wanted to be an artist. Her annoyance quickened her footsteps and she reached home in no time at all.

She would have been intrigued to learn that as Theo walked

back to Thornton Hall, he too was replaying the chance meeting, and she would have been even more surprised to know that, to the contrary, he had found her intelligent and entertaining. That her frank way of speaking and her sense of humour showed no trace of the superficiality common in many of the young women with whom he was acquainted. And what was more, she was beautiful. He sincerely hoped he would meet her again.

4

'May God's blessing be upon us and remain with us always.'

The rector's final words signalled the end of morning service in All Hallows Church. Verity waited patiently for those she had shared a pew with to shuffle out into the aisle. A bright May sun lanced the stained-glass windows in the east wall, coloured patches of light dancing on the beamed ceiling and the faces of the people below. Smiling inwardly, she watched the shiny, bald head of a stout gentleman turn scarlet and the cheeks of his plump wife a ghastly green. Then, making a move, she followed the slow-moving congregation out into the gloomy porch where the rector stood shaking hands or chatting with his parishioners. He didn't give Verity a second glance.

Out in the sunlight, she turned her face to the sun's warmth then, lowering her gaze, she searched the faces of the people standing in groups and talking convivially before making their way home. She had attended the service in the hope of finding a familiar face, perhaps the daughter of one of Aunt Martha's visitors that she had occasionally met during the brief spells she had spent in Almondbury. It would be nice to share the company of someone her own age. But she recognised no one, and none of them paid heed to the tall girl wearing a pin-tucked, white shirtwaist and a fine, woollen jacket and skirt in a delicate shade of mauve: a parting gift from Aunt Flora to ease the guilt she felt at sending Verity back to live with her father. It was the first time she had worn it and as she had pinned on her straw boater, her reflection in the cheval mirror had told her she looked quite elegant. *I might as well not have taken the trouble*, she thought miserably. *My appearance has gone unnoticed.* Disappointed, she walked along the paved path and at the gate, she paused before stepping out into Westgate.

Two girls passed by, arms linked and heads close together. They were deep in a conversation that made them laugh, and Verity felt envious. She could tell by their cheap muslin dresses that they were working-class girls, and as they continued walking towards the cemetery that was a short distance from All Hallows Church, she felt an unexplainable urge to follow them. The shorter of the two had lank, mouse-brown hair and a well-rounded figure but her companion was slender and a good head taller, her red-gold hair gleaming in the sunlight. She carried a canvas bag, the shape inside leading Verity to assume it held a large book, and the other girl clasped a bunch of wildflowers by their wilting stems.

Verity kept her distance, dogging their footsteps and when they reached the graveyard, the girls made straight for a newly dug, unmarked grave topped with loamy earth and small stones. The smaller girl laid the posy on the flat top of a nearby tomb and went off in the direction of the sexton's hut. Her friend perched on the tomb and took a book and a tin from her bag. Curious, Verity sauntered up to a grave with an enormous headstone in the shape of an obelisk, and half-hidden behind it, she observed the red-haired girl.

The red-headed girl opened up her book and then the tin and was busily drawing when her friend returned with a jam jar filled with water. Carefully, she arranged the flowers in the jar and then pushed it into the soft soil on the new grave. Verity moved closer, near enough to hear their voices, and lingering in front of another headstone, she pretended to read the weathered, ancient, gothic script.

'What's tha drawing, Dolly?' the flower-arranger asked.

'The baby angel on that grave,' she said, pointing with the pastel she held between her dusty fingers at a massive memorial directly in her line of vision. At the foot of a huge cross embellished with climbing roses, a larger-than-life stone cherub lay sleeping. 'Do you want me to make a picture of your flowers so that you can show your mam, Nellie?'

'Ooh, would you? She'd like that. She's going to miss me granny summat shocking.'

Dolly and Nellie: Verity mused on how she might strike up a conversation with them. She turned, ready to give them a smile of introduction, but Dolly had swivelled round on the tomb, her back to Verity as she focused her attention on the flowers in the jam jar, and Nellie stood looking over Dolly's shoulder.

Feeling rather foolish yet still hoping the girls might acknowledge her, Verity walked between the graves until she was in a clear position for them to see her but Dolly was concentrating on drawing the flowers, and Nellie seemed to look right through her. Overcome with a sense of loneliness, and feeling ashamed of the need to find friends, Verity hurried away. *How pathetic I am?* she chastised herself as she retraced her the path out of the cemetery. *I might well be invisible*, she fumed. *I went unnoticed at the church and then in the graveyard, and it's the same when I am at home, the Medleys too busy to spend time in my company, and Father avoiding me at all costs.*

But she had not gone unnoticed in the cemetery.

'She wa' tall, wasn't she, that girl who wa' looking at the graves,' Nellie commented.

'Aye, she was. She reminded me of a picture I saw in one of my library books. It was of a heroine in a Greek myth, and that's what she looked like – statuesque – and her mauve suit was very elegant,' Dolly replied as she added a final touch to the picture of the posy. Carefully, she tore off the sheet of creamy paper. 'Here, you can give that to your mam.' She handed the drawing to Nellie.

'It's lovely, Dolly. Thanks.' Nellie perused the picture but her mind was still on the tall girl in the fine suit. 'You do use some fancy words, Dolly. I've never heard anybody say stach-ooo-esk.'

'It means tall and shapely,' Dolly explained as she put her pastels back in the tin.

'She wa' that all right,' said Nellie. 'I thought she looked a bit lost an' lonely.'

'Aye, she did, but I've no idea who she is. I've not seen her round here before.' Dolly put her sketchbook and pastels in her bag. 'We'd best be getting back for us dinner. Mam gives off stink if she has to keep it warming.'

'Aye, so does mine, but you can't spoil scrag end of mutton.' Nellie pulled a face at the thought of eating the cheap meat. 'It's that greasy, you could oil wagon wheels wi' it.'

The girls walked back the way they had come, stopping for a moment at a grave marked with a lozenge of stone and bearing only a number. Dolly thought how sad it was that her three siblings lying beneath the soil didn't have angels to watch over them. She said a little prayer. Then the girls walked on to the gate. By now, the other girl was out of sight.

Verity had left the village behind and was walking back to Far View House. The hedgerows were a riot of dandelions and corn marigolds, their yellow petals bright against the lush fescue and meadow grasses. In the fields, young lambs stumbled on unsteady feet after their mothers and on catching them, nuzzled at drooping udders, their innocent bleating sweet on the midday air. A pair of thrushes trilled their joyful song and a bold blackbird whistled his jaunty tune, but Verity neither saw nor heard the splendour of the hour. Her heart as heavy as her tread, she trudged up the hill to the house that didn't feel like home, contemplating yet another day without company, and only her books for comfort.

A savoury aroma met her nose as Verity stepped into the hallway. Clara emerged from the dining room, her flushed face breaking into a welcoming smile. 'Tha timed that well, Miss Verity. Sunday dinner is ready to be served,' she said cheerily, then lowering her voice to a conspiratorial whisper, 'It's toad-in-the-hole made wi' them sausages you bought.' She flicked a thumb at the dining-room door and at the same time gave Verity a look that she couldn't interpret. 'The master's already at the table.'

Verity unpinned her boater and hung it on the hallstand then went into the dining room.

'Aah, Verity, there tha is,' her father boomed, his jowls wobbling as he beamed at her. 'Clara tells me tha went to church. Didst tha enjoy the service?'

Verity, taken aback by his welcome, was lost for words. Then, finding her voice, she told him she had, and took her place at the table.

'Thas looking well, lass,' Jeb said, nodding his head at her mauve suit. 'Tha should dress up more often.'

What on earth had come over him, she wondered as she thanked him for the compliment. He appeared to be relatively sober and in an exceptionally good mood.

He was. Last night, at the gaming tables in the White Hart, Jeb had won a tidy sum of money and celebrated his winnings by tumbling a pretty young wench. He had plenty to feel happy about. He didn't, of course, convey any of this to Verity, and he gave an involuntary shudder as he recalled having wagered Far View House on the turn of a card. But luck had been on his side and now he felt like master of all he surveyed.

Clara served soup followed by toad-in-the-hole, the sausages spicy and the Yorkshire pudding crisp and golden. Jeb praised her fulsomely as she cleared away the plates. In between the courses, Verity and her father talked about the fine weather, and Jeb asked Verity about her recent trip into Huddersfield and wanted her opinion of the town.

'It seems to be thriving judging by the great variety of shops and the grand new buildings,' she said. 'I visited the library and reading rooms. They have a fine selection of books.' She paused, thinking what else she might say to interest him, and also to steer the conversation towards what she was about to ask him. 'There were plenty of townsfolk in the streets doing their shopping, and it's good to see that they have the money to do so. The mills and other industries must be faring well to keep so many people in employment.'

'Aye, they are, lass,' Jeb agreed as he filled his glass with brandy. 'Huddersfield's mills are t'best in t'world an' it all started here in Almondbury tha knows. I remember my grandfather tellin' me how his father wove the grandest kersey in all o' t'Colne Valley. That was in the days they did their weaving at home on handlooms an' sold their cloth outside All Hallows. Draped it over the walls they did so that folks could judge the quality for themselves. Then along came looms that 'ud make a piece in a quarter of the time. That's when thy great-grandfather, Ezra, put every penny he had into building

Lockwood Mill. We've never looked back since,' he said expansively.

'He must have been a very enterprising man,' Verity said.

'Oh aye, he wa'. Even when them bloody Luddites came smashing up the machines, Ezra stood his ground. Tha knows who t'Luddites were, don't you, lass?'

'Yes, Father. They were the men who objected to the mechanisation of the mills.'

'Aye, they did that. They had these bloody big hammers called Enochs after t'fellow that made 'em, an' when the Luddites came a-wrecking, they'd shout, "Enoch makes 'em, Enoch breaks 'em."' Jeb chortled, brandy dribbling down his chin. 'In them days, he sold his cloth in t'cloth hall up Cloth Hall Street, tha knows, the place that's a market now. We don't need it any more 'cos these days, we sell us cloth direct, all over t'world. Only the finest Yorkshire worsted comes out of Lockwood Mill, lass, an' don't you forget that.'

Verity was surprised to hear him talk so enthusiastically about a business he so foolishly neglected. 'I take it then that Lockwood Mill is thriving,' she said.

Jeb gulped at his brandy. He didn't care for where this conversation was going. 'So tha enjoyed thi trip into town? Didst buy owt nice?' he deflected.

Verity's cheeks turned pink. 'A ribbon and other womanly things,' she lied airily. She wasn't going to mention her embarrassing visit to Berry's butchers, but with that in mind and Jeb being in such a pleasant frame of mind, she decided to broach the subject of the Medleys' unpaid wages and the running of the house.

'Thank you for telling me about our family's history, Father. I'm fascinated by it.' Then deliberately adopting an amazed expression to add impact to her words, she said, 'It's rather awesome to think that all these years later, Great-Grandfather Ezra's mill is still in your possession and that we Lockwoods are living in the house that he built.' She paused to take a deep breath. 'And talking about the house, Father, has got me thinking.' Her voice wobbled. 'If I'm to run the house as a good daughter should do for her father then I will need to learn from you to do it justice.' She put her head meekly to one side to judge his reaction.

When Jeb nodded affably, Verity's confidence grew. Giving him her sweetest smile and buttering her tone, she continued, 'You're a man with years of experience of running both the mill and our home, therefore I will need your guidance if the house is to function properly.'

She half-expected an angry response, but Jeb seemed flattered and smiled benevolently.

Verity took another deep breath.

'It has been brought to my attention that certain matters have been let slip, no doubt because you are so busy dealing with the mill, and I intend to be of assistance and put them right. It's only fair that I should take some responsibility and not leave you to carry the burden. As I've already said, you are a busy man.' The lies slipped easily from her tongue.

Jeb looked puzzled. His brow furrowed as he asked, 'What matters might these be?'

Verity's heart thudded painfully and her mouth went dry.

'The Medleys have not been paid their wages for some two months, and the tradesmen are anxious for their bills to be settled,' she said, her voice so low, it was barely above a whisper. She felt like raising her hands to shield her head from the abuse she was sure was about to be hurled at her.

To her amazement, Jeb gave a guttural laugh and slapped the table with the flat of his hand. 'Is that it? Wages to be paid and bills to settle.' He guffawed loudly. 'Then let's set about putting matters right.'

He shoved his hand into his jacket pocket and pulled out a wad of notes. Peeling off a large, white five-pound note, he slapped it down on the table then riffling through the wad, he added three one-pound notes, and feeling magnanimous, he plunged his hand in his pocket and tossed a handful of silver and copper coins on top of the paper money.

'There! Tha can start by doing thi duties wi' that.' He guffawed again before adding in a slightly sneering tone, 'Run my house *properly*,' and, pocketing the remaining notes, he got to his feet. 'I must be off; a busy man has things to do,' he jested, the money burning a hole in his pocket. He'd start by going to the Woolpack and paying what he owed the landlord then he'd have no need to take the trap into Huddersfield. The thought of restoring his reputation and being able to quench his thirst nearer home made him feel almost euphoric.

'Th... thank you... Father,' Verity stuttered. 'I'll p... p... put the money to good use.'

Jeb blundered into the hallway and rammed on his bowler at a jaunty angle. It being a Sunday, the Woolpack would be closed to the public, but Jeb knew that a knock on the rear door and the offer to settle his bill would gain him access to both strong drink and good company; laws were made to be broken in Jeb's book.

Stunned, Verity sat glued to her chair staring at the pile of money: a king's ransom. And all got so easily without any rantings and ravings or begging and pleading. Really, wonders never ceased. Feeling quite dizzy with excitement, she scooped up the notes and coins and headed straight for the stairs to the basement.

'The toad-in-the-hole was delicious, Mrs Medley,' said Verity as she walked into the overly warm kitchen that housed the large stove in which Clara cooked the meals. She was clattering dishes in the sink. Drying her hands on her apron, she turned and smiled.

'I'm pleased tha enjoyed it, Miss Verity. And the master?' She cocked her head and pursed her lips.

'He ate every pick, and furthermore,' Verity was bubbling with excitement, 'he said to give you what you are owed.' She flourished the pound notes.

'Eeh, Miss! What did tha say to get him to gi' thee that?' Clara's shocked expression matched the one that Verity had worn only a short while ago when her father had handed over the money.

'I simply brought the matter to his attention.'

'Well, bless me cotton socks, an' bless you, Miss Verity.'

* * *

The mellow days of May slid pleasantly into a sunlit June, and although Verity felt easier about the financial affairs of Far View House, she still worried about her father's drinking habits. Jeb had stocked his cellar with several bottles of brandy, and at 2s/6d a bottle and nights spent carousing in the Woolpack and other drinking dens, his apparent good fortune must be seriously depleted by now.

More pressing was the problem of how she might spend yet another day in what to her seemed a very worthless life.

Clara gently scolded her when she busied herself doing household chores. 'Nay, Miss Verity, tha shouldn't be dusting an' polishing; that's my job,' she had said whenever she came across Verity in the drawing room plumping cushions or in the dining room rubbing the patina on the old oak sideboards to a gleaming finish, her chiding making Verity feel as though she was interfering with Clara's routine. Taking long walks in the countryside without the pleasure of company had waned, and there was only so much reading one could do. There were days when her life seemed so empty and humdrum that she felt like screaming.

She hadn't enjoyed living with Aunt Flora or her cousins, but the house in Leeds had always been filled with noisy chatter and frequent comings and goings, whereas Far View was rather like a mausoleum, and Verity was beginning to dread the long hours of silence broken only by Jeb's drunken rantings when he returned home late at night. There had been no further occasions when they had shared a meal or indulged in pleasant, interesting conversations. In fact, it seemed as though Jeb was avoiding her again and when their paths did cross, he was surly and morose.

I have to do something positive with my life, she thought, setting aside her book and going to gaze out of her bedroom window at the unkempt garden. Then, as Verity's eyes roamed the neglected lawn and borders, she was filled with a sudden urge to be out in the afternoon sunshine doing something productive. She ran downstairs and out of the front door.

In amongst the overly long grass and plots thick with weeds, fluffy-petalled scarlet peonies drooped their large, spherical heads, and spiky yellow, pink and white dahlias were tangled in chickweed. In the borders, salvias and lavender struggled through clumps of meadow grass, unable to show off their bright-red and purple splendour. Only the camellia and forsythia bushes stood proud, too tall to be lost in the undergrowth.

The air was heavier than indoors, and she wandered further into the garden, the long grass thick beneath her tread. On the magnolia bush, a ladybird crawled over a glossy leaf. She held out a finger, tempting it to climb on, but it suddenly took flight. *Ladybird, ladybird fly away home.* To be perfectly truthful, Verity had never really considered Far View House to be her home; it had simply been a place to which she came when she wasn't being sent to live somewhere else. But now, as she silently acknowledged that this was where she belonged, she felt the urge to make her mark on it.

Such beauty, she marvelled, gently fingering the petals of a white camellia. It somehow seemed sinful to allow God's handiwork to be spoiled by such neglect, and feeling that it was her duty to amend it, she went back into the house and hurried down to the kitchen.

Clara was on her knees applying blacklead to the large iron range.

'May I borrow one of your black aprons, Mrs Medley? And will Bert object to my using some of his gardening tools?'

Verity's flushed, pink cheeks had Clara looking up at her with a puzzled frown. She got to her feet too hastily for comfort.

'Why, Miss? Whatever are tha bound to do?'

'I would have thought that obvious, Mrs Medley. I'm going to put the front garden to rights. There are lots of beautiful flowers and shrubs struggling to show off their best out there but they are choked with weeds.'

'Eeh, that's not a job for the likes of you, Miss Verity. 'Tis man's work,' Clara exclaimed, flapping her blackened hands at the very idea. 'I'll tell Medley to see to it.'

'I don't want Bert to do it. He has enough to do. I, on the other hand, have all the time in the world, and I *want* to do it. And for your information, Mrs Medley, I'm just as strong and capable as any man. Why is it that women are always cast as fragile, useless creatures? Look at you. You scrub and polish and wash the laundry, and when you're not doing that, you're ironing or cooking. Hard enough tasks, all of them, yet you don't consider them beyond your capabilities. Surely, I'm perfectly able to do something as simple as pulling out weeds.'

'Well, if you insist, Miss Verity.' Clara begrudgingly fetched a black apron from the scullery, her scowl letting Verity know that she heartily disapproved. 'Medley's out there chopping logs for the fires. He'll give you the tools.' She dropped back to her knees and vented her disapprobation on the door of the range.

Bert had finished chopping logs, judging by the neatly stacked pile under the overhang of the coach house, so Verity went in to see if he was there. He was cleaning the pony's stall, wielding a stout besom that brushed up piles of trampled straw and dust. He looked up in surprise when he saw her.

'The master's away wi' t'trap if tha wa' lookin' for a ride into town, Miss Verity.'

'I'm not, Medley. I want some gardening tools. I'm going to tackle the front garden.'

Unlike his wife, Bert voiced no objections. Although he tended the vegetable plots in the rear garden, he drew the line at taking on what he considered was a paid job for a gardener. Putting aside his broom, he led the way to the potting shed. As they walked across the yard, he stated the reasons as to why he didn't tend the front garden.

'You see, Miss, it's like this. I'd be doin' some chap out of a job, an' I've enough to do what wi' driving the master in an' out of Huddersfield at all times of day and night afore walking back here like I had to do today, 'cos he's taken t'trap on to Honley. He said he had business there,' Bert groused, his tone suggesting that Jeb's trip to Honley had nothing at all to do with business.

'I on'y grow veg so as Clara has summat to cook, 'cos by rights, it's a gardener's job,' he continued, ducking inside the potting shed and returning with a trug holding a trowel, a fork and a pair of shears. 'There, that'll do thi,' he said, handing Verity the trug. 'Now, if that's all, Miss, I'll get back to cleanin' out Bess's stall whilst she's away.'

Verity smiled and thanked him. 'You love that little pony, don't you, Medley?'

It was Bert's turn to smile. 'I do, Miss. Her an' me spend a lot o' lonely hours together when we're waitin' to bring the master back home.'

Verity knew that Bert was referring to the long, late nights he had to hang around the town, sometimes in the pouring rain, waiting to bring a drunken Jeb back to Far View and put him into bed before retiring to his own.

'Thank you, Medley. I don't know how we'd manage without you and your good wife.'

Feeling rather sad, Verity left him to carry on cleaning out the stable and made her way round the house and into the front garden.

Two hours later, she stood at the top of the drive to admire her labours, her grubby hands pressed into her aching back. To one side of the paved flags in front of the house, a huge pile of chickweed, dandelions, purslane and crabgrass awaited disposal, and Verity was just thinking of going to ask Bert for a wheelbarrow when he appeared round the corner.

'By, Miss Verity, thas done a grand job,' he said, gesturing at the borders of lavender where deep purple clumps now prettily delineated the edges of the driveway.

Verity smiled. 'Tomorrow, I'll clear the weeds from the peonies and dahlias and let them show off their true colours, and,' she pointed to the pile of weeds, 'for now, I need to get rid of those.'

'Nay, Miss, you leave that to me. I'll go an' get the barrow.'

Verity willingly let him go, and placing the trug and the tools on top of the weeds, she went indoors to wash her hands in the kitchen sink.

'Eeh, Miss Verity, you'll ruin your hands takin' on such tasks,' Clara moaned as she watched Verity scrub the dirt from under her fingernails and in between her fingers. 'A grand lady needs to keep her hands soft. An' the hem of your skirt's all mucky.'

Verity laughed. 'I don't think of myself as a grand lady, and as for the gardening, I found it very therapeutic. I feel as though I've done something really worthwhile today. Like I said, Mrs Medley, I intend to make changes.'

'Aye, well, getting your hands dirty might be thepa... whatever you called it, but gentlemen don't care for ladies wi' rough, calloused hands. Now, give me back my apron an' get yoursen cleaned up for dinner. T'master said he'd be back about six.'

Still smiling at the notion of a gentleman finding her hands not to his liking, Verity went upstairs to change her skirt. As she put on a clean one, she mused on Clara's words. *Where and when am I likely to meet a man who cares about my appearance? The only person we entertain at Far View is Aunt Martha, and it's not as if I have any sort of social life.* That thought made her feel sad and friendless, and out of the blue, she recalled the Sunday a few weeks ago when she had followed two girls to the cemetery and how envious she had felt as they had walked by with their arms linked, heads close together, chatting and laughing.

Jeb arrived home in time for dinner, sufficiently intoxicated to be in a foul mood. He slumped over the table toying with his food and filling his glass again and again. His trip to a bawdy house in Honley hadn't been entirely satisfying and it had used up the last of his cash.

'Did you notice that I've cleared the lavender borders of weeds, Father?' Verity's attempt to lighten the unpleasant atmosphere fell on deaf ears. Further pleasant remarks met with a sullen silence and she admitted defeat and watched her father grow more irascible by the minute, almost jumping out of her chair when Jeb let out a roar.

'Medley! This blasted decanter's nigh on empty. Fill it up an' be quick about it.'

Clara, bringing in the rice pudding dessert, banged down the tray and, snatching the decanter, she fled back to the kitchen. 'He's bawling for more brandy,' she puffed.

Bert hurried into the cellar, his expression tight. He had filled the decanter to the brim as Clara had set the table. 'Is there no quenchin' that man's thirst,' he grumbled to his wife as he stamped up the stairs to the dining room.

The decanter filled, Jeb set about emptying it, his mood surly and unapproachable.

Finding it extremely repulsive to sit and watch her father drink himself into a stupor, Verity excused herself from the table and went up to her room. She read for a while then, tired out by her unaccustomed hard labour, she fell into a deep sleep.

5

The glaring sun streamed through the glazed roof in Lockwood Mill's weaving shed, its golden shafts descending through a haze of shimmering dust motes to glint on the oily machinery below. The grinding roar and throb of the looms reverberated from wall to wall and floor to ceiling as shuttles trailing fine yarns flew back and forth, interlacing wefts with warps and the beaters thrashing faster than the eye could see. Pick on pick, row on row, smooth, Yorkshire worsted lapped the thickening cloth beams, the weavers keeping a sharp eye out for loose ends, broken threads or empty bobbins.

Dolly ran her index finger under the edge of her turban that not only protected her hair from the rising dust but also prevented it from getting caught in the loom should she have to lean in to catch a loose end; many a girl had been scalped when her flowing locks had tangled with the weft and warp. Her finger moistened as she wiped the sweat from her brow. Today was a scorcher and the intense heat in the shed made minding her loom less than pleasant. *Oh, to be out on the moors in the clean, fresh air,* she thought, risking a quick glance to her right to try and catch Nellie's attention.

Across 'weaver's alley', the space that separated the two rows of looms, Nellie was changing an empty bobbin. When that was done, she looked in Dolly's direction and grinned. Dolly raised two fingers to her lips, giving the signal that she was about to speak. The noise of the machinery made normal conversation impossible, but all the women in the weaving shed were adept at mouthing and lip-reading, and gossip flowed as easily as it would if they were sitting in their own parlours over a cup of tea.

'I'm sweating cobs,' Dolly mouthed.

'Me an' all,' Nellie mouthed back, 'an' I'm dyin' for me breakfast.'

Dolly swiftly skipped sideways, peering round the edge of her loom to look at the huge clock on the far wall of the shed before dodging back to catch a loose end. The thread secured, she signalled again, and Nellie responded. 'Five minutes to go,' Dolly mouthed, her alabaster cheeks flushed with heat and exertion.

She turned her eyes back on her loom just in time to see the yarn in the shuttle snap. She groaned out loud. 'Dammit,' she cried, pulling on the lever that brought the heddle to a standstill. Stepping into the alley under the overhanging leather belts that were attached to the drums and pulleys that powered the looms, she looked left then right. Neither the Mrs Weaver who was in charge of all the weavers nor the overlooker were to be seen. An idle loom was frowned on, and it was up to the weaver to see that it was back in action as soon as possible.

Dolly lifted the empty shuttle from its bed. Threading the shuttle was an onerous task that involved placing the thread into the shuttle's eye then sucking it through with one quick intake of breath. Dolly abhorred 'kissing the shuttle' as the girls called it. Sucking dust and fluff into her lungs was something to be avoided if she wanted to stay healthy, and if Isaac Horsfall, the elderly loom tuner, had been on the spot he would have done it for her. But Isaac, now the mill's only loom tuner since Jeb Lockwood had sacked the other two, was busy warping a loom at the other end of the shed and was so overworked that Dolly knew she would have to thread the shuttle, like it or not.

The blast from the mill hooter signalled breakfast time and the looms ground to a halt. She'd leave the shuttle for now. With any luck, Isaac might be free when breakfast was over, so joining Nellie and the other women hurrying to the shed doors, she went out into the mill yard. It was just gone half-past eight, the morning still young and the sun had yet to reach its zenith, but the heat in the mill yard was only slightly cooler than that in the weaving shed.

Dolly and Nellie and some of the other women raced for the shade of the dyehouse wall, and flopping down on the cobbles, they opened their snap tins and started tucking into their breakfasts. Dolly had cheese and pickle sandwiches. Nellie had dripping. The Haighs lived hand to mouth. Nellie and her younger brother, Pip, were the only members of the family in employment. With a crippled father, an ailing mother and five younger siblings to feed and clothe, money didn't run to the luxury of cheese.

'Swap you one of mine. I love drip bread.' Dolly held out a cheese sandwich for Nellie to take. Nellie shot her a grateful smile and accepted the exchange. She knew Dolly was only doing it out of the goodness of her heart.

'It's bloody scorching in that shed,' Hetty Lumb commented as with her hand inside the front of her overall, she mopped sweat from under her ample bosom with a grubby rag. 'T'sweat wa' runnin' down shucks o' my arse that fast, you'd think I'd peed mesen.'

Dolly laughed at the older woman's crude remark. She was used to 'mill talk' although she didn't engage in it for fear of a tongue-lashing from her mother. Florence Armitage firmly insisted that her offspring should speak properly, no 'thee and thy' where 'you and your' should be used, and certainly no use of foul language.

'Only ignorant people curse,' she told them.

Before her marriage to Clem, Florence had worked as a maid for the Cartwrights at Denby Hall, as had her grandmother and mother before her. Penelope Cartwright, mistress of the house and a benevolent employer had taken it upon herself to educate her maids, and it was there that Florence had learned to speak correctly, and to read. Considering both attributes important, she had passed them on to her own children.

'Did your mam like the apple pie my mam sent round for you?' Dolly asked as she eased the cork out of the bottle of cold tea to wash down her sandwich.

'She thought it wa' lovely. It made her cry, but she cries at everything since me gran died. It wa' bad enough before but now, livin' in our house is bloomin' awful. Me mam weepin' an' me dad grumblin' 'cos he can't work any more.'

Dolly's heart went out to Nellie. Her dad had been crippled in a mining accident and had to walk with crutches. She thought fondly of her own dad, a joiner working for J T Ellis the furniture maker whose factory was on the spare ground at the end of Silver Street, right next to where they lived. Then she thought of her mam. Mam never cried. She was unfailingly cheerful and never complained even though she worked all day with the stink of vinegar and onions in the bottling plant at Shaw's pickle factory. Hers was a lucky family, Dolly silently acknowledged. Four people all in work and wanting for nothing.

'I'm sorry things are bad at home, and if there's anything I can do to make it better, I will,' Dolly said, squeezing Nellie's hand. 'And I know it's only Monday and we have the rest of the week to work, but if it's fine next Saturday, what do you say to taking a picnic up to Castle Hill? I'll bring the sandwiches and stuff and you just bring yourself.'

'I'd love that. You are a good friend, Dolly.' Nellie blinked away threatening tears.

Just then, George emerged from the dyehouse, his handsome face streaked with sweat and dark wet patches under the armpits of his coarse blue shirt.

'Look at you two, you're like a couple of wallflowers lolling in the sun,' he scoffed when he saw the girls leaning against the dyehouse wall.

Nellie gave him a winsome smile. She fancied George and lived in hope that one day, he might see her as someone who wasn't just his sister's friend – all being that he got fed up of Amy Dickenson and her moaning, spiteful ways.

'Feeling the heat are you, Georgie boy?'

Dolly's sarcasm made him laugh.

'Not as much you will, sis, if you don't get your bum off the cobbles and get back to work. The hooter's about to blow, and Sam Firth's looking nastier than usual.'

The piercing blast had the girls and women scrambling to their feet, and under the baleful eye of the unpopular overlooker, they began to make their way back to the shed.

'Hold on there, Sam. I want a word.' Oliver Hardcastle's imperious shout wiped the ugly look off Sam's face, and stopped the weavers in their tracks.

Tall, broad and darkly handsome in his crisp white shirt,

sleeves rolled up to his elbows, the mill manager hurried up the yard to stand by the overlooker at the weaving shed door. He gave the women clustered in front of him a friendly, sympathetic smile. They smiled back. They all admired Oliver.

'Ladies, I can't control the weather or the heat in the shed, but I can help alleviate it.'

He turned to Sam. 'Make sure that there is plenty of fresh water for the women to drink as and when they need to, and if any of them are feeling faint, allow them outside until they're refreshed.' Oliver's firm command was accompanied by a stern glare at the overlooker.

'I will, Mister Hardcastle,' muttered Sam, giving an obsequious smile.

'See that you do.' Oliver did not return the smile.

'Mr Hardcastle, sir. Can I have a minute?' A woman in the crowd pushed her way up to the front. 'I've not roved a pick all mornin', Mr Hardcastle. Me loom needs warpin' and Isaac's that busy he hasn't got round to seein' to it.'

Oliver sighed audibly. 'I'm sorry for that, Connie. With only one tuner, we have to be patient. I'll attend to it myself as soon as I've fixed the carding machine.' He looked fit to be tied as his gaze ranged from the women to one of the carders who was frantically beckoning him from outside the carding room where raw wool was passed through a machine to prepare the fibres for spinning. 'It appears to have broken down again.'

The women muttered sympathetically. They understood his predicament. Too many workers had been let go, every department shorthanded, and at each stage in the process of making cloth, Oliver was beset with problems. They all knew that Jebediah Lockwood was a drunken sot who cared nothing for his mill or their livelihoods. Every corner he cut and every wage he didn't have to pay put more money in his own pocket to squander on his profligate way of life. They also knew that the mill would stumble to a halt if it wasn't for Oliver's efforts, and that they would be on the scrapheap.

'Thanks for the offer of the water, Mister Hardcastle,' Dolly sang out.

'If I feel faint, wilt tha come an' carry me out in thi strong arms, Mister Hardcastle?'

Annie Wilkinson weighed all of sixteen stones and the women and Oliver roared with laughter.

'It will be my pleasure, Annie,' he said, flexing his muscles. 'Now ladies. Back to work if you will.' He stood to one side to let them troop into the shed. 'You, Firth, fetch the water.' Oliver strode back to the carding room and, looking as black as thunder, Sam Firth went to fill two buckets from the tap in the dyehouse.

'The rotten old beggar's not best pleased at being given orders to be nice to us,' Dolly said as she watched Sam stomp across the yard.

'I wouldn't put it past him to piss in it,' Hetty sneered. 'Mek sure tha smells it afore tha sups it, lasses.'

Most of the women laughed, but one or two of them exchanged concerned glances. Sam Firth was a nasty old sod. He bullied the weavers and found fault with their work so that he could extort fines that were deducted from their wages. When they complained at his unfairness, he demanded sexual favours to offset the fine. The older women held him in contempt, and the young ones feared him.

As the women trooped back inside the weaving shed, Isaac Horsfall, the elderly loom tuner, was working on the loom next to Dolly's. Giving him a warm smile, she asked him to thread her shuttle. Isaac took the shuttle in his gnarled hands, and with one quick suck, he drew the yarn through. By now, the other looms had roared into motion, and Dolly mouthed, 'Thanks, Isaac. You're a good man.'

'You're a grand lass yersen, Dolly,' he replied, his smile as warm as her own. He trudged back to the loom he was warping.

For the rest of the morning, Dolly and her companions toiled on, the heat in the shed intolerable. Every now and then, the perspiring women nipped to the buckets of water near the cubby hole that Sam called his office.

'Eeh, a fair needed that,' May Sykes gasped after quaffing a cup full then dipping her hands in the bucket and dabbing at her flushed face.

Sam watched as one woman after another came to refresh herself, leering lasciviously when some of them wet their hands then slid them inside their overalls, breasts jiggling as they sought to cool their overheated bodies. But, to his annoyance, there were those who were taking full advantage of Oliver's kind gesture. Sam had refilled the buckets twice already.

When he saw Lily by the buckets again, he let out a yell and blundered out of his cubby hole. 'Are you trying to bloody drown yersen,' he barked. 'That's third time in t'last half-hour thas left thi loom.'

Lily splashed her face and neck, then loosening the top of her cross-over pinny, she wet her hands again and slowly and sensuously slipped one hand inside, raising her breasts so high that he could see her nipples. Sam's eyes boggled with lust.

'Is this hot weather makin' thi feel all hot an' bothered, Mister Firth?' Lily drawled as she dabbed water under the pert, pink mounds in the sure knowledge that in the shed full of women and Isaac, Sam hadn't the nerve to do anything else but look frustrated.

'Get back to your bloody loom,' he growled. 'Don't try my patience.'

'Is that what I'm doing, Mister Firth?' Lily sneered. She sauntered back to her loom, leaving the thwarted overseer struggling to suppress the bulge in his britches.

* * *

Up at Far View House, although it was another perfect day for gardening, Verity decided to leave clearing the weeds from the peonies and the dahlias for another day; her back ached. *My bones are lazy and unused to manual work*, she chastised herself as she lifted her breakfast dishes onto a tray then carried it down to the kitchen.

It being a Monday, Clara was in the scullery bent over the washtub, up to her elbows in hot, soapy water. She pulled up one of Jeb's shirts and rubbed the grimy cuffs vigorously on the corrugated zinc washboard. Hearing the gush of the tap and the rattle of crockery, she let the shirt slide back into the water and hurried into the kitchen, drying her stinging knuckles on her voluminous, grey apron.

'Eeh, Miss Verity, tha shouldn't be doin' that,' she expostulated when she saw Verity at the sink washing dishes. 'I've told thee afore. That's my job.'

'And now it's mine,' Verity chirped. 'I don't see why I can't wash a few dishes when you have a mountain of clothes to wash.' She lifted the empty porridge pot from the stove and plunged it into the sink. 'It was for my benefit that the pots and dishes were dirtied. It's only right that I should clean them.' Even so, she had to hide a wave of nausea as she scraped the slimy residue of boiled oats from inside the pot.

'It's very kind of thi, lass,' Clara relented. 'Washdays are allus thrawn.' Muttering her thanks, she went back into the scullery.

Verity, feeling awfully domestic and rather righteous, pulled out the plug. The scummy water swirled round the sink and gurgled down the plughole, leaving behind a vile detritus of food particles. Ignoring it, she lifted the drying cloth, and humming a little tune, she dried the dishes and pots and put them back into the huge cupboards that filled one wall of the kitchen then glanced about her for a further task. Finding none, she trotted into the steamy scullery.

Clara was turning the huge iron mangle's handle, soapy squirts coiling from the shirt passing between the giant wooden rollers.

'Oh, might I do that?' Verity asked gleefully.

The housekeeper looked doubtful. But seeing the eager look on her mistress's face, she said, 'Aye, if it pleases thi. But I'll feed the clothes through the rollers. I don't want thi trappin' thi fingers.'

Verity gripped the handle. Clara plunged her hands in the tub and brought up a petticoat. 'Wind when I gi' thi a nod,' she ordered, pushing the petticoat into where the rollers met. Verity turned the handle, watching with delight as the flattened garment crept through the rollers and plopped into a tin bath filled with cool rinsing water. Clara inserted a shirt then some undergarments and Verity kept winding until the tub was empty and her arm aching.

Within the next hour, the whites were washed, mangled and rinsed then mangled again, and shirt, aprons, caps and petticoats dipped in Dolly Blue and finally starched and mangled for the last time. Verity looked proudly at the wicker baskets filled with clean linens. 'I'll peg these out on the line to dry,' she said enthusiastically as she lifted a basket.

Resigned to her demands, Clara looked pained but said, 'Aye, if tha insists.'

In the rear garden, Verity pegged merrily, and when Clara brought out the other basket, Verity said, 'They'll be dry in no time in all this glorious sunshine.'

Clara gazed in dismay at the haphazard display on the washing line. She herself had a regimented routine: shirts pegged by their tails, undergarments by the shoulders or waists, and finally aprons and caps. Now, some shirts dangled by the neck whilst others were tossed over the line and pinned at the armpits, and all interspersed with a jumble of badly pegged undergarments and aprons. *Never mind*, she silently told herself. She'd peg them properly when her mistress tired of helping.

'Thas done a grand job there, Miss Verity. Cut my work by half the time,' Clara said, but she felt anxious as to what the master might say if his daughter told him she had done the washing. It wasn't fitting, and furthermore the greedy, drunken sot might decide to dispense with her services if he knew his daughter could do the chores. Thinking on her feet, she craftily added, 'That leaves just the bedlinens to do, but we'll have to wait for the copper to boil afore we tackle them so you get off an' enjoy the sunshine.'

Verity, still glowing under Clara's praise and the feeling of having done something worthwhile, discovered she was relieved to hear it. *I'm not used to expending such energy*, she silently admitted with a tinge of disgust. When she said, 'Then I'll walk into town, Mrs Medley, and visit the library,' Clara breathed a sigh of relief.

Up in her bedroom, Verity stripped off the blouse and skirt she was wearing and put on her blue dress: the same dress her Leeds cousins had made sneering reference to by saying, 'It must be summer. Miss Longshanks is wearing the blue', or, 'You can tell it's not winter; she's not wearing the brown wool'. She would have liked a new dress and had been tempted to buy one with some of the money her father had given her, but fearing that it might be a long time before he handed over any more, she had resisted; the Medleys must get their next wages, and food had to be bought if they were not to starve. She would have preferred to wear her mauve suit but it was too hot for the high-collared, neat-fitting, woollen jacket and skirt.

The blue dress had a boat-shaped neckline, a loosely bloused bodice and elbow-length sleeves. Verity had grown an inch or two since it had been bought and now the draped skirt was fashionably short and showed off her trim ankles. Gazing at her reflection in the mirror, she decided against rolling her long, chestnut hair, and draping it over her ears, she fastened it back with a blue ribbon. Then she pinned on her straw boater.

I look quite presentable, she thought, and anticipating the pleasure of choosing two new books, she picked up her basket, skipped downstairs and went out into the sunshine. She glanced at the peonies, telling them she'd rescue them soon, and walking down the drive, she admired the freed-up lavender. *I'm learning to be useful in more ways than one*, she told herself, feeling pleased with her early-morning labours.

At the foot of the hill, she paused at Aunt Martha's gate then walked up the path and into the house. 'Good morning, Aunt Martha,' she called out as she stepped into the hallway.

'Is that you, Verity?' her aunt called back.

'It is,' Verity replied, walking into the parlour to find her aunt sitting in a chair by the window nibbling on an oatcake smeared with treacle. Martha waved a sticky finger at a chair opposite to the one in which she was seated.

'Sit thi down, child, and tell me what's going on up the hill.'

Verity, knowing that her aunt was referring to Jeb's behaviour, suppressed a sigh. Just lately, Martha seemed obsessed by her brother's profligate lifestyle and each Friday when she came for dinner, she rebuked him soundly. She might well have not troubled herself, for Jeb either bawled her out or sat in surly silence and drank.

'Much the same as usual, Aunt,' said Verity as she reluctantly sat down; she had not intended to stay any length of time. 'He comes and goes at all hours and is often the worse for wear.' Then unexpectedly feeling rather loyal, she added, 'But perhaps he is attending to the mill. The other day, he went to Honley to discuss business, so Medley told me.'

'He'll need to do a lot more than that if he's to stay afloat,' Martha replied dryly. 'I've said it afore, and I'll say it again: you need to take him in hand, Verity, or it'll be ruin for all of us.' She stuffed the last of the oatcake into her mouth and munched noisily.

Verity stood. 'I'll do what I can, Aunt.' And eager to curtail the conversation, she said, 'I'm going into town. Is there anything you need?'

Martha pursed her sticky lips. 'Aye, bring me back some liquorice. It helps move me bowels. You'll find it in the dispensary in Byram Arcade.'

Loath to dwell on the subject of Aunt Martha's bowels, Verity bid her good day and walked down into the town. It being Monday and market day, the streets were busy and as Verity reached the junction of Kirkgate with Lord Street, the throng thickened with folks making their way to the open market on Great Northern Street. As Verity waited on the corner to cross the street, a cart with high sides trundled past, bleating lambs pushing their noses through the slats: a pitiful sound heralding a more piteous end. They were heading for the beast market to be sold and slaughtered. *The world can be a cruel place at times*, Verity thought as she continued on her way to Westgate.

However, such grim thoughts left her mind as soon as she entered Byram Arcade. Its cathedral-high glass ceiling and floors of terracotta and blue tiles, and the two balconies with elegant, iron balustrades were indeed a pleasing sight. There was all manner of shops on the ground floor and the two upper storeys, and finding the dispensary, she stepped inside, her nose assailed by the smells of cough linctus, camphor and sweet-smelling soap. After buying four ounces of liquorice for Aunt Martha, she window-shopped on the ground floor then climbed the steps to the upper galleries admiring hats, capes and dresses, none of which she could afford to buy but it didn't stop her dreaming.

Her mind's eye filled with images of feathered hats and embroidered tunics, she left the arcade, intent on going to Church Street and the library. On the corner, with her back to Rushworth's Bazaar, Verity waited for a tram to rattle along John William Street before she could cross the road. Above the clanking of the tram's wheels on the iron rails, she heard raised voices. Then someone shouted her father's name.

'Jeb Lockwood! That's who's to blame. Bloody Jebediah Lockwood!'

Shocked by the impassioned cry, Verity turned to see who it was that was shouting.

What she next saw and heard clutched at her heart and she stood feet glued to the pavement, her senses whirling.

A shabbily dressed young man, tears streaming down his cheeks, was holding on to the arms of a young woman in such a manner that Verity was unsure whether he was about to shake her or simply in need of her support. The woman gave no sign of being afraid for her safety as she gazed imploringly at him, her careworn features pale and drawn. Two small children of maybe two and four years clung to the tails of her frayed shawl, their grimy faces smeared with snot and tears.

'Aye, I was in the pub, Emmy, but I took no drink. Honestly, I wa' lookin for work,' the young man pleaded, and letting go of her arms, he reared his head, his contrition changing to anger as he snarled, 'Work I wouldn't be seekin' if bloody Lockwood hadn't let me go.'

'Don't cry, John, not here in front o' the childer an' all,' Emmy softly begged as, adjusting her shawl, she drew the children into its folds. They buried their faces in her tattered skirt. 'It wa' just that I saw thee comin' out o' The Swan Wi' Two Necks that gev me the wrong idea. I'm right sorry.' Oblivious to Verity and passers-by, Emmy reached up and stroked John's face. 'Like you said, love, you're not to blame. You did nowt wrong at t'mill. He sacked you to save his brass.' Emmy's lip curled with distaste. 'An' all so he can pour it down his throat an' piss it up against the wall.'

'Aye, you're right about that,' John grunted.

'Summat'll turn up, lad, never fret.' Emmy sounded falsely brave.

The pathetic scene brought tears to Verity's eyes and she blinked them away, her heart bleeding for the poor couple's distress. John stooped, and picking up the youngest child, he nuzzled its neck with his tear-stained face. 'Aye, I'll just keep on lookin', lass, but for now, let's go home.' Emmy took the hand of the older child and the sad little family plodded along John William Street united by love and misery.

Only a few minutes had passed, but to Verity, it felt like an hour since she had last moved. She stared at the trams and carts trundling past but she wasn't seeing them. The young woman's pale, weary face and the defeated man's pitiful hopelessness was etched on her mind's eye. To think that her father had reduced them to such misery made her seethe with rage.

From a distance, she heard the clock of the Parish Church strike eleven. Gathering her wits, she crossed the road and walked briskly down Kirkgate, her trip to the library forgotten. She was going to the mill: her mill.

6

The sun had almost reached its zenith, the strong rays beating down on Verity's head as she hurried towards Aspley Wharfe. Dazzling glares reflected from the glazed roofs of the mills into a haze of smoke and sunlight, the air oppressive, not a breath of wind. By the time she arrived at the wharf, her brow and upper lip were moist with perspiration and damp patches darkened the underarms of her dress.

As she approached the open mill gates, she slowed her pace, dithering uncertainly and swapping her basket from one hand to the other, its handle slippery with sweat. Should she go in? Or should she leave it for another day, when she felt less hot and more in control of her temper? A picture of the hapless John and Emmy clouded her vision, and Aunt Martha's wittering concerns sprang to mind. The need to find out what was going on at Lockwood Mill gave her courage.

She took a handkerchief from her dress pocket and dabbed her face then rubbed the square of cotton between her hands in order to feel presentable. Her thudding heart steadied as she gazed around her at the blackened mills and warehouses, a hive of industry in the heart of the cloth-manufacturing town. On the nearby canal, a barge loaded with bales moved serenely along the waterway, the greasy waters swirling in its wake. The incessant throb of machinery pulsated in Verity's ears, and all at once, she felt revived and ready to complete her mission. The mill gates were open and unmanned. Pushing back her shoulders, she walked into the yard. *I have a right to be here*, she told herself. *This is my father's mill, and I am his heir.*

Oliver Hardcastle emerged from the carding room, head down as he brushed lint from his trousers. He did not see the young woman in a blue dress as she stepped inside the mill office situated at the top of the yard and close by the gate.

In the unattended office, Verity saw the clutter of ledgers and invoices, loom patterns and yarn samples on the desk, and the open drawers of the filing cabinet. No one here to attend to the business, she noted, but plenty in need of attention. She had expected to find a clerk or the manager at his desk and now she was uncertain what to do next. Backing out of the office, she all but collided with Oliver.

'Begging your pardon, Miss. Were you looking for someone?'

Verity turned to find herself being scrutinised by a pair of sharp blue eyes. Her breath caught in her throat, and feeling extremely embarrassed, she was temporarily lost for words.

Furthermore, she looked so nervous and guilty that Oliver had to suppress a smile. He noted that her silver-grey eyes were almost – but not quite – on a level with his own. At six-feet tall, he was used to lowering his gaze to look into a pretty face, not that he thought her pretty. Even so, she was not without a certain sort of beauty, her high cheekbones and determined chin well-defined and interesting. What was her business? he mused. She didn't look like a mill girl, her dress well-worn but of fine quality and her bearing that of a woman of means.

'How may I be of assistance, Miss? I'm Oliver Hardcastle, manager of Lockwood Mill.'

Verity's composure recovered she held out her hand. 'Verity Lockwood, Jebediah's daughter. I'm pleased to make your acquaintance, Mr Hardcastle.'

Oliver liked the sound of her well-modulated, rather musical voice. So... this was Jeb's daughter. The one who had recently returned to live at Far View House having been away since she was a child. He'd heard it from Clara Medley's sister, Elsie, who worked in the spinning shed. Jeb hadn't mentioned her at all.

'I'm pleased to meet you, Miss Lockwood. However, your father isn't at the mill today; he... he... is elsewhere on business.' Oliver looked discomfited as if to say, *Don't ask me where*, then calmly added, 'I presume it was him you came to see.'

Verity heard the hesitancy in Oliver's response and noticed that his cheeks had reddened. *He's lying*, she thought, *making excuses to save me embarrassment. He has no more idea than I as to my father's whereabouts but he has his suspicions; what public house is he gracing with his presence as we speak?*

'I didn't come here to see my father, Mr Hardcastle. I came to see you, and to ask how the mill is faring.' She smiled, keen to put him at ease. 'I'd like to see how the mill works.'

Her request came as a shock. Oliver rarely felt out of his depth, but at that moment, he felt himself floundering. Had Jeb sent her? Was this some ruse to find him wanting?

'Did your father ask you to come?' Oliver wasn't about to play games. He didn't trust his employer and he wasn't about to be made a fool of.

This time, it was Verity's cheeks that flushed. 'He doesn't know I'm here, and I'd prefer that you did not mention my visit when next you see him, but I am interested in learning how the mill works. Will you give me a tour of the premises, please?'

Stranger and stranger, thought Oliver. But who was he to refuse the girl who would one day inherit Lockwood Mill – if it survived that long?

'As you wish, Miss Lockwood. Where would you like to begin?'

'I know nothing about the manufacture of cloth, Mr Hardcastle, so I'll leave you to lead the way.' Again, Verity smiled in a friendly fashion, and Oliver noticed how her intelligent grey eyes lit up her handsome face.

'Then we'll begin with the production of shoddy mungo.' Oliver, still doubtful as to why she had come and eager to get rid of her, set off walking briskly across the mill yard to a low building with one small window and a pair of double doors.

'I'm familiar with the terms shoddy and mungo but I've no idea what they mean,' Verity said as she matched his stride, 'but I was told by my own father that my great-grandfather was a weaver of fine worsted. Is that not why he founded the mill?'

Oliver's neck reddened. She'd caught him out. He had thought that if he showed her the worst aspect of what the mill produced, her interest would wane, and she'd leave – in a hurry.

'That's true, we do weave fine worsted,' he admitted, coming to a halt outside the double doors, 'but the production of shoddy and mungo were a principal part of the mill's success in the early days.'

'Then I'm more than interested to see what that entails, Mr Hardcastle,' Verity replied in a tone rich with confidence. 'I wish to learn all I can about the mill.'

'Well, let's begin your education right here.' He pulled open one of the wide doors. A putrid, overpowering stink belched out, and Verity visibly recoiled. Oliver hid a wry smile. 'After you, Miss Lockwood.'

Holding her hand to her nose to filter the foul stench, Verity stepped inside, desperate not to eject the breakfast she had eaten several hours before.

'This is where the shoddy mungo begins its process.' Oliver gestured at the huge bales of rags stacked high against the walls and then at a large, foul mound of tattered cloth around which eight ill-clad girls and women in shawls and broken-down boots picked out unwanted objects such as buttons and bits of wood and paper, their filthy, nimble fingers tossing the rubbish into wooden skips and throwing the freed rags onto another heap. With their heads down, the women doggedly carried on ferreting through the mounds of stinking waste but raised curious eyes when they saw Verity, puzzled to see a grand lady staring at them, clearly appalled by what she saw. They looked from her to Oliver, their frowns changing to smiles as he greeted them.

'How is young Alfie, Mary? Has he recovered from the croup?'

'Aye, Mister Hardcastle, he's doin' rightly.' Gratitude lit the woman's face.

'And what about you, Katy? Is your mother's leg healed?'

'It's nearly better, sir.' The young girl blushed prettily at the enquiry. Oliver addressed each of the women in turn, his manner warm and friendly.

Further down the shed, two men tinkered with a monstrous machine.

'Jim. Norman.' Oliver called out cheerily then grimaced. 'Don't tell me... it's broken down again.'

'No, Mr Hardcastle. We're just cleaning the teeth.'

Verity watched all this with a mixture of surprise and horror. Amazed that he seemed to know all their names and their problems – she didn't think her father would – and aghast that anyone had to earn a living doing such a filthy job.

Sickened, Verity turned to meet Oliver's steady gaze. 'Why on earth are they doing this?' she gasped. 'It's absolutely disgusting. Positively evil. Surely...'

'They do it so that the mill can produce cheap fibres out of which we make blankets, and yes, it is disgusting,' he replied, his words almost drowned by the roar of the machine into which the men were now feeding bundles of rags. A thousand teeth chewed ravenously then spewed out tangled fibres. 'The machine shreds the rags ready for spinning into yarn,' he yelled, and seeing Verity's distraught expression, 'I take it you've seen enough?'

She nodded, her stomach churning and the chattering rattle of the machine making her head spin as Oliver ushered her out into the smoky but fresher air.

Verity gulped and breathed through her mouth to rid herself of the stink that was clinging to the inside of her nose and throat. Then she shook her head to dispel the sight of the downtrodden women and girls that was stamped on her eyeballs.

'Those girls and women...' She looked as though she might cry.

'Yes, there are some jobs in the making of cloth that are vile but necessary if we are to stay in business.' Oliver sounded bitter. 'Now, shall we continue or have you seen enough?'

He eyed her coolly as though he was merely tolerating her presence.

He thinks I'm some silly, privileged girl come to poke her nose into her father's business just for amusement, Verity told herself, believing that he had chosen to show her the very worst part of the mill in order to get rid of her. She drew herself up to full height and met his gaze. 'Lead on, good man.'

Goodness me, I sound like Aunt Martha, she thought as she accompanied him down the mill yard.

A whirlwind tour ensued, Oliver delivering terse explanations as they progressed from one part of the mill to another, Verity learning that some parts were called 'sheds' and others 'rooms'.

'Scouring shed,' Oliver announced in the hot, steamy atmosphere of a place filled with vats of boiling water. 'Washing the wax out of the raw wool.' He exchanged a few friendly words with the two men pushing raw wool into the vats and stirring it with long poles before indicating for Verity to move on.

He led the way up a flight of wooden stairs to where women toiled over huge machines that spun the fibre into yarn, the dust clogging in Verity's throat and the whir of the giant frames assaulting her ears as she watched yarn twist round fattening bobbins.

'Loose twist for plain, woollen cloth, tight twist for worsted,' Oliver said, and Verity none the wiser other than that the spinning shed was yet another place where women sweated in the intense heat. They all acknowledged him with smiles, and an older woman called out, 'I see thas got a lady to keep thi company today, Mister Hardcastle.'

Oliver and the women laughed.

In the dyehouse, steamy and stinking of natural and aniline dyes, a rather handsome young man with reddish hair addressed Oliver. 'We're short on indigo to complete this order, Mr Hardcastle. We'll need a fresh order tomorrow.'

'I'll see what I can do, George,' said Oliver but he sounded less than hopeful.

George gave him a sympathetic grin, one that suggested they shared the problem.

Finally, they entered the weaving shed and walked slowly down the 'weavers alley', explanation impossible as the looms rattled and roared, but it did not prevent the weavers from giving

Oliver a smile or a wave. Three looms stood idle. An elderly man was fixing the warp on one. The unemployed women watched, dismal and impatient. Oliver had a word with the man, who gave him a weary smile. Then he seemed to share a joke with the women, for they giggled and nudged one another.

Verity, feeling shut out, turned back into 'the alley', looking from left to right at the sharp-eyed, quick-moving weavers as they darted back and forth catching at loose ends, refilling pirns and keeping their eyes on the flying shuttle as the beaters thrashed and the woven pieces lengthened. As she noted their sweat-stained overalls and brows as they toiled relentlessly weaving worsted for her father – a man who cared nothing for their wellbeing – she experienced a surge of anger.

Seething inwardly, she waited for Oliver. As they retraced their steps, he stopped to speak to one of the women, and it was then that Verity spotted a familiar face. It belonged to the red-haired girl she had seen in the cemetery at Almondbury. The girl glanced up from her loom and for a fleeting moment, their eyes met.

The girl looked across 'the alley' and raised two fingers to her lips, seeking the attention of another girl that Verity knew she had seen before. Lips moving, eyes lighting up, smiles on their faces they made a swift, inaudible exchange. Were they talking about her?

Verity stood, alternately blushing and trembling, as several other weavers turned their eyes on her, the expressions on their faces ranging from the curious to the envious or downright contempt. Suddenly, she felt shrouded in shame – shame that her life was so easy, that she had the audacity to pride herself on helping with the laundry and pulling up weeds.

'We had better keep moving, Miss Lockwood,' she heard Oliver say directly into her ear. She felt his hot breath on her neck and his hand gently nudging her elbow. Her breath caught in her throat, the skin under her sleeve tingled, and she felt quite shocked by how his touch made her feel. 'The hooter's about to go and we don't want to be trampled in the rush for the door,' he said.

On feet that felt as though they belonged to someone else, Verity let him shepherd her out into the yard. A piercing blast and the rattling, clacking looms ground to halt, the noise changing to a chorus of women's chatter as they streamed out to find a shady place to eat their dinnertime snap. Verity suddenly realised she too was hungry. Oliver set off walking towards the gate, and she kept pace with him.

At the gate, he held out his hand. 'I hope you found your visit interesting, Miss Lockwood, and that your curiosity has been satisfied,' he said, a smile twitching the corners of his mouth.

Verity couldn't decide whether she liked him or not. There was an arrogance about him, and his attitude towards her was verging on disdain – she didn't like that – but then she recalled his compassion towards the women in the shoddy mungo shed and the friendly smiles and respect he'd received from the workers in all the sheds and rooms they had visited. She didn't quite know what to make of him, and yet there was something solid and reliable about him: a man you could trust. She decided to make clear the reason for her visit.

She took his hand in hers and gave it a brief shake. Then drawing herself up to her full height, she looked directly into his eyes, and in a resolute voice that barely hid suppressed annoyance, she said, 'Mr Hardcastle, my visit today was not merely to satisfy my idle curiosity; it was to allay my concerns. It has been brought to my attention that the mill is in trouble due to my father's neglect. I came to see for myself how bad things are.'

Oliver's eyebrows rose and his rather unctuous smile was wiped clean off his face.

Verity pressed on, her eyes alight with zeal. 'I saw for myself the poor working conditions, the idle or temperamental machinery and the overworked employees. Now, what I want to know is, how can we rectify the problem to ensure the mill's prosperity, not for my benefit but for those in its employ? If it is to fold – and my informant predicts that that might well be the case – it will put all those poor souls out of work.'

She spoke with such fervour and compassion that Oliver was immediately regretful.

'Miss Lockwood. I owe you an apology. I completely misunderstood your intentions.' His handsome face creased in contrition, and his straight white teeth bit into his lower lip in consternation. This girl was nobody's fool. She was brave and caring, putting the workers' needs above her own. Silently admitting that he had wrongly judged her, he said, 'Please, Miss Lockwood, allow me to make amends. I usually have something to eat at this time of day. Will you join me in the office so that we can discuss the matter over a sandwich?'

'Thank you, Mr Hardcastle. I appreciate you giving me your time. I will join you.'

Out in the yard in the shade of the dyehouse wall, Dolly exclaimed, 'I knew it was her the minute I saw her. You'd remember somebody with her bearing.'

'Aye, I recognised her as well,' Nellie said before biting into a slice of drip bread. 'But what's she doin' here?'

'Maybe she's a lady friend of Mr Hardcastle's and he was just showing her where he works,' Dolly replied as she opened her snap tin.

In the office, Oliver and Verity sat at opposite sides of the desk that Oliver had hastily cleared and as they chewed on cheese and pickle in thick white bread, they talked.

'We are small compared to many of the mills in the valley but we produce a decent quality of cloth. However, our looms are dated and badly maintained due to your father insisting we can manage with only one tuner. And then there is the problem of obtaining supplies when the bills go unpaid. We are ticking over, and no more. I fear that closure or a sell-out is on the cards, and that may well result in our mill hands losing their livelihoods. Jobs are hard to come by in the present climate.'

'I'm aware of that,' Verity said, feeling much more in control now that her belly wasn't grumbling. She went on to tell Oliver what she had witnessed earlier that morning in the street outside Rushworth's Bazaar. 'They were desperate,' she concluded.

Oliver saw how much it had pained her.

'That would be John Halstead. He was a tuner, and a good one at that. He's sorely missed.' Oliver rubbed his hand over his face despairingly.

'Yet my father let him go.'

'The master's laid off a dozen and more men in the past three months. We're down to only three men in the dyehouse where there should be five, two carders are expected to do the work of four, as are the men in the wash house, and as you saw for yourself, we only have one loom tuner. There's not a week goes by that he doesn't sack someone.'

Oliver's disconsolate shrug spoke a thousand words.

'Why does he do that?'

Oliver hesitated. 'He... he says we can't afford their wages, what with the price of raw materials having increased this past year and the selling price of worsted fallen. The blankets we weave from the shoddy bring in next to nothing, and our machinery is constantly in need of repair.' Then, deciding to be perfectly honest, he added, 'But that's only part of it. The delivery of raw wool and aniline dyes has been stopped until he settles the bills.'

'Then the business is indeed most precarious, Mr Hardcastle.'

'I have to agree, Miss Lockwood. We can't match our competitors in the valley when production is low and investment even lower.'

'Then what are we to do?'

Oliver sat back in his chair, and raising his arms, he clasped his hands at the back of his head. What could she do? It was plain that she had been touched by John Halstead's plight and the arduous working conditions in the mill, but she was just a young, privileged woman who more than likely had no influence over her father and whilst she might be showing an interest now, how long would it last? He stretched his arms wide and gave a deep sigh.

Verity found herself fascinated by the way in which his white shirt stretched across his broad chest and the sinews in his arms rippled. She'd never before looked at a man in this way, and now she found herself wondering what it would feel like to be wrapped in those strong arms.

'Forgive me,' she said, suddenly aware that Oliver was still speaking. 'I was distracted for a moment. What was it you were saying?'

'That we need to give the matter careful thought. Perhaps you should go and reflect on what you've seen this morning and then ask yourself what can be done about it.' Oliver gave her a deep, meaningful look that said he believed her interest in the mill would fade when she contemplated its problems and how her involvement in rectifying them might affect her life. A spurt of rage pierced Verity's chest.

'You're still thinking I came here on a whim to satisfy my idle curiosity,' she cried. 'That I'll go away and forget what I've seen and heard today in pursuit of something else that interests me. Well, you are wrong, Mr Hardcastle, very wrong!'

Her voice had risen an octave, and her cheeks were blazing. Oliver thought she looked quite magnificent, and he realised that yet again, he had misjudged her. However, conscious that time was ticking away and that there were other things requiring his attention, he got to his feet. Verity also stood.

'Very well, Miss Lockwood. I appreciate your concern, but I'm still of the opinion that you should give it more thought before committing yourself to such an overwhelming task.'

'I will most certainly be giving it serious consideration, Mr Hardcastle. Like you, I intend to make sure the mill doesn't founder so I'll leave you to get back to work. I'm sure you have plenty to do.' She picked up her basket and walked to the door. Oliver held it open.

'Indeed, I have. I told Isaac I'd lend a hand with the broken-down looms.'

Verity recalled how a lock of black hair had fallen endearingly over Oliver's brow when he had bent his head to talk directly into the loom tuner's ear. 'Yes. you did, Mr Hardcastle,' she chirped, at the same time wondering why she had remembered the incident in that way.

'What this mill needs right now is an influx of hard cash to pay off its debts so that we can buy the supplies needed to keep up production,' Oliver said by way of reinforcing the momentous task she seemed so keen to take on.

'Sadly, Mr Hardcastle, I have no personal wealth that would instantly solve the problem, but I'm pleased we've met and that we can work together.' She walked out of the office, head held high, and her shapely hips swaying as she walked across the cobbles to the gate.

Oliver watched her go. *She's a woman to be reckoned with*, he mused, as he hurried to the weaving shed.

* * *

'Did you see the girl that Oliver Hardcastle was showing round the mill this morning?' Dolly asked George as they walked home that evening in the rain. Earlier that afternoon, thunder clouds had massed over the town, dispelling the intense heat in a torrential downpour that had dissipated into a fine drizzle, the sort that wets one through in a matter of minutes.

'Aye, Mr Hardcastle brought her into the dyehouse. He was—'

George got no further. Dolly interrupted, as she so often did when talking to her brother.

'Well, me and Nellie saw her in Almondbury cemetery when we went to put flowers on her granny's grave. She was wandering round looking at the headstones. She looked lonely.'

'Did she now?' George grinned. It was just like soft-hearted Dolly to be sensitive to how she thought other people were feeling.

'We wondered who she was,' Dolly said, pulling her shawl further over her head.

'Well, for your information, she's Miss Lockwood, Jeb's daughter.'

'Ooh! I told Nellie that maybe she was Mr Hardcastle's lady friend come to see where he worked.' Dolly giggled at her mistake then, her smile slipping, she said, 'Jeb's daughter, eh? Why do you think she came to the mill? If she was looking for her dad, she was looking in the wrong place. She should have tried the Pack Horse pub.'

'Aye, you can say that again. And can we have less talk and walk a bit faster? I'm getting soaked.'

'All right, clever clogs. I'm just curious, that's all.' Dolly lengthened her stride, her boots squelching in the puddles.

'Whatever the reason, Mr Hardcastle gave her a full tour of every shed and then they sat in his office and talked for ages.'

'How do you know all this, Mr Know-All?'

'I keep my eyes and my ears open on anything to do with the mill. My job and yours relies on it, and we all know Lockwood's isn't doing as well as it could.' George frowned. 'We've run out of indigo dye to complete an order and Jarmain's won't deliver any more until they get paid for the last lot. That's how bad things are.'

'We'd umpteen looms standing idle and Isaac running rings round himself trying to fix them until Mr Hardcastle came and helped him,' Dolly said despondently.

'Aye, Oliver's a good 'un,' George agreed, 'and if it wasn't for him, Lockwood's 'ud be in a worse mess than it already is.'

George would have been surprised to learn that at that same moment, Verity Lockwood was sitting in the drawing room at Far View House thinking exactly the same thing. Maybe Oliver Hardcastle was the shining light at the end of a dark tunnel. Granted, at the start, his rather condescending attitude had annoyed her, but during their conversation over lunch, she had come to realise that he was putting his heart and soul into keeping the mill a going concern. But, as she sat mulling over the meeting and trying to make sense of all she'd seen and heard that morning, she had yet to reach a solution as to how she might help him. However, she was determined to try.

Earlier that afternoon as she'd walked back to Far View, her thoughts had been as black as the gathering clouds, and when thunder rumbled over the hills, it had sounded as angry as she felt.

She had arrived home, drenched, to find Clara in a tizz. 'Eeh, Miss Verity, where hasta been all this time? An' look at the state of thi dress. Thas missed thi lunch an' I wa' beginnin' to think summat had happened to thi.'

Touched by her concern, Verity told her that she had had lunch with a friend. Clara, looking puzzled, had refrained from asking who, which was just as well, thought Verity as she watched the rain trickle down the window. It would have been unwise to tell Clara of her visit to the mill, but the housekeeper would have to get used to her being out of the house in the forthcoming days. Lockwood Mill had to be saved, and she intended to do just that.

But where and how should she start? Without any capital to invest in the mill, it seemed like an impossible task. And yet, if orders were still being fulfilled then the mill must be in receipt of some money, enough to pay the reduced workforce, and allow her father to freely spend the profits on drinking and gambling, so why was there a mountain of debt?

Puzzled as to how this could be, she waited impatiently for her father to arrive home. Some pertinent questions needed to be asked and if Jeb was relatively sober, he might give her some sensible answers. *That's my problem,* she despondently told herself, *I don't know enough about how the mill works. It was all right for Mr Hardcastle to whisk me through the sheds and rooms showing me the various processes in cloth-making – it was valuable information – but it's the financial aspect I really need to understand.*

'Will tha tek thi dinner now, Miss Verity? It's gone seven.'

Verity's troubled reverie broken, she turned to see Clara standing in the drawing-room doorway looking displeased.

'I'm waiting for my father, Mrs Medley.'

'Aye, well, he's not here, an' like I say, it's gettin' late.'

'Sorry, Mrs Medley. I'll take it now,' said Verity, aware that the sooner the evening meal was done with then the sooner Clara could go and visit her mother and her children.

After she had eaten and bade Clara goodnight, Verity returned to the drawing room. With her ears pricked for the sound of wheels on the gravel and only the ticking of the clock on the mantelpiece for company, she began to read, but the travails of the sailor, Marlow, in Conrad's *Heart of Darkness* would not hold her interest as her thoughts strayed to the mill.

When the clock chimed eleven, Jeb had still not returned, and admitting defeat, Verity went to bed. She decided that tomorrow, she would pay another visit to the mill.

7

The next morning, Verity wakened later than she had intended. She'd spent a restless night mulling over the problems at the mill then dozing off only to wake up and begin thinking all over again. Now, laid back on her pillows, she planned what she was about to do. She'd go to the mill, demand to look into the ledgers that recorded the mill's finances, and later, with that information under her belt, she could approach her father in the sure knowledge that she knew what she was talking about. If she sounded as though she had a firm grasp of the situation and her father was in a receptive mood then they might discuss matters in a business-like manner, hopefully at dinner that evening. Pleased with her notions, she climbed out of bed.

Drawing back the curtains, she saw that the sun was promising another fine day. She gazed across the distance at the lush, green fields and hedgerows scattered with gold, and on the horizon, Castle Hill. *So much beauty in the world for all to see, and yet so much ugliness*, she thought as a picture of the women in the shoddy mungo shed suddenly came to mind. Lowering her gaze to the garden below her window, she spied the dark red peonies still choked with weeds. *You'll have to wait; I have more pressing issues to deal with*, she silently told them, *the least of which is what shall I wear today? Not that I have much choice,* she thought, giving the blue dress that she would have chosen had it not suffered badly in yesterday's downpour a dismayed glance. It was now draped over the back of a chair, still damp and crumpled.

She walked over to the wardrobe and finally settled on a dark blue, crepe skirt and white, pin-tucked shirt that was slightly frayed at the collar and cuffs. Both were well past their best. *I must be the shabbiest mill heiress in the county*, she thought, as she pulled the skirt up over her long, slender thighs. Fully dressed and filled with determination to get on with the first part of her plan, she went down to breakfast.

'Has my father already eaten?' she asked on meeting Clara in the hallway.

'Medley says the master didn't come home last night. The trap's not back.' Clara sniffed her disapproval and walked into the dining room with the tray she was carrying. Verity followed, feeling extremely annoyed. Jeb was as elusive as a needle in a haystack.

Breakfast over, Verity prepared to leave the house. She was standing in front of the hallstand's mirror pinning a dark blue hat trimmed with white feathers atop her neatly rolled hair when Clara came up from the kitchen to clear the table. Clara recognised the hat. It had belonged to Verity's late mother. *He must have missed that,* she thought, recalling the terrible night Jeb had burned Leila's possessions. But Verity didn't need to know about that so Clara said, 'Off again today, Miss Verity?' her curiosity tangible.

'I am, Mrs Medley. Don't make lunch for me.' Verity picked up her gloves. She would have liked to confide in the housekeeper but first, she needed to have some news that was worth divulging. She gave Clara a warm smile. 'Thank you for all you do, Mrs Medley. You're very good to me.'

Leaving Clara pink with gratitude and her inquisitiveness unsatisfied, Verity stepped out into the sunshine and walked briskly down the drive.

She arrived at the mill shortly after ten o'clock to find Oliver in the office, his shirt sleeves rolled up, a pen in his hand and his head bent over a ledger. As she entered, he was running the fingers of his free hand through his thick black hair, making it stand up in tufts. *Quite endearing*, she thought, as startled, he looked up at the sound of her voice.

'Good morning, Mr Hardcastle.'

He dropped the pen and hastily got to his feet, his eyebrows still raised in surprise as he replied, 'Good morning, Miss Lockwood. Back so soon.' Verity thought he did not look best pleased but she was undeterred.

'Mr Hardcastle, yesterday you told me to go away and think carefully before I made a commitment to the problems facing the mill. I have thought of little else since then and have reached the conclusion that I need to understand more about the mill's finances. I have a lot of questions that require answers. Are you willing to supply them?'

'If I can,' he said rather wearily, at the same time thinking how efficient she looked in her neat blue skirt and white blouse. Today, her glossy, brown hair was rolled into the nape of her long neck, not loosely tied as it had been the day before, and she looked altogether ready to take on the world. 'Please, sit down, Miss Lockwood.'

Verity sat across from him and removed her gloves. Oliver noted that her hands were finely shaped, her fingers long and her sensible, clipped nails a pretty pink with half-moons of a paler shade. He gave a discreet cough and wondered why he was captivated by this triviality when more important matters awaited his attention. However, his dour expression gave Verity no inkling that he found her attractive or that he felt rather pleased to see her.

She decided to employ a different tack, establish a friendship and be open and honest. 'Mr Hardcastle, we are both aware that my father neglects the mill and spends much of his time in the inns in town, drinking. I'm worried that he does not know how to stop. He will not listen to me or my aunt, who is the one who told me that the mill was in trouble.' She felt ashamed to have say this. She did not expect Oliver to read the riot act to his master, but it comforted her to share the problem.

Oliver was touched by her artlessness. To admit that her father was a drunkard was brave and he admired her courage. 'I cannot interfere in that matter, but I can sympathise with you, Miss Lockwood. Your father seems to be a very unhappy man.'

'And I am part of the cause of his disillusionment. He wishes I had been a son, or...' her sarcasm was thick as treacle as she added, 'or beautiful enough to attract a wealthy husband.'

'I'm sorry things are the way they are, Miss Lockwood,' Oliver said, his voice rich with sincerity but he was at a complete loss as to where her confession was leading.

Verity's eyes narrowed and she leaned across the desk to add emphasis to what she was about to ask. 'How often does my father come to the mill? And how is it that if the mill is in dire straits, he has money to spend freely round the town?' She delivered the questions with such asperity that Oliver reckoned it would be useless to tell her anything but the truth.

'He comes often enough, but his visits are fleeting. He shows no interest in the working of the mill but he does keep his eye on the ledgers to keep abreast of production. He knows what orders we have and when they are likely to be completed. That way, he knows what's owing and when payment is due. Then, as the money comes in, we deduct the workers' wages and a few other expenses, and the master takes what's left.'

Verity frowned. 'But what if payment for the orders isn't met on time? How then do you pay the wages?'

Oliver gave a wry smile. 'I'll have you know I spend a great deal of my time chasing payments to make sure that doesn't happen. It's been a close shave more than once just lately, but fortunately, most of our clients know me well and they pay up on receipt of the goods.'

'And what are the other expenses you mentioned?' Verity felt that she needed to understand all the machinations of running the mill if she was to be of any use.

'Money to purchase the things we need to fulfil the orders,' Oliver said.

'Then why is it that you have a list of unpaid debts and can't buy dye or raw wool?'

'Because the amount to cover expenditure is limited to such a degree that we cannot pay for the things we need and we are constantly in debt.' Oliver sounded weary.

'In other words, my father takes all the profit and leaves you with a reduced workforce and nothing to pay for supplies or repairs,' Verity summed up bitterly.

'That's it in a nutshell, Miss Lockwood.'

Angered by what she had learned, and saddened by Oliver's despondence, Verity said, 'Then let's get to work.'

Oliver showed her the ledgers and patiently explained how he recorded his accounts. Credits and debits written in small, neat copperplate blurred before Verity's eyes and she marvelled at how he kept track of it all. As her quick mind got to grips with the columns of figures and each balance, she was dismayed to see the amounts of money her father regularly creamed off to fund his disgusting habits, and how little was left to purchase supplies and settle the mounting debts.

She looked at Oliver, her dismal expression letting him know she understood the precarious situation. He returned the look and was just about to show her another ledger when a woman in a turban appeared in the doorway.

'Mister Hardcastle, sir, come quick. Isaac's tekken a turn. He's lyin' on t'weaving shed floor an' he can't get a breath.'

'Good God, Maggie!' Oliver dashed to the door, calling out, 'Wait here, Miss Lockwood.' Then he raced across the mill yard, Maggie hard on his heels.

Suddenly abandoned, Verity deliberated on whether she too should go and find out what had happened to the loom tuner. But thinking she would not be of any use, she stayed where she was, making a pretence of studying a ledger but too confused to make sense of it. She stayed this way until, some fifteen minutes later, the hooter signalled dinnertime. She stood and, looking through the office's small window, she watched the mill hands stream out into the yard. A gaggle of women walked past the office door and round the corner into the shade of the gable wall. Crouched on the cobbles, they began to eat their dinner and chatter.

Verity couldn't face returning to the ledgers – the mill's finances were depressing to say the least – so she went and stood in the doorway, taking deep breaths of soot-laden air. Distasteful as it was it, it was preferable to the stuffy atmosphere in the cluttered office. The women's voices rose and fell, and keen to hear what they were talking about, she tuned in her ears to their gossip.

'Poor Isaac, he's worked himself to death to keep them looms goin' an' all for what?'

'So that greedy bugger, Jeb Lockwood, can piss it up against a wall.'

'I heard tell he wa' carried out o' t'Swan the other night. He wa' that drunk, he didn't know where he wa'.' The informant gave a throaty cackle.

'My old man told me he'd seen him gambling in the White Hart an' when he lost, he'd started a fight an' the landlord chucked him out.'

'Disgraceful, that's what I call it. Any mill master worth his salt wouldn't carry on in that fashion, an' his mill runnin' to pot.'

Verity's heart sank as she listened to the angry complaints. This was her father they were talking about.

'I've not earned a penny this morning,' a voice moaned. 'Me loom's been waiting on Isaac to come an' fix the heddle. Now the poor old beggar's laid low an' can fix nowt. I'll be lucky if I finish me piece this week.'

'Aye, it's allus same. The looms are buggered an' for all Isaac Horsfall's a grand tuner, he can't keep up wi' what needs doin'.'

'Isaac says that miserly sod Jeb Lockwood told him there's nowt wrong wi' 'em. But then, he could never tell shit from chocolate could Jeb. Mind the time he used to visit yon dirty hussy at Bank Bottom, an' him what had a lovely wife at home.'

'Aye, poor soul that she was. It no doubt wa' him that made her as sick as she was. Death musta come as a blessed relief after livin' wi' the likes of him all them years.'

'I heard she took herself off to Cornwall for months at a time just to get away from him.'

'Would you blame her?'

'Indeed, I would not. They say he wa' out in the town whorin' an' drinkin' an' gamblin' on the night the poor soul passed. God rest her.'

Verity felt sick. Not because the women had such a low

opinion of her father; it matched her own. It was the thought of her mother gradually losing her hold on life as her husband caroused the town satisfying his own filthy needs that made her feel faint. Had her mother known of his adultery?

'He has no shame hasn't that one, an' that's the long an' short of it, but talkin' about him's a waste o' breath. Let's talk of summat else.'

'Aye, talkin' about Jeb Lockwood turns me dinner sour.'

Before they could start on another topic, someone cried, 'Look, the're tekkin Isaac away.' A cart trundled from behind the weaving shed, a driver up front and Oliver and Isaac in the back. Dolly and two other women ran across the yard, Dolly shouting, 'How is he, Mr Hardcastle. Is it serious?'

'I'm taking him home. I've sent for the doctor. We'll find out then,' Oliver called back.

Verity, unsure as to what she should do, dithered inside the office doorway.

'Good luck, Isaac,' a chorus of voices cried as the cart drove away. The women went back to sit on the cobbles, bemoaning Isaac's misfortune. 'He'll not want to pay for a doctor, won't Isaac,' Hetty Lumb declared.

'Aye, he'll not. Why, on'y last week, I paid a shillin' for t'doctor to tell me our Stanley has a bad chest. We bloody knew that,' Lily scoffed.

'Jeb Lockwood should pay. It's his fault.'

Dolly's comment met with a hail of approval.

The mill hooter signalled the women back to work, and hearing the scrape of their boots on the cobbles as they prepared to return to the weaving shed, Verity slunk back into the office and slumped into the chair behind the desk. She felt ashamed.

I must do something, she thought, and hopeful that it would diminish the feeling of uselessness, she began tidying the desk, stacking the ledgers, making neat piles of invoices in date order, and replacing pens in a pot. That done, she lifted screwed-up balls of paper from the floor and put loom pattern cards in one pile and yarn samples in another. And as she worked, she gave serious thought to the present situation.

'She's here again today. Miss Lockwood. I saw her at the office window,' Dolly said as she walked across the yard with Nellie and Lily.

'Mebbe she's seein' to t'mill now that her dad's never here,' Nellie opined.

'Sumbdy needs to,' Lily scorned. 'We'll all be skint at t'end o' t' week if us bloody looms needs fixing, an' wi' Isaac tekken badly, there's not much chance o' that happenin'.'

'Poor Isaac, I hope he's not too poorly,' said Nellie.

'We'll soon find out,' Dolly said as the cart rattled back through the gate and Oliver jumped down. 'How's Isaac, Mr Hardcastle?' she cried.

'A little better, Dolly. The doctor's with him now. He says he needs complete rest so we'll have to make do without him for the time being.'

The women groaned loud enough for Verity to hear. She stopped tidying and peered through the window. Oliver was walking towards the office.

'How is Isaac?' she asked as soon as he entered.

'As well as can be expected. He's suffering from exhaustion. I don't expect him back any time soon, and it's impossible to keep the weaving shed going without a loom tuner.' Oliver looked at the end of his tether.

'Then you must rehire the man my father dismissed. What was his name? John Halstead, I believe,' Verity said, airing the first of the ideas she had had whilst tidying. 'And tell Isaac Horsfall that I will pay the doctor's bill. We don't want him worrying at a time like this.'

Oliver's jaw dropped. He gave Verity a piercing look then let his gaze travel round the office. He gave a slow smile. 'You have been busy,' he said, gesturing at the tidy desk, 'and no doubt as you tidied, you gave serious thought to running the mill.' His smile widened. 'I think we'll make a mill master of you yet – or should I say mistress?'

Verity blushed at the jesting compliment and laughed too. 'Thank you, kind sir.'

'It's not going to be easy,' Oliver said, 'and it cannot continue without attracting your father's attention. Your presence at the mill has not gone unnoticed, and there are some who will be only too eager to make him aware of it.' He was thinking of Sam Firth, the predatory overlooker.

'I've thought about that and I will tell my father at the first opportunity. If I can persuade him to let me take some responsibility for running the mill then he might be glad to share the burden. I know I'm not the son he hoped for but I am capable of doing the work of one. Father's interest might be renewed if I can make him believe that I too have the mill's best interests at heart. I will put the matter to him this evening.'

'Very wise, Miss Lockwood. It would be foolish, if not impossible, for us to go behind the master's back. If you can reason with him as to the state the mill is in, and assure him of your assistance in putting matters right...' Oliver gave helpless shrug, 'although I have tried on many occasions and failed miserably... he could well listen to *you* and be pleased by your offer. Perhaps your first task should be to persuade him to take less for himself from the incoming money so that we can purchase the supplies we need to fulfil our orders. If we don't do that then...' He threw up his hands. 'We're on a knife edge,

Miss Lockwood. What the mill needs right now is an injection of hard cash.'

'Oh, for goodness' sake, Mr Hardcastle! If we are going to work together, call me Verity, and I'll address you as Oliver.'

'As you wish... Verity.' He gave a courteous little bow.

'Then I will speak with him tonight.' With a determined toss of her head, and the brisk pulling on of her gloves, she chirped, 'I'll see you tomorrow, Oliver.'

'I'll look forward to that,' he said, his smile encouraging as he held open the office door.

'Good day, Verity.'

'Good day, Oliver.'

By the time Verity reached the foot of Far View Hill, she felt so invigorated by the plans she was making to approach her father about the mill that she almost ran up the slope.

'I'm back, Mrs Medley,' she called as she entered the house and skipped down to the kitchen. Clara saw the bloom on her cheeks and the sparkle in her eyes.

'Well, Miss Verity, whatever tha wa' at this morning, it's put some colour in thi cheeks an' a smile on thi face.'

Verity laughed. 'I feel as though I'm on the top of the world, Mrs Medley. I'll just go up to take off my things and then I'll be back down for a cup of tea, please.'

Up in her bedroom, she peered at her reflection in the mirror. She really did look different, as though a fire had been lit inside her and was burning brightly. *No more than two weeks have passed since I left Leeds and my miserable existence with Aunt Flora and my silly cousins, and in that short time, my life in Almondbury has changed so dramatically that I can barely believe it,* she silently told the happy face looking back at her.

8

On his way home that evening, Oliver called on Isaac Horsfall in Smithy Yard, an enclave of four houses behind the pickle factory. Oliver walked down the narrow passage that led from Rose Street into the yard, the strong smell of vinegar biting his nose. Knocking on the door of the nearest house, he was welcomed in by Isaac's wife, Maria.

'How is he?' Oliver asked.

'Feelin' a bit better, Mr Hardcastle. T'doctor says it's nowt too serious.'

'I'm glad to hear that. He had me worried.'

'I'm all right,' Isaac called out from his chair by the fire, his tall, gangly frame stretched out and his feet on a footstool. 'She's just fussin' over me.'

Oliver crossed the cosy little kitchen to stand in front of Isaac. He smiled down at him.

'There's nowt wrong wi' me that a couple o' days rest won't cure,' Isaac protested. 'I just took a funny turn 'cos I wa' that thrawn wi' all I had to do.' His drooping whiskers and tufted eyebrows were shaggy and greying. He reminded Oliver of a faithful old sheep dog. Years of toil in the mill to provide a home for the family of seven that he and Maria had raised had taken their toll and Isaac looked much older than his fifty-odd years.

'Don't you worry about those looms, Isaac. Just do as the doctor ordered. I want him to give you a clean bill of health before you return to work.'

'Nay, I've no use for a doctor, Mr Hardcastle. They cost too much.'

'Lockwood's will take care of his bill, Isaac. The next time he calls you, just refer him to me for payment.'

'Eeh, that's right good of thee, Mr Hardcastle,' Maria said. 'Wilt tha tek a cup of tea?'

'No thank you, I've another call to make. I'm going to ask John Halstead to come back.'

Isaac looked alarmed. 'Does that mean I'm finished. Are thi givin' him me job?'

'No, Isaac. John will stand in for you until you're well, and when you come back to the mill, he'll work under you as before,' Oliver reassured. 'We can't do without you.'

'Tha had me freetened for a minute, lad. I nearly took another turn.' Isaac chuckled. 'Has Jeb Lockwood come to his senses and started hiring again?'

'Not yet. It's Miss Lockwood who gave me permission to pay the doctor and take John back on. She's planning to make some changes for the better.' Oliver sounded far more convincing than he felt. 'Now you just concentrate on getting fit. I'll be off round to John Halstead's and give him the good news.'

Maria saw him to the door. 'Thanks, Mr Hardcastle. You're a good lad.' She patted his arm in a motherly fashion.

Oliver's next port of call resulted in screams of delight and tears. John shook Oliver's hand so vigorously, Oliver though it was in danger of being broken off at the wrist, and Emmy hugged him then blushed furiously at her audacity.

'Sorry, Mister Hardcastle... I'm just that overjoyed...' Tears prevented her from saying more. 'Wilt tha tek a cup of tea?' she asked, eager to show her appreciation.

'No thank you, Emmy, I must be on my way,' Oliver said, aware that every tealeaf was precious in a house as penurious as the Halsteads. 'My mother will have my dinner ready.'

'Does this mean I'm back for good? Even when Isaac's fit again?' John looked anxious.

'Yes, John.' Oliver hoped that was the truth.

Farewell cries ringing in his ears, Oliver left the Halstead's house and made his way to his own home at the foot of Almondbury Bank where he lived with his mother and two sisters. The substantial end terrace house that his father, Mark, had inherited from his own father was one of the better houses in the area and the Hardcastles were comfortably off, Oliver's grandfather having been a well-to-do iron master who had made his money on the railway line that ran through the Stand Edge tunnel from Huddersfield to Manchester. Mark had been an engineer and there had been enough money to provide Oliver with a sound education at King James Grammar School in Almondbury. After Mark's death, fourteen-year-old Oliver had gone to work as a clerk in Lockwood Mill and had been promoted to manager two years ago at the age of twenty-five. Now, with the welcoming lamps in the parlour in view and the thought of a tasty dinner awaiting him, Oliver quickened his pace. He was hungry and weary.

'You're late, son. What kept you?' His mother, Evelyn, began piling a plate with potatoes and braised pork as his sister, Rose, helped him off with his coat, the two women fussing round him and urging him to sit down and eat. His youngest sister, Maud, gave him a vacant smile. Both of his sisters were spinsters, twenty-nine-year-old Rose bossy and interfering and Maud, twenty-three, quiet and what their mother termed as 'light-headed'. They looked on their brother as their property.

Oliver sat down, and in between mouthfuls, he told them the events of the day. They showed genuine concern when they heard about Isaac and disparagement when he mentioned Jeb Lockwood, and were avidly curious about his daughter.

'She's a very forthright young woman with a good brain, and she seems determined to make her father come to his senses and save the mill from going bankrupt. She's already made it her business to understand the mill's finances, and I get the impression she's not afraid of hard work. I'm confident she'll bring Jeb round to her way of thinking.'

'From what you say, son, Miss Lockwood sounds as though she's a rare piece of work,' his mother commented.

His sisters nodded agreement.

'She is,' Oliver said, sitting back, his belly full and his spirits high.

* * *

The euphoria that had carried Verity home from the mill began to fade as the afternoon wore on. She might have established a working relationship with Oliver, but would her father be as amenable? He was difficult at the best of times, and just lately, he seemed even more opposed to her presence in the house. How would he view her presence at the mill? As evening approached, she became increasingly nervous of the undertaking she had promised.

Her father's feckless behaviour was the root of the problem, she bitterly admitted, and until he came to his senses then it would remain so. But how did one get a man like Jeb Lockwood to abandon his drunken habits and face up to his responsibilities? Verity's head swam at the very idea. But it was up to her to see that he did, and with her heart in her mouth, she went downstairs to wait for him to arrive home for the evening meal.

He arrived shortly after seven o'clock, inebriated and dishevelled. Clara served up cold pie made from pigeons Bert had caught. Slumping into a chair at the dining-room table, Jeb glared at Verity. She trembled. Had he already heard about her visits to the mill?

Her fears were groundless. Jeb was glaring because he was in a particularly sour frame of mind. He had lost heavily at cards and was feeling decidedly cheated in more ways than one. He had no wife to comfort him, and he'd had to make do with a doxy that he now feared might have given him the pox. And he had no son and heir to take over the responsibility of the mill and turn a profit. All he had was a gawky, plain-as-a-pikestaff daughter who at that moment was looking down her nose at him.

'What's tha staring at?' he growled.

'I was just thinking that you looked weary, Father,' Verity replied sweetly. If she was to make a start on reforming Jeb then she must stay calm and ease him into a receptive frame of mind. 'Did you have a hard day at the mill?'

'What does tha care? Mill business is nowt to do wi' women like thee,' Jeb sneered, and reached for the brandy.

'Women like me. What do you mean by that, Father?' Verity kept her tone playful.

Jeb, his mouth turned down at the corners and an ugly scowl creasing his florid face, slopped brandy into his glass before answering.

Verity forked up a piece of pie and popped it in her mouth.

'I mean women that are brought into this world to live off men like me. Useless bitches that never do a day's work an' know nowt about business,' Jeb snarled.

Stung by his callousness, the mouthful of pie stuck in Verity's throat. She swallowed noisily and reached for her glass of water. *Don't let him rile you,* an inner voice advised. *You need to keep control if you are to persuade him to see your point of view.* She drank deeply, forcing herself to stay on track.

'Then what would you say to me taking an interest in our mill, Father? Learn how it works and take the weight off your shoulders. A shared burden is much lighter to carry.' Verity leaned across the table and gave him a dazzling smile to emphasise her sincerity.

'I'd say keep thi blasted nose out o' my business, tha useless lummock.'

Jeb's coarse reply seemed to amuse him judging by the nasty laugh that turned into a phlegmy cough. He swigged at his brandy then gave Verity a challenging look.

'If tha really wants to help me then t'best thing tha can do is get thi sen a rich husband. One wi' gammy eyesight so's he overlooks thy shortcomings an' daft enough to bail me out 'cos I'm up to me eyeballs in debt, lass,' he jeered.

Verity's blood boiled, her resolve to stay calm in tatters. She jumped up, her grey eyes flashing like honed steel and, placing the flat of her hands on the table, she leaned forward, glowering back at him. 'Is that all you think I'm worth, Father? Do you intend to sell me off so that you can squander the money on drink?'

Taken aback, Jeb reared up in his chair. 'Don't thee raise thy voice to me, lass. I'm master in this house an' I'll do as I bloody well please.'

'And it pleases you to drink yourself stupid and neglect the mill,' Verity sneered. And hurt by Jeb's low opinion of her, and extremely annoyed at failing to keep her temper, she marched out of the room.

Jeb filled his glass. The decanter was almost empty. If she'd been a lad, he'd have given her a thump. But all his sons were dead and buried. His morose thoughts stirring up an uncontrollable anger, he thrust back his chair and barged into the hallway.

'Medley,' he roared.

Below stairs, Clara raised her eyes to the ceiling. 'Why can't he ring the bell like a normal person,' she huffed.

'Cos he's a bloody madman,' Bert growled and mounted the backstairs.

'Get me another bottle,' Jeb ordered then staggered into the drawing room.

Up in her bedroom, Verity sat by the window staring out into the distance. Castle Hill stood sentinel-like over the valley, its stark outlines a blackness that matched her thoughts. All her plans to make her father see the error of his ways had gone awry. She had hoped for a sensible discussion about the mill, tell him about her visits and encourage him to tell her about his financial difficulties and how they might find a way to settle the debts. Then she might have cautiously addressed the prickly subject of his excessive drinking. But she had failed to do either. Tears sprang to her eyes. She had so wanted to present Oliver with a solution when next they met.

Oliver. What was it he had said just before they had parted that morning? Ah, yes. *What this mill needs is an injection of hard cash.* Verity pressed her fevered brow against the coolness of the window pane and closed her eyes.

Where were they likely to come by that? Jeb creamed off any

profit the mill made and the coffers were empty, the bills unpaid, machinery in need of repair, and necessary supplies denied. Oliver urgently needed indigo dye to fulfil an important order.

Feeling crushed with disappointment, she prepared to go to bed. Deep in thought, she sat at her dressing table brushing her hair. As she made the swift downwards strokes, she had a sudden revelation. The brush fell from her hand. She stared at her reflection in the mirror. A pair of amazed grey eyes stared back. Had she found the answer to the mill's immediate problems? Opening the middle drawer, she reached into the far corner, her fingers moving over a variety of objects until she found what she was looking for.

* * *

Verity rose early the next morning and, dressed in her mauve suit, she went downstairs to breakfast. 'Has my father had his, Mrs Medley?' she asked as Clara placed a boiled egg and toast in front of her.

'He's asleep on the couch in the drawing room, Miss Verity. Best not disturb him till he's ready,' Clara replied, disapproval written large on her plump cheeks.

'I have some business I need to attend to in town, Mrs Medley. I might be late back. Don't make me any lunch.' Verity cracked the top of her egg with the back of her spoon. Would that she could crack Jeb's head just as easily and knock some sense into it.

Clara hovered at the table. 'Tha seems awful busy of late, Miss Verity.' She cocked her head to one side, waiting for Verity to satisfy her curiosity.

'Better to be usefully employed than doing nothing,' Verity replied airily.

Disappointed, Clara went back to the kitchen. 'She's up to summat is that one,' she said to Bert. 'Three days in a row out and about in the town. An' all dressed in her best today. Does tha think she's met a man?'

Bert looked up from tying his bootlaces. 'If she has, it'll please t'master. He's never wanted her here. He'll be glad for sumbdy to tek her off his hands.'

'Aye, sumbdy wi' a bit o' brass so he can sponge off him,' Clara scoffed as she clattered a pan on the range ready to make soup. The larder was looking bare again, the money Verity had given for the housekeeping all but spent.

The torrential rain of the previous day had cooled the air and as Verity walked down into the town, she was glad of it. Had it been as hot as yesterday, she would have felt uncomfortable in her mauve suit. It was important that she should look like a woman of means, otherwise she might arouse suspicion. Today, to complement her outfit, she carried a grey soft kid handbag that she had found in what had once been her mother's bedroom.

When she arrived in the town centre, she made straight for Market Walk and a jeweller's shop she had once visited with her mother on one of the rare occasions Leila had been well enough to leave her bed. Then it had been to take a locket for repair. Now it was for an entirely different purpose. She gazed into the shop window at the beautiful merchandise on display: velvet trays holding serried rows of rings, necklaces spread on satin pads and brooches nestling in little boxes. Behind them, a backdrop of shelves holding silver and porcelain ware.

Verity entered and walked up to the long, glass-topped counter, thankful that there were no other customers. Behind the counter, an elderly man in a dark suit and high-collared white shirt waited to be of service.

'Good morning, madam. How may I help you?'

Verity opened her bag and took out what she hoped would be the answer to her prayers. 'I'd like you to value this for me,' she said coolly and calmly, even though her heart was racing and her stomach performing somersaults.

The jeweller took the brooch and placed it on a velvet pad on the counter top. Then reaching for a jeweller's loupe and placing it in his eye socket, he began to examine the fronds of sapphires and seed pearls that flared from a polished cabochon to form a delightful spray of flowers. Then he turned it over to examine the gold pin.

'One moment, madam.' He disappeared into the rear of the shop. Verity's palms felt clammy inside her grey kid gloves.

When he returned, he slid a piece of paper over the counter. 'In our opinion, that is the estimated value, madam. It's a pretty little piece.'

Verity read what was written on the headed notepaper and choked back the gasp that threatened to spoil her demeanour. She took a deep breath. 'I'd like to sell it, if you would care to buy it,' she said. 'It holds too many painful memories and I would rather someone else take pleasure from wearing it.'

That was a lie. Verity didn't treasure the brooch, nor had she ever worn it. It had originally belonged to her maternal grandmother, and then her own mother. Given to Leila by her parents before they disowned her. 'Take it,' Leila had said one day when Verity was about twelve years old. 'It holds only bitter memories for me and I will never wear it again.'

Verity had put the brooch in the drawer where it had remained until now. She had no qualms about selling it. It was hers to do with as she pleased. She had her mother's Bible and a few of her possessions to remember her by. What had become of the other jewellery her mother had owned, she did not know. She had the brooch, and she held her breath as she waited for the jeweller's response.

He gave a discreet cough then asked, 'May I enquire as to your name and the address of your residence, madam?' One had to be so careful when buying second-hand goods. It was imperative to check on rightful ownership of the piece; it might be stolen property.

'Verity Lockwood of Far View House, Almondbury, daughter of Jebediah Lockwood of Lockwood Mill in Aspley,' she replied at length in order to verify her authenticity.

The jeweller seemed satisfied. 'I can make you an offer, Miss Lockwood, and if you agree then we will buy the brooch.' He named a sum slightly lower than that written on the paper. Verity frowned, then smiled and accepted the offer. It was still far more than she had expected.

She left the shop on winged feet, her bag clutched to her chest.

In a flurry of excitement, she hurried into Market Place and hired a hackney carriage to take her to the mill. Alighting in the mill yard, she ran to the office to share her triumph with Oliver. He wasn't there, but outside the dyehouse, Verity had spied a young man.

'I'm looking for Mr Hardcastle. Do you know where I might find him?'

George recognised her. 'Wait in the office, Miss Lockwood, and I'll fetch him.'

A few moments later, Oliver entered the office, his hands black with grease and a dark streak of it on his white shirt. 'Verity, good to see you,' he said, wiping his hands on a piece of cotton waste. Then hastily donning his jacket to hide the stain, and thinking that she looked elegant in her mauve suit, the colour of which enhanced her beautiful grey eyes, he asked, 'What can I do for you?'

'It's more a case of what I can do for you, Oliver,' she replied, liking the sound of his name on her tongue. A mischievous smile curved her lips. She opened her bag and taking out the bundle of notes, she placed them on the desk.

Oliver stared at them. Had she persuaded her father to give back the money he had taken on his last visit to the mill? If so, her powers of persuasion equalled those of one of the characters in a Jane Austen novel that he read some time ago. He hadn't particularly enjoyed the book and he couldn't remember the name of the character but there was something about Verity Lockwood that brought it to mind.

'Did your father give it to you?'

Verity heard the incredulity in his voice. She laughed. 'Oliver, we both know that's highly unlikely. My father doesn't have that kind of money, and when he does, he cannot wait to spend it foolishly. That is my money – and now it's ours to settle the debts, buy the dyes and whatever else the mill needs.' She was positively fizzing with pleasure.

'Begging your pardon, Verity, but you told me you had no personal wealth.'

'Neither do I, but I did have this.' She handed him the bill of sale that the jeweller had given her. Oliver read it. He looked shocked.

'But... but... you can't sell your possessions to keep the mill functioning.'

'I can, and I have. It was mine and I had no use for it. In fact, I had forgotten I owned it. Then last night, as I dwelt on what we had discussed, I recalled what you said – the mill needs hard cash. Well, now we have some, Mr Hardcastle.'

'It doesn't seem right to accept it,' Oliver said.

'You have no choice. I told you I mean to keep the mill functioning, for after all,' her eyes twinkled as she archly said, 'one day in the future, it will be mine, and if I'm to be a good mill mistress, like you said, then I order you to take it.'

9

'I can't begin to tell you what satisfaction it gives me to do this, Verity.'

Oliver signed an invoice with a flourish and laughed out loud. She laughed along with him. It was Thursday morning and they were in the office selecting which of their suppliers they would pay first from the money her brooch had raised. Choosing the most urgent, Oliver then went off to settle the debts, leaving Verity to see to the running of the mill.

'She looks happy today,' Dolly mouthed to Nellie as Verity walked down 'weaver's alley'.

'She looked lovely when she came in yesterday,' Nellie mouthed back. 'She wa' wearing that mauve suit she had on that time we saw her in the cemetery.'

'She's a good-looking woman.'

'Oh, I don't know about that.' Nellie pulled a face.

Completely unaware that she was the topic of the girls' conversation, Verity gave them each a smile as she made her way down to where John Halstead was warping a loom.

'How are you getting on, John?'

'Fine, Miss. I'm managing to keep on top of things, an' Isaac starts back on Monday.' He gave her a grateful smile. 'I can't thank you enough for givin' me me job back, Miss.'

'It's us that should be thankful. We need you, John.'

Her next port of call was the dyehouse. 'Your worries should be over by the end of today, George,' she told him. 'Mr Hardcastle is on his way to Jarmain's dye works as we speak.'

'That's good to hear, Miss Lockwood. Production on Grigson's order is at a standstill, and although we're working on Bostock's, we're low on that particular shade of green.'

'Grigson's order can go ahead as soon as Mr Hardcastle returns,' she assured him, 'and all is in hand for Bostock's. Indigo dyes, green dyes, we'll have them running out of our ears before the day's over.'

George smiled at her departing back. Things were looking up.

By late afternoon, they were in receipt of the dyes they so desperately needed, and just before the end of the working day, a delivery of raw wool arrived. As Verity signed and paid for it, she felt the thrill of achievement. Turning to Oliver, she gave him a triumphant smile. Their eyes locked, gleaming grey meeting darkest brown, as they silently basked in the glow of their success.

* * *

On Friday morning, Jeb arrived at the mill looking dishevelled and hungover, the bags beneath his eyes like purple plums and his side whiskers unkempt. He stomped into the office. Oliver greeted him warily.

'How's that order for Grigson's comin' along?' Jeb asked.

'It will be completed by the end of today, sir,' Oliver replied evenly although he didn't say that it wouldn't have been completed at all if Verity hadn't provided the money to pay off Jarmain's debt and purchase the indigo dye.

'Good, good...' Jeb rubbed his hands – *that 'ud bring in plenty cash* – 'an' owt else come in this week?'

'Hartley's settled the bill for the blankets, and Shaw's for the worsted pieces, and a few smaller items have been paid for.' Oliver flipped open a ledger and pushed it across the desk. 'The receipts are all accounted for on that page. I've made the usual deductions... wages... necessary expenses... but we're still showing a deficit of...' He pointed to the figures at the foot of a balance sheet. He and Verity had decided it would be unwise to make Jeb aware of the money she had injected into the business.

Jeb grunted. 'Aye, well...' His eyes darted to the strongbox. 'Let's be havin' what's left then.' He took his key from his stained waistcoat pocket and unlocked the box, scooped out the money and stuffed it into his jacket pocket. Oliver had difficulty hiding a smile at the thought of Verity's money hidden in a cabinet in a dark corner of the office. Thank God Jeb didn't know about that, otherwise...

'I'll be off then.' Jeb strutted to the door. 'See that tha keeps production up, an' make sure Grigson's order goes out on time.'

'I'll do that, sir.' Oliver followed him to the door and out into the yard. Sam Firth was lingering by Jeb's trap, an obsequious smile on his face.

'Morning, Master Lockwood, I wa' hopin' to catch thi. I'd like a word wi' thi,' he said as Jeb approached. Oliver looked with distaste at the slimy overlooker. A weasel of a man, Sam was never happier than when he was making someone else miserable. In Oliver's opinion, he should have been dismissed long ago, his harsh treatment of the women weavers bad enough and his sexual abuse of the young girls far worse. But Sam and Jeb were birds of a feather, and although Oliver had protested on numerous occasions that Sam should be got rid of, Jeb had pooh-poohed the idea, saying, 'There's now wrong w' a bit o' slap an' tickle, an' if he keeps them lasses hard at it, he'll do for me.'

Sam was now filling Jeb's ear, a spiteful gleam in his eye and a sneer curling his lips.

Jeb's face, already florid, turned puce. He wheeled round. 'Hardcastle! Get thi' sen over here right now.'

Oliver reluctantly walked over to the trap; he knew what was about to be said.

'What's this about my lass comin' to t'mill? Tha never said owt about that.'

'I didn't see the need of it. I thought Miss Lockwood came at your bidding, sir,' Oliver said smoothly. 'She asked to see the mill, and I showed her what we do.'

'Well, you'd no bloody right without my say so, an' in future, Hardcastle, you ask my permission before showin' anybody round my mill. Do you hear me, Hardcastle? I'll not have any bloody nosy parkers lookin' into my business – an' that includes my daughter.'

'Understood, sir.' Oliver was seething, but for Verity's sake and all that they planned to do, he held himself in check. Sam gave him a nasty, satisfied smirk, the stumps of his blackened teeth repulsive. Oliver glared balefully at him then addressed Jeb. 'Will that be all, sir?'

Jeb, still puzzled as to why Verity had visited the mill, took stock of his manager's level gaze. Hardcastle was a reliable man, an excellent mill manager and as loyal and honest as the day was long, Jeb silently acknowledged. He'd not want to lose him.

'Aye, well, think nowt of it. I wa' just surprised, that's all.' And feeling in need of a strong drink, Jeb hastily brought his visit to a close. 'Thas a good man, Hardcastle,' he said as he climbed into the trap. A flick of the whip and the pony cantered out of the mill yard.

'Get back to work, Firth,' Oliver bawled at the overlooker, who slunk back to the weaving shed. Oliver went back into the office, deep in thought. Should he warn Verity that her father knew of her visits? But how? He couldn't call at the house in case Jeb had returned there. He could, however, send a lad with a note. He went to the spinning shed. Pip Haigh seemed like a reliable lad. He'd send him.

Pip had recently started work as a doffer, and was just taking the full bobbins off a spinning frame when Oliver tapped him on the shoulder and said, 'Come with me, Pip.'

Pip tossed a bobbin into a crate and stood, his knees wobbling under him as he followed Oliver out into the mill yard. What had he done wrong? He looked at the sturdy frame of the handsome mill manager, prepared to take his punishment although his sister, Nellie, and her best friend, Dolly Armitage, had told him Mr Hardcastle never treated the workers badly.

'I have an important job I want you do, Pip. Do you know where Far View House is?'

'Aye, sir. It's where Master Lockwood lives.' Pip looked extremely anxious. Was the mill master angry with him?

'Good. I want you to take a note for me. You must give it to no other than Miss Lockwood. If she is not at home, bring it back to me.'

'Aw, right, Mr Hardcastle.' Pip's relief was patent. He wasn't about to be punished.

Oliver gave him the sealed note. 'Go at once, and don't dawdle.'

Pip set off at a run. Nellie had told him that the young lady whom Oliver had shown round the mill was Miss Lockwood, the mill master's daughter, and that Dolly had thought she was Mr Hardcastle's lady friend. Maybe it was a love letter he was about to deliver. The thought excited him, and he ran all the faster.

* * *

Jeb had not gone back to Far View House. He was sitting in the snug at the Pack Horse, a brandy in front of him. Why was his daughter ferreting about his mill? he wondered. She was a funny lass, was Verity, her nose always stuck in a book. And now it seemed she'd been sticking it in his business. He took a swig of brandy, swirling it round in his mouth as he recalled what she had said the other night over dinner. She'd asked him what he thought about her helping him run the mill. He took another swig. The daft bugger, what did she know about making cloth? And why did she want to know? She should be out looking for a husband instead. He emptied his glass.

'Landlord,' he shouted. 'Another brandy an' be quick about it.'

* * *

Verity, dressed in her oldest skirt and blouse and one of Clara's aprons, was pulling weeds from the bed of peonies when Pip arrived with the note.

'From Mr Hardcastle, Miss,' he panted. 'He said to give it to you an' nobody else.'

Verity read it and frowned. The note was brief.

V, your father has learned of your visits to the mill. He is angry. Be prepared when next you see him. O.

So, her father had found her out and was displeased. Ah, well, it had only been a matter of time.

'Thank you, Pip,' she said. 'Wait here a moment.' She slipped into the house, coming back with a sixpence that she gave to him. 'Tell Mr Hardcastle that you did a splendid job.'

'Ooh! Ta, Miss Lockwood,' Pip gasped and, marvelling at the coin in his hand, he set off back to the mill.

Verity tucked the note in her skirt pocket and continued weeding and pondering on what to do. She wouldn't risk going to the mill in case her father was still there. To do so might put Oliver in an invidious position. She tore angrily at the weeds, her bad temper adding impetus to her work and the peonies and the camellias benefitting from her ire. Her father was a pain in the backside.

She was still contemplating the situation when it was time to go indoors and wash and change for dinner. What would Jeb do if and when he returned home? Putting on her blue dress that Clara had washed and ironed, she went downstairs into the drawing room, her anxiety mounting as she waited for her father's and Aunt Martha's arrival.

The crunching of gravel outside signalled her aunt's arrival, and Verity put down her book and ran to the door to greet her. Martha's short but corpulent body swathed in black bombazine almost filled the cart to overflowing, and as the carrier helped her down, his knees buckled under her weight. She grabbed at him, and he at her, knocking her braided bonnet askew. Verity was reminded of the huge, black hen in Bert's chicken coop when it puffed up its plumage before attacking the other birds. Suppressing a giggle, she hurried to assist. She had never been more pleased to see her aunt; her support could prove invaluable.

'Come in, come in,' Verity cried, helping the old lady up the steps and into the house.

Puffing and panting, Martha divested her cape and bonnet then waddled into the drawing room. She plumped down on the couch. 'Is your father not here?'

'Not yet, Aunt, and I'm glad he isn't for I have something to tell you.'

Martha's curiosity aroused, she sat up straight, her beady eyes glinting.

Verity told her of her visits to the mill and her meetings with Oliver Hardcastle. 'He's a good, reliable man,' she praised then went on to tell her how they had discussed the mill's finances and that she had found a solution to their immediate problems.

'I remember that brooch. It was a lovely thing but your mother said she hated it because her mother had given it to her as a sop for disowning her.' Martha shook her head ruefully. 'That poor lass never should have married our Jeb.'

When Verity told her about using her initiative when the loom tuner had been taken ill, Martha complimented her. 'Tha did the right thing. Paying for the doctor for Isaac an' giving Halstead his job back just goes to show that you've a kind heart and that you'd be more than capable of running the mill.'

Verity glowed under the praise, but it didn't make her feel any less anxious about her immediate problem. 'Thank you for your vote of confidence, Aunt Martha, but now that Father knows what I've been up to, I'm dreading his reaction.'

Martha sucked her teeth. 'I doubt he'll be pleased. He can be a right nasty piece of work if anybody goes against him.' She gave a grim smile. 'He allus wa' a cantankerous beggar even when he wa' young,' she said, giving a despairing shake of her head. 'He bullied your mother something shocking. Blamed her for not bearing a son. An' in the days when he did look after the mill, he wa' a hard taskmaster.'

Verity, saddened to be reminded of how cruel he had been to her mother, felt a spurt of violent rage burn her chest. 'I don't care in the least if he is angry. I'll give as good as I get. I'll tell him that from now on, I'll see to the running of the mill. I will not allow him to drink it into the ground.'

'Well, lass, tha has my support – tha allus has,' said Martha, experiencing a twinge of guilt when she recalled how she had sent her young niece away at her late husband's bidding.

She would have said more but the rattle of the trap in the driveway had her exchanging an apprehensive glance with her niece. 'We'll know soon enough what frame he's in, lass. But don't let him get the better of thi.'

Outside the front door, Jeb fell from the trap, so drunk, he could barely stand. It was fortunate for him that the pony knew its way home. He staggered up the steps and threw the door open so vigorously that it screeched on its hinges and crashed against the wall.

'Medley!' he roared, 'see to that bloody pony.'

Bert came running up the backstairs. Jeb lashed out at him as he ran to the front door. Bert ducked and leapt down the steps, eager to see that the pony had come to no harm.

'I doubt tha'll get much sense out of him tonight, lass,' Martha opined wearily as Jeb burst into the drawing room. 'An' you, sit thi sen down afore tha falls flat on thi face,' she barked at her brother. Verity's spirits sank even lower.

Jeb stumbled across the room to the sideboard and slopped brandy into a glass. Then he turned to address them, the baleful look on his face frightening.

'Sit me sen down? Sit wi' a snooper like that. Not bloody likely,' he snarled, wagging his finger at Verity. She quivered. 'Does tha know what she's been up to? Going behind my back and sneakin' round my mill wi'out so much as my say so. I'll not bloody stand for it.' He emptied his glass in one gulp.

'Stop thi blartin' an' come to thi senses, Jeb. The lass is tryin' to help thi, an' if tha hadn't pickled thi brains, you'd welcome her wi' open arms.'

'I don't need her to help me. I never did need her,' Jeb bawled, his hand shaking as he refilled his glass and raised it to his lips.

Verity sprang to her feet. 'Yes, you do, Father. The mill is almost in ruins and—'

She got no further. The glass sailed across the room and struck her on the temple. She reeled under the blow, her eyes widening in disbelief as she stared at her father.

'Jeb Lockwood! You should be ashamed of thi sen,' screeched Martha, and struggling to her feet, she tottered to Verity's side.

Just then, Clara, all agog at hearing raised voices, tapped the door and marched in. 'Dinner's ready to be served, master,' she said, her eyes darting from Jeb to Martha, who was bright red with fury, and then to Verity, who was holding a handkerchief to her forehead.

'I'll not eat wi' the likes o' them,' Jeb spat. 'They're all again me an' I want nowt to do wi' 'em.' He reached for another glass and filled it.

'Come Verity, we're wastin' our time an' I'm hungry,' Martha said, taking Verity's free arm and leading her out of the room. Clara followed, but not before she'd given Jeb a look of utter disgust. There was no pleasure in working for him this past while back, she thought, but then there never had been.

In the hallway, Verity lowered the hand that she had been holding to her forehead.

'Did he hurt you, Miss?' Clara pointed to the handkerchief that was spotted with blood. Verity, too stunned to speak, nodded. Clara peered at the small wound. 'It's only a little nick,' she said. 'Come wi' me an' I'll clean you up.' Too shocked to do otherwise, Verity allowed Clara to take her down to the kitchen.

Verity and Martha ate alone that evening, Martha consoling her niece and berating her brother, and Verity declaring that she wasn't intimidated by her father and was all the more determined to stand her ground. They sat talking long after they had finished eating and Clara had cleared the table. As the hour drew late, Clara came and asked at what time did Martha want Bert to bring round the trap to take her home. 'Give me five more minutes,' Martha said, and when Clara had gone back to the kitchen, she warned her niece, 'Keep out of his way tonight, Verity. You can't reason wi' a drunken man.'

'But when can I reason with him, Aunt? He's always intoxicated, and I can't stop him drinking. I just pray that he'll—'

A resounding thud and the crash of iron on stone from the drawing room brought her up short. She leapt to her feet and Martha, giving a little scream and moving surprisingly fast for a woman of her bulk, followed Verity into the hallway only to meet Clara and Bert rushing up the backstairs.

'What wa' that?' Clara cried. 'It fair shook the house.'

They crowded through the doorway into the drawing room then stopped and stared, horrified. Jeb was sprawled on top of the overturned club fender that stood round the fireplace with his head and shoulders in the hearth amongst the toppled fire irons. Blood poured from his scalp and his face was twisted in an ugly rictus.

Verity dashed over to where he lay. 'Go fetch the doctor, Bert. Mrs Medley, bring cloths and warm water. Aunt Martha! Please stop screeching and bring me a cushion.' She stepped over the heavy brass fender and, kneeling in the hearth, she carefully raised Jeb's head and cradled it in her lap, heedless of the blood seeping on to her dress. When Martha handed her a cushion, she gently placed it beneath her father's broken head. 'I never wanted it to come to this,' she sobbed.

10

'He's suffered a stroke, Miss Lockwood: a rush of blood to the brain,' Ernest Clegg explained as he knelt beside Jeb's body. 'The head injury is minor,' the doctor continued, getting to his feet and brushing the knees of his trousers, 'but should he regain consciousness – and he may not – the damage could be considerable. He might not walk or talk again and will need to be cared for day and night.'

Verity shuddered. She did not want her father to die, neither did she wish for him to be incapacitated, and yet if he was to die... She shook her head to dispel the wicked thought.

'What do we do now, Dr Clegg?' she asked, gazing down at Jeb's prone body.

'Have you a room on this floor that we can carry him to, make him comfortable whilst we wait for the outcome? It would be unwise to take him upstairs even if we could – he's a considerable weight – and if in the long term he survives, it will be handier to have him close by.' He turned to Clara, who was sniffling into her apron. 'We can't have you running up and down stairs a hundred times a day, can we, Mrs Medley?'

Clara nodded grim agreement.

'We could put him in the little back sitting room,' Bert suggested. 'Nobody ever uses it. Me an' Clara can bring that single bed down from t'guest room an' set it up.'

'That will do, Medley. I'll lend a hand.' Dr Clegg walked to the door and the Medleys led the way upstairs.

Meanwhile, Verity stared down at Jeb's contorted face, at his sagging mouth and bruised cheeks. His eyes were closed, the left one no longer in alignment with the right. She watched his chest rise and fall with every faint breath as he clung on to life, oblivious to what had befallen him, and his situation filled her with horror and an unexpected compassion. Martha was sitting on the couch sobbing noisily.

'He was drinking too heavily but I did not see how I could stop him.' Verity's voice was barely above a whisper.

'Nobody could, lass,' Martha replied brokenly. 'He allus was pig-headed. Now look at him.' She began to wail even louder.

'Please, Aunt, don't cry,' Verity begged, the sound of Martha's grief more than she could bear. 'Stay with him whilst I go and help prepare the room.'

After much heaving and banging, the bed was got downstairs into the sitting room. Verity made it up with fresh linen, and Dr Clegg and Bert carried Jeb, still unconscious, from the drawing room and into the bed. Breathless, the two men stood looking down at the patient and Verity and Clara arranged the bedcovers. Martha waddled in, still sobbing.

Jeb stirred. A guttural noise escaped his throat and his eyelids fluttered. The lid to the left one stayed closed. Dr Clegg leaned over him. 'Mr Lockwood. Jeb. Do you know where you are?'

Jeb rolled his head to one side, drool slipping from the corner of his mouth and his open eye unfocused. 'Uugh, uugh,' he grunted, raising his limp right hand and flapping it weakly. Dr Clegg examined him more closely.

'I believe the stroke has left him paralysed down the left side. He may eventually regain the power of speech but it's unlikely he'll walk again. Only time will tell.'

Martha began to wail again.

Verity digested Dr Clegg's words. In such a short space of time, her life had dramatically changed yet again.

* * *

The following day, when Verity broke the news to Oliver, he was shocked and dismayed. 'What will you do now?' he asked, his dark eyes filled with friendly concern.

'We will look after him the best we can, although he does not know who we are or where he is,' Verity replied, her voice in danger of cracking under the strain. 'I will need to employ a nurse. Clara Medley can't be expected to do that as well as her other duties. I would nurse him myself but I have no experience, and I would prefer to be here at the mill doing the job my father should have been doing.'

'I'll do anything I can to help,' Oliver said, 'and maybe I can make a start by suggesting you employ Ada Brook, a friend of my mother's. She's a trained nurse and was until recently caring for an aged woman in Moldgreen who died last week. Ada lives in one of the cottages close by All Hallows so she wouldn't have far to travel.'

'That sounds splendid,' said Verity, heartened by Oliver's offer of help. 'I'll call on her on my way home.' She paused to give Oliver a searching look. 'Will you have any objection to me coming to work at the mill on a daily basis? I think I could make myself useful in all sorts of ways.' Her smile wavered.

'None whatsoever, Verity. After all, with your father indisposed, you are now the mill mistress and have every right to run the mill as you see fit.'

Verity's wan smile turned into a deprecating grimace. 'Oh, Oliver, I will merely be assisting. We both know it's you that runs the mill. I couldn't possibly do it without you.'

'Thank you for having faith in me. I think we'll work well together.' His solemn words were accompanied by a warm smile.

'Oh, I know we will,' Verity said fulsomely and returned the smile.

Then they stood silently, each lost in their own thoughts. Verity was thinking how exciting and rewarding it would be to spend each day working with Oliver to make her mill flourish. Oliver, to his surprise, was thinking much the same. In fact, he was looking forward to it. Their eyes met as they shared delighted and somewhat complicit smiles.

* * *

'Miss Lockwood's spending a lot of time at the mill since her dad had his stroke,' Nellie said to Dolly as they entered the mill yard one sunny morning at the end of August. 'She's here most days workin' in t'office or checkin' that everything's runnin' to order.'

'Well, it *is* her mill now that Jeb's bedridden. And she's doing a better job that he did. We don't have to wait ages for our looms to be fixed now we've got Isaac and John doing the tuning, and our George says working in the dyehouse isn't half as hard now that she's set on another man. And he says they don't run out of dyes like they used to because she pays the bills on time.'

'Aye, her an' Mr Hardcastle have made some grand changes lately. It's stopped folks sayin' that Lockwood's was runnin' on borrowed time,' Nellie agreed.

'I like the way she comes into the weaving shed and bids us good morning, and she seems to know all our names,' Dolly said as they went inside the shed. 'She always asks after them that she knows have sick children or parents to care for. It makes you feel she's really interested in us as people, doesn't it?'

The hooter blew and they hurried to put on their turbans and overalls. Within minutes, the weaving shed roared into action, looms weaving fine worsted and the girls watching for loose ends or anything else that would mar the cloth. It was six o'clock and another two and a half hours before they would have their breakfast.

It was nine o'clock when Verity arrived at the mill, just in time to see the weavers trooping back to the shed. 'Good morning, ladies,' she called out as she made her way across the yard. This was met with a chorus of, 'Morning, Miss Lockwood,' and friendly smiles.

'You got a warm welcome,' Oliver said as she stepped into the office where he was sorting blueish grey yarn samples and loom patterns.

'A happy workforce is a productive workforce, Oliver.'

Verity's pert reply made him grin.

'Are those the yarns and patterns for Hepworth's order?' she asked, taking off her hat and gloves.

Oliver said they were, and went on to explain how the new loom pattern would weave a complicated herringbone design. A pattern they had not used before. Verity was fascinated by the Jacquard loom cards into which small holes were punched. These interchangeable cards were placed in the loom's heddle and controlled which warp threads should be raised to allow the weft threads in the shuttle to pass under.

'They're so clever,' she marvelled, running the tip of her forefinger over the little holes, 'and I'd love to own a dress in that shade of grey.'

Oliver chuckled. 'Then you'd better help yourself to a length when it's woven up.'

'I could, couldn't I?' Verity's eyes widened with delight. 'When do we start weaving?'

'Today. Isaac and John are going to set up the looms as soon as I get these over to them,' Oliver said, bundling the Jacquard patterns together. 'We'll start with two looms and work our way down the shed as the others become free until we've got twenty looms working on the order. That way we'll meet the deadline with time to spare.' He walked to the door.

'Then I'll let you get on, and I'll attend to these invoices.' Verity slipped into the chair behind the desk. Left alone, she felt like hugging herself for sheer joy. Now that Jeb was no longer bleeding the coffers dry, and they had the money realised by the sale of the brooch, the mill was slowly but surely making a recovery. Some of the dismissed workers had been rehired, and the outstanding debts were gradually being reduced. Oliver predicted that by Christmas, they might be showing a small profit, and with this new order from Hepworth's, a highly respected tailoring business in Sheffield – that Oliver had worked hard to pull off – and the capacity to produce fancy woven worsteds instead of just plain cloth, they could compete with their rivals. Verity couldn't have been happier.

The invoices done, she wiped her inky fingers and went to stand in the office doorway for a breath of fresh air. She had not expected to see Dolly sitting on the weaving shed step, her head bent over something in her lap. Curious, Verity strolled across the yard.

'Hello, Dolly. What brings you out here at this time of day?' It was still more than an hour before dinnertime.

Dolly looked up and smiled. 'Isaac's setting up my loom with the new jacquard pattern. Mr Hardcastle said it was all right if I sat in the sun until it's ready so I'm taking the opportunity to find out to what happens to Umbopa after Gagool sentences him to death.' She held up a copy of *King Solomon's Mines*.

'You can read?' Verity's tone registered her surprise and she immediately felt like biting off her tongue. She had sounded condescending.

'Oh, yes, Miss Lockwood. I love reading. It takes you to different times and different places. Have you read this?' She gestured with the book, and Verity nodded. 'Imagine going across deserts and almost dying of thirst then getting lost in the deep, dark jungle,' Dolly continued, her enthusiasm making Verity smile and agree.

'I too get lost in books. I can't remember a time when I didn't.'

'Me neither. Mam taught me and our George. You see, her mam was lady's maid to one of the Cartwrights up at Denby Hall an' my mam was educated with the children there.'

'That's most unusual.'

'Aye well, seeing as how it was a member of the family got my granny pregnant, they sort of felt obliged to let her keep her position, and educate my mam.' Dolly grimaced and gave a little shrug. 'I borrow books from the library. I feel sorry for people who can't read.'

'So do I,' said Verity, intrigued by Dolly's forthrightness.

'Dolly, your loom's ready.' Unnoticed, Oliver had appeared in the weaving shed doorway.

'Right you are, Mr Hardcastle. Thanks.' Dolly leapt to her feet and went into the shed.

'She's an interesting girl,' Verity remarked as she and Oliver crossed the yard to the office.

'Aye, and a bright one too. The Armitages are good stock. Her brother, George, runs the dyehouse like a tight ship.' Oliver flicked his hair back from his brow. 'Had either of them been born in different circumstances, they could go far.'

'How do you mean – different circumstances?'

Oliver smiled wryly. Verity still had a lot to learn about the working classes. 'I suppose I mean had they been born into your family – or even mine for that matter. However, George and Dolly are the children of hard-working parents who have only ever been paid a pittance for their labours. Education is a luxury, Verity.' He looked at her to see if she understood. Her lips pursed and her brow furrowed, she nodded.

'Whilst ever the owners of the mills and factories keep wages at a minimum, the workers will never have the opportunity to break the mould. Some of them do no more than survive,' he continued with a regretful shake of his head. 'You and I are fortunate. We have both been well-schooled and have never known poverty but many of those in your employ could not even afford to attend school. The coppers it cost were needed to put food on the table. And those who did have schooling left at the age of ten – a little learning but not enough.'

'Thank you for your interesting lecture, Mr Hardcastle.' Her slightly mocking tone made Oliver smile.

'It's a serious matter,' he protested.

'Indeed, it is,' Verity agreed. 'And you've given me an idea.'

'And what might that be?'

'One that requires some thought and necessary preparation.'

She left him staring after her with a frown on his face as she walked out of the office.

11

August melted into September, the days cooler and work in the weaving shed more tolerable for Dolly and Nellie, and for George in the dyehouse. They still toiled daily, but there was no more waiting for looms to be fixed and the fear of not being able to finish a piece and earn a decent wage at the end of the week. George no longer worried over not having the alkaline dyes to complete an order, and throughout the sheds from scouring to baling there was the united feeling that Lockwood Mill wasn't such a bad place to work.

Verity had never been busier. She kept the ledgers, thus leaving Oliver free to attend to the processing of each stage of manufacturing cloth. She dealt with invoices and receipts and chased orders, visiting garment manufacturers in Halifax and Bradford to persuade them to buy Lockwood cloth, the male-dominated businesses surprised, and somewhat shocked, to be dealing with a young woman.

At home, Jeb's health showed no improvement. Ada Brook proved to be an efficient and pleasant nurse. She fed and cleaned her patient with good humour, jollying him into accepting her ministrations without a struggle. When, before Ada's arrival, Verity and Clara had attempted to do this, Jeb had grunted and growled, flailing his good arm to fight them off.

His sister, Martha, visited him daily, and even though he did not recognise her, she was undeterred. As her knitting grew row on row, she kept up a lively chatter, reminiscing about days when they had been young. Jeb made no response, but Martha seemed not to care and appeared to have a greater affection for him now than she had ever showed when he was in full health. Verity sat with him in the evening reading extracts from the *Leeds Intelligencer*, the newspaper he had always favoured, but she could never be sure if he was listening.

He laid propped on his pillows, the lid of his left eye permanently closed and his right eye unfocused. His face drooped to one side and his skin was an unhealthy shade of grey. He ate little, and then only softened food, for he had difficulty swallowing. Every evening, Verity gave him a drink of brandy, holding the glass to his lips as he slurped and dribbled. Only then did he show any signs of pleasure. His bleary eye would brighten, he'd grunt and smack his lips and something resembling a smile lit his twisted face when the brandy was finished.

Verity felt only pity for him. She wished she could feel love, but theirs had never been a loving relationship. One night, as she sat waiting for Jeb to fall asleep, she recalled a visit she and her mother had made to a house in Grimscar when Verity had been about six and Leila was feeling well enough to take tea with her old school friend, now Mrs Phoebe Halliwell.

The Halliwells had four children ranged in age from five to ten years old. It had been a glorious spring day, and whilst her mother and her friend had sipped tea on the lawn, the children's father had taken the youngsters into the nearby woods. Whilst the young Halliwells gambolled ahead, Verity had hung back, unused to the company of other children. When she felt Mr Halliwell's big, warm hand clasp hers, she had been utterly charmed. Jeb had never held her hand.

'Chase us, chase us,' the Halliwell children had cried, and encouraged by their father, Verity had run with them, heedless of trampling the carpet of bluebells and giggling delightedly when, as he caught them in turn, he hugged and tickled them. No one had ever done this to Verity, and oh, how she'd wished for a father like that.

Sitting that night by Jeb's bedside, she gazed at the ravaged man and mused on how much they had both missed: she, the love of a good father, and he, a loving daughter.

And so, her days occupied with mill business and her nights with Jeb, it wasn't until late September that Verity began to nurture the seed that Oliver's little lecture on poverty and inequality had planted.

'May I have a word with you, Dolly,' she asked one morning as the women were sitting on the cobbles at the gable end of the office eating their breakfasts.

Dolly looked up, startled, and hastily swallowed a mouthful of bread and fish paste.

'Certainly, Miss Lockwood.' She got to her feet, and under the quizzical eyes of the women, she followed Verity round the corner and into the office. She didn't feel at all nervous; her work was good, she knew that, and rather than looking annoyed, Verity had seemed rather excited. Bursting with curiosity, Dolly waited for her to speak.

'I have a proposition to put to you, Dolly, but before you accept it, I need your advice,' said Verity, feeling rather self-conscious. 'I know that, like me, you're a reader and take great pleasure from the books you read, and with that in mind, it occurred to me that many of our workers will never know the joy of reading because they have not had the opportunity to learn. Therefore, I thought that... with your help... we could start reading classes, teach those who want to learn and are willing to give an hour or so of their time one or two evenings a week. What do you think?' Verity twisted the fingers of both hands, a hopeful gleam in her eyes.

Dolly's brow puckered, and she pressed her lips together. Verity held her breath.

Eventually, Dolly said, 'I myself think it's a grand idea, Miss Lockwood. Everybody should be able to read, even if it's only the newspapers, but most of the women will think it's a waste of time.' She sounded almost apologetic.

'So, I'd be foolish to put it to them.'

Verity's downcast expression tugged at Dolly's heart. She wanted to help, but she didn't want the mill mistress to be scorned by the rougher women in the weaving and spinning sheds. They enjoyed making cruel fun of people.

'I just don't know, Miss Lockwood. Some of them might think you were trying to make little of them. They'd not like showing their ignorance in front of you but...' she paused, deep in thought, 'but some of the young ones might be keen. Nellie Haigh 'ud be interested. I've been teaching her for ages, but she finds it hard, and she has so much to do at home helping her mam with the young ones, she doesn't have time to practice.'

'What if we made the classes more of a social affair?' Verity was unwilling to give in. 'I could provide tea and biscuits, and if we were to hold the lessons immediately after work, they wouldn't have to travel back and forth, and could leave at whatever time they liked.'

'You really want to do this, don't you, Miss Lockwood?'

'I do! Really, I do. It will be such an advantage to them if only they...' Verity shrugged.

'Then in that case, I'll help you. When do you want to start?'

* * *

The last Sunday in September was the mellowest of early autumn days. Verity had spent the morning laboriously copying out the letters of the alphabet and simple phrases onto stiff card that had once held samples of yarn. *The cat sat on the mat* she printed in a large, neat hand. A pile of cards sat at her elbow ready for the start of the reading classes. Her wrist aching and her fingers stained with ink, she decided she was in need of fresh air, and after dressing for the outdoors and informing Aunt Martha and Clara of her intentions, she set out for Castle Hill.

The beech trees at the end of the driveway had started to scatter their summer foliage, the gravel now a burnished copper carpet, and in the lane, long-fingered, yellow horse chestnut leaves crunched under Verity's boots. The grassy banks each side of the steep slope sported bright yellow hawkbit, spiky, purple thistles and harebells as if to say winter is still far off.

At the foot of the hill, she continued on into Lumb Lane then turned south-west towards the hill, the road rising before her. As she walked, she conjured up a group of eager pupils sitting wide-eyed and marvelling as she made the alphabet letters form familiar words that they used every day. She imagined their delight as they learned to write their own names and read simple phrases, the letters on a page no longer mystifying ciphers but words that conveyed meaningful thoughts and feelings. The vision was so real and her belief in the importance of women's education so passionate – she saw only female faces in her imaginary class – that she barely noticed the road she took or the passage of time.

* * *

At home in the house in Almondbury Bank, Oliver was feeling restless. He'd eaten a stodgy Sunday dinner and was feeling the need to work it off. 'I'm going out for a long walk,' he announced to his mother and sisters. Disappointment clouded their faces.

'Oh, must you? We were going to have a game of canasta, you and I against Maud and Mother.' Rose pouted and looked to her mother to intervene.

'We can't play without we have a fourth member,' his mother said.

Maud gave a vacant smile and went back to chewing the corner of the cushion pressed under her chin.

'Then you'll have to choose another game,' Oliver replied, walking to the door, as eager to be out in the fresh air as he was to escape his domineering mother and clinging sisters. Of late, he'd been absorbed in thoughts that did not sit easily with him. He often caught himself dwelling on unimportant incidents that had taken place in the mill office, a certain movement of a chestnut head or a playful comment and other things he couldn't quite pinpoint. He'd never experienced these feelings before and a brisk walk might help settle his mood.

His long stride took him up Almondbury Bank, across Dog Kennel Bank and past the Longley estate that was home to the wealthy Ramsden family. Without giving too much thought to the direction he was going in, he headed towards Castle Hill.

Verity had arrived at that part of the road the locals called Catterstones. The hillside rose steeply, the path to the ancient ruins rough and winding. She paused before making the climb, letting her gaze roam across the valley to the hamlets and villages nestled there: Berry Brow, Hanging Stone, Stile Common and Newsome. And in the distance, the dense urbanisation of mills, factories and houses that was the heart of the cloth-making industry. This was her town. This was where she belonged, and today, she felt more at home than ever before. This was the place where she was planting her dreams, letting them take root, and waiting for them to bloom. She didn't expect it to be perfect but at that moment, life felt wonderful and beautiful. A surge of gratitude had her turning to ascend the hill.

Oliver was feeling refreshed by the time he reached Catterstones. Up ahead, he saw a woman wearing a mauve jacket and skirt, her tall, shapely figure familiar. He quickened his pace. 'Verity,' he called out.

She looked back over her shoulder, surprise then pleasure lighting her face. Three long strides brought him abreast of her.

'Oliver. How unexpected and nice to see you.'

'And you,' he said, his eyes lingering on her face. *How lovely she looks*, he thought, gazing at her slightly flushed cheeks and grey eyes soft as a dove's wing. So intense was his gaze that Verity's heart fluttered. By mutual agreement they fell into step, climbing the steep and winding path up the hill, Oliver taking Verity's hand when they arrived at a precipitous incline covered with loose scree. She liked the feel of his strong, warm hand, and was sorry when he released it as they reached firmer ground.

At the top of the hill, they strolled across the grass cropped short by the flock of ragged sheep that wandered aimlessly and fearlessly among the huge stones that were the remains of an ancient castle's ramparts. So far, they had exchanged only a few words, both of them comfortable in the silence that denotes good friendship.

'Isn't it wonderful up here? So wild and free. And I love the way you can see for miles and miles across the landscape.' Verity climbed atop a large slab of stone.

'That's most likely why people settled on the hill four thousand years ago. A great vantage point for seeing your enemies before they saw you,' Oliver said, thinking how striking Verity's tall, slender physique and her proud stance was. 'Perched on that rock, you look like Cartimandua, Queen of Brigantia, surveying her territory,' he said.

'Queen who?' Verity jumped down. 'Tell me more,' she demanded.

Oliver told the story of the ancient Celtic warrior queen, and then pointed to the ruins of what had been an ale house near to where the present pub stood. It being Sunday, it was closed for business, otherwise he would have suggested they quench their thirst. He went on to relate more history as they walked over the sheep-cropped grass. Verity was fascinated.

'The De Laceys, a prominent family in this area, built a castle here in the twelfth century, and about fifty years ago, a group of local businessmen formed the Victoria Prospect Tower Company to erect a tower in honour of Queen Victoria.'

Verity gazed about her as if to locate the tower. Seeing none, she asked, 'Why didn't they build it?'

'Sir John William Ramsden objected to it. His family have tremendous influence in the valley. Then someone suggested they erect the tower to honour the Duke of Wellington. He's the one who established a regiment of soldiers about four hundred years ago that fought in all the major wars. Our local West Riding regiment was formed in his name.' They stopped walking and rested on a low wall as he continued his story.

'I know about the duke. He was called Arthur Wellesley and was victorious at the Battle of Waterloo,' said Verity, keen to show that she wasn't entirely ignorant before adding, 'Good enough to give his name to a boot but not enough of a hero to have a tower named for him.'

Oliver laughed at her wit. 'No, they argued that it would spoil the landscape, that it would serve no useful purpose, and it took so long to raise the money that eventually, the scheme was abandoned.' He gave a disappointed shrug then continued by saying, 'A pity really. They'd already engaged an architect, a chap called William Wallen who designed the George Hotel in Huddersfield, and he wanted to build a tower tall enough that if you stood on top of it, you'd be able to see the North Sea.'

'My goodness!' Verity exclaimed. 'That would be a sight worth seeing.'

'Indeed, it would,' Oliver agreed, getting to his feet and cupping Verity's elbow to assist her. When they continued walking, he kept his hand there. It felt nice and she leaned into it. Then, slipping her arm over his, she linked his, taking pleasure from being close to him.

'How do you know all this?' Verity, astounded by Oliver's knowledge, urged him to go on.

'I attend the Philosophical Society meetings,' Oliver replied, his cheeks colouring and his modest tone indicating that he didn't want her to think he was a know-all. 'They give lectures on our heritage and a variety of topics. Last week, we discussed how we might address the poverty that afflicts those living in slums in the town.'

'That would be a mammoth task,' Verity said with feeling, 'but we can do something about working conditions in the mill. I've been toying with the idea of—'

Oliver didn't have a chance to enquire what the idea was because just then, a voice sang out, 'Good afternoon, Miss Lockwood, Mr Hardcastle. Fancy meeting you up here.'

They turned to see Dolly, sketchbook in hand, smiling at them, and Nellie close behind with four young children in tow. 'Glorious day, isn't it?' Dolly's hazel eyes glinted impishly.

Verity glanced at Oliver. His expression told her that he too was thinking they had been caught doing something they should not be doing.

'Dolly, how lovely to see you.' And gathering her wits, Verity asked, 'Have you everything ready for tomorrow evening?'

'I have, Miss Lockwood. I cut out lots of easy-to-read headlines from the newspapers like you told me and stuck them on card with flour and water paste.'

'This will be for your reading class, I presume,' said Oliver with a wry smile.

'That's right. We're holding the first class after work tomorrow evening.' Verity spoke confidently even though she was aware that Oliver thought it would fail miserably.

'Then I wish you both luck with that.' He sounded far more convinced than he felt. He anticipated that few would attend and he disliked the idea that Verity would be disappointed. Eager to change the subject, he asked, 'Is that a drawing book, Dolly?'

'It is, Mr Hardcastle. I was sketching the views from up here.'

'May we look?' Verity held out her hand.

Dolly handed her the book.

'These are really very good,' Verity exclaimed, unable to hide her surprise as she looked at how Dolly had captured the contrast between the pretty hamlets and the stark grimness of the town, and the undefined vista of the moors and mountains on the horizon.

'Indeed, they are,' Oliver agreed as he peered over Verity's shoulder. 'You've quite a talent for drawing, Dolly.'

Dolly flushed. 'Thank you,' she said modestly as a shout from Nellie grabbed her attention. 'I'd best go and help Nellie. She has her hands full with them rascals. See you tomorrow.' Dolly took back the sketchbook and skipped off to join her friend.

'Not only does she appreciate literature; she has a good eye for the visual arts. She's certainly not the sort of girl you'd expect to find working in a weaving shed. So, why is she?' Verity sounded puzzled.

'Simply because she can earn more in the mill than she would in a shop or an office,' Oliver said as they set off walking round the tower and to the edge of the hill. 'There, the wages are fixed no matter how hard you work whereas in the mill, if she flashes her pieces, she can make more than two pounds a week. And Dolly does that most weeks.'

'Flashes her pieces?' Verity realised how much she didn't understand about the mill.

'Aye, managing more than one loom and weaving quickly and efficiently. Not all the women do that,' Oliver replied, his tone matter of fact. 'Her brother's the same. The dyehouse functions like it does because George uses his brains. They're both a cut above the rest.'

They had come to the edge of the steep, rough incline and they stopped and gazed into the distance, both of them lost in their own thoughts: Verity wondering how best she could help Dolly achieve her full potential, and Oliver thinking how pleasant it was to be in the company of a woman that he could converse with on an equal level about his work and his interest in history.

His thoughts strayed to Lucy Whittaker, a young woman he had taken to concerts in the Town Hall. She detested what she referred to as 'mill talk' and made it quite clear that whilst she found Oliver desirable, she would have preferred it had he been a professional man. Her own father was a bank manager, and she herself stayed at home and kept house. Just lately, she had given Oliver the impression that she was expecting a commitment from him. Since then, he had avoided her the best he could which was difficult seeing as how she was his sister Rose's best friend and called regularly to visit her.

'Can we see our mill from here?' said Verity, pointing towards the town, its huge, grim, gritstone buildings and tall chimneys the very centre of the Yorkshire wool trade.

Oliver said he thought not. 'It's dwarfed by our more prosperous competitors,' he jested. 'Hidden in the bowels of a rapacious industry.'

'But the dark, satanic mills don't really spoil the landscape, do they?' she asked, loosely quoting William Blake's poem.

Oliver gazed at the lush, green fields and woods below the hill then into the distance at the density of blackened mills, and beyond them to where they blended into the vast moorlands and the hills surrounding them. 'No, they're the very heart of it,' he agreed.

'And look over there,' Verity cried, pointing to the hillsides higher up the Colne Valley where the late afternoon sun winked on the upper windows in the rows of small cottages that had once held the handlooms where cloth had been woven before the advent of the huge mills. 'Those rows of little windows on the upper floor provided them with light to weave by for as long as the day was long,' she said.

'Aye, their handlooms took up the whole of the top floor of their houses, the stink of raw wool in every crevice of their homes and the danger of fire from all the grease. They were hard times,' Oliver said, his tone sombre. 'We've come a long way from when entire families toiled over a single piece of kersey to take to market each week.'

'My father told me that my great-grandfather lived in a small cottage like those before he borrowed the money to build our mill. He fought off the Luddites, you know, when they tried to smash his spinning frames and looms.' Verity's pride in her ancestry shone through.

'And it's a good job he did or we'd both be out of a job.' Oliver laughed. 'And the job's going well. We too have come a long way, Verity.' He gave her a warm smile and she returned it, thinking how nice it was the way he said 'we'. Their partnership was a good one even though she was the mill mistress.

They continued walking and talking until the sun was low in the sky, the bracken on the moors glowing a rusty red. 'We should be making our way back. It's getting late,' Oliver said.

During the descent of the hillside, when they came to a tricky bit, Oliver took Verity's hand, and he did not let it go. Hand in hand, they made their way to the foot of the hill and only then did he loosen his hold on her. The warmth of his calloused palm had felt lovely against the softness of her own and Verity felt rather disappointed as they continued walking sedately side by side along Lumb Lane.

They hadn't gone far when a youth on a bicycle came careering towards them, the front wheel of his machine wobbling out of control. 'Watch out,' he yelled as he whizzed by them so close that Oliver grabbed at Verity's arm and pulled her out of its path.

Pressed to his chest, Oliver felt the trembling of her heart – like a captive bird in a cage that beats its wings in an attempt to escape its confines – but he held onto her, relishing the moment. Verity felt the thud of his heart against her own and felt faint with pleasure. Not since childhood had anyone held her so close, and the human contact brought tears to her eyes. She blinked them away and when, at last, he let her go, she suddenly felt bereft.

Oliver stepped back a pace so that he could look into her face. His dark eyes smouldered.

Verity's heart beat a rapid tattoo. She returned his gaze, the warmth in her eyes turning silver-grey to a pale shade of violet. She had never before looked more beautiful, and Oliver drew a deep breath, then slowly released it. Verity looked at him expectantly.

'Do you like music, Verity?'

Taken aback, she hesitated. What had she wanted him to say? She didn't really know but it wasn't that she'd wanted to hear.

'If you do, I wondered if you'd accompany me to a concert in the Town Hall next Friday evening,' Oliver continued, anxiety colouring his tone of voice. Then looking abashed, he added, 'You don't think it presumptuous of me, considering that you are...' His voice trailed off in confusion.

'Not at all, Oliver. I'd be delighted,' said Verity, her spirits rising.

'It's the local choral society. They're giving a performance of Mendelssohn's "Elijah",' Oliver told her, his relief patent.

Verity walked on air as they made their way back into the village. That a man like Oliver should find her interesting and attractive enough to want to be her escort warmed the cockles of her heart. It was a whole new experience and it made her feel desirable and womanly.

12

The mill hooter's piercing blast had split the air almost ten minutes ago, the hubbub of noise that had followed as the mill hands departed fading into silence. Verity took a deep breath and nervously listened for the sound of clogs on the cobbles outside the baling shed, her heart leaping into her throat when the door was pushed open. Six women trooped in, Dolly leading the way and Nellie at her heels. Verity's breath whooshed from her throat; they had come. She hadn't been made to look foolish after all.

The women perched on the bales Verity had dragged into place round a long table used for cutting off lengths of cloth, and after the women had consumed the welcome mugs of tea and tasty biscuits, she called the group to order. Then, feeling as nervous as a kitten but not letting it show, she pointed with a pencil to the large black symbols she had written on the big sheet of card, and thinking it was wise to credit them with knowing more than might prove to be true, she said, 'Now I'm sure you all know what the alphabet is.'

Heads nodded, some more assuredly than others.

'These are the letters that make up the words we speak and read,' she said, her confidence growing as tapping each letter, she sang out, 'A, B, C, D...' until, rather breathlessly, she arrived at Z. The women giggled. 'Now, you sing them after me.'

What happened next turned out to be great fun, the women repeating the sounds in loud, drawn-out, sing-song voices and laughing at their efforts. Then Verity picked out individual letters for them to call out. Amid much joshing when mistakes were made, they identified the letters that denoted their Christian names.

'Well done, Connie,' Verity praised as a young girl pointed to the letter C.

'Miss, Miss, I can do me dad's name,' shouted young Katy, jumping up and tapping the letters B-O-B. Her friends clapped and cheered. Then Dolly handed out pencils and paper and with help from Verity and Dolly, the women all copied out the letters that spelled out their names. 'I'll practice this then I'll not have to sign t'rent book wi' me mark any more,' an older woman crowed. 'That'll be one in't eye for my bloody landlord.'

Forty-five minutes later, five happy women left for home, chattering excitedly and clutching the pages on which they had written their full names and several small words.

'That went well,' Dolly said, rolling up the big alphabet card.

Verity was putting the mugs and the large teapot that she had brought from home into a cardboard box along with the empty tins that had contained the biscuits she and Clara had made the previous evening.

'It was a start, Dolly. And they were all so eager to learn, it brought me close to tears.' She flopped down on one of the bales of cloth, suddenly feeling quite weary. 'I do hope they come again.'

'Course they will, Miss Lockwood. You wait and see. There'll be more come next week, even if it's only for the lovely tea and biscuits.'

'Thanks, Dolly. You're a wonderful helper.' Verity's voice was rich with sincerity. 'Now you get off home. I'll see you tomorrow.'

'Goodnight, Miss Lockwood.' Dolly trotted out of the baling shed, glowing under the praise and thinking that the mill mistress wasn't a bit like her horrible dad, Jeb.

Verity picked up her basket, locked the shed and walked across to the office. Oliver was at his desk writing in a ledger. Verity looked at the top of his head bent over the book, his thick black hair gleaming in the lamplight. A surge of gratitude, then a deeper feeling she couldn't quite explain for this lovely, hardworking man flooded her veins. He looked up with a tired smile.

'Well, was your reading class a success?'

'It was. Dolly and I had five very keen pupils,' Verity said, her eyes shining. 'We expect more will join given time. At least, Dolly thinks so.'

'I'm pleased for you,' he said, pushing aside the ledger. He'd had his doubts. He'd heard some of the women scorning the idea, asking who did she think she was making out they were as ignorant as muck? Oliver's smile widened. 'Then it won't be long before Lockwood Mill has the most educated workforce in the valley,' he quipped.

'Don't make fun of me, Oliver. The more changes we make can only be to our benefit.'

'You may well be right,' he said, getting to his feet and pulling on his jacket. 'Come on, you can give me a lift as far as Somerset Road in that fancy little trap of yours for I'm sure you're as hungry and tired as I am.'

At the gate, Oliver gave instructions to the nightwatchman, and with Verity at the reins, the pony clopped out of the mill yard. When they reached Somerset Road, Oliver asked to be set down. 'I'll walk from here,' he said when she protested that she'd drive him to his door. 'Almondbury Bank's too steep for this little chap. Somerset's a much easier road.' He patted the pony. 'Goodnight, Verity. Sweet dreams.'

He watched the trap until it disappeared into the twilight then set off walking. He was looking forward to taking her to the choral concert on Friday.

Verity travelled the rest of the way to Far View with a song in her heart. The reading class had been successful, and although her small mill could never compete with the production of larger mills in the valley, she would in a different way make it into one of the happiest, safest places where workers were as valued as all people should be. She began to render a slightly out of tune version of 'The Ash Grove', a favourite from her schooldays and as she sang, she wondered if she would like the music at the concert on Friday night. She didn't really care. She was going with Oliver and that was enough.

* * *

Verity liked to walk round her mill, and the next morning, not long after she arrived, she set out across the mill yard. The morning was pleasant, a mild September sun breaking through the clouds and she decided to go down by the canal and enter the mill at the rear. The slick, oily water glistened purple, green and brown and slinky green reeds clung to the walls, the placid scene making her feel uplifted and glad to be alive. Then, retracing her footsteps, she approached the rear of the gaunt, black edifice that was her inheritance.

She heard the whimpering and the grunts before she turned the corner, and rounding it, she came to a sudden stop, shocked rigid. Sam Firth had young Maisie Booth pressed up against the wall, one hand clasping her throat and other hand holding his rigid manhood.

'Lift thi skirts an' get thi britches down,' Sam ordered Maisie.

Maisie's tears streamed down her cheeks and she struggled to free herself. 'Don't, Mister Firth. Let me go. I'm on'y fourteen. I don't do this.'

Sam tightened his grip on Maisie's slender neck, pushing all the harder, and Maisie yelped as the rough stone bit into the back of her head. Sam, engrossed in satisfying his filthy needs, hadn't yet spotted Verity. 'Tha'll do as I bloody well tell thee if tha values thi job,' he barked.

'No, she most certainly won't!' Verity yelled as, hitching up her skirt, she charged at him.

Caught completely unaware, Sam swung his head in her direction, his jaw hanging open.

Verity lunged at him and lashed out, slapping forcefully at the hand that imprisoned Maisie. Sam, a head and more shorter than Verity, lost his grip, reeling as her flailing hand swiped his startled face again and again. Cowering under the torrent of blows, he staggered backwards, putting distance between them. Verity dropped her fists.

'Collect your things and get off my premises. You're dismissed, Firth,' she panted, her grating tones and flashing eyes brooking no opposition.

Just for a moment, Sam looked panic-stricken. Then, speedily recovering his bombast, he barked, 'Nay! The bloody hell. I'll—'

'You'll do nothing! And if you've any sense, you'll get out of my sight before I do you further damage.' Verity took a threatening step towards him. 'And do up your trousers,' she sneered. 'There's a pathetic appendage dangling from them.'

'You cheeky bitch. You can't sack me,' Sam snarled as he adjusted his britches.

'I just have. Now, leave this instant.'

Muttering threats, Sam shambled round the corner and Verity turned to the quivering, weeping Maisie. The little girl's eyes were wide with fear and she trembled from head to foot. 'Am I goin' to get t'sack an' all, Miss Lockwood?'

'No, of course not, Maisie.' Verity rubbed her stinging palms together and tried to still her own tremors. Her violent attack on Sam had quite shocked her but she did not regret it. She cradled the weeping girl in her arms. 'Come now, let's go to my office and we'll both calm down over a cup of hot, sweet tea.'

When they reached the mill yard, they saw that Sam had got there before them. He was standing at the office doorway that was blocked by Oliver's sturdy frame. He had listened to Sam's garbled version of what had taken place, that he'd only been 'mucking about with a willing girl' and that Verity was being high-handed, but detesting the man as he did, Oliver chose to side with the mill mistress.

'She can't sack me,' Sam yelled. 'It's not her bloody mill. Jeb Lockwood's my boss. We'll see what he has to say about this.'

'Don't be a fool, man. Jeb Lockwood can't help you now. If Miss Lockwood says you're fired then that's good enough for me. Be off with you, and don't come back.' Oliver's fists curled and the grim set of his mouth let Sam know he meant business.

Sam scuttled towards the gate.

'Tha'll be sorry for this. I'm not done wi' thee,' he bawled when he caught sight of Verity. 'Tha'd better watch thi bloody back cos—'

Oliver leapt from the doorway, sped across the yard and delivered a swift kick to Sam's backside. Sam pitched forwards, and as he struggled to regain his balance, Oliver kicked him again. 'Don't you dare threaten Miss Lockwood. Get out! Now!'

* * *

'Whooh, Mr Hardcastle. You do have a hot temper.' Verity giggled, her eyes full of admiration as she sat in the office sometime later over yet another cup of tea made on the gas ring that she had installed the week before. Maisie, somewhat recovered from her ordeal, was back in the weaving shed all smiles and sure of her job, and bursting to tell the other women of Sam's demise and sing the praises of the wonderful Miss Lockwood.

Oliver, now conversant with what had really occurred, was sitting opposite Verity, her cheeks still flushed from the altercation, and his eyes glowing with admiration.

'I wasn't going to stand there and let that guttersnipe threaten you. I've had all I can take of his filthy ways. He got what he deserved. And not before time. From what Maisie said, you weren't too easy on him yourself.'

Verity laughed then shook her head. 'That poor little girl. She was terrified, but now that we've got rid of Firth, that should put an end to girls like her living in fear of his abuse. I won't stand for that in my mill.' There was fire in her eyes, and Oliver fleetingly thought of the warrior queen he had told her about on Castle Hill.

'And rightly so,' he said. 'Let's hope that's the last we see of him.'

Buoyed by her success, Verity spent the days that followed feeling that she was indeed proving to be the mill mistress, and that Oliver was perhaps more than just a colleague.

* * *

A New Dawn for the Mill Girls

On Friday evening, Verity and Oliver joined the throng of people in Ramsden Street making their way to the Town Hall, Verity wearing a well-cut skirt and jacket made from an offcut of the grey and mauve herringbone cloth woven in her own mill, and Oliver in a smart black suit with a grey waistcoat and crisp white shirt. They made an attractive couple.

When Verity had discovered that a length of the herringbone cloth had a slight flaw and wasn't fit to be included in the client's order, she had immediately taken the piece along to a dressmaker in the Imperial Arcade, telling her that she needed the suit as a matter of urgency. The clever needlewoman had been able to fashion the suit without having to use the flawed section and had completed it in time for Verity to collect it that Friday morning. It fitted perfectly, and her delight at wearing something new for the occasion now doubled when Oliver complimented her on her appearance.

'You look splendid, Verity and...' he paused for effect, 'you're a beautiful advertisement for the cloth we weave.'

She blushed prettily. 'Perhaps I should have attached a little sign saying, "Woven by Lockwood's",' she said airily.

Oliver laughed out loud and, feeling easier in his company, Verity linked her arm through his. He smiled approvingly and patted her hand.

Huddersfield Town Hall in Ramsden Street, built in the late 1870s, had been extended to provide a large concert hall with access from Princess Street. It was an impressive edifice in the classical Corinthian style with long windows above and on either side of a wide, stone portico. As they approached it, Verity commented on what a splendid building it was, and Oliver told her that it was built from local stone quarried at Crosland Moor at a cost of £40,000.

'Did you learn that at the Philosophical Society?' she asked with an impish grin.

'As a matter of fact, I did. And I remember seeing it being built whenever I came into town with my mother. I must have been about ten or so when it was finished.'

Verity liked hearing snippets of information about his life, and she imagined him as a small, dark haired boy out shopping with his mother. 'I don't recall anything about the town when I was young,' she said. 'I was sent away to school in Leeds when I was seven.'

Oliver heard the regret in her voice. 'That must have been hard at such a young age.' He wanted to hear more about her childhood but by now, they had reached the entrance to the Town Hall and, with his hand under her elbow, he shepherded her into the spacious vestibule and up a flight of stone stairs to the concert hall.

When they were seated, Verity gazed in awe at her surroundings. The walls were decorated with giant, ornate pilasters, and above where they sat, there were two galleries supported by iron columns under a coved ceiling with moulded beams. The most fascinating aspect was the huge Father Willis concert organ that filled the recess behind the orchestra pit, its golden pipes gleaming in the soft light. Then the orchestra, choir and soloists took their places and a hush fell over the hall.

Verity had never before attended an oratorio, the pursuits of Aunt Flora and her cousins being of a much more frivolous nature, and she tensed as the conductor raised his baton. Oliver felt her stiffen and placed his hand over hers. 'Do you know the story of Elijah?' he whispered. Not wishing to appear ignorant, she said she did, although she knew little more than that he was a Biblical character, and when Elijah's curse rang out in a fine tenor voice, she shuddered. But as the voices rose and fell, and as a turbulent orchestral overture depicted the tragedy, Verity was more aware of Oliver's hand now holding hers than she was of the music. When the soloists and chorus begged for God's help, the music washed over her and she wanted for nothing more than to sit with her hand tucked inside Oliver's forever.

'I enjoyed that immensely,' Verity said as they walked back down Princess Street in the chill night air.

'Then we must do it again,' said Oliver.

She rejoiced at his words and wondered if he intended to court her. She thought she would like it if he did. As the idea of being romanced by Oliver set her heart fluttering and her veins tingling, common sense kicked in. Perhaps she was reading too much into it. After all, one night out at a concert was hardly a proposal of marriage.

Oliver was wondering what people might say if they saw him with his employer outside working hours. Would they label him a social climber worming his way into the affections of a mill heiress? With that in mind, he hailed a hackney cab, and as they travelled back to Almondbury, they talked about the oratorio and the mill. Verity would have preferred to walk back with him under the starlit sky and too soon, the cab drew to a halt outside Far View House.

'Would you care to come in?'

'It's late. I'd better let the driver take me home.'

Oliver longed to go inside and prolong the evening, but in all the time he had worked for Jeb Lockwood, he had not once been invited into the mill master's home. Any time he had called on urgent mill business, he had been kept on the doorstep.

'Thank you for a lovely evening, Verity. Will I see you tomorrow?'

She knew that tomorrow being a Saturday and the mill working only until midday that he probably saw no reason for her to be there, and disappointed at his refusal to stay a little longer, she said, 'Maybe. And thank you. I've had a delightful evening.'

He saw her to her door then climbed back in the cab and was gone.

* * *

Autumn days faded into a cold and often wet October. When rain lashed the mill yard where the mill hands usually ate their breakfasts and dinners, they were confined to the sheds and rooms where they worked, every mouthful tainted with the dust and fluff or the stink and fumes of their labour. And today was one of those days.

When the midday hooter blew, Verity peered through the office window at the driving rain. 'It's still pouring,' she told Oliver as she reached for her umbrella. 'I'll take a walk round the mill whilst it's quiet.'

She stepped out of the office without waiting for his reply and walked across the yard to begin her rounds. She took pleasure from making her presence known to all the mill hands, getting to know them and what their work entailed. It was important that she learned about all the processes. *And I am learning,* she told herself, as she reached the weaving shed.

Only the week before, Verity had had water boilers installed in the weaving shed and the spinning room so that the workers throughout the mill could make hot drinks at mealtimes. 'With winter fast approaching, it's only right they should have something to warm them,' she had told Oliver when he had shown amusement at her concern, and doubt at the expense.

Now the weavers were crouched on the greasy, cold floor

close to the water boiler and so busy eating and chattering that when Verity entered the shed, she went unobserved.

'I blooming hate having to eat my snap in here. It's like eating fluff and dust butties,' Dolly complained as she sat cross-legged on the floor with her snap tin on her knee.

'Aye, an' sittin' on this floor's freezing my arse off,' May grumbled.

'Brierley's have a canteen, the lucky buggers,' said Lily enviously.

Verity felt rather guilty at their discomfort, despite the fact that she had provided them with hot water. Then, to make them aware of her presence, she said, 'Sorry about the awful weather, ladies. Is the tea urn working as it should?'

Heads turned in her direction and a number of voices chorused, 'It is, Miss Lockwood.'

'Aye, it's grand to get a warm drink 'cos I can't stomach cold tea,' Hetty commented.

'Me neither, Hetty,' said the woman hunkered beside her, 'an' I never thought I'd live to see t'day I'd have a hot cuppa wi' me snap in Lockwood Mill.'

The grateful comments went some way to easing Verity's conscience.

'I'm glad to hear that. I'll leave you to your lunch, ladies.'

As she walked to the door, Dolly got to her feet and followed her.

'I made the extra cards for tonight's reading class, Miss Lockwood. Did you remember to get more pencils?'

'I did – and some more rubbers,' Verity replied with a forbearing grin; the class members liked to eradicate their mistakes.

They talked like friends rather than mistress and servant for Verity had encouraged Dolly to do so. Then leaving Dolly to finish her dinner, Verity went up to the spinning room to be met with more praise for providing the tea urn but it didn't dispel the sympathy she felt for the mill hands, and as she walked from one floor to another, an idea began to take root.

The weather might be foul, Verity thought, but the mill was doing well. The order book had acquired three new entries that week and production was no longer hampered by too few mill hands, broken-down machinery or shortages of raw wool and dyes. Oliver's prediction that they might turn a profit by Christmas might well be realised.

And now she had a new project to consider.

With that in mind, she went to investigate a room at the rear of the mill that contained old bits and pieces no longer fit for use. Standing amidst the clutter, she pictured how it could look. *With benches and tables and a couple of women to serve food and drink, the room would make an ideal canteen.* Her stride purposeful, she went back to tell Oliver what she had in mind.

'A canteen!' Oliver's eyebrows shot up. 'Whatever next? A trip to the seaside?'

'That's for the summer, Oliver. You can make arrangements for the charabancs.' Verity's somewhat testy response had Oliver shaking his head in bemusement. 'You have to admit a canteen makes sense,' she continued. 'Look at the weather. And Brierley's and Crowther's both have canteens, so why not us?'

'Maybe because we're not as prosperous as Brierley's or Crowther's.'

'But we could afford to offer a little comfort,' Verity demurred.

'And where are we to house Miss Lockwood's luxurious tea rooms?'

Oliver's sarcasm didn't deter Verity. She told him about the disused room. 'Get some of the young hands to clear it out, then we'll hire someone to limewash the walls.'

'Your wish is my command, Miss Lockwood, but don't you think we're getting ahead of ourselves? We're not yet breaking even, and a canteen will cost more than just the hiring of a couple of women for a few hours a day. You'll need tables and benches, and if you're to provide food, it will have to be paid for.' He gave a sympathetic smile. 'I think this idea needs careful consideration, Verity.'

'I've given that some thought already,' she replied pertly. 'We've already got the hot water urns to make tea, and we could make soup to ward off the cold. Medley always grows more vegetables than we can use, and if we charge for it, the soup will pay for itself.'

Oliver smiled at her naivety, but he could tell she wasn't about to take his advice. He held no strong objections to the mill having a canteen and he found himself wanting to please this ambitious girl who let her heart rule her head, and at the same time affected his heart.

'That still leaves the matter of tables and benches but...' he gave her a tantalising smile, 'I happen to know where we might get those. The old Fellowship Hall on Glebe Street is to be demolished to make way for a new engineering factory. I'll ask one of the members if we can buy the furnishings cheap.'

'Oh, Oliver! You are the most enterprising, helpful man in the whole world!' For one moment, Oliver thought that she was about to throw her arms around him but at the last minute, she made do with patting his upper arms. Looking rather embarrassed, she said, 'So can I go ahead with my plans?'

'You may,' he said, this time shaking his head in the same way that a doting father might do to his rebellious child.

Over the next few days, Pip Haigh and four other young lads

cleaned out the cluttered room but with no idea of why they were doing it. Men were hired to limewash the walls, and the tables and benches were delivered at night after the mill had shut down for the day.

Much to Oliver's amusement, Verity didn't disclose her reasons for altering the room to any of the mill hands; she wanted to surprise them. But when it came to finding two women who would serve the food, she sought Dolly's help.

'Ooh, Miss Lockwood, a canteen. That's marvellous.'

'I'm glad you think so, but don't mention it to anyone until everything's in place.'

Feeling privileged to be in on the secret, Dolly promised not to say a word, and the next day, she reported that she had found two women who wanted the work. 'Mona's a widow with a houseful of children but her mother will mind them for a few hours each day,' she said. 'She'll be glad of the work. And Bertha's a friend of my mam's. She worked in the kitchen at Carr Green House until the new owners moved in and brought their own staff with them.'

'Tell them to call at the mill tomorrow morning, and remember, not a word to anyone.'

'It's our secret,' Dolly said and winked.

The mill mistress was full of surprises.

* * *

The following morning, Pip Haigh strutted across the mill yard full of his own importance. Not five minutes ago, the mill mistress had taken him into her confidence then ordered him to fetch the tea urns from the weaving shed and spinning room. *A canteen, eh?* His eyes twinkled mischievously He liked the idea of being sworn to secrecy. He marched into the weaving shed.

A New Dawn for the Mill Girls 167

'Hey! Pip Haigh. Where does tha think thas goin' wi' that?' Lily yelled as Nellie's brother disconnected then lifted the hot-water boiler and headed for the weaving shed door.

'Put it back, Pip,' Nellie shouted. 'Miss Lockwood gave it us to make hot drinks.' Half in and half out of her overall, she made to block the lad's way. 'You tell him, Dolly.'

But Dolly paid her no heed, seeming to concentrate on covering her bright-red hair with a green, striped turban.

'Aye well, thas not havin' it in here any more,' said Pip, dodging round his sister and out into the yard, laughing loudly under a hail of catcalls and curses.

'I knew it were too good to last,' Hetty groaned. 'Give wi' one hand, tek back wi' t'other. They're all t'bloody same are t'bosses, an' she's no different.'

'Don't you dare say that.' Dolly jumped to Verity's defence. 'She's been good to us, and she always treats us like we matter.'

'Aye, as long as it suits,' Lily sneered, tying a turban over her mop of blonde hair.

'You'll be eating your words, let alone your snap, come breakfast time,' Dolly quipped, a smug smile curving her lips as she trotted to her loom under the watchful eye of the overlooker. Hildred Bottomley had replaced Sam Firth, and although he had none of Sam's disgusting proclivities, he was dour and short-tempered.

The thump of machinery bounced off the walls and as Dolly worked at her loom, she anticipated her workmates' surprise.

Shortly before half-past eight, Verity went out into the yard, her umbrella aloft to shield her from the mizzle that threatened to turn into a downpour. Her steps light, and her heart lighter, she hurried to the canteen. Bertha Strong and Mona Hepplethwaite greeted her with beaming smiles. 'Everything's ready, Miss Lockwood,' said Bertha, gesturing to the boiling urns and the two huge pots of soup – pots that had last been used in Verity's grandfather's days when Far View hosted large dinner parties and hadn't been used since. Clara had been glad to see the back of them.

'Thank you, Bertha, Mona,' Verity said as the breakfast hooter let out its piercing blast.

In the weaving, spinning and carding sheds, the machines ground to a halt.

'It's mizzlin' out there,' Lily said, going to the weaving shed door. 'We'll have to stay in here again.'

'I'm not. I'm off to the canteen to eat my breakfast.' Dolly casually walked to the door.

'Canteen?'

An uproar of voices high with curiosity bombarded her.

'What are you talkin' about?'

'Has tha lost thi marbles, Dolly?'

'Where do you think you are? Brierleys?'

'No, Lockwood's. It's in that room at the back of the mill where the rubbish was kept. I'm off to let the spinners and the others know about it.' She ran to deliver her message as Verity had asked her to do.

'Canteen?'

'In the rubbish room?'

'That's what she said, an' she'd be the one to know. Her an' Miss Lockwood are as thick as thieves.'

Exchanging bemused glances, the weavers headed to the rear of the mill where they were joined by scourers, carders, dyers and spinners, the air rife with inquisitiveness and unanswered questions as they converged on the new canteen.

'Gerra bloody move on,' a voice yelled from the back of the queue as those who had been the first through the doors stopped and stared in amazement at the benches and trestle tables, and smelled the fragrant aroma of soup.

'Welcome to your new canteen,' Verity shouted above the chatter as the workers crammed in. 'Help yourself to tea from the urns. Soup is free today to celebrate the opening, and after that, it will be a penny a bowl.' She repeated this several times in between fielding words of praise and helping Bertha and Mona dish up soup.

'By, this's grand, Miss Lockwood.'

'There's not a better mill in t'valley to work for.'

The compliments came thick and fast.

'Eeh, this is a godsend, Mr Hardcastle,' an elderly spinner called out as Oliver entered and made his way between the tables and benches to Verity's side.

'Another success, Miss Lockwood.' Oliver gave her a lopsided grin.

'I can't take all the credit, Mr Hardcastle. I couldn't have done it without your help.'

Dolly watched as they exchanged words. She saw the look in the manager's eyes, and the way Miss Lockwood's cheeks glowed. She nudged Nellie.

'There's something going on between them two,' she whispered. 'Look at 'em. You don't look at one another like that if there's not. There's more to it than just mistress and manager, believe you me.'

'Aye, well, anybody 'ud fancy Mr Hardcastle. He's ever so handsome,' Nellie said.

'So's Miss Lockwood,' Dolly replied with temerity. 'She's beautiful.'

'Ooh, I wouldn't go as far as that,' Nellie scorned and went back to slurping soup.

'Little you know about beauty, Nellie Haigh.' Dolly felt hurt for Verity's sake.

'Mind you, you could be right. Look at him now.' Nellie nudged Dolly.

Oliver was gazing deep into Verity's eyes, a gentle smile twitching the corners of his lips as he was speaking, and she was gazing back at him and hanging on his every word.

'Told you so.' Dolly smirked then draining her mug, she looked round at her workmates all enjoying their breakfasts in the warm, dry canteen. Miss Lockwood had triumphed again.

13

'He's not showing any improvement, is he?' Verity kept her voice low as she stood by Jeb's bed looking down at his twisted features, his skin the colour of putty.

Ada was wringing out a flannel in a bowl of warm water. 'No, he's deteriorating by the week,' she replied softly. 'His muscles are wasted, and he eats no more than a baby bird.' She moved to the head of the bed, flannel in hand. 'Come on, lad, let's get you washed.'

Jeb's bleary eye rolled and he grunted and groaned as Ada wiped his face then his hands. When she lifted his nightshirt, he let out a guttural moan, thrusting against her hand as she washed his manhood and his bony buttocks.

Verity looked on, pity and something close to rage tumbling in her head: that her father had brought himself to this. A wreck of a man who had ruined his life with drink. He who had inherited a sound business and could have now been reaping the benefits had he applied the same dedication to the mill that he had to drinking and gambling. What a dreadful waste.

Jeb's ablutions completed, she helped Ada to prop him up on

his pillows and make him comfortable. Then holding his wizened hand in both her own, she talked about the mill. Jeb gazed vacantly into space, making no sign that he heard or understood. Drool ran from his blubbery lips and she gently wiped his chin. She might not love him but she would not neglect him as he had neglected her. When his eye drooped and his head rested on his chest, she released his hand feeling utterly at a loss, his rasping breaths setting her nerves on edge. How many more months would he linger in this half-life? she wondered. She didn't wish him dead, but he might as well be, she thought sadly as she got to her feet.

Ada saw Verity's despondence, and almost as though she had read her mind, she said, 'He hasn't long for this world, Miss Lockwood. His organs are gradually shutting down. He has difficulty peeing and his breathing's not good. It'll be a blessing when the good Lord takes him.' Her tone was matter of fact as one might expect from someone who had spent long years nursing the dying.

Tears sprang to Verity's eyes. 'Such a waste,' she murmured.

'Aye, it seems like it, but maybe he didn't think it was when he had his health.'

'You're probably right. He had a good innings as the saying goes, but he could have done so much more with his life if only he'd chosen a different path.'

'He could,' Ada said sagely. 'Now it's up to you to do it all in his name. And from what I've heard tell, you're making a good hand of it. So, you get off, and don't be moping about what might have been. Live for the day.'

With Ada's advice ringing in her ears, Verity set out for the mill. A damp November fog hung over the town, wrapping the tall mill chimneys, the rushing river and the lazy waters of the canal in a thick grey blanket. By late afternoon it had lifted, and

Verity was looking forward to taking the reading class that numbered nine women and five men and was now always held each Friday after the last shift.

When the hooter signalled the end of the working day, she walked from the office to the weaving shed to have a word with Dolly. It was a dark, desolate evening and Verity shivered as she crossed the yard. Thankfully, the canteen where the reading classes now took place retained the heat from the boilers that earlier that day had produced hot drinks and soup and she was consoled by the fact that it provided her readers with warmth as they learned. As for herself, Verity was always warmed by the enthusiasm of her students and her own deep sense of satisfaction. Teaching the skills that she had taken for granted – so precious now to the young women and men who came each week – was without doubt one of her greatest pleasures.

She entered the shed, the waning thrum of machinery and the smell of hot oil assailing her ears and nose. Gertie Spragg, the Mrs Weaver stood arms folded across her ample bosom at the head of 'weaver's alley'. She was very large and square with a face like a box: one that Verity did not wish to open. Her eyebrows were a thick straight line across her broad brow, and cold, grey eyes above a squat nose and wide chin looked Verity up and down.

'Miss Lockwood, what can we do for thi?' The wispy, greyish hair on her upper lip rose and fell as she spoke, her tone as usual unfriendly.

Verity, popular with all the women in the shed, had asked Dolly why it was that the Mrs Weaver so clearly disliked her. 'Oh, take no notice of her, Miss Lockwood. She's Sam Firth's sister, that's why,' Dolly had told her.

'I just came to have a quick word with Dolly Armitage,' Verity said briskly.

'Aye, well, she's busy tidying her loom, but I suppose tha can seein' as tha can do as thi pleases,' Gertie sneered, her animosity not lost on Verity.

'Indeed I can, Mrs Spragg, and you would be wise to remember that,' Verity retorted.

Gertie paled. 'Right you are, Miss Lockwood,' she muttered.

Dolly was checking that her piece was in good order when Verity arrived at her side.

'Reading class is ready when you are, Dolly. Gather the others and I'll be in the canteen.'

Dolly's face fell. 'They'll not be coming tonight, Miss Lockwood – and neither will I,' she said, her expression apologetic.

Verity's heart missed a beat. What had gone wrong? Had Gertie Spragg got to them? She'd been very vocal about her objections to the classes. On more than one occasion on class nights, Verity had heard her urging the women to, 'Get off home wi thi, lasses. Tha doesn't want to be wastin' thi time on stuff above thi station.'

Verity's disappointment palpable, Dolly gabbled, 'Tonight's bonfire night, Miss Lockwood. We're all going up Castle Hill to have a bit of fun.'

Verity breathed a sigh of relief. 'Oh, I see. Wish them all a good time from me, and you too, Dolly.' She waited for Dolly to ask her to join them and when no invitation was offered, she realised how foolish it was to think it would be; she was the mill mistress. But it didn't prevent her from feeling friendless and lonely.

'No reading class tonight. They're all going to Castle Hill,' she said to Oliver when she went back into the office. 'I'd quite forgotten it's Guy Fawkes' night.'

'So it is,' he said, looking up with a smile and closing the ledger in front of him. Again, Verity waited, wondering if he was joining the festivities and if so, hopeful that he might ask her to accompany him. The chattering voices they could hear in the mill yard faded into silence as the mill hands left for home. Oliver stood, pulled on his jacket and then looked expectantly at Verity as if to ask had she anything more to say.

Verity looked at his handsome face, the locks of dark hair that fell over his brow and curled round his ears.

Oh yes. She had a thousand things she wanted to say, such as why had he not invited her to the most recent concert in the Town Hall, or why he refused her offers to drive him home in the trap, and why did he look at her in a certain way that spoke of more than friendship but then suddenly become cool and impersonal. But she didn't say any of these. She simply smiled and said, 'If we're finished for the day, I'll get off home.'

'Be careful how you go,' he advised as he went and opened the door for her. 'Watch out for young lads throwing squibs that'll scare the pony. I don't want it running away with you.'

'I will,' she said, thinking at that moment that she would like to run away with him.

He walked with her to the trap. The pony was nuzzling at a bag of hay. Oliver helped untether it and put it between the shafts. Then he handed Verity up. The sky was a lake of purple velvet with a handful of stars. The lamps at the mill gate cast long shadows on the stark blackness of the silent mill.

'Will you ride with me?' she offered.

'Thank you, no. I'm going in the opposite direction. Off you go, and take care.'

Verity flicked the reins and the trap rattled out of the yard. The nightwatchman gave her a wave. Oliver waited until she was out of sight then set off walking in the same direction. He walked slowly, his tread and heart heavy. He needed time to think. Shoving his hands deep into his overcoat pockets, he walked on, a prisoner of his own thoughts. Nine months ago, he had never given Jebediah Lockwood's daughter a thought. And now...

A gang of young lads came whooping towards him and suddenly, the pavement at his feet erupted in a flash and a bang as a squib exploded. They ran on, laughing. Oliver kicked at the dead firework. It skidded into the gutter and down a drain and he wished that the thoughts now troubling him could be disposed of just as easily. Were Verity's feelings for him as genuine as his for her? Or did she see him as just another of her employees? Showing him the same respect and kindness that she gave to all the others.

But then, what of the special moments they shared, the warmth or sparkle in her dove-grey eyes, and her words of admiration that seemed to speak of something more? Surely, he wasn't mistaking those. Yet... she was the mill mistress. If he pursued her, would people see him as a fortune hunter? That she had no great fortune wouldn't prevent them from assuming that he was rising above his station by setting his sights on a mill heiress.

Overhead, the sky spread like an endless, dark sheet but here and there in the yards behind the houses, the hot glow of bonfires lit the night, sparks flying, and the excited cries of small children splitting the air. At the foot of Almondbury Bank, and his home in sight, a small crowd were gathered round a huge bonfire on a piece of spare land. Tongues of flame leapt upwards but none of them burned as fiercely as the one in Oliver's heart.

* * *

At the same time as Oliver arrived home still dwelling on his thoughts, Dolly, Nellie and Pip were making their way up the steep incline that led to the top of Castle Hill. Behind them came

George and Amy. She was hanging onto his arm and complaining that the rough ground was playing havoc with her new boots.

'Tha shoudn't have worn 'em then,' Nellie called over her shoulder, jealousy flaring as she wished she was the one hanging on George's arm. She'd have no complaints, and she hadn't had a new pair of boots in ages, the ones she was wearing being her mother's cast-offs. 'Amy Dickenson's as miserable as sin,' she whispered to Dolly.

'She has no capacity for joy unless it's boasting about her new clothes,' Dolly agreed.

At the top of the hill, they joined the crowds already there. The massive pyre of wood had just been lit, clouds of blue-grey smoke swirling upwards as hungry flames licked the dry tinder. Spitting and crackling, the fire began to burn brightly, and as the onlookers lit their fireworks, the night exploded in sparks and stars. Squibs banged, Roman candles ejected streams of brilliant colours and Catherine wheels on sticks whizzed round and round in whooshing circles. Rockets soared high in the sky, their glittering showers winking and blinking as they slowly descended on the hilltop that was now a magical conflagration of blazing branches, shimmering air and floating ash.

'How many fires can tha see?' Pip asked, pointing to the surrounding countryside and the glow of bonfires in Berry Brow, Taylor Hill and the other hamlets below the hill.

'I make it eleven,' Dolly answered.

'I can only see seven,' said Nellie.

'George, the smoke's making my eyes water,' Amy whined.

George ignored her.

'My hair smells and my coat's covered in ash,' she cried, brushing at her shoulder.

Dolly and Nellie exchanged frustrated glances. 'Let's leave

'em to it and go and enjoy ourselves. If I have to listen to her any longer, I might throttle her,' said Dolly, skipping away from her brother and his moaning girlfriend. She felt sorry for George.

Her arm linked in Nellie's and Pip close behind, they circled the fire, laughing and jumping at the fire crackers that the lads threw at their heels. Some foolhardy boys and men were chasing each other with burning brands, or daring their mates to jump over the low-lying embers that had spread from the fire.

'Don't thee be doin' that,' Nellie warned Pip. 'If tha burns the arse out of thi trousers, Mam'll kill thi.'

Pip ignored her, and heedless of scorching the seat of his trousers, he joined his friends in their risky game.

By now, the flames were licking into the heart of the wooden mountain, the blaze creeping higher and the flames eating at the stuffed straw legs of the effigy of Guy Fawkes. As he slowly disintegrated, his turnip head rolled into the ashes, the spectators whooping at his ritual death. Someone started to sing 'Little Brown Jug' and everyone joined in. Dolly and Nellie linked arms with their neighbours and were dancing round the fire when, above the happy sound, they heard bloodcurdling shouts and curses. The singing faded, the dancers' steps faltering, and Dolly and Nellie stopped cavorting.

A gang of marauding youths armed with burning sticks were bearing down on another group of young men who were fleeing for their lives.

'What's up? What's happening?' Dolly shouted at a lad she recognised from the mill.

'Them bloody toffs are tryin' to gerroff wi' our lasses,' he bawled.

'We're gonna beat the shit out o' them,' another fellow cried, waving his burning brand.

Nellie screamed and ran off to find Pip, and before Dolly

could take flight and follow her, she found herself right in the thick of the melee as all hell broke loose. The sudden violence rooted her to the spot and she glanced round, wild-eyed, as the local lads punched and kicked at the young men dressed in fine jackets and boots. Where was Nellie?

Just as Dolly was in danger of being trampled underfoot by the brawling men, she felt herself wrapped in a pair of strong arms. Her feet left the ground and she screamed at the top of her lungs, her screams turning to cries of relief when she found she was being carried away from the mob. Twisting her neck to get a look at her rescuer, she saw that it was none other than the boy she had met in Penny Spring wood at bluebell time.

Puffing and panting, he set her down against the remains of an ancient rampart. 'Are you all right?' he gasped, pushing his blonde locks back from his forehead and smiling.

'I am now. For a minute, I thought I'd had it,' she spluttered, breathlessness making her voice husky. 'Thanks for rescuing me, kind sir.'

'Don't you remember me?' he asked, disappointment wiping the smile from his handsome, flushed face.

'Course I do. You're the lad who looked at my drawings. Theo, isn't it?' she said as she straightened her coat and smoothed her hair.

'That's right,' he said, his smile reappearing. 'And you're Dolly.'

'Oh! You remember that, do you?' She sounded surprised.

'I most certainly do. How could I forget a girl with hair as fiery as the setting sun? I've tramped the woods several times hoping to see you again.'

Dolly blushed. She had gone to the woods a few times in the summer and now she felt rather grieved to learn that their paths had never crossed.

By now, the yelling and cursing had subsided, the local rabblerousers lust for blood having been quenched by older and wiser men, and the toffs making a hasty escape. The singing started again. Dolly felt uncomfortable standing in the shadows with a boy she barely knew.

'I'd best go and find my friends,' she said, moving away.

'Can I come with you? It seems a shame not to, now that we've found one another again.' Theo proffered his arm and Dolly, feeling rather discombobulated, accepted.

'Who started the fight?' she asked as they walked back to the bonfire.

'The locals. The fools I was with tried to get off with their girls and all they got was a hiding for their troubles.'

'Are those toffs your friends?' Dolly sounded annoyed.

'No, they're guests up from London and staying at Thornton Hall. I was roped in to show them the way here so that they could enjoy a good old Yorkshire Guy Fawkes Night. Somehow, I don't think they did.' He laughed. 'I did warn them that the mill hands are rough customers.'

'We're not all rough,' Dolly retorted, stung by his low opinion of her people. She removed her hand from his arm and began pushing through the crowds, searching for Nellie. Theo followed her. She found Nellie and Pip standing with Lily and her husband, Frank. Nellie looked disgruntled.

'Where wa' thi? I thought tha'd beggared off an' left us,' she snapped.

Dolly's friends stared curiously at Theo, looking him up and down and noting the silk stock at his throat and his well-cut jacket and knee-high boots. Their lips curled.

'Beggared off!' Dolly exclaimed. 'It was you that left me. I nearly got trampled to death, and would have been had it not been for Theo. He dragged me clear of the fighting, and not a minute too soon.'

Nellie looked askance at Dolly when she said, 'Meet my knight in shining armour, Theo Beaumont from Thornton Hall.'

'Pleased to meet you,' Theo said, nodding from one gaping face to another.

'He's one o' them toffs,' Lily sneered.

'No, he's not,' Dolly cried, jumping to Theo's defence. 'He works at the Hall. He showed the toffs the way here, that's all.'

Lily tugged at Frank's arm and they walked off.

Nellie and Pip's ugly expressions softened but they made no attempt to be friendly. Instead, they began poking sticks into the huge circle of the dying fire's red-hot embers, hunting for potatoes that they'd thrown in earlier. Theo gallantly raked out four potatoes, handing one each to Dolly's friends before giving one to Dolly and keeping one for himself. They tossed them from hand to hand until they cooled then sank their teeth into the crispy skin and the soft mush inside.

Then, as they stood munching and watching the fire die, a fine tenor voice began to sing 'The Four Loom Weavers', the sorry lament signalling the end of the festivities, and reminding them that they had work the next morning.

A pale moon sifted through the clouds, giving just enough light for Dolly, Theo, Nellie and Pip to keep their footing as they made their way back down the hill. When they reached the road, Nellie walked ahead with Pip, leaving Dolly and Theo a few paces behind, Nellie's long stride and her rigid back letting Dolly know she was cross with her. Trying not to mind, Dolly made casual conversation with Theo as they ambled down Lumb Lane. When they reached All Hallows Church and the parting of their ways, Theo down Helen's Gate to Thornton Hall and Dolly down Somerset Road into the town, they stopped walking.

'Can we meet again?' he asked.

Dolly's heart lurched. She'd had a few boyfriends in the past, but they had been lads she had grown up with, and none of them had held her attention for long. Theo Beaumont was different, not aristocracy but certainly a cut above the mill hands she was used to. She hesitated, her heart battling with her head. Her heart won.

'I'd like that,' she said.

His rewarding smile made her heart flutter. 'When and where?'

'Tomorrow afternoon. I don't work then, but...' She was thinking on her feet. They would have to meet in a place where they were unlikely to be seen together. 'I'll meet you at the top of the Rookery in Somerset Road at two o'clock. Do you know where that is?'

Theo said he did, and Dolly bade him a hasty farewell for by now, Nellie was looking back and scowling. Dolly ran to catch up with her. Theo strode off into the darkness. He wondered what his father would say if he knew that his son had arranged to meet a mill girl.

'What wa' tha talkin' about wi' him?' Nellie sounded put out.

'We were making arrangements. I'm meeting him tomorrow.'

'What! You never are! He's not our sort, Dolly. Tha wants to be careful.'

'Careful of what?' Dolly tossed her head dismissively. 'He's nice, and I'm just going for a walk with him. What's the harm in that?'

'He most likely thinks tha'll be easy 'cos you're a mill lass.'

'Nellie Haigh, you do have a dirty mind.' Dolly laughed.

'Aye, well, his sort are on'y out for one thing. Don't say I didn't warn thi.'

They walked down Somerset Road in silence, Dolly wondering if she should take Nellie's advice, and Nellie struggling with jealousy and real concern for her friend.

'See you tomorrow,' Dolly said as they arrived at the place where she would leave them to go to Silver Street and Nellie and Pip up into the town to Tinker's Yard.

'Aye, it'll come soon enough,' Pip said as the distant chimes from St Peter's clock tower struck eleven times.

Dolly ran the rest of the way home.

'You're a late bird,' her mother said as she burst through the door. 'Our George's been back ages. He said Amy didn't like the smoke so they came away early. Did you enjoy it?'

'I did,' said Dolly, tossing her coat over the back of a chair. 'I had a lovely time.'

'I can see that,' Sarah laughed. 'What did you get up to?'

'Oh, you know. We sang and danced round the fire, and now I'm jiggered.' Dolly wasn't ready to divulge the real reason for her flushed cheeks and sparkling eyes. She'd wait to see how things turned out before mentioning Theo Beaumont.

* * *

Verity had watched the blazing fire on Castle Hill from her bedroom window. The flame-washed sky had seemed like a lure calling to her and she felt an intense loneliness. She'd wondered if Oliver was there enjoying the fun and had mused on how exciting it would have been to stand close to him in the heat of a roaring fire and watch the night sky come alight with soaring rockets. Perhaps he might have put his arm around her to ward off the chill evening air. But nobody had invited her, not even Dolly, she thought dismally. *And all because I'm the mill mistress, and as such, not really a true friend. I'm neither one thing nor the other.*

14

November had run its course. Days of fog and rain and bitterly cold nights had followed one after the other and now, late in the afternoon at the end of the first week in December and the weather still harsh, there seemed little to feel cheerful about. Verity closed the ledger and leaned with her chin rested on her hands, her elbows on the desk. 'It doesn't look as though we're going to make that profit you predicted after all.' She didn't sound too disheartened, and Oliver shrugged and gave her a sympathetic smile.

'No, we're not yet in the clear but then, we didn't know the full extent of your father's debts,' he said. 'But look on the bright side. You've settled most of them, and the mill is in good shape. We have orders to complete, and the mill hands are showing their appreciation of the changes you've made by working to the best of their ability. We're producing cloth as fine as any mill in the valley, even if it's still in a small way. All credit to you, Verity. You're doing a good job.' He sat back and stretched, his shirt tightening across his broad chest. 'And now it's time to call it a day. I don't know about you but I'm ready for home.' He got to his feet.

You might be looking forward to going home, but not me, Verity thought, her eyes fixed on his rippling chest and then on his broad back as he turned and unhooked his jacket from the wall. *The only time I feel that life is worth living is when I'm here at the mill doing something worthwhile, and being near you. There's no life in Far View House.*

She stood reluctantly and took her coat from the hook behind the office door. Oliver, ever the gentleman, took it from her. 'Here, let me,' he said, and as she slipped her arms into her coat sleeves, she smelled his cologne and felt his warm breath on the back of her neck. She had to resist leaning in to him. Oliver suppressed the temptation to wrap her in his arms.

They stepped out into the mill yard. The cobbles glistened under a covering of hard frost. The nightwatchman had the pony and trap waiting. Verity climbed aboard, and to her surprise, Oliver said, 'I'll ride with you tonight, if that's all right.' An unexpected warmth flooded her veins as he climbed up beside her. The journey they were about to undertake would be brief but for both of them it prolonged the pleasure of being together. Sadly, neither of them would admit to this out loud.

Although the air was chill, a bright moon shone and brittle stars glittered and winked. Verity wished they could travel like this forever, and Oliver felt the same. Tossing aside his misgivings about courting the mill mistress, he took a deep breath of frosty air.

'The choral society are putting on a performance of Handel's "Messiah",' he said. 'Would you care to go with me?'

'Oh, yes. I really would. It's a perfect way to celebrate Christmas so I've been told,' she gushed, her hands tightening on the reins to such an extent that the pony was startled.

Quick as a flash, Oliver covered her hands with his and controlled the skittering pony.

'Oh, dear me. I wasn't concentrating,' Verity gasped, looking extremely embarrassed.

'Ice on the road,' said Oliver, excusing the mishap yet feeling awfully pleased with himself, and her eager acceptance of his invitation.

At the bottom of Somerset Road, Oliver climbed down and, her spirits raised, Verity watched his departing back before continuing her journey.

Minutes later, just as she was almost level with where Rookery Lane met the road, she was surprised to see Dolly standing at the top of the path. She opened her mouth to call out then swallowed her words as Dolly, oblivious to the approaching trap, suddenly ran across the road and into the arms of a young man hurrying towards her. They held each other tight and their lips met. Verity felt envious. She had never been kissed. She flicked the reins and urged the pony on.

* * *

'Theo! Your nose is freezing,' Dolly giggled when the kiss ended. This was their fourth time of meeting. Up until now, they had just met on Saturday afternoons but a week apart now seemed too long and Theo had suggested they meet on Wednesday evenings too.

'Where will we go?' Dolly asked anxiously.

'I don't know,' said Theo, 'but let's start walking. My blood's turning to ice.'

Although neither of them had put it into words, they had both decided that it would be wiser to spend their time together in places where they were unlikely to be seen by anyone who knew them, Dolly unsure of her mother's reaction to the son of a land agent, and Theo doubting that his father would approve of him courting a mill girl. Dolly already knew Nellie's opinion of Theo. She hadn't minced her words when she'd objected to her friend spending her Saturday afternoons with him rather than with her as she usually did.

'Don't come crying to me when he's had his mucky way with you,' Nellie had said when Dolly told her she was meeting Theo again.

And so, on the first two Saturdays after Bonfire Night, Dolly and Theo had strolled through Penny Spring wood and in the lanes surrounding it, fairly sure that none of their acquaintances would be walking in the woods at this time of year. As they walked, they had learned about each other's histories. Dolly had talked happily about her family and friends and Theo had told her about his parents' divorce and how awful it had been to be separated from his father. He'd been sent to boarding school – a cold, cruel place, so he'd said – then in the school holidays, he'd been shunted between his mother's new home and whatever estate his father was working on. Dolly's kind heart had ached for him. She couldn't imagine not having a loving home and a proper family.

The other two Saturdays had been spent walking round the town, Dolly familiarising Theo with what it had to offer, and if she happened to spot a neighbour or a fellow mill worker, she had dropped back or hurried forward, putting a short distance between herself and Theo, as though they were not together. Theo, unaware of her tactics, had no similar concerns; the town's people didn't know him.

She'd shown him the grand façade of the railway station with its six huge columns and neo-classical pediment in St George's Square, and the George Hotel where the wealthy mill owners met, then on to window-shop in Rushworth's Bazaar and browse the stalls in the covered market. On one occasion, the bitterly cold weather being against them, they had gone into the Boy and Barrell public house in the Beast Market, a pub that catered for the men from the slaughterhouse, and one that Dolly's friends wouldn't dream of frequenting, it having a bad reputation.

There they'd sipped hot toddies, Dolly declaring, 'My dad 'ud kill me if he knew I was in *this* dump,' and Theo blithely replying, 'What the eye doesn't see, the heart doesn't grieve about.' Dolly had laughed then because no matter where she was with Theo, it was exciting.

Whenever they were together, they chattered nineteen to the dozen, and in Dolly's opinion, that was one of the nicest things about Theo.

Now, as they walked down Somerset Road in the blistering cold air, each wondering where they might go in order to prolong the subterfuge that ruled their meetings, they told each other how they had each celebrated Christmas when they were young. Theo recalled the workers' children's parties on the estate where his father had then worked, and Dolly painted a picture of wassailing round the doors singing carols and munching on the mince pies and walnuts the householders gave them.

Whilst it was fun to swap happy memories, it didn't prevent the icy chill and the frost-rimed pavements underfoot from biting into their bones and their enthusiasm soon waned. It wasn't a night for walking the streets, and by the time they reached the bottom of King Street, Dolly was shivering and her feet were numb. 'I'll catch my death if we stay out much longer,' she groaned. 'Where can we go?'

'In here,' Theo said, tugging her arm and leading her into a dark passage that led to one of the yards at that end of the street. It was the entrance to Tinker's Yard where Nellie lived.

'We can't stop here,' Dolly cried, fearing that Nellie or Pip might appear at any moment.

'Yes, we can,' said Theo, wrapping his arms around her. 'I'll keep you warm.'

Dolly readily admitted that it felt good to be out of the biting wind, and warmed by Theo's kisses, she began to enjoy herself. His lips were tender, and he made her giggle by kissing the tip of her nose then her forehead and chin. He told her she was the loveliest girl he'd ever known, and that he wanted her to be his girl and nobody else's. His kisses became more passionate and although Dolly couldn't help but respond, in the back of her mind was Nellie's warning: *his sort's only out for one thing.*

Panic fluttered inside her and she pushed him away. 'I've got to go,' she cried.

To her relief, Theo didn't protest. He gave her a lopsided grin and said, 'Sorry, Dolly. I got carried away. Forgive me.' Looking utterly contrite, he added, 'You know I'd never do anything to hurt you.' The grin returned. 'And you have to agree we're much warmer now.' Then clasping her hand, he ran with her down the passage and back onto the street.

A long patch of ice had formed on the pavement outside a butcher's shop. Letting go of Dolly's hand, Theo skated over its glassy surface then turned back, urging her to have a go. Laughing, she skidded towards him and he caught her in his arms. They walked briskly and talked about books they had both read until they reached Silver Street.

'Will we meet on Saturday?' he asked, afraid that she might refuse after what had happened in the passage.

'Two o'clock at the usual place,' Dolly said, knowing that she had nothing to fear from Theo.

They kissed and parted, and Dolly hurried to her front door, the joy of her friendship with Theo clouded by the lies she was about to spin.

'How's Nellie's mother? This bitter weather can't be doing her much good,' Florence said as Dolly took off her coat.

Dolly couldn't look her in the eye as she said, 'She's doing as well as can be expected.'

Lying to her mother about where she had just been and about where she went on Saturday afternoons didn't come easy. People of her mother's generation were particularly wary of the upper class, and with good reason. Her own mother was the bastard child of a relative of the house where her grandmother had been a maid. As for Nellie, she had argued that, 'the son of a land agent who worked for a Sir Somebody-or-Other' was most definitely not in the same class as herself or Dolly.

Upper class! Lower class! Dolly fumed inwardly as she ate a drip sandwich for her supper and listened to her mother's gossip. What was the point of having reading lessons or striving for anything that might better oneself if you weren't allowed to transcend the classes? Aspirations gave people hope: the girl in the weaving shed who wanted to be the Mrs Weaver, the lad in the dyehouse who hoped one day to be the Master Dyer, or a girl like herself who craved to be an artist. So what if she wanted to be courted by the son of a land agent? What had that to with anyone else?

'And talking of sick people, how's Miss Lockwood coping with her father? I heard he's getting no better.'

Florence's comment broke Dolly's angry reverie. She hadn't even been aware that her mother had been telling her about a dying neighbour.

'I... I... we... we don't talk about him,' Dolly floundered. 'Miss

Lockwood keeps her personal matters to herself.' *Just like I'm doing,* she thought guiltily.

* * *

Jeb Lockwood was fading fast. Just as Ada Brook predicted, his internal organs were gradually ceasing to function. 'He'll be lucky to see Christmas,' she confided in Clara as they changed the soiled sheets on his bed.

'I'm surprised he's lasted this long,' Clara said as they slid Jeb from one side of the bed to the other. He grunted and groaned and rolled his eye, a helpless bundle of skin and bone. 'There tha is, Master. All clean an' comfy,' she shouted at the top of her lungs, believing that Jeb had lost his hearing as well as the power of speech.

'How will you celebrate Christmas?' Ada asked as they bundled-up the dirty bedding. 'I'm for Evelyn Hardcastle's. She kindly invited me to have dinner with them.'

'I'll mek summat here for Miss Verity an' her Aunt Martha then me an' Bert'll scoot off home for t'rest of the day. It'll just be for the two of 'em 'cos he'll not be eatin' owt.' Clara nodded at Jeb and raised her eyes. 'There's nowt much to celebrate in this house these days.'

* * *

Verity would have agreed with her, but she didn't dwell on it. The mill was busy and she was buzzing with yet another bright idea. So, on the Friday morning in the week before Christmas Eve, she burst into the mill office and announced that she wanted to give the workers a bonus. Oliver's jaw dropped and his eyebrows shot up. For the next ten minutes, he adamantly advised caution but Verity passionately overruled him.

'The improvement in the cloth they're producing has to be acknowledged,' she urged. 'And if we put a bonus in their wage packets this week, they'll have that bit extra to buy things for Christmas, and know that we appreciate their efforts.'

Oliver reminded her of the money spent on the canteen, and that the mill had still to turn a profit. 'We're not out of the woods yet.'

'We will be in the new year,' she confidently replied.

Despite Oliver's protestations, when the wage packets were handed over just before dinnertime that day, an air of jubilation flooded every corner of Lockwood Mill. The hooter blasted, and when Verity and Oliver went out into the yard, profuse thanks flowed from the mill hands' lips as they made their way to the canteen.

'See what spreading a bit of happiness does for morale,' she said.

'Not to mention what it does to the bank balance,' Oliver replied gloomily as they walked over to where the gatekeeper was waiting with the trap. They were going to meet a new client at the George Hotel. Verity was wearing her good blue-grey suit she'd had made from their own worsted and Oliver his grey waistcoat with his best jacket and trousers.

'Tha looks like Prince Bertie an' Princess Alexandra,' Lily shouted as Oliver handed Verity into the trap. They smiled, both used to Lily's cheeky remarks.

'They make a lovely couple,' Dolly said dreamily. She was still nursing her own secret romance and now she thought, *You wouldn't say they were the same class, Miss Lockwood being the owner of the mill and Mr Hardcastle her employee, but that doesn't seem to bother them. After all, he must be courting her if he takes her to concerts and walks out with her.*

She watched the trap trundle out of the yard then followed the women on their way to the canteen still commenting on what a smart couple they made.

A short while later, Oliver and Verity arrived in St George's Square. The railway station and the George Hotel, both impressive buildings, dominated the square. A statue of Robert Peel stood guard in the centre of the square as if to indicate that law and order abided here.

Leaving the pony and trap in the care of a stable boy, Oliver and Verity went into the hotel, Oliver carrying the samples of their latest cloths. There, in the comfort of one of the hotel's grandiose sitting rooms, they met with Levi Ruddiman and his wife. Levi owned two garment factories and a chain of tailors' shops in Bradford, Halifax and Dewsbury.

Introductions made, the little Jewish tailor rubbed the cloth samples between his long, bony forefinger and thumb and peered at the weave through wire-framed glasses perched on the end of his nose. Mrs Ruddiman admired the delightful shades and patterns. A moderate order was placed, and whilst Oliver dealt with the details, Verity talked to the tailor's wife.

'It's most unusual to meet a young woman in your position, Miss Lockwood,' the elderly lady remarked. 'Running a mill is a great responsibility, and I must say your cloth is of the finest quality.'

'Thank you,' said Verity, her heart pumping at the size of the order. It would offset the mill hands' Christmas bonus that Oliver had argued against. 'My father's incapacitated and I have taken over his duties...' she paused and smiled, 'with Mr Hardcastle's invaluable help.'

'Very noble, my dear. Do tell me more.' Elsa Ruddiman

caught the eye of a hovering waiter and ordered tea and cakes. When they arrived, she took over in a motherly fashion.

'I have worked alongside my husband for the past thirty years, and I admire women who don't shy away from what is considered men's work,' she said as she poured tea for everyone, adding two heaped spoonsful of sugar to her husband's cup before handing it to him. 'We are often wiser and kinder when it comes to keeping our employees happy,' she continued. 'Remember that, my dear. We can't do without them.'

She expanded on the theme by telling Verity about the women they employed in their sewing factories. Verity responded by talking about the reading classes, the canteen and the Christmas bonus, and in between sipping and nibbling, Elsa Ruddiman listened, then said, '*Yasher koach*' and, turning to her husband, she said, 'Levi, this is a girl after my own heart.'

Flattered and curious, Verity asked, 'What does *yasher ko*—'

'It means you have done well, used your initiative,' Elsa praised in her rich, husky voice.

She turned to address her husband again, and in Yiddish, she told him something that made him laugh. He then spoke to Oliver, and this time, it was Oliver's turn to laugh, but Verity hadn't heard what was said because Elsa was enquiring about her father.

They parted on the best of terms, and as they left the hotel, Verity asked what the tailor had said to make Oliver laugh. 'That his wife told him you were the sort of person she wanted to do business with and that he should double the order on the Jacquard grey and mauve herringbone.'

'And did he?' Verity's eyebrows shot up.

'He said he trusts his wife's judgement implicitly so yes, he did.'

'Oh, Oliver! That's wonderful. What a start for the New Year.'

Her eyes sparkled and her cheeks, still flushed from Elsa's praise, glowed even more delightfully. 'I feel like dancing round the square,' she cried, doing a little twirl.

Oliver yearned to take her in his arms and dance with her but propriety overruling desire, he took her arm and led her to the trap. They chatted excitedly all the way back to the mill, thrilled by the Ruddiman's order, and what the future might hold.

* * *

Spirits remained high in the week running up to Christmas, and on the night before Verity and Oliver were to attend the performance of the 'Messiah', which was on the Wednesday, Oliver told his mother that he had invited Verity to take tea with them before going to the concert.

'Why ever would you want to do that, son?' Evelyn Hardcastle, a big-boned woman with a helmet of steely grey hair gave a troubled frown.

'I like her. She's good company – an interesting girl,' he said, a sudden reddening of his neck speaking a thousand words.

'You might well like working for her, but she's not for you. She's the mill owner. Her sort moves in different circles.'

'Miss Lockwood doesn't – I think she's quite lonely and in need of the company of a family like ours.'

'Then I think you'd be wrong. Mixing business with pleasure is never a wise move.'

'And what about Lucy Whittaker?' Rose intervened pettishly. 'Why are you not taking her to the "Messiah"? Is she not as *interesting* as Miss Lockwood?'

Oliver frowned at Rose's barbed comment.

'Lucy is your friend, not mine,' he snapped, feeling slightly guilty at seemingly having used Lucy for his own entertainment.

'She'll make a better companion than your boss,' Evelyn said sourly. But she'd begrudgingly agreed to put on a spread.

* * *

Verity had been excited by the prospect of the concert from the moment Oliver had asked her to accompany him, and to be asked to take tea with his family pleased her all the more. As they drove to his house on Thursday evening, she felt rather nervous. It was a long time since she had socialised and she dearly wanted to acquit herself in an appropriate manner.

'You're very welcome, Miss Lockwood.' Oliver's mother's smile didn't quite reach her cold, blue eyes as she took Verity's coat and bade her take a seat in the parlour. Oliver was greeted in quite a different fashion. His mother and his sister flapped round him, Evelyn helping him off with his coat and Rose plumping the cushion in his chair before he sat down. Verity sensed immediately that he was the privileged one, the darling boy, the cock of the roost. *After all*, she reflected, *it is a man's world and he is master of the house.*

Tea was served. Slices of pork pie with a thick golden crust, ham sandwiches with the crusts cut off, buttered scones and fruit cake. Verity ate sparingly due mainly to having to field Rose's interrogation. Where had she gone to school? Where had she lived before coming back to Almondbury? What did she do at the mill, and what did she think of the new billowing sleeves in dresses and blouses that were now so fashionable?

'I intend to buy one of those blouses,' Rose twittered, fingering the neck of her overly frilly dress that did little to enhance her plump figure or her heavy jawline. Her features resembled Oliver's but whereas his were handsome, Rose's were unattractive in a woman.

Verity answered as best she could, her head ringing under the bombardment. Maud said nothing but occasionally, she gave her a slow, somewhat vacant smile. Oliver ate steadily, leaving the conversation to the women. At one point, when his mother went into the kitchen to replenish the teapot, he followed her.

'I believe he's taking you to hear the "Messiah",' Rose prattled.

Verity, her mouth full of buttered scone, nodded.

'He usually takes Lucy Whittaker. I'm surprised that he didn't ask her. They have an understanding, you know – but maybe he did and she had a prior engagement.' Rose sounded innocent enough but Verity detected a malicious gleam in her eyes.

When Oliver came back into the parlour, he said, 'We should be leaving soon. We don't want to be late.'

Verity stood. She couldn't get away quickly enough.

Oliver helped her into her coat, and Evelyn accompanied them to the door.

'It was nice to meet you, Miss Lockwood.' She didn't offer a future invitation, and Verity didn't expect one. She wished she hadn't come.

Out on the street, Oliver collected the trap from where they had left it in the lane beside the house. As they drove into the town, Verity pondered on Rose's words. Eventually, the question burning on her tongue, she voiced it.

'Who is Lucy Whittaker?'

'Lucy? Oh, she's Rose's best friend.' Oliver sounded disinterested.

'Not yours then.' The words slipped out before Verity could stop them.

'Mine?' Oliver gave her a puzzled glance then turned his attention back to guiding the pony into an ostler's yard close by the Town Hall. 'She works with Rose in Rushworth's Bazaar, and yes, I know her.' He handed the reins to the ostler's boy then helped Verity alight, his frown indicating that he understood Verity's line of conversation. Rose had been prattling.

'What makes you ask that?' He wasn't sure he'd like the answer.

'Something Rose said,' Verity replied. 'Something I must have misunderstood.' Then afraid that further probing would spoil the evening entirely, she gave Oliver a winning smile and tucked her hand in the crook of his arm, as if to say the matter was forgotten.

Oliver fumed inwardly as they walked to the Town Hall. *Damn Rose.* He had a good idea what Rose had said, and the malicious pleasure she would have derived from saying it.

'You shouldn't listen to Rose. She's full of witless prattle,' he said as they entered the building and mounted the stairs to the auditorium. Verity thought he sounded annoyed. She wondered if there was more to it than he was leading her to believe.

The concert was magnificent, and as the Hallelujah chorus raised the rafters, Verity had almost dismissed Rose's cruel jibe – but not quite.

15

The morning after the concert, Oliver was already at his desk when Verity bounced into the mill office. The delightful evening at the 'Messiah' had left her feeling magnanimous and she wanted to spread her happiness.

'I've been giving some thought as to what we should do tomorrow, it being Christmas Eve,' Verity announced brightly.

'And...?' Oliver eyes narrowed, his curiosity aroused. He wondered if he would like what he was about to hear. Several times in the past few months, the new mill mistress had taken him by surprise as she mooted her 'ideas' and all too often, he had been forced to rein in her enthusiasm, arguing that the idea was unaffordable or in one or two cases downright nonsense. Now, as he looked into her eyes alight with excitement, he hoped that whatever it was she was about to suggest had something to do with their personal lives and nothing to do with the mill.

'I want to close the mill today at six and let the workers have a free Christmas Eve,' she said emphatically. 'If you include Sunday which, being Boxing Day, they are already entitled, that will give our mill hands three full days to enjoy the festive season.' Her beaming smile was like that of a child who had just discovered she could do something that had previously eluded her.

Oliver's jaw dropped, and interpreting the look, Verity opened her mouth, ready to overrule his objections, but he beat her to it. 'Woah!' he raised his hand in protest. 'Another day's paid leave? We're already going to pay them the Union rate for Christmas Day and Boxing Day, and as for giving them tomorrow, well...' He jumped to his feet. 'That's utter nonsense, Verity. We've always worked on Christmas Eve. All the mills do.'

'But we don't have to, Oliver. We can set our own agenda, and it's only one extra day.' Verity's disappointment was palpable.

'A day that we should be using to get the frames and looms ready for the Ruddiman order,' Oliver reminded her tersely. 'We have to start full production immediately after the holiday if we're to meet the deadline. What's more, you're spoiling the mill hands.'

Verity pouted. 'I'm not spoiling them,' she denied strenuously. 'If anything, I'm manipulating them. When they return on Monday, they'll be working flat-out to produce the finest cloth we've ever made. I'll let them know that the Ruddiman's order has to be perfect, that it's a new venture for us that will secure their jobs for years to come.'

'Not only are you soft-hearted, you're also cunning, Miss Lockwood,' Oliver mocked.

'It's my Machiavellian streak coming out in me, Mr Hardcastle.'

She had hoped that her arch response would bring a smile to Oliver's face. It didn't.

'You can't afford to indulge the workforce, and neither is it wise to break with tradition.'

Verity placed her hands on her shapely hips and stared him

down. 'What is the point of me being the mill mistress if I can't do things my way?' she snapped, his disabuse of her idea making her angry.

'I'm merely offering advice.' Oliver's tone was forcedly reasonable. 'But it's your mill.' Grabbing his jacket from where it hung on his chair, he marched out of the office.

They were still at loggerheads in the afternoon when they did the rounds of the mill, and it was then that Oliver made his peace with Verity. As they crossed the mill yard, Oliver asked Verity how she would spend Christmas Day.

Verity sighed. 'Very quietly. I'll eat dinner with my aunt, and sit and read to my father. We don't entertain at Far View House.'

'Neither do we. Apart from Ada Brook, it will be just the family,' he said glumly. 'We'll eat too much and play a few tedious card games. I don't expect to enjoy it, but look... on Monday, there's the hunt at the Upper Royal George. They usually hold it on Boxing Day but with it falling on Sunday, it's been deferred until Monday. It's usually a good day out. Would you like to go?'

Verity clapped her hands to her mouth as she gasped her surprise, and seeing her delight, Oliver said, 'Then if you're still intent on giving them an extra day's holiday, why not give them the Monday instead of Christmas Eve? That way, we won't be breaking with tradition and annoying our competitors.'

'Then that's what we'll do. How clever of you, Oliver.'

'So, we're agreed that the mill hands work Christmas Eve?'

Verity nodded. 'I've never followed the hounds,' she said, her eyes sparkling at the thought of spending the day with him. Her smile slipped. 'But I can't ride a horse.'

'You don't have to. We follow on foot so wear sensible footwear.'

Suddenly, the prospect of Christmas had taken on a different hue.

Verity had already resigned herself to the fact that when the mill closed for the holiday, she and Oliver would spend it apart, each in their own homes. Now, the thought of being with him for an entire day somewhere other than the mill made her heart sing and she had to hold herself back from hugging him. Instead, she gave him a rapturous smile and when they crossed the mill yard, she felt like dancing.

As they moved from shed to shed, Verity announced that the mill would shut down at six o'clock on Christmas Eve and not reopen until Tuesday and that the hands would be paid at a fixed rate for Monday. Some of the hands gave a resounding cheer.

Oliver shuddered at the expense.

One of the carders grumbled, 'I don't know why you're bloody cheering. They're on'y givin' us summat we're entitled to, what wi' Boxing Day fallin' on Sunday.'

When they arrived in the weaving shed, Dolly saw them coming, and once again, she thought what a lovely couple they made. She automatically caught at a loose end of thread on her piece, for although she didn't neglect her work, her mind wasn't really on her loom. She had arranged to meet Theo that evening, snatching a last chance to see him before the holiday because both of them would be busy elsewhere: Dolly with her family on Christmas Eve and the day itself, and Theo at Thornton Hall attending to the visitors.

She still hadn't told her parents about him, but telling lies, duping her mother and abandoning Nellie left her feeling wearily guilty. She didn't want to cause any ructions during the festive season, but once it was over, she intended to make a clean breast of it.

Now, as Oliver and Verity passed by her loom, Dolly told herself, *If Oliver Hardcastle can court the mill mistress, then I should be able to go out with a land agent's son. Nobody has the right to tell me how I should lead my life.*

All around her, her fellow weavers were whooping and cheering now that they didn't have to work on Monday, and half-heartedly, Dolly joined in.

* * *

'Where are you for this evening?' Florence asked her daughter as Dolly put on her Sunday best cloche hat in the mirror above the sideboard.

'Wherever it is it must be a dressy do,' George remarked. 'She's wearing her new clothes under her coat, and she spent an hour doing her hair.'

Dolly's face reddened, and she continued staring into the mirror. Trust George to notice she was wearing her new brown skirt and emerald-green blouse, bought with her Christmas bonus, and chosen to compliment her fiery red hair that now hung in glossy curtains down below her shoulders.

'Aye, what's the special occasion?' her father asked.

If it was possible for Dolly's cheeks to turn a deeper shade of red, they did as she lied, 'Me and Nellie and a few of the other girls are going to the dance in Moldgreen church hall.' Even to her own ears, she could hear the wobble in her voice.

Her mother gave her an enquiring look.

'Are you sure you're all right, Dolly? You hardly touched your tea – and it was lovely piece of poached haddock.'

'I just didn't fancy it,' Dolly mumbled, heading for the door, eager to escape.

'You do look a bit flushed, love.' Florence looked more closely at her.

'I think she must have her eye on some fellow she's hoping to see at the dance,' said George. 'Is it Bob from the carding room?'

Dolly had no answer to that. 'I'll be off then,' she said, hurrying out of the kitchen, the blatant lies she had just told making her feel queasy.

Theo was waiting for her at the Rookery. 'You look beautiful,' he said, taking her hand and leaning in to peck her still slightly flushed cheek. The night air was crisp, and the sky a velvet black sheet studded with a million stars.

'The stars are shining specially for us,' Dolly said, and seeing them as a good omen, she pushed aside the risk of them being seen by anyone who knew her and suggested they walk to Greenhead Park. Theo hadn't been to the park before, and he readily agreed. Dolly led him through the back streets – just in case – to the very top of the town and into the park that was one of Huddersfield's most beautiful assets. It had been opened with great pomp and ceremony some six years before and was a perfect place for the townsfolk to take their leisure, but on a cold December evening, Dolly was banking on there being few people about.

By the light from the tall, ornate gas lamps that cast a pale gleam on the pathways, they strolled round the lake to the stone-built arbour with its crenelated top and arched entrances. Lured by the deep shadows and a bench to sit on, they went inside. Theo removed Dolly's hat and ran his fingers through her silky hair, his breath hot on her face. He was holding her and kissing her as if he would never let her go and she returned his kisses with equal ardour.

Although she loved the feel of his hands and lips, she was mindful of what they might lead to and after a while, she pushed him away. He groaned, throwing his arms wide and his face crumpling, his eyes pleading for more.

'I'm sorry, Theo,' she said, her voice barely above a whisper, 'but it 'ud be wrong to do what we both want to do. It's too soon.' She sat up straight to regain her composure and strengthened her tone. 'I'm fed up of meeting in secret and telling lies to the people I love. I want us to be a proper courting couple. For you to meet my family and... if we stay in love... we can get married. Then we can do as we please.' She got to her feet. There, she'd said it. Let him know she wasn't an easy girl. That she demanded respect and commitment.

'Do you love me?' Theo sounded doubtful.

'I think I do. I've never been in love before so I don't really know what it feels like. What I do know is that I love being with you, that you make me happy, and that I'd like to spend my life with you, but...' she paused and gave a deep sigh. 'I hate sneaking around as though we were doing something we shouldn't. Do you love me?'

Theo jumped up from the bench and threw his arms round her, raising her to her feet. 'You know I do, Dolly. I've loved you from the day I saw you sitting in the bluebells.'

'Then will we let everyone know? Stop acting like thieves in the night,' she said against his chest, surprised by how firm and in control she sounded even though her heart was thudding and her tummy turning somersaults.

'I... I... suppose we can.' He was thinking of what his father would say.

Dolly didn't hear the hesitancy in Theo's answer. He'd said he loved her, and that was enough. Pulling herself free, she ran beneath the arch, calling, 'Race you round the lake.'

Roaring with laughter, Theo chased after her. When he caught her, he rained kisses on her face. 'I love you, Dolly

Armitage,' he said, his breathless words making her laugh. She heard the sincerity in his voice and rejoiced in the fact that he hadn't forced her to prove her love for him.

They walked back into town, and reaching Market Place, they stopped to listen to the Salvation Army Band, and caught up in the mood, they sang along with the carol singers. Dolly felt that a weight had been lifted from her shoulders now that they had decided to let everyone know they were in love, and as they continued on to Silver Street, she had never felt happier. She'd tell her mum and dad about Theo, and who knew, her mam might say, 'Bring him to meet us.' New Year's Day would be ideal to do that.

She was just about to put her thoughts into words when Theo said, 'The Hall's heaving with visitors. The first lot arrived from London yesterday. Sir Arnold's invited half the countryside for Christmas and New Year and I have to help with their luggage and get the horses ready for the Boxing Day hunt. Then I'm to be on duty to assist the young men if any of them want to ride round the estate.' He grimaced at that. 'There's also a shooting party on New Year's Day.' He'd dropped Dolly's hand as he spoke, and with his hands plunged deep in his overcoat pockets, he mooched on beside her. 'I don't know when I'll be able to see you again, Dolly.'

Dolly's heart plummeted. By the time they shared a parting kiss on the corner of Silver Street, she had convinced herself that this was Theo's way of saying he wasn't prepared to wait any longer for her to give herself to him. But she was too proud to argue.

'Goodnight, Theo, God bless,' she said softly then ran down the street blinded by tears.

There would be no call to tell her mother about Theo, no

need for any more deceit but the thought didn't take away the hurt of losing him.

* * *

At the same time that evening as Dolly and Theo made their way to Greenhead Park, Oliver called into the Pack Horse Inn and ordered a pint of ale and a hot whisky chaser. He had just taken his first sip when a hand clapped his shoulder. Oliver turned to see Clarence Hargreaves, the owner of a mill in Kirkburton, and an old acquaintance from his school days, leering at him.

'Ah! Hardcastle. What's this nonsense I hear about Lockwood's? A canteen and reading and writing lessons,' Hargreaves sneered. 'Pandering to their whims and educating them beyond their need is bad for business, old chap. Next thing you know is all the hands in the valley will be making demands.'

'Everybody has a right to eat their meals in some comfort, and as for learning to read, they have a right to that also.' Oliver's cool, level gaze indicated the conversation was at an end. He turned back to his pint.

'Not in my mill, they don't.' Hargreaves sniggered, settling on the bar stool next to Oliver's. 'Noses to the grindstone, that's my motto.'

'I'm sure it is.' Oliver downed his whisky in one gulp.

Like Lockwood's, Hargreaves's mill was a small, family-run business that couldn't compete with the larger mills. However, it still managed to provide Clarence with a profligate lifestyle, and unlike Lockwood's, it was best known for producing inferior quality cloth, paying low wages and doling out cruel treatment.

'And what's this rumour about that mistress of yours giving her hands a Christmas bonus. Is there any truth in it?'

Oliver's silence said it all.

'Ah, so there is,' Hargreaves scoffed. 'That doesn't sit well in my book. It sticks in my craw.' He took a swig of his drink and smacked his blubbery lips before snarling, 'And I'm not alone. There are some in the valley who don't take kindly to her. Heed my advice, Hardcastle, and curb your do-gooding Miss Lockwood before she ruins us all.'

Oliver had heard enough. He downed his pint. 'I'll do no such thing, Hargreaves. Miss Lockwood is the finest woman you are ever likely to meet. She's worth ten of you.' His eyes as black as pitch, he glared murderously at Hargreaves. Then he marched out of the Pack Horse, the drink curdling in his stomach.

He understood the reason behind Hargreaves's threats. Unrest in the mills was a historic and common problem, the mill hands demanding higher wages and better working conditions. In the past, this had led to riots and damage to property, the mill owners out of pocket until the workers had been coerced into accepting their lot. And although Oliver did not agree with everything that Verity suggested, he did condone much of what she had already done, and he would defend her to the limit when it came to dealing with a greedy taskmaster like Hargreaves.

Even so, he felt uneasy.

***

Florence Armitage was standing with her back to the fire and her hands on her hips when Dolly entered the kitchen. Clem sat by the hearth, his lips clamped, and when neither of her parents returned her smile, Dolly's blood ran cold.

'Well, have you had a good time?' Her mother's tone was almost sneering.

'Ye... yes... Nellie got...'

'Stop there, lass.' Clem raised a staying hand. 'Don't lie to your mother.' His face wore a look of deep disappointment.

Dolly hung her head and stood wringing her hands, shrouded in shame.

'It's odd you saying that you had a good time with Nellie, 'cos she was round here looking for you. She also said you hadn't spent a Saturday together for ages,' Florence said icily, her eyes glinting with anger.

'Oh, Mam.' Dolly's reserves crumbled and she began to weep. 'I'm sorry for lying to you. I never would have, only...' She looked helplessly from one parent to another.

'Take your coat off, sit down, and start by telling the truth,' Clem ordered.

In between sobs and sniffles, Dolly told them all about Theo. Who he was, and how they'd met, then how he saved her from being trampled underfoot at the bonfire. 'And... if it hadn't been for him... I could have...'

Florence's lip curled 'And you thought you'd repay him by doing whatever he wanted.'

Her tart interjection cut Dolly to the bone.

'No, Mam! No! It's not like that. Theo loves me and I love him.'

'Aye, he'll say that as long as he's getting his way.'

At Florence's scornful remark, Clem reared up. 'Nay, Florrie. Thas accusing the lass of summat she might not have done.' He looked at Dolly, the pain and love in his expression begging for her to confirm that he was right. It made Dolly feel sick. Causing such hurt to the people she loved most tore at her heart. 'Tell her she's wrong, Dolly,' Clem begged.

'She can't tell the truth so why should we believe a word that comes out of her mouth?' Florence wasn't going to be so easily appeased. Her precious daughter had let her down.

'Please, Mam. Listen to me before you condemn me.' Dolly grabbed at her mother's arm. Florence shook her off. 'We haven't done anything wrong. I wouldn't, and neither would Theo,' she continued hotly. 'I know I shouldn't have lied to you, but I knew from the start that you'd disapprove and stop me from seeing him. I didn't want to be deceitful, and I hated having to sneak around but the more I got to know him, the more I knew I loved him.' The fire went out of her and Dolly slumped in her chair, wiping away her tears with the sleeve of her blouse.

'And are you still a virgin?' Florence kept her voice deliberately low.

Clem got to his feet. 'I'll leave you two to talk,' he muttered; this was women's business.

He looked at Dolly and shook his head, his face creased with dismay and sympathy as he pulled on his jacket. 'I'm off to t'Somerset for a pint,' he grunted.

Dolly started to cry again.

When he'd gone, a silence fell over that kitchen, so deep that Dolly felt bathed in it.

'In answer to your question, Mam, I am. And I will remain so until I'm married,' she said stoutly, and tossed her head to add impact to her words.

'And has he asked you to marry him?'

Dolly sighed. 'It's too soon for that, but I thought he might.'

Florence pursed her lips. 'A land agent's son, eh? You're getting ideas above your station, my girl.'

A spark of rebellion made Dolly's hazel eyes flash. 'And what exactly is my "station", Mam? You've always told me I'm as good as anybody, that because I can read and write and speak properly that I'm their equal. And now you're castigating me for daring to go out with a land agent's son.'

'Aye, well, they're different from us,' Florence huffed. 'They mix with the aristocracy, and think and act like them. They're not working class like us. You say that lad's been educated at a boarding school. His father won't want to think he's wasted his money if his son marries a mill girl.' Florence's face crumpled and she looked tenderly at her daughter. 'I'm only saying this for your own good, love. I don't want to see you get hurt.'

Dolly jumped up and embraced her mother. 'I know, Mam, and I'm sorry for all the trouble I've caused, but you've no need to worry any more. Theo's broken it off.' Swallowing her tears, she released her hold on her mother. 'He said he couldn't see me again until he didn't know when.' It pained Dolly to have to admit it, and she felt such a deep stab of loss that her breath caught in her throat. 'I think it was just an excuse,' she croaked.

'Aye, well, it's perhaps for the best, love.' Florence patted Dolly's arm affectionately, putting the quarrel behind them. 'You'll have some making up to do with Nellie, lass. She's not best pleased at you neglecting her.'

'I will, Mam. I'll go round now and apologise.'

Florence glanced at the clock. It showed ten past ten. 'It's late to be calling,' she said.

'I know,' said Dolly, pulling on her coat, 'but I'll sleep better if I've made my peace with Nellie.' She hurried to the door thinking she'd never sleep peacefully again now that Theo was no longer part of her life.

16

Dolly ran through the dark streets to Tinker's Yard and knocked on the Haigh's door. Nellie answered and when she saw Dolly, her mouth turned down at the corners, her expression petulant and spiteful. 'What do you want?'

'To ask you to forgive me for not being a true friend.'

'Aye, well, I can do wi'out friends like you, Dolly Armitage. It's late an' I'm off to bed.'

Nellie pushed the door to close it. Dolly pushed it back.

'Please, Nellie, hear me out. Let me in so that I can explain.'

Her cry was so heartfelt that Nellie begrudgingly opened the door wider and Dolly slipped inside.

Once again, Dolly repeated the whole sorry story.

'I know it seemed mean putting him before you, Nellie, but we can still be friends, can't we?' Dolly gave her a winning smile.

Nellie, still feeling aggrieved and a little bit jealous, asked, 'Are thi on'y sayin' that 'cos he's let thi down?'

It took quite a lot of cajoling and eating humble pie on Dolly's part, but eventually, Nellie relented, and by the time Dolly left for home, they were the best of friends again.

On Christmas Eve, they went with George and Amy to the Somerset Arms. The pub was packed with mill workers and at first, Dolly joined in with the rowdy fun then making the excuse that she'd promised to help her mother prepare the goose and the vegetables for the next day, she went home and to bed. She should have been thrilled by the prospect of three days of long lie-ins, and carol singing round the doors, along with the fun of neighbours dropping in at all hours for a nip of Christmas cheer, but not being able to share any of this with Theo had put a damper on things.

* * *

Christmas Day in Far View House was a miserable occasion. Aunt Martha had a queasy stomach. After picking listlessly at the goose Clara had cooked, and refusing the brandy pudding, she now sat at Jeb's bedside, burping and farting as she rubbed her corpulent belly.

Verity, fully aware of her aunt's voracious appetite, was worried it might be something serious and suggested they call the doctor, but Martha pooh-poohed that. 'It's Christmas Day. Leave the poor man in peace, Verity.' She emitted a belch, and easing her bottom off the chair, followed it with a trumpeting expellant of smelly wind that wafted unpleasantly round the overheated room. She sighed. 'Once I get me bowels moving, I'll be right as rain.'

Opposed to dwelling on that subject, Verity sat holding Jeb's lifeless hand. Earlier that day, she had undertaken Ada Brook's role and had washed him and spooned broth into his slack mouth. As she made him comfortable Jeb had spluttered, 'Soth thee.'

'It's too late to be sorry, Father.' Verity had whispered, but even so, she'd felt pity mixed with gratitude that finally he was apologising for being cruel to her. She'd stroked his cheek.

It was perhaps as well that she would never know that Jeb had actually said, 'Sod thee.'

He was now lying on his back, his eyes closed and his mouth agape. His breathing was shallow, his heavy bottom lip fluttering with every intake of air. Ada had been reluctant to take the day off to go to the Hardcastle's for Christmas dinner but Verity had insisted, at the same time as almost envying her, but not quite. Her one and only visit to Oliver's home had left her with no desire to spend time in the company of his mother and sisters, but she would have liked to be with him. Her thoughts wandered to the Boxing Day hunt and she shivered with excited anticipation. Maybe on Monday...

In the gloomy stillness of the stuffy room, Aunt Martha dozed, little snores bubbling from her lips, and Verity, left to her own devices, indulged in daydreams. Eventually, she too slept, wearied by the tedium of the day.

She wakened with a start. Outside the window, dusk had fallen, the trees in the back garden stark against a looming, black sky.

Verity glanced at her aunt. Martha's head lolled to one side, a dribble of saliva seeping from the corner of her mouth. Then Verity turned her gaze on Jeb. He lay inert, no rise and fall of his chest, his eyes closed and his twisted face relaxed and almost its former shape. He looked at peace. Verity leaned over the bed, her ear pressed to his lips. Nothing. No wavering breath brushed her cheek.

She felt a small, cold wind blow over her shoulders. Her father was dead.

* * *

Boxing Day dawned, the grey light seeping slowly into the room and lighting on the weary faces of the two women at the bedside and the corpse in the bed. Verity roused herself; there was much to do.

She and her aunt had sat with Jeb through the long hours of the night, Martha weeping and Verity numb. Over cups of tea, they had reflected on his wasted life and waited for daylight and a respectable hour before sending for the doctor. 'No point in draggin' him out of bed, lass. There's nothing he can do,' Martha had said in between sniffles and hiccups.

Now she lolled dozing in her chair, her fat cheeks tearstained and her lips put-put-putting as her ample bosom rose and fell.

Voices in the basement signalled the arrival of the Medleys and Verity ran downstairs to tell them the news. Bert hurried straight off to fetch the doctor, and Verity and Clara returned to Jeb's room. When Clara saw the dead body of the man whom she had cursed every day of her working life, her heartrending wails roused Martha.

Anyone would think she had loved him dearly, Verity thought irritably as Clara's cries rose to a crescendo, and when her aunt added to the cacophony, Verity covered her ears and ran from the room. In the hallway, she paced the floor, waiting for Bert to return with the doctor, her thoughts tumbling disjointedly. She would have to deal with the undertakers and organise a funeral, an unpleasant task at any time but more so at Christmas. Unbidden, an ugly thought crept into her mind. *How typical of you, Father, to ruin my opportunity to spend the day with Oliver at the hunt.*

One shouldn't think ill of the dead, she chastised herself as the rattle of the trap outside alerted her. Feeling rather guilty, she went and opened the door.

Ernest Clegg, irritated at having his day ruined from the

start, gave Jeb a brief examination, scribbled a death certificate and dashed away. Then, Aunt Martha declaring she was hungry, Clara hurried down to the kitchen and fried eggs and bacon. Martha, her grief temporarily allayed, tucked in heartily, and Verity forced herself to eat a few mouthfuls; it would be a long day.

After breakfast, she sent Bert to tell Oliver that her father had died, and that she would not be available to attend the hunt. Oliver returned with him, and now he stood feeling awkward and helpless as he gazed down at the man who had so often made his life a misery. He yearned to console Verity, but her cool, stiff demeanour seemed to reject sympathy in any degree and certainly not the sort that involved taking her in his arms and stroking her hair as he yearned to do.

'Don't let me detain you, Oliver. I'm sure you must have things to do.' Her silvery-grey eyes met his as she calmly gave him the opportunity to leave.

He looked askance. 'I wouldn't leave at a time like this,' he said. 'I'll stay with you.'

'As you wish,' she said and crossed the room to greet two of her father's manufacturing associates who had come to offer their condolences. They had met Dr Clegg on his way back into the village. This then became the pattern of the day for in a small town, news travels fast. And whilst Jeb Lockwood might not have been the most popular of men, there were still plenty who called to pay their respects if not to mourn his passing.

Clara was run off her feet, and Bert and Oliver assisted by answering the door, serving cups of tea or something stronger as the occasion demanded. When the vicar arrived, Verity asked Oliver to sit with them as they made arrangements for the funeral. Much later, when it seemed that there would be no more callers, Verity walked Oliver to the front door.

'Thank you for today. I don't think I could have seen it through without you.'

Her face was pale and drawn but she had lost her cold, stiff attitude and her voice was rich with sincerity.

'It's the least I could do.' Oliver stepped outside into the crisp, night air, the grass and shrubs in the garden glittering under a fine coating of frost.

'I'm sorry I won't be able to accompany you to the hunt tomorrow.'

He gave a little shrug. 'Will you be all right?' he asked, his dark eyes looking deep into hers and his voice thick with concern.

Verity hesitated before answering him. 'It's strange, isn't it? As long as he was alive, I never really felt that the mill was mine. And even though he could offer no help, he was there in the back of my mind, and it was his mill. Now I feel the full weight of responsibility and I suddenly feel very alone.' She shivered and sounded so small and lost that Oliver could no longer restrain his feelings.

'Verity. Dearest.' He clasped her hands in his. 'You're not alone. I'll always be with you if you'll have me.' Feeling no resistance, he let go of her hands and folded her in his arms.

She felt the thud of his heart beating in tandem with her own. Slowly, she digested his words. *If you'll have me.* He wanted her, wanted always to be with her. She lifted her face to his. Oliver covered her lips with his, so sweetly, so tenderly, that she felt bathed in warmth and sweetness and her womanhood blossomed as she kissed him back.

* * *

Jebediah Lockwood was laid to rest in All Hallows graveyard. The funeral, specially arranged to take place after the mill closed at midday, saw the mill hands out in force, more out of respect for Miss Lockwood than their erstwhile master. As she stood at the graveside to accept their condolences and shake their hands, she felt an utterly inappropriate urge to sing out, *Oliver loves me, and I love him!*

Dolly was one of the last to make her way to Verity's side. 'I'm sorry for your loss,' she said, and as she shook Verity's hand, she saw that her employer looked somehow different. Her grey eyes glowed and there was a softness in her features that hadn't been there before. In fact, she seemed to be positively blooming. Oliver stood beside her, his hand rested in the middle of Verity's back and his expression was one of fond admiration.

The mourners drifted away, and when Verity left the graveside, Oliver stayed behind to have a final word with the gravediggers. Verity fell into step with the girl she now looked on as a friend rather than an employee. She'd noticed that Dolly looked unusually downcast and presuming it couldn't possibly have anything to do with Jeb's death, she asked, 'Is all well with you, Dolly? You don't seem your usual happy self.'

Dolly pulled a sad little face. 'Aw, take no notice of me, Miss Lockwood. I've just had a big disappointment but...' she shrugged, 'I suppose I'll get over it in time.'

'I'm sorry to hear that, Dolly. Do you want to talk about it?' Verity's smile was sympathetically encouraging.

Dolly's respect and admiration coupled with the belief she had in Verity ran deep. Without thinking twice, she poured her heart out.

When Oliver came towards them, he saw that they were holding an intense conversation and that Dolly's face was stained with tears. He deliberately hung back.

'Now it looks as though I'll never see him again,' Dolly concluded shakily. 'Do you think I was setting my sights above my station, Miss Lockwood?'

Filled with the euphoria of her own love affair, Verity's heart went out to Dolly. 'True love transcends all boundaries, Dolly. If Theo really loves you, he'll come to you. And if he does, you both have to be brave enough to withstand any objections others might have. It's your life, Dolly, and you must live it as you please.'

'Oh, Miss Lockwood. I knew you'd understand.' Dolly smiled for the first time that day. Then she gave a perky nod. 'Mr Hardcastle's waiting for you.'

Dolly trotted away to where Nellie and George lingered by the church gate, and Oliver joined Verity. 'What was that all about?' he asked, tucking her hand in the crook of his arm.

'A very sad story about a broken romance. Much of the blame lying at the door of the silly, stupid, upper-class, lower-class nonsense people still believe in,' she said hotly as they walked through the cemetery. 'When are they going to acknowledge that we're all born equal? And when two people are in love, it shouldn't matter whether we're high or lowly born.'

Her cheeks were pink and her eyes radiated defiance of the odious class system. Oliver loved her all the more, but he couldn't help reflecting on his own position: a mill manager in love with a mill heiress.

17

By mutual agreement, Verity and Oliver told nobody of the change in their relationship. It was too soon after Jeb's death to announce an engagement and they decided to wait until a decent length of time had elapsed before making their intention public. However, behind closed doors, it was a different story.

Oliver's frequent evening calls to Far View House raised no suspicion – it was usual practice for the mill manager to visit the home of his employer to discuss business even though Jeb Lockwood had never encouraged it – and if Clara and Bert Medley wondered what went on in the drawing room in the long hours Verity and Oliver were closeted there, they kept their thoughts to themselves, for now that Jeb was dead, their jobs were far easier and they had no complaints.

And if their mistress often seemed in a dreamy state, her cheeks flushed and eyes shining after Mr Hardcastle's visits, they put it down to the success the mill was now experiencing. It was common knowledge that Lockwood Mill had turned a corner and was now considered to be one of the most thriving small mills in the valley.

As for Verity and Oliver, their love deepened by the day. Verity, who on the night of her father's death had never before been kissed until Oliver's lips met hers, revelled in the evenings spent in his arms as in between kisses, they learned everything there was to know about each other. When Oliver heard about her dysfunctional childhood and Jeb's cruel treatment, it tore at his heart. He had been showered with love from birth, and he determined that this beautiful, kind woman would never again know unhappiness.

Towards the end of January, the mill delivered the Ruddiman's first order. It was well received and further orders were placed. Oliver had also secured a new and better contract for the shoddy/mungo blankets, and two new clients had ordered a quantity of fancy Jacquard.

'It seems that 1898 is to be our year in more ways than one,' Oliver said to Verity as they did their rounds at the end of the day, checking that production was up to scratch in all departments.

'Indeed, it does,' she replied, 'and if anyone had told me that at this time last year, I would have laughed in their faces.' She pulled a sad face. 'There was I, still living with Aunt Flora in Leeds, and she desperately seeking a prospective husband for me and now...' she giggled delightfully and gave him an impish smile, 'I've found one for myself.'

'Indeed, you have,' Oliver said. 'One who can't wait to marry you.'

They returned to the office and continued working until after seven o'clock then, in the trap, they left the mill to go to Fair View House. Oliver often took his evening meal there with Verity, much to the disapproval of his mother and his sister, Rose. Evelyn disliked this because in her opinion, her son was being used by Verity to further her own ambitions and she feared that when these were achieved, he would be cast aside. Rose, on the other hand, still favoured Lucy Whittaker as a potential sister-in-law.

However, Oliver chose to ignore Evelyn's 'Stop making a fool of yourself, son', and Rose's 'Why don't you ask Lucy out any more?' and spent his evenings with Verity making plans for the mill's future and, of course, sharing kisses and declarations of love.

For her part, Verity was in her element in Oliver's company, and although she was impatient to make their relationship known, she abided by his advice to keep it secret and suppressed her yearnings by immersing herself in improving her mill.

As winter gave way to early spring, there wasn't a corner of her mill that did not receive her attention, and she was ever on the lookout for making improvements in one way or another. Bearing in mind something Mrs Ruddiman had told her, she had embarked on yet another idea to better the lot of her women weavers and spinners.

The sewing classes started shortly before Easter. A sewing machine had been brought down from Far View House and a second-hand one purchased. Installed in the canteen, they allowed the women to mend or alter old clothes and to make new skirts or children's coats and trousers out of the mill's scrap wastage.

The sewing sessions were a roaring success. The adept needlewomen helped those who weren't as skilled and week on week, the women added to their own and their families' wardrobes. It warmed Verity's heart to know she was making a difference and she looked forward to the evenings spent in their jolly company.

'Eeh, Miss Lockwood, you shoulda seen the looks I got when I went to chapel in me new skirt an' weskit,' one of the spinners crowed. 'I told 'em they were made from Lockwood's worsted, t'finest cloth in t'valley.'

'Aye, an' our little Jimmy looks a right toff in his new overcoat, even if I did sew the sleeves in wonky,' Lily chortled.

'Aye, an' if I hadn't helped her mek 'em sit right, the poor little bugger 'ud have looked as if his arms were on back to front.'

May's remark had the women howling with laughter as they bade Verity goodnight and went off home bearing the fruits of their labour.

'You do make a difference to people's lives, Miss Lockwood,' Dolly said as they cleared away at the end of a session.

'Thank you, Dolly. I do take pleasure from helping where I can, and what better way to use our own worsted scraps than to clothe our own people.'

'It's not just about letting them have something better to wear; it's the way you make them feel. They love it when you call them "ladies" and ask after their families like a friend does.'

'They are my friends – or should I say, I like to think of them as such.'

'Aye, but you're still the mill mistress,' Dolly reminded her. 'There's not many mill owners in the valley treat their workers like you do. They think it's beneath them.'

'That's the upper class versus the lower class raising its ugly head again,' Verity scorned, 'and talking of that, have you heard from the young man at Thornton Hall?'

Dolly shook her head. 'No, and I don't expect to. Not after all this time.' She turned and put the cover on the sewing machine, but not quickly enough to hide the tears that sprang to her eyes.

'It still makes you sad, though,' said Verity and, at a loss to offer comfort, she asked, 'Do you still spend your time drawing and painting?'

'Oh, yes. It fills many a lonely hour. I did some lovely pastel drawings up on Castle Hill during the winter. When it snows, Wessenden Head and West Nab look smooth and soft like mountains of ice cream, and the valleys are crystal-white blankets. It even makes the mills look pretty when it hides all the soot.' Dolly gave a wistful smile. 'I'd be happy drawing all day, but that's just a dream.' She put on her coat, ready to go home.

'We all have our dreams, Dolly. It's what makes life worthwhile,' said Verity, following her to the door. 'Hold on to your dreams. One day, they might come true.' *As will mine when I marry Oliver,* she thought as they walked across the mill yard, each lost in their own thoughts.

On her way back to Far View House, Verity mused on their conversation. She would love to make this lovely, talented girl's dreams come true. She had no idea how she might do that but the thought stayed with her until she reached home. Oliver had gone to a meeting of the Philosophical Society and the rest of the evening stretched in front of her without his company. When she entered the hallway, she saw a crisp, white envelope in the tray on the hallstand. Addressed to her in flamboyant handwriting, she wondered who it could be from and opened it. It was an invitation. The same hand had written to request her company at Dogley Grange on May Day for afternoon tea. It was signed Letitia Hargreaves.

Verity stared at it. Letitia Hargreaves wasn't an acquaintance, but if she lived at Dogley Grange then she must be the wife of Clarence Hargreaves, a fellow mill owner. She had never met him, but she had heard gossip about the inferior quality cloth his mill produced, and that he was a hard taskmaster. Although she didn't like the sound of him, she did feel rather flattered to be invited to the Grange. Was this invitation her introduction into the society of other mill owners?

Were they accepting her now that her own mill was prospering?

'Go if you must,' Oliver said the next morning as he read the wording on the thick embossed card. 'Personally, I can't stand the fellow, but don't let that prevent you from accepting.'

Oliver's repugnance surprised Verity. 'It's very kind of Mrs Hargreaves to invite me,' she said pettishly.

'She's not Hargreaves's wife; she's his sister.' Oliver marched out of the office, the subject dismissed. Had Verity been able to read his mind, she would have learned that the cause of his irritation was two-fold: firstly, his dislike of Clarence Hargreaves, and secondly, his uneasiness about his own position. She was being accepted by the mill-owning fraternity and invited to their gatherings because she had been born into it, whereas he had not. In their eyes, he would always be a man who had worked his way up the ladder and they would never consider him to be on a par with them, not even when he married his boss. He shuddered at the thought of it.

Later that evening, Verity, oblivious to his feeling, sat at her desk and replied that she would be delighted to attend the Hargreaves's tea party. She gave it to Bert to deliver.

* * *

On the last Sunday in April, Dolly was at a loose end, nowhere to go and no one to go with but the sun was shining after a week of showers and she itched to do something pleasant. The book she was reading failed to capture her imagination and every now and then, she just gazed into space, her expression woebegone.

Florence frowned as she looked at her daughter. For some time now, she'd noticed that Dolly wasn't the same bright, bubbly girl she had once been. She suspected that it was to do with the lad from Thornton Hall, the land agent's son, but she considered it more of a blessing than a sorrow since there had been no more mention of him. She didn't want her Dolly messing about with his sort.

'Are you not going out with Nellie this afternoon? It's a lovely day.'

'What... what did you say?' Dolly almost jumped. She'd been miles away. Her mother repeated her question. 'Nellie's needed at home,' Dolly replied. 'Her auntie's coming from Lindley to see her mam and she has to make the tea. Her mam's really poorly.'

'Oh dear, that's sad. But there's no need for you to sit moping. Get out into the fresh air and clear your head.' Florence spread a clean white cloth on the table. 'And anyway, you'll not want to be here when our George brings Amy round. He's wanting me to back him up in telling Amy why it's not a good idea to get married yet.' She chuckled. 'He's like your dad, soft as tripe when it comes to hurting folk's feelings.'

'If he had any sense, he'd dump her, and quick,' said Dolly, putting her book aside and getting to her feet. 'She does nothing but moan, and she wants, wants, wants all the time. Our George can't afford her. She has him skint as it is what with wanting flowers and chocolates at every dog dance.'

Florence sighed. 'I know what you mean, love. All this nonsense about him getting her a house of her own. He says she's even chosen the furniture. Asked him to put a deposit down on it, she did. I think he's fed up to the back teeth with her. He'd like to end it but he wants to let her down gently.'

'And he's expecting you to do his dirty work.' Dolly laughed. Her own love life, or lack of it, suddenly didn't seem too bad compared with her brother's. 'I'm off out. Good luck in getting rid of your prospective daughter-in-law, Mam.' She picked up her bag that held her sketchbook and pastels. 'I'll be back in time for tea. Make sure Moaning Minnie's gone by then, and tell our George from me that he'd be better off without her.'

* * *

Dolly strolled up the Rookery and into Somerset Road. Although it brought back painful memories, she was going to Penny Spring woods; the bluebells would be out again. She tramped into the wood, her footsteps muffled by the mossy carpet and unbidden, her feet took her to where she had first met Theo.

He was there. Sitting on a tree stump, his head in his hands.

Dolly faltered to a stop. She felt weak, trembling, and unsure whether to run or stay.

The trees were not yet in full leaf and a ray of sunlight lanced through the branches, turning Theo's fair hair to gold. A blackbird took flight, chirruping to his mate and Theo raised his head. He rubbed the backs of his hands over his eyes, amazement lighting his face.

'Dolly! Oh, Dolly!' He leapt up, and swaying on unsteady legs, he opened his arms wide, his joy replaced by a look of anguish when Dolly stayed where she was, staring stonily at him.

She longed to fly into his arms and feel his lips on hers, but an inner core of hard feelings held her in check. He had been gone without a word for three long months. She steeled her thudding heart and coolly said, 'Hello, Theo. It's been a long time.'

He took three tentative steps towards her. Dolly stepped back, her arms folded as if to protect her heart. She looked into his eyes. They were so full of tenderness and regret, she was forced to look away. But she'd lost count of how many times she had walked to the Rookery, hopeful that Theo might magically appear, or the number of long, fruitless walks she'd taken past the Thornton Hall estate. She wasn't going to let him hurt her again.

'Dolly. Please let me explain.' His tone was flat, defeated.

'There's not much to say, is there, Theo? You walked out on me, and if you think we can just take up where we left off, you're sadly mistaken.' She felt her resolve weakening and she hardened her voice. 'Did you get bored and suddenly think you'd come and find me, have a bit of fun then beggar off again?'

Theo shook his head in denial, his teeth clamped on his bottom lip and his face screwed up as though he was in pain. 'Stop, Dolly! Just stop!' He raised his hands, his beseeching cry startling the blackbirds on a nearby bush. Wings flapping, they swooped over his head. 'Just listen to me,' he pleaded.

Dolly gave a resigned shrug.

'I'm only just returned from Devon. The day after New Year's Day, Lady Thornton's father took ill and she insisted that I had to go and help with the horses and carriage and their blasted luggage,' he cried. 'I got back yesterday.' He gave her a hopeful look, begging her to understand. When he saw the disbelief on her face, he gabbled, 'I didn't dare come to your house the night before I went but I did hang about at the end of your street just in case I might see you. I waited for ages but...' His voice trailed off and his arms hung loosely by his sides as despair overwhelmed him.

'You came looking for me?' Dolly croaked. 'You still want us to be friends?'

'Friends! Oh, Dolly, we're more than friends. Surely you must know that. I love you.'

Theo's strangled cry broke Dolly's last reserves.

'And I love you,' she said, her voice barely above a whisper.

They stared into each other's eyes then they fell against one another, cheeks then lips meeting and arms clinging as though they might never let go again.

* * *

'Your walk seems to have done you a power of good,' her mother remarked, noting the bloom on her daughter's cheeks as Dolly entered the kitchen some three hours later.

'It was grand. The bluebells always cheer me up,' said Dolly, her heart beginning to race as she silently told herself, *And the love of my life has come back to me.*

'You missed a right ding-dong,' Florence said as she poured boiling water on the leaves in the pot. 'Madam Amy told our George that if he doesn't marry her before May is out then they won't be getting married at all.'

Dolly looked askance. 'But that's only four weeks away. Why so soon?'

Florence grimaced. 'She says she's waited long enough.'

'Where's our George now?'

'Out. He went off in a right temper. He says there's no way he'll let her bully him into marrying her. He says he'll do the asking as and when the time is right.'

'Good for him,' Dolly cheered. She began buttering bread to go with the brawn and tomatoes Florence had arranged on four plates and mused on what her mam would say if *she* was to announce that she was thinking of getting married before the year was out.

Clem came in from his pigeon loft and went to wash his hands under the tap. He'd got offside as soon as Amy had arrived. He didn't care for the girl.

'Where's the happy couple?' he asked, looking round the kitchen as he dried his hands.

Dolly's lips twitched, amused by Clem's hint of sarcasm.

'Not so happy now,' Florence replied and went onto tell him what she'd told Dolly.

'He did right to refuse,' Clem grunted. 'He's well rid.'

'Aye, well, I'm not sure he'd agree with you.' His wife shook her head, her dismay apparent. She was always upset when her children were unhappy.

The kitchen door scraped open. George came in. All eyes turned on him. His angry face spoke a thousand words.

'Sit down, lad. Your tea's ready,' his mother said gently.

'I'm not hungry,' George growled. 'And before any of you start giving me your two-pennyworth, remember I'm my own man and I'll do as I please.' He barged upstairs.

Dolly popped a slice of tomato into her mouth and wondered if she would be brave enough to be her own woman and do as she pleased when it came to telling her mam and dad that she was going to marry Theo.

18

'Before t'end o' May? Why?' Nellie's eyes boggled as Dolly told her about George and Amy.

It was Monday morning and the girls were in the weaving shed getting ready to start work.

Dolly began buttoning her overall. 'I don't know. I think it's all a bit strange, and George won't talk about it.' She tied her turban over her hair.

Nellie glanced round to make sure they weren't being overheard by the other women. 'I din't say owt before 'cos I don't like spreadin' gossip but I heard Lily Cockhill tellin' May Sykes that she'd seen Amy wi' another fellow.'

'When? Where?' Dolly's jaw dropped.

'She said they wa' canoodlin' in't baker's shop doorway at t'end o' Maple Street when she wa' goin home from the pub.' Nellie gave Dolly a bemused look. 'If she's two-timin' your George, why is she in such a hurry to marry him?'

Dolly's hazel eyes glinted. 'There's only one reason that I know of for somebody wanting to get married in a rush.' She gave Nellie a meaningful look.

'Ooh! Do you think she's...' Nellie clapped her hand over her mouth.

One long, piercing blast from the hooter had Dolly and Nellie and the other women hurrying to their looms before Gertie Spragg, the Mrs Weaver, could bawl them out. She liked nothing better than to push and shove them with her big, meaty hands if she thought they were dawdling.

Dolly kept her eyes on the flying shuttle and the bobbins on her loom but her mind was on George and Amy and what Nellie had just told her. At breakfast time, she took Lily to one side and quizzed her.

'Aye, I've seen her wi' him more than once when I've been on me way home from t'Somerset.' Lily liked her nightly drop of beer. 'I'd say he's a fair bit older than her, smart you know, an' he wears a hat wi' a wide brim like Mr Hardcastle. I thought it wa' him but I couldn't see his face, so I'm not sure. I think it's a shame 'cos your George's a nice lad, but it's not up to me to say owt to him.'

'I'm glad you said something to somebody, Lily.' Dolly gave her a grateful smile.

* * *

On Wednesday at midday on the day that Verity was going to take tea with Letitia Hargreaves, she put on her coat ready to go home and dress for the occasion. Oliver watched her from out of the corner of his eye but he passed no remark.

'I'm going now. Will I see you this evening to tell you all about it?'

'I can't wait,' he said, forcing a smile as she left in a flurry of excitement.

Oliver sat, deep in thought. *Please don't let them steal her from me, change her into a society butterfly or a grasping mill owner; she's perfect as she is,* he told himself. But he was conscious of her lack of experience as to how the world at large worked, and more so as to how the mill-owning fraternity conducted itself – he'd heard the gossip about what went on at their parties – and he was aware that no matter how gentlemanly her fellow mill owners might outwardly appear, it was a dog-eat-dog society underneath all the charm. Exposure to it could leave Verity vulnerable and unable to detect the hidden motives behind their interest in her, and he feared that Verity's new circle of friends might take advantage of her. Still, she had to learn somehow and he hoped for her sake it wasn't a baptism by fire.

* * *

Up in her bedroom at Far View House, Verity had no such qualms. Excited by the prospect of her visit to Dogley Grange, she had purchased a tea gown from Rushworth's in soft, grey, silk tulle trimmed with tape lace on the bodice and hem that accentuated her slender figure and enhanced the colour of her eyes. Now, as she pinned a black, saucer-shaped hat with a bunch of grey feathers on the brim over her carefully rolled chestnut hair then pulled on her long black gloves, her elegant reflection in the cheval mirror told her that she looked like a mill heiress about to take tea in a prestigious mansion with her mill-owning counterparts. She had contemplated wearing all black since it was less than a year since her father's death, but she had been assured by the matronly shop assistant that to do so was outmoded, and as she draped a soft grey woollen cape trimmed with black braid over her shoulders, she was glad she had taken her advice. Giving a satisfied smile, she went downstairs.

'Eeh, Miss Verity, tha looks proper beautiful,' Clara gushed when Verity went down into the kitchen to tell her she was leaving, and secretly wanting the housekeeper's admiration. Delighted when she got it and refusing Bert's offer to drive the trap, she sashayed out feeling like a woman of the world.

Thankful that the sun was shining and the breeze gentle, she drove through Almondbury village, down Helen's Gate then Fenay Lane and onto the road leading to Kirkburton. When, shortly after three o'clock, she arrived at Dogley Grange, she was met by a gatekeeper who gave her directions to the front of the house. Steering the pony up the winding, tree-lined drive, she came to a large gravel sweep where a young lad waited to take care of the pony and trap. *Very grand*, she thought. Hargreaves's mill must be more prosperous than she had been led to believe if one was to judge it by the number of servants they employed. Verity handed the reins to the lad and stepped down.

The mansion, built from red brick that was partially hidden by Virginia creeper that trailed prettily over its walls, had a columned porch with two windows on either side and six above. The paintwork gleamed, and Verity compared it to the shabbiness of Far View House.

A maid in a smart black and white uniform stood in the open doorway. As Verity handed over her cape, a plump-faced young woman with a mop of yellow ringlets came trotting towards her, hands outstretched and her smile revealing a set of prominent, crooked teeth. 'You must be Miss Lockwood. I'm Letitia Hargreaves,' she twittered in a high, squeaky voice. 'I'm so glad to meet you.' She clasped Verity's hand, and as Verity offered her thanks for the invitation, she was whisked through the ornately decorated hallway into an opulent drawing room. Her eyes widened when she saw the crowd of men and women already there. She had imagined that she might be the only guest, or that there would be no more than one or two of Letitia's lady friends in attendance. The room buzzed with chatter and the clink of teacups on saucers.

Letitia clapped her chubby hands, and as a partial silence fell over the room and heads turned, she announced, 'Ladies and gentlemen, allow me to introduce Miss Verity Lockwood of Far View House and Lockwood Mill.'

Verity felt her cheeks pinking as several pairs of eyes were trained on her. A rumble of voices made her welcome and she acknowledged them with nods and a hesitant smile. Then the assembled company went back to whatever they had been doing before the interruption.

'I'll leave you to circulate,' chirped Letitia, and ringlets bouncing, she tripped back into the hallway in a froth of pink lace, ready to greet more guests.

Verity was filled with regret. She felt hot and rather foolish. Her gaze travelled nervously over the room's deep burgundy walls, the lavish drapes and furnishings. What on earth was she to do now?

In an attempt to appear less conspicuous, she shrank into a space between two large consoles, her back against the wall. Close by, two gentlemen stood with their backs to her.

'Aye, she's Jeb's daughter,' she heard the corpulent one say, 'but she's not a chip off the block.' He chuckled nastily. 'She's as soft as tripe. Gives 'em reading lessons, and makes like they're her equals so I've been told. Jeb wouldn't have stood for that.'

'She's a bloody fool, if you ask me,' the tall, sour-looking one replied. 'Hargreaves says she's upped the weavers' rate for a piece by twopence and the same for spinners for a frame o' bobbins. An' she's given 'em a canteen. Jeb 'ud have let 'em freeze their arses off before parting wi' a penny. She'll be bankrupt afore long.'

Verity wanted the floor to open up and swallow her. Is this what they thought of her?

Her palms felt clammy and every nerve in her body tingled. The tension was so great that she found herself trembling with rage – and disappointment.

Her anxiety was short-lived. A small, pretty young woman hurried over to her. 'Come, my dear. Let me introduce you to the company.' She took Verity's hand. 'I'm Millicent Shawcross, married to Henry, the son of Alfred. You're no doubt familiar with Shawcross Mill at Lindley,' she continued and gave a little groan. 'Henry's there now, holding the fort but my in-laws – or should I say outlaws – are over there.' She pointed to a stately couple at the far side of the room.

Verity began to relax in the company of this perky young woman, liking her somewhat irreverent attitude as they did the rounds of the room. Introductions were made, the mill owners telling Verity that they had known her father and Millicent whispering witty remarks at the expense of them and their wives as soon as they moved out of earshot.

'Roland Briggs is a dinosaur, and his wife is so full of tittle-tattle, it's a wonder she doesn't rattle when she moves,' she said about the couple Verity had just met, Roland booming, 'Nay, I never thought I'd live to see the day. A lass running a mill. There's summat not right about that.' And Mrs Briggs sniffing and saying, 'Most unladylike.'

Even so, there were some who openly admired her, and when they asked about the mill, Verity surprised them with her knowledge of how her mill worked and the cloth she produced. 'Good on thi, lass,' an elderly mill owner praised. 'Jeb 'ud be proud of thee.'

Verity couldn't entirely agree but she was thrilled by the

compliment. Gradually, she began to feel accepted in what she thought of as an illustrious circle of fellow mill owners.

However, not all were as friendly. The two men she had overheard discussing her nodded sourly, and an elaborately dressed woman looked down her nose at her.

'Steer clear of her,' Millicent advised. 'She's as malicious as typhoid fever.'

Verity had difficulty suppressing her laughter, and as they sat down to partake of the delicious spread on the low tables scattered about the room, Verity had to admit she was enjoying herself. Wafer-thin slices of bread and butter, savoury tarts and cucumber sandwiches, pastries, scones with jam and cream, and Madeira cake sat temptingly on fine porcelain plates with matching teacups and saucers.

'Earl Grey or lapsang souchong, madam?' The servant with a teapot in either hand hovered at Verity's elbow. She had never heard of the latter so she chose Earl Grey, and as she and Millicent sipped and nibbled, they got to know one another. 'Please, call me Millie,' the mine owner's daughter from Barnsley said. Verity liked her all the more.

'I'm so glad I met you, Millie. And thank you for coming to my rescue. I was all at sea when Letitia left me stranded.'

'Letitia's a ninny. She holds these tea parties in the hope of finding a husband for herself and a wife for her brother. Have you met Clarence?' Millie grimaced and drew her finger across her throat. 'Oh, speak of the devil, here he comes.'

A fat young man with pale, fair hair and protruding teeth was striding towards them.

'Miss Lockwood, accept my humble apologies. I have neglected you but business called me away.' He didn't explain that the business involved taking advantage of a buxom housemaid, new to the job, who happened to bring his freshly cleaned boots up to his bedroom as he dressed for the tea party. Her struggles had excited him and now he felt like a lion.

'No need to apologise, Mr Hargreaves. Mrs Shawcross has looked after me splendidly.' His limp, moist hand was still holding hers and Verity didn't like the feel of it. Neither did she care for the way spittle clung to the teeth hanging over his lower lip. She felt even more disgruntled when Millie's mother-in-law came and took her away and Clarence wedged himself into the space Millie's departure had left on the small velvet sofa. His thigh pressed against hers and she felt crowded by his presence.

'Please, if we are to be friends, you must call me Clarence, and may I call you Verity?' he burbled, and in between bites of cucumber sandwiches, he began to quiz Verity about her mill. She answered his questions readily and proudly, sometimes boastful. Clarence, satisfied with his interrogation, then began oozing charm and flattering her.

'I must say, I find you a most intriguing woman, Verity. Not only are you exceptionally intelligent, your beauty is most pleasing to the eye,' he gushed, his gaze lingering on her bosom before leering into her face. He clasped both her hands in his and continued to sing her praises, his body too close to hers. At one point, his spittle wet her cheek.

By now, Verity was feeling exceedingly uncomfortable and was relieved when Millie returned. Clarence let go of Verity's hand and waddled off to join his cronies.

'You seemed to be rather engrossed with Miss Lockwood,' said his chum, giving a naughty wink and a dirty chuckle. 'Are you smitten?'

Clarence sniggered. 'Face like a horse and a bit too long in the shanks for me, old chap. But she has some interesting assets, and one doesn't look at the mantelpiece when poking the fire,' he smugly replied, laughing at his own wit.

Before the afternoon ended, Verity was approached by several mill owners whose curiosity was aroused; a young woman in charge of a mill was a rarity. Verity, flattered by their attention and eager to be accepted, revelled in discussions about cloth-making, priding herself on being able to hold her own in the experienced company. It was all new and exciting and by the time she was ready to leave, Verity was of the opinion that her venture into society had been a success. She hadn't much cared for Letitia or Clarence, but she had made a new friend in Millie Shawcross who had promised to keep in touch, and she believed she had shown the mill-owning fraternity that she was indeed capable of running Lockwood Mill.

* * *

When Dolly finished her shift at the mill, she went in search of Amy. She hadn't said anything to George about what she had heard. She wanted to hear Amy's version first. Now, concealed in the doorway of a disused shop in Maple Street, she waited. When she spied Amy leaving the bakery and walking towards her, Dolly stepped out, barring her way.

'Dolly!' Amy blinked her surprise. 'What are you doing here?'

'I've come to have a word with you.'

Amy flinched at Dolly's sharp tone.

'If you've come interfering in what's going on between me and George, you're wasting your time,' Amy said peevishly as she attempted to flounce past Dolly.

'Hold on! Not so fast, lady.' Dolly flung out her arm and caught Amy's elbow. 'I want you to tell me about this chap you're seeing behind our George's back.'

The biting delivery of Dolly's request made Amy stagger, her face at first bleached white then turning to a deep shade of puce under Dolly's glare.

'I... I... don't know what you're talking about,' Amy stammered.

'Aw, come off it, Amy, everybody in Lockwood Mill's talking about it.' Dolly tightened her hold on Amy as she struggled to break free. 'You've been seen with him more than once. Who is he?'

'He's nobody you know,' Amy mumbled. 'And there's nothing in it, I promise you. Don't tell George, please.' Amy began to cry.

'Nothing in it but there's something in your belly, I'll bet.' Dolly looked deeply into Amy's wet, crumpled face. 'You're pregnant, aren't you? That's why you set a deadline. And it's not our George's baby, is it? He wouldn't disrespect you in that way.'

Dolly's sneering tirade hit home. Amy blanched again and hung her head.

'Oh, Dolly, please don't tell anybody.' Amy clutched at her and begged for mercy. 'I didn't know what else I could do. I just thought that if I...' Dolly's stern face turned Amy's pleas into a piercing wail that disintegrated into shuddering sobs.

Dolly pushed her away. 'You just thought you'd foist somebody else's baby on our George, you rotten bitch. Well, that's never going to happen now. I'll make sure of it.'

Amy ran down the street howling.

With a heavy heart, Dolly trudged home, and convinced of her suspicions, she told George what had transpired. They were sitting in his half of the bedroom, George horrified at what he was hearing.

'I knew there was something funny going on 'cos more than once she's made excuses not to see me,' he said brokenly as he rubbed his jaw with his large, dye-stained hand. 'I used to think I loved her. She's so neat and pretty, and she can be lovely when she wants to be. Mind you, just lately she's been so demanding that she put me off, Dolly. She even tried to get me to make love to her, but I'd not do that out of wedlock, even when I wanted to.' He gave his sister a bemused look. 'She always seemed to want more than I could give her and I told her over and again that I needed to save my brass, not fritter it on baubles if we were to start married life in a home of our own.'

'Well, now she's got more than she wanted.'

Dolly's sage remark caused George to give a watery smile. 'Not from me, she hasn't.'

'You've had a lucky escape, Georgie boy.' Dolly patted his hand.

George pulled her to his chest in a big hug. 'I'm glad I have a sister like you.' He let her go and said, 'Don't be saying anything to Mam and Dad about Amy. Just let them think I decided to call it a day and Amy agreed.'

'They'll know the reason soon enough give or take seven months.'

George's face creased with anxiety. 'I hope nobody thinks it has anything to do with me.'

'I'll make sure they don't. And if I don't, Lily Cockhill will. She's already spread the gossip about Amy seeing another chap to the lasses in the weaving shed. I'm surprised you didn't hear it.'

George grimaced. 'What is it they say round here when a chap's cheating on his wife, she's always the last to know. Well, it seems it's the same for us men an' all.'

Dolly laughed, glad to see that her brother wasn't a broken man. For the moment, his love life was on hold, but what about her own?

* * *

A few days later, when Dolly met Theo in Penny Spring wood, she told him what she was about to do. 'I'm going to ask my mam if you can come to tea next Saturday,' she said as they strolled through the leafy glades hand in hand. 'We shouldn't have to keep meeting in secret.'

Theo looked thoughtful. 'I'd like that. And I'd like you to meet my father.' He stopped walking and, letting go of Dolly's hand, he ran his fingers through his hair, the gesture coupled with the frown on his face expressing his frustration. 'I can't for the life of me see what the problem is, but you seem to think that your folks will see me as some sort of bounder who couldn't possibly love a girl who earns her living by working in a mill.'

'But that's the way my mam thinks, Theo. The women in her family and my mother all worked in service for the toffs and she has a firm belief in "knowing your station" as she calls it. She's convinced that everybody has their place in society and should keep to it,' Dolly said, throwing up her hands, exasperated. 'Why, she even told me that a butler in a grand house would never court a scullery maid with the intentions of making an honest woman of her. And it's the same with the gentry. They'll dally with chambermaids and the like but it's only to satisfy their urges. It's not because they love them. She's never got over the fact that she's the bastard child of a member of the family her mother worked for.'

Theo plumped down on the trunk of a fallen tree and pulled Dolly onto his knee. 'Why do people insist on making boundaries?' he scorned. 'Upper class, middle class, lower class, who cares?' He gave a bitter laugh. 'My dad for one. He considers himself to be far better than working class even though he works day and night for his master.' Theo gave a shrug and a helpless smile. 'What are we to do, Dolly?'

'We'll grasp the iron whilst it's hot. Face up to them. And if they object, we'll ignore them and go our own way. We are the masters of our own destiny, Theo.' She giggled, her cheeks pink with determination as she added, 'I read that in a book.'

Theo pushed her off his knee then leapt up, catching her in his arms and swinging her high into the air. 'I love you, Dolly Armitage,' he cried before setting her down and kissing her roundly. 'We'll beard the lions in their dens.' He smirked. 'I read that in a book.'

They strolled back through the wood, busily making plans.

* * *

'Where's our George?' Dolly asked as, less than an hour later, she sat with her mother and father drinking tea.

'He's taken Nellie up to Castle Hill to see the works for that tower they're going to build to commemorate the queen's diamond jubilee,' Florence said, her smile showing she approved both the tribute to Her Majesty and George's interest in Nellie. 'She came round here earlier looking for you then she went off with our George because, of course, you weren't here.' This last comment was delivered with both disapproval and suspicion.

Dolly took a deep breath. Now was the time to carry out her plan: get it over and done with once and for all. 'I went to meet Theo,' she said boldly before her courage failed her. 'You know, the boy I was going out with before Christmas. The one who's the son of Sir Arnold Thornton's land agent. The one you think is too good for me – above my station.'

She tossed her head defiantly then immediately regretted taking such a belligerent stance; it invited an argument. She lowered her head and from under her lashes, she looked contritely at her mother. Florence's lips were pursed, her eyes narrow, ready to protest.

'Sorry, Mam. That was rude of me,' Dolly said before Florence found her voice. 'Can I begin again?'

'You can stop being so damned cheeky speaking to your mother like that,' Clem said. 'If you've summat to say, be reasonable about it.'

Dolly's cheeks reddened. Her father rarely reprimanded her, and now it hurt.

'Please, this is really important to me,' she began, her voice low and wobbling with emotion. 'You see, I love Theo and he loves me. It's been a year since we first met, a year in which we've got to know each other and I know I'll never feel this way about anybody else.' She paused.

Her mother sniffed.

'All I'm asking is that you meet him and judge for yourself what a wonderful young man he is,' Dolly continued, and seeing her mother's doubt as to Theo's credentials, she added, 'Not once has he expected anything of me that I wasn't willing to give. He loves and respects me too much for that.' Her hazel eyes were brimming with tears as she begged, 'Do I have your permission to ask him to tea next Sunday?'

'I can't see there'd be much harm in meeting the lad,' Clem opined.

Dolly cheered inwardly. Her dad was always on her side.

Florence pressed her fingers to her lips as she made up her mind. 'Aye, go on then; we'll see what we make of him,' she said flatly.

Dolly's grateful smile flitted from one parent to the other as she gushed, 'Thanks Mam, and thank you, Dad.' She wondered if they could hear her heart thudding against her ribs. She'd won the first round.

19

Verity had just arrived back from her first visit to Millicent Shawcross's home at Lindley. She felt pleasantly weary and at the same time exhilarated by her new friend's jolly company. The Shawcross house was nowhere near as grand as that of Clarence and Letitia Hargreaves but it was still far more elegant than Far View House and as Verity moved from the hallway into the drawing room, she was aware of how shabby everything looked. She'd need to do something about it if she were to invite Millicent to tea.

Clara heard Verity's footsteps and came bustling up from the kitchen. She had grown used to her mistress spending her days at the mill or 'gadding about the countryside'; as she termed it and, apart from mealtimes, they saw little of one another. These days however, her young mistress's busy life gave Clara no cause for concern.

At one time, she had worried about the lonely girl who'd hung about the house all day waiting for her drunken father to come home, and her only company her Aunt Martha. Since Jeb's death, Martha no longer made the journey up the steep slope from her own home at the foot of the hill, and it was left to Verity to visit her, which she did two or three times each week. Just one of the many changes in Far View House that had taken place in the last year.

Now, she popped her head round the drawing-room door. 'There's steak and kidney pie, cabbage and potatoes keeping warm in the stove, Miss Verity,' she announced. 'Do you want me to serve it now or will you help yourself?'

'I'll see to it, thank you, Mrs Medley. You get off home,' said Verity, peeling off her gloves and unpinning her hat.

Clara noted that Verity was wearing another new dress, the second bought in as many weeks. It was cream tulle embroidered with tiny pink and blue flowers. 'You look very pretty, Miss Verity,' she said, recalling the day when the poor girl had but two dresses to her name. 'I'll say goodnight then, Miss. See you tomorrow.'

'Goodnight, Mrs Medley, and thank you.'

Verity sounded distracted but Clara took no offence. She plodded back to the kitchen still musing on the change in her mistress. She did look pretty these days, had done for some time now. Back in the kitchen, she shared her opinion with Bert.

'"Grett ugly gawk" her father used to call her,' Clara remarked as she put on her shawl, 'an' she's still long an' lanky, but her skin's as clear an' smooth as a baby's bum, an' she carries her height like a proper lady, no stooping an' hunchin' into hersen like she used to do,' she continued as she tied her bonnet strings. 'An' has tha noticed how she dresses her hair in the latest fashion an' has tekken to wearing powder an' lipstick?'

Bert grunted that he hadn't and told her to hurry up.

'She once told me she was going to make some changes,' Clara told him as they stepped outside. 'Well, she has done and most of 'em are to herself.'

Not long after Clara and Bert had departed, Oliver arrived. Verity ran to greet him with a warm kiss. 'You look beautiful tonight,' he said, holding her at arm's length and appraising her fondly. 'Another new dress?' He asked this lightly but there was the slightest edge to his tone of voice, one that escaped Verity's notice.

'One has to keep up appearances,' she trilled.

Oliver flinched. Just as he had on the night after Verity had attended Letitia Hargreaves's tea party. He'd listened patiently to her excited recount of the event and hidden his annoyance when she mentioned Clarence Hargreaves. Verity, of course, had omitted to mention Clarence's admiring declarations. Since then, she had attended two further parties and now, as she related her afternoon spent with Millicent Shawcross and her friends, he didn't want to hear it. The girl he had fallen in love with had shed her cocoon and was now a butterfly in full flight and it made him feel uneasy. Was there more of Jeb Lockwood's nature in his daughter than Oliver had ever thought possible? He dearly hoped not.

They sat down to eat, Verity chattering about the people she had met that afternoon and Oliver telling her that the new patterns for fancy Jacquard weaving had been delivered and that associates of the Ruddimans had placed an order. Verity praised Oliver for his efficiency almost dismissively then began to enthuse about the Shawcross's beautiful home and the invitations she had received to visit the houses of other mill owners in the valley. He listened with half an ear, his spirits sinking.

They were raised somewhat when later in the drawing room sharing kisses and fond embraces, they agreed to announce their engagement at Christmas and marry in the spring. When it was time for Oliver to go, Verity stood in the doorway watching his broad back disappear into the shadows. Oh, but she loved that man and she still found it hard to believe that someone as wonderful as Oliver returned her love. A yellow May moon glimmered in then out of the clouds, its pale light shining for a moment on the garden and the field and hills beyond then suddenly plunging them into stark blackness. Verity watched the changes; *my life has been like that*, she thought. Fleeting moments of sunshine that were swallowed by dark, despairing days and years. But not now. Her future was looking rosy and she was going to enjoy it to the full.

* * *

On Sunday afternoon, Dolly waited at the Rookery for Theo to arrive, her nerves as tight as an overstrung violin. Earlier, she had helped her mother set out a spread of egg and cress sandwiches and freshly baked scones. The best teacups and saucers had been brought out and a new white cloth put on the small table in the parlour. Now, she looked anxiously in the direction from which he would come.

When she spied him, her heart leapt into her mouth. He was wearing his lovat-green jacket with a matching waistcoat, and fawn, moleskin trousers. Inside the collar of his shirt, a dark green, silk cravat sat beneath his firm jaw. Dolly's breath caught in her throat and she struggled with mixed feelings. He looked strikingly handsome – but at the same time, he looked like a toff.

Theo's face broke into a wide, confident smile when he saw her. 'Are we ready to beard the lions in their den?' he jested before dropping a kiss on her flushed cheek. He kept up a lively line of chatter as they walked to Silver Street in the hope of stemming the nerves that churned in his stomach. Dolly responded distractedly. *Please God let thing go well.*

Clem shook Theo's hand rather too vigorously and told him

he was welcome. Florence gave him a tight smile, her sharp eyes taking in his fine clothes and assured manner. George jumped up and clasped his hand in a firm grip accompanied by an encouraging grin; he pitied the poor fellow. Facing Florence Armitage when she was in one of her moods wasn't easy.

'Take a seat, Theo.' George pulled a chair away from the kitchen table.

'We're taking tea in the parlour, George.'

Florence's reprimand made George laugh.

'You're being honoured, Theo,' he said, taking him by the arm and leading him through into the room that was rarely used. 'It's not Christmas, nor Easter, and it's not a funeral either but I suppose it's a special occasion.'

George's bonhomie had Theo laughing, and Dolly could have kissed her brother.

Florence carried the loaded tray into the parlour. Dolly came behind with the teapot.

'Help yourself, lad,' said Clem when they were all seated and plates passed round.

'So, what brought you to Thornton Hall?' Florence asked as if she didn't know. Dolly had told her exactly why he was there.

Dolly's cup rattled in her saucer.

'My father's Sir Arnold's land agent,' Theo said calmly then swallowed noisily. 'I come from a long line of land agents. My grandfather and father worked for the Eccles estate near Harrogate but when that was sold off, my father came to work for Sir Arnold.' He paused, his neck reddening as he added, 'My parents are divorced. My mother remarried and I chose to live with my dad.' He leaned forward, his hand trembling as he helped himself to a scone.

Florence gave him a long, hard look. At least the lad was open and honest.

'An' will you be a land agent one day?' Clem's question eased the tension.

'My father hopes I will, and I suppose I do too,' Theo replied, his confidence restored. 'I did have a notion of joining the Bays but it no longer appeals.'

He glanced in Dolly's direction. She smiled warmly and gave an imperceptible nod, her eyes letting him know he was acquitting himself in a satisfactory manner.

'And you and our Dolly have known one another for a year or so,' Florence commented dryly. She was still in two minds as to whether or not she would give her approval.

George nudged Dolly and winked at Theo. 'You managed to keep that quiet,' he chortled. 'Mind you, you didn't fool Nellie. She knew what you were at.'

Dolly noticed her brother's face soften and heard the pride in his voice as he mentioned Nellie. She laughed and said, 'Trust Nellie.' And although she grimaced, her tone was affectionate. She glanced at her mother, then at Theo.

Theo took up the strain. 'I disliked being deceitful, Mrs Armitage,' he said, looking directly at Florence, 'but we were afraid you'd put an end to our friendship before we'd had a chance to get to know one another. My intentions towards Dolly are entirely honourable. I love her and...' his eyes slid to Dolly's, 'I think she loves me.'

'I can see that,' Florence said emphatically, 'So we'll have no more sneaking around and telling lies. We all know where we stand, and we'll see how things go from here.' She smiled at Theo, her first proper smile since he'd entered the house.

Dolly stood and flung her arms about her mother, almost unbalancing Florence's chair.

'Steady on there,' Florence said gruffly. 'I only said we'll see how things turn out.'

'It'll be grand,' Clem put in to lessen the emotions that filled the room. He gave his wife a fond smile that said she'd done the right thing.

George clapped Theo on the shoulder. 'Mind you treat my little sister properly,' he joshed. 'She can be a right handful at times.'

Dolly and Theo exchanged triumphant smiles. They'd won the second round.

* * *

On Friday evening after the reading class that now had twenty members, Dolly told Verity about Theo's visit. 'Do you recall me telling you I'd met a boy that I thought my parents might disapprove of,' she said as she packed the alphabet cards and simple reading books into a crate.

Verity told her she did.

'Well, he came to tea on Sunday and my mam likes him.'

'Oh, Dolly. I am pleased for you. He's the land agent's son at Thornton Hall, isn't he?'

'Yes, and that was one of Mam's objections. She seemed to think I was getting above my station and that he was only using me to get his wicked way,' said Dolly, raising her eyebrows. 'She's old-fashioned when it comes to forming opinions about people connected with the gentry, but Theo was so open and down to earth that she couldn't find anything to criticise.' Dolly's eyes sparkled, her joy at no longer having to hide her romance poignant.

Verity felt envious, and not for the first time, she asked herself why she and Oliver were still carrying out the subterfuge of being just mill mistress and manager? Her father had been dead for almost six months, and she couldn't honestly say she was mourning his passing, but Oliver had advised her to keep their relationship secret for the time being. He didn't want people to think that he was setting his sights too high. People could be cruel, their gossip malicious if they believed he only wanted to marry her because she was a mill heiress.

'I wish you and Theo well, Dolly. Don't let anything or anyone come between you.'

* * *

Theo poured his father a tot of whisky and went to sit beside him at the hearth in their home on the Thornton estate. He had been working hard all day, following his father's instructions and paying careful attention to the detail as they checked the farmland and livestock, and collected rent from the tenants. He desperately needed to catch him in a good mood, and now seemed the right time.

Joshua Beaumont had been hurt by his wife's adultery and she was to blame for his black moods and irascible temper. In order to overcome this slight to his manhood, he threw himself into his work, toiling day and night to run the estate to the best of his ability. He loved his son and had been pleased when Theo chose to live with him but he was sparing when it came to showing his affection. Now, as he looked across at Theo, he felt a fondness for him that was deepening by the day. The lad was shaping up well and had the makings of being a good land agent in the future.

'Dad, I've got something to ask you.' Theo broke the comfortable silence and leaned forward in his chair, his face anxious.

'Ask all you like,' Joshua replied, presuming that it was related to their work.

'I have a confession to make,' said Theo, his anxiety increasing. 'For some time now, I haven't been honest with you.'

Joshua's brow creased. Did the lad want to go back to his mother? He'd miss him if he did. He nodded for Theo to continue. Theo took a deep breath.

'When I told you I'd made friends with the stable lads and that I was spending my free time with them, it was only partially true. Most of my days and nights off have been spent in the company of the loveliest girl you could ever wish to meet.'

Joshua raised his eyebrows and an amused smile twitched his lips. Was the girl one of the house servants, or better still, was she one of Sir Arnold's many illustrious visitors? The lad was handsome, his manners presentable. Had he attracted the attention of a daughter of an aristocrat?

'And who might this young lady be?' he asked jovially.

'She's Dolly Armitage. She lives in the town and works at Lockwood Mill.'

'A mill worker!' All trace of amusement was wiped from Joshua's face.

'A cloth weaver,' Theo explained and, aware that his father was of the opinion that mill girls could be rough, he hastened to add, 'but she's educated and a wonderful artist, and her parents are decent, hardworking people who...' His voice trailed off and he buried his head in his hands as he witnessed his father's intransigence.

'Whatever made you take up with a mill girl? You've had plenty of opportunity to meet girls from the better classes since you came to live here.' Joshua sounded bemused. He closed his eyes and pictured a weaver clad in clogs and shawl. Nay, a chambermaid would have been preferable. He shook his head to dispel his disappointment.

'I can tell you're disappointed, Father, but you won't be once you've met her. Dolly's an absolutely splendid girl and she makes me happy.'

Joshua gave a knowing leer. 'Oh, I'm sure she does,' he crooned before adopting a firmer tone. 'Look lad, we all like to sow a few wild oats when we're young. It's a rite of passage, but it doesn't mean we have to get too involved.'

Theo reared up. 'I haven't been sowing wild oats, Dad. I love and respect her,' he said hotly. 'Her parents have accepted me, and I'd like you to do the same with Dolly.'

Joshua saw and heard the passion in his son's face and voice. He took a sip of whisky, swirling it over his tongue as he recalled his first love. She had been a scullery maid in the house in Harrogate. Beautiful, gentle, yet full of fun. He'd never forgotten her. He downed the rest of his whisky and passed the glass to Theo for a refill. As he waited for his drink, he thought bitterly of how he'd cast the kitchen maid aside and chosen instead to exalt his position by marrying the daughter of a wealthy farmer. And look what good that had done him. She had betrayed him at every turn. Still, she had given him a son to be proud of, and he didn't want to lose him.

Theo handed him the glass, his expression tense and questioning. He dearly wanted his father to agree to meet Dolly, but if he refused, Theo knew he would have to go his own way.

'What's it to be then, Dad?' he asked softly.

Joshua's face creased into a slow smile.

'If you have chosen her and really love her then who am I that I should disagree. Bring her whenever you like. I'll make her welcome.'

'Thanks, Dad.' Theo's reply gushed out on a release of pent breath, his relief patent.

20

Throughout the summer, Verity continued to accept invitations to the tea parties, picnics and soirees that the mill-owning families in the valley hosted – too many in Oliver's opinion, but conscious that she delighted in them, his kind heart wouldn't allow him to voice his objections.

Verity, oblivious to his misgivings, was in her element. Her mill was prospering, and she so enjoyed Millie's company that she rarely refused to join her in the company of the mill owners who offered her their advice and flattered her for being the only woman in the valley to run her own mill.

Encouraged by Millie, Verity bought new dresses and, delighted by her own appearance and enamoured by the attention she received from the old men and the young, she revelled in their admiration. Clarence Hargreaves was her most ardent admirer, and although he didn't stir in her the same feelings that she had for Oliver, it did feel lovely to have the approval of more than one man. Clarence's interest in her also meant that she always had someone to escort her into dinner or to dance with, and she was no longer the wallflower she had been at those dreadful parties her Aunt Flora had organised.

'Clarence thinks we should increase productivity on the herringbone Jacquards,' she told Oliver one evening after she had attended a tea party at Dogley Grange.

'That idiot! What would he know?' Oliver said dismissively.

'He seems to be very well respected by the other mill owners,' Verity replied tersely, feeling slightly annoyed that Oliver should think her new admirer was an idiot.

'That's only because they held his father in high regard. Edward Hargreaves manufactured some of the finest cloth in the valley. He must be turning in his grave at the stuff his son produces. And they toady up to him because they're impressed by the fact that his late mother was the daughter of Sir Somebody-or-Other. In my opinion, Clarence Hargreaves is an ignoramus.'

'He always shows me the most utter respect and interest,' Verity hotly countered.

'Does he now?'

Oliver's scathing reply had hurt Verity. It seemed to her that he didn't think she was worthy of another man's attention, or that she deserved to be accepted into the circle of her fellow mill owners. However, his curt dismissal of the clique of manufacturers that, to his dismay, she found so fascinating had not deterred her.

Oliver silently made excuses for her naivety when she repeated their dubious opinions or enthused over how much they admired her, but it did little to allay his fears that one day he might lose her. She did not appear to love him any less for all her newfound interests. They still spent pleasant evenings in the drawing room at Far View espousing their feelings and sharing things that pleased them, Oliver frequently chastising himself for doubting her. It was perhaps as well he didn't attend the tea parties or the occasional evening soirees for if he had, he would have been even more worried.

Letitia Hargreaves sent regular requests for Verity to take afternoon tea with her, and although Verity found her rather vacuous, it seemed churlish to refuse. Letitia talked about affairs of the heart, her twittery little voice encouraging Verity to divulge her own feelings, but Verity kept her love for Oliver close to her chest. Not before Christmas would they let the world know of their intentions. The had agreed on that.

'Constance Hartley has become engaged to Sydney Hepplestone. Isn't it exciting?' Letitia squeaked one afternoon as she and Verity sat in the garden at Dogley Grange. 'I do so love it when there's romance in the air.' Her squinty little baby-blue eyes rolled and she pouted her lips as though she was about to be kissed. Verity couldn't help thinking, rather unkindly, that Letitia looked like a piglet rooting for its mother's teat.

Dismissing the vulgar thought, she said, 'A union of hearts and mills,' for the engaged couple were the scion of two mill owners in the valley.

'And what about you, Verity?' pressed Letitia, agog with inquisitiveness. 'Have you given your heart to anyone, or are you still free?'

Verity was saved from having to answer as Clarence swooped across the lawn on his short, slightly bowed legs. 'Ah, the divine Miss Lockwood,' he brayed. 'How fortunate for me that I left the mill early and find you still here.' He flopped down on the grass at Verity's feet and gazed up at her. 'May I say how beautiful you look?' His fleshy pink face, squat nose and blubbery lips made Verity think of piglets again.

'Thank you, Clarence.'

Her cool reply did not deter him. He continued telling her

how fascinating she was, and how intriguing he found her. She had heard it all before. Whenever they met, he commandeered her, and much to her annoyance, he acted as though they had an understanding. Now, he placed his hand on her ankle, stroking it with his sausage-like fingers.

'Such pretty feet,' he said, gazing up into her face lasciviously as Verity angrily shook her foot free from the offending hand. She stood and stepped over his outstretched legs.

'I must be going,' she said. 'Thank you for a lovely tea, Letitia.'

Clarence, hindered by his portly belly, struggled to his feet and his sister got to hers, chorusing, 'Oh, must you go so soon?' Clarence scowled at Letitia. She caught at Verity's arm, stammering, 'But... but... Clarence has only just got here. He'll be so disappointed if you leave now.' She looked to him for approval.

Verity was adamant. 'I'm sorry, but I really must. I have things to attend to at the mill.' She began walking across the lawns, Clarence trotting alongside using several ploys to detain her. First, it was to stop and smell the roses, then to admire the fountain and finally, to ask how the mill was faring. Was production up? Was she making a healthy profit?

At this last attempt to hold her back, Verity was reminded of how often, in between his silly flattery, he quizzed her about the mill. 'Lockwood Mill is fine, Clarence,' she replied, her eyes cold as she looked down with distaste into his florid face; he was a full four inches shorter than herself. 'Now please let me go.'

'I will think of you every minute we are apart,' he burbled, striving yet again to charm her as they arrived at the rear of the house and the stable yard. This remark was lost on Verity. Hastily mounting the trap, she drove off at a good clip and did not look back.

She laughed when later she told Oliver about the silly incident, but he wasn't amused. 'He has his eye on your mill,' he growled. 'He sees how well you're doing and wants a share in it.'

Verity met this comment with mixed emotions: anger that Oliver was right about Clarence's interest in the mill and saddened to think he held the opinion that no man could desire her for herself.

Shrugging aside her sensitivity, she said, 'Then he's wasting his time.'

'I'm glad to hear that,' Oliver replied, sounding more assured than he felt.

* * *

Autumn days moved on apace in a riot of gold and russet, the fields humming with the sound of reapers as the harvest was gathered. Hedgerows glittered with dew-drenched spiders' webs, and in the far distance, the moors and hills wore browning bracken and heather.

Up on Castle Hill, the Jubilee Tower was beginning to take shape and as Verity made her way to the mill on a misty morning in the last week of October, she breathed in the mellow scents of the dying season and thought that, like the tower, her life was on an upward trajectory.

Oliver met her with a broad smile as she entered the office. He waited until she had taken off her gloves and unpinned her hat before speaking. He thought how lovely she looked in her green suit made from a new batch of their own cloth, the jacket's nipped-in waist accentuating her slender figure and the close-fitting skirt short enough to show off her trim ankles.

'I've been checking the order book and double-checking the ledgers and I think I can safely say that you don't owe anyone a penny, that you have a healthy profit in the bank, and orders to see you through to next spring, Miss Lockwood.' Smiling broadly, he sat back with his hands behind his head in the way that Verity found so endearing.

'Oh, Oliver! That's marvellous,' she cried and, quite forgetting where they were, she skipped round the desk and planted a kiss on his upturned face. He responded willingly. Then, both of them aware that at any minute, one of the mill hands might appear at the door, they broke apart, laughing.

Verity regained her composure but her eyes still sparkled as she said, 'To know that Father's debts are finally cleared is a weight off my shoulders. And a full order book and a profit, what more could we ask for?' She gave a huge, satisfied sigh. 'And it is *we,* Oliver. I couldn't have done it without you.' She gave him a look so full of love, he felt his heart melting. 'And furthermore,' she continued chirpily, 'come Christmas, when we announce our engagement, it will be *our* mill, yours and mine.' She placed a finger to her lips and looked thoughtful. 'Will we call it Lockwood and Hardcastle's or the other way round? After all, I'll soon be Mrs Hardcastle.'

Oliver smiled at her childlike excitement. 'Plenty of time to think about that,' he said. 'In the meantime, we'll keep on making it our success.'

Across the yard in the canteen, the prospect of an engagement was on someone else's mind. As Dolly and Nellie quenched their thirst with steaming cups of tea – such a treat after all the dust and fluff they'd been breathing in – and Dolly swapped one of her cold bacon butties for Nellie's drip bread, she was bursting to tell Nellie her latest news. She'd been hugging it close to her chest for the past two-and-a-half hours as she worked at her looms because in her opinion, it was too important to convey by mouthing over the cacophonous roar of machinery. Now, she let it all spill out.

'Theo and I are getting engaged on November the fifth 'cos that's a special night for us,' she gabbled. 'We were up at Thornton Hall and when we told his dad, he made a joke about young love setting the world on fire.' Dolly raised her eyebrows. 'And when Theo walked me home and we told Mam, she said it was romantic.'

'Ooh, Dolly, I'm ever so pleased for you,' Nellie said sincerely.

Not for the first time Dolly noticed that just lately, ever since Nellie had started spending a lot of her free time with George, that she rarely said 'tha' and 'thi' and that her manner of speech was more refined. Dolly put that down to George's influence.

'We'll not get married till next spring. I want it to be a day when the sun is shining and the birds are singing,' Dolly continued dreamily, 'and I want you to be my bridesmaid.'

'Aw, Dolly!' Nellie almost leapt across the table. 'Thanks, I'd love to be.'

The mill hooter signalled them back to the weaving shed and for the rest of the morning, Dolly wove cloth for Lockwood's and daydreamed about her wedding. Things had turned out far easier than she ever had imagined. After meeting Theo on several occasions, her mam had cast aside her prejudice, declaring, 'That lad has no airs and graces. He's a decent, working man with good manners, and he respects our Dolly.'

Likewise, Joshua Beaumont had immediately taken to Dolly. His concept of rough mill women had been dashed from the start when he'd found Dolly to be an intelligent, interesting young woman and, as his son had told him, a talented artist. His opinion of her had rocketed on the day Lady Sybil Thornton, the wife of Sir Arnold, had insisted on buying one of Dolly's drawings of Thornton Hall.

Dolly had been at Thornton Hall on a glorious autumn

Sunday afternoon and, captivated by the colours of the trees surrounding the house and the Virginia creeper adorning its walls, she had taken out her sketchbook and pastels. As she sat, head bent and fingers dusty, Lady Sybil had strolled by. Curious as to the stranger sitting in a shady spot diligently sketching, she had stopped to enquire, and when she saw the finished result, she had asked if she could have it. Dolly had been thrilled and would have given the drawing willingly, but Lady Sybil had said, 'Talent like this deserves a reward' and had given Dolly ten shillings.

Now, the money was secreted in Dolly's bottom drawer until it would eventually go towards buying a wedding dress and items for their new home. Theo was hopeful that he would be offered a cottage on the estate, and on the last Saturday afternoon in October, as she and Nellie were shopping in Heywood's department store, Dolly was deliberating over towels and sheets in anticipation of becoming Theo's wife.

'You are lucky. I'd love to be buying stuff for my bottom drawer,' Nellie said wistfully.

'Your turn will come, Nellie,' said Dolly as she paid the assistant for two white towels. 'Just you wait. Like me, you'll find the man of your dreams.'

'I've found him already,' Nellie muttered, her remark falling on deaf ears as they walked out into the street.

'Aw, look! It's drizzling,' Dolly said and, quickening their pace, they hurried across the town to the shops in the Lion Arcade.

'I hope it's not raining tomorrow; George is taking me to Beaumont Park.'

Nellie's casual remark didn't fool Dolly for one minute even though her friend was trying hard to hide her excitement. The park was a beauty spot popular with courting couples and as

Dolly paid for a pair of white pillow cases, she reflected on how often George sought Nellie's company now that he no longer courted the dreadful Amy who, according to the gossips, had been sent away to relatives in Lancashire to hide her shame.

When they left the arcade under the watchful gaze of the huge stone lion on top of the building's façade, the rain had stopped. 'Thank goodness for that. Let's hope it stays away for tomorrow,' Nellie said, and Dolly was touched by her friend's need for the outing with George to take place.

'You and our George seem to be making a right go of things just lately,' she said, the pleasure in her voice not escaping Nellie's notice.

She blushed. 'I'd like to think we'll go on doing that forever,' she said, her voice wobbling and her smile wishful.

'And why not? You make a lovely couple.'

Nellie positively glowed, and their shopping done, the girls sauntered homeward, happily discussing their love lives and heedless of the dark clouds gathering overhead.

'Oh, look, there's Mr Hardcastle.' Dolly pointed to the other side of the road.

Oliver saw them and doffed his hat.

'Good afternoon, sir,' the girls called out.

Then Nellie gave Dolly a nudge. 'Eh!' she hissed. 'You know when Lily said that the chap who got Amy Dickenson in the family way wore a hat like Mr Hardcastle's; you don't think it was him, do you?'

'Don't be daft! Mr Hardcastle wouldn't look twice at Amy Dickenson,' Dolly scoffed. 'I still haven't forgiven her for trying to pin that baby on our George, the scheming hussy. I'm glad they sent her away.'

'So am I.' Nellie's reply was heartfelt, and Dolly knew she was thinking of George. 'But I was just saying,' Nellie continued, 'you don't see many other chaps wearing hats like that. When he tipped it at us, it got me thinking.'

'Well don't, Nellie Haigh! When you start thinking, you're dangerous,' Dolly jested.

'Cheeky beggar,' Nellie laughingly retorted, then cried, 'Oh no!' as the heavens opened and the rain began to pour.

* * *

It being Saturday, the mill closed and Oliver, in need of cigarettes, was making his way into the town to the tobacconists on Cross Church Street. After buying two packets of Capstan Navy Cut, he left the shop to find that the drizzle had turned into a downpour. Hurrying across the road, he ducked into the Sun Inn and ordered a pint of stout. Then spying Jack Rangely, another mill manager, he crossed the bar to join him. 'How do, Jack. How are things at Bairstow's these days?' Oliver sat down.

'Not bad, Oliver. We've plenty of work on. An' I hear Lockwood's is doing all right.'

They chatted convivially about the mills. Oliver was drinking his second pint of stout when Jack said, 'After puttin' up wi' yon drunken bastard, Jeb Lockwood, for all them years, it must mek a change workin' for his daughter. Does she know owt about runnin' a mill or does she leave it all up to thee?'

'Miss Lockwood is very knowledgeable, and she's a fair employer,' Oliver said.

'I hear that Clarence Hargreaves has set his cap at her.' Jack supped on his pint.

Oliver's hand tightened round his glass. 'Who told you that?'

'Our Emily. She's a maid at Hartley's an' her chap, Fred Oldroyd, works for Hargreaves up at Dogley Grange. She told me it's common gossip in t'big houses,' Jack continued. 'He's been after her for months. Fred says he's lookin' to get his hands on Lockwood's seein' as how his own mill's a bloody shambles, the cloth they turn out that rotten, nubbdy'll buy it.' He lifted his glass and drank deeply.

The beer in Oliver's belly soured. 'And is Miss Lockwood willing?'

'Eeh, that I couldn't tell thi, but Fred says she's not much of a looker so she might be glad of Hargreaves's interest in her, even if he is a slobbering little bugger. Our Emily says your Miss Lockwood's that tall that Hargreaves needs a stool to stand on to kiss her.' Jack laughed and swigged his glass empty. 'Does tha want another one, Oliver?'

'Not for me, Jack.' Oliver stood, his heart in his boots.

As he walked back through the town, Oliver pondered unhappily on what Jack had told him. Heedless of the puddles left by the downpour, he reflected on how often Clarence Hargreaves's name came up when Verity was relating what had been said or done at the parties she attended. He found it hard to believe that there was any truth in what he'd just heard but he couldn't deny that of late, he'd more than once had his own doubts and it made him feel confused and heartsore as to the future.

* * *

Rain drizzled down the tram's windows and the air, stuffy with the strong smell of wet wool and tobacco smoke, made the journey unpleasant but preferable to getting soaking wet had Verity travelled by pony and trap. She was on her way to Lindley to visit Millie, who was now in her fourth month of pregnancy. Yesterday, she had sent a note to say she was still confined to the house having been advised to rest by her mother-in-law, and begging Verity to visit her.

Each week since the Hargreaves party, they had met, just the two of them, but of late, it being Millie's first pregnancy, she had been plagued by morning sickness and had had to forgo their meetings. Verity had been disappointed for she not only found Millie's witty chatter amusing; she also found it healing to talk about her own life, past and present, with a woman of her own age. As the tram rattled along the lines, she realised how much she had missed Millie and was glad when she reached her destination.

She was met by a maid who took her cape and umbrella then showed her into a cosy parlour where Millie was sitting with her feet resting on a footstool, a blanket over her knees and a sardonic expression on her pretty face.

'The Ma-in-Law, she who must be obeyed, has taken me prisoner,' Millie quipped as Verity sat down. 'I am to rest till the weekend when I will be allowed to attend the Blamire's evening soiree. The old chap's celebrating his eightieth.' She pulled a face and groaned. 'Oh, what fun we'll have. Will you go?'

'Joseph Blamire is one of the most respected mill owners in the district so I suppose it would be rude not to attend,' said Verity. 'And if I do, I hope beyond hope that that crass fool, Hargreaves, won't be there.' This time, she was the one to pull a face.

'No chance of that happening. He'd attend the opening of a box of biscuits, he's so desperate to be seen as one of the big wheels in the valley. Silly little man.' Millie gave Verity a sympathetic grin. 'Is he still pestering you?'

Verity grimaced. 'The last time I took tea with Letitia, he had the audacity to grope my ankles, and the day after and yesterday, he sent me flowers, and when I had the misfortune to meet him at the Hartley's, he smothered me with attention and...' she threw up her hands, horrified, 'he even tried to kiss me when he thought no one was looking.'

'Oh, my goodness! The horrid little man. What are you going to do about him?' Millie began to giggle, her hands on her little bump. 'Even the baby's disgusted. He's rolling over.'

Alarmed, Verity cried, 'Oh, I'm sorry. Did I upset you?'

Millie laughed out loud. 'No! I was just imagining Hargreaves stretching up on tiptoe and pushing his blubbery lips to yours. It made us both squirm.'

Verity joined in the laughter. Clarence was ridiculous. But even so, his pursuit of her was extremely embarrassing and totally unwelcomed. On the one hand, common sense told her that she could avoid him if she were to refuse invitations to the social gatherings, but on the other hand, she did not see why she should let the silly buffoon deny her the pleasure of feeling part of the mill-owning community in the valley; it was important for business.

'I'll just do my best to avoid him,' she told Millie. 'He'll soon tire of being spurned.'

'Ah, but... maybe it will only increase his ardour,' Millie predicted wickedly.

'Oh, my goodness!' Verity clapped her hand to her mouth. 'That would be the worst thing that could happen.'

Millie laughed. She was enjoying the idea of toying with Verity's love life. It eased the boredom of being cooped up, and she wondered how else she might interfere.

* * *

'And how was Millie? Did you find her in good health?' Oliver asked later that evening. The question sounded innocent enough, but inside his head, Jack's information still rankled.

'Oh, Millie's fine, but rather bored by her ma-in-law's cossetting,' Verity replied as she snuggled up to him on the couch in the drawing room.

'Who else was there?' Oliver probed, aware that other members of the mill-owning elite might have been in attendance. 'You know, like the Hartleys or... the Hargreaves.'

'No, it was just me, thank goodness. Millie is of the same opinion as I am where Letitia Hargreaves is concerned. She drives me insane with her silly twittering, and that odious brother of hers...' Verity pulled a face and gave a little shudder. 'I cringe at the very mention of his name.'

Oliver should have felt pleased, but Verity's protestations seemed a little too strong. Was she being deliberately evasive?

Just as he was thinking that, she cupped his face in her hands and kissed him. 'I'm so lucky to have a man like you, Oliver,' she said, her eyes shining with love.

With the warmth of her kiss still on his lips and the tenderness in her gaze speaking a thousand words, Oliver pushed his doubts to the back of his mind.

* * *

Dolly popped her head round the office door and said, 'Pardon me, Miss Lockwood, may I have a word? Saturday's the fifth of November and it's a special day for me and Theo and we're having a small party in the evening to announce our engagement. I'd like to invite you and Mr Hardcastle if you think that's all right.'

'Why, thank you, Dolly. That's most kind. Where will the party be held?'

'At home in Silver Street. It's just for a few friends and family. I'll understand if you refuse. Maybe it's wrong of me to ask, you being the mill mistress, but I think of you as a friend.' She flushed. 'You don't mind, do you?'

'Of course not. I'll be delighted and if Mr Hardcastle is free, I'll bring him along.'

Dolly smiled. 'Then we'll expect you about seven. Thank you, Miss Lockwood.'

On her way home, Verity wondered if she and Oliver should hold a party to celebrate their engagement. But when? Christmas was such a busy time for everyone. And where would they hold it? Not Far View – it was far too shabby to entertain her new friends. And not at Oliver's home either. She hadn't felt welcome there. Furthermore, who could they invite? They didn't have any mutual friends. Giving the reins a sharper flick than intended, the pony visibly flinching, she abandoned the idea. Theirs was a-hole-in-the-corner romance and it troubled her to think why it was so.

At the foot of Far View Hill, she slowed the trap and came to a halt at Aunt Martha's gate. She visited her elderly aunt at least twice each week, often feeling guilty at neglecting her. But the elderly, housebound woman had little to proffer in the way of interesting conversation and was inclined to reminisce on her own and Jeb's younger days, painting them in a rosy glow. This irked Verity, her memories of the drunken bully still painful.

A large, shiny motor car was parked by the gate. Verity wondered whose it was as she went to the door and let herself in. 'Hello, Aunt Martha,' she called out as she went through to the parlour where Martha spent her day.

The couple sitting with her aunt greeted her. Verity couldn't recall the last time she had seen Joseph Boothroyd's niece, Cora, and her husband, Cecil. They had been in the habit of visiting her aunt's husband when was he was alive, but since Joseph's death, they had neglected Martha. She wondered what had brought them here after all this time. She was soon to find out. Over cups of tea and small talk, they informed her that they were taking Martha back with them to stay in their home in Pateley Bridge.

'It will do her good to have a change of scene, and we'll be able to take her out and about in our motor car. Did you see it by the gate?' Cora looked smug.

Verity resisted saying she would have to be blind not to have done and looked quizzically at her aunt.

Martha was all smiles. 'Betty's packing me things,' she said.

'I'll go and give her a hand,' said Verity, and excusing herself, she crossed the hall into the room her aunt now used as a bedroom. Betty Oldroyd, the woman Verity had employed to care for Martha, was folding garments into a large valise. 'How did all this come about?' Verity asked.

Betty pulled a face. 'She wasn't for it at first but they talked her round,' she said, stuffing a woollen wrap into the bag. 'She said summat about her stayin' till Christmas an' New Year. If you ask me, they've got their eyes on her property. Him in there had a good nosy round afore you came. They most likely think she's not long for this world an' they want to be in wi' t'first shout for what she leaves.'

'Good Lord! Do you think so?' Verity felt even more guilty if this was true. She too had neglected Martha. She hurried back into the parlour and sat as close as possible to her aunt. 'Are you sure about this, Aunt Martha?' she whispered. 'What about leaving your house empty for so long.' She looked pointedly at Cora.

'Betty'll come in an' air it every now an' then, an' you'll keep an eye on it for me, won't you?' Martha said complacently.

'It's all arranged,' Cecil said testily. 'We'll take good care of her.'

I'm sure you will, and you'll wheedle your way into making sure it's to your benefit. But Verity, seeing that her aunt was delighted to be going to Pateley Bridge, kept her thoughts to herself.

At Cecil's brisk, 'We'd best be getting off,' she hugged Martha and told her she would miss her, at the same time thinking she might never see her again.

My family circle gets smaller and smaller, she thought as she drove up the hill.

* * *

Oliver saw no harm in accepting Dolly's invitation. 'It was thoughtful of the girl to ask us, and she's not just any weaver. You and Dolly have grown quite close what with the reading and sewing classes,' he had said with a wry smile. 'We can pop in for a short while, show our faces and leave when we think fit.'

On the day of the party, Oliver suggested that they spend the afternoon together and take a walk up to Castle Hill to see how the tower was progressing. It was bitterly cold and overcast but Verity, wrapped up warmly in a new, heavy tweed coat, was delighted to be sharing the afternoon and evening with him. As they climbed the hillside, they were overtaken by gangs of young boys who were dragging branches and pieces of wood up to the hilltop to fuel the bonfire that would be lit later.

'I used to love chumping,' Oliver said, his eyes twinkling at the memory, and Verity asking him to explain what he meant. 'A gang of us raided the woods for days before bonfire night looking for fallen branches or we'd call at people's houses asking for old tables and chairs: anything that would burn. It was a competition to see who could collect the most.'

Verity, who had never chumped, thought how narrow her childhood had been. She had only ever run wild through the woods but once, many years ago with the Halliwell children and their father, and she'd never been part of a gang of happy children. It made her feel sad.

The four-square tower was by now several feet high and already dominated the landscape. Several yards away, in an open patch of ground, a huge pyre of wood was being added to by the gang of whooping boys. Verity recalled how she had watched last year's bonfire burn from her bedroom window and how lonely she had felt then, but now she was no longer alone; she was with the man she was going to marry. Kicking up her heels, she began running round the base of the tower, revelling in the pure joy of the moment. Oliver stared after her. Then he smiled fondly; she was the same sweet Verity at heart. When he caught up with her, she fell into his arms, laughing and feeling thoroughly exhilarated. Then, as he kissed her, she felt as though she might explode into a million tiny pieces of happiness.

Later that evening, after a meal in Far View House, they made their way to Dolly's home in Silver Street. It being Guy Fawkes Night, the air was smoky, the sparks from little backyard bonfires lighting the sky like fireflies and children squealing their delight as rockets soared and squibs crackled and banged. Verity, still feeling elated, said, 'It's magic, isn't it.'

Dolly had spent the afternoon in a flurry of excitement and now, after helping her mother put the finishing touches to the preparations, she had dashed upstairs to wash and change into her new chartreuse-green dress, bought with the money Lady Sybil had given her for the drawing of Thornton Hall. It had a tight-fitting bodice and slender skirt that showed off her figure, and with her fiery red hair pinned in loops to the crown of her head and stray tendrils caressing the nape of her neck and face, she looked the picture of loveliness as she bounced back into the kitchen.

'Aw, Mam, it's a feast fit for a king,' she cried as she cast her eye over the kitchen table that was loaded with three different sorts of sandwiches: thinly sliced ham, cheese and pickle and egg and cress. Florence, having long since put aside her misgivings about Theo and only too pleased to put on a good show for her daughter, had baked scones and buns, and Dolly had called at the dairy for clotted cream, a rare treat, as were the iced fairy cakes. It all looked rather splendid, and Dolly's cheeks were rosy with excitement.

When Theo arrived with his father, he told Dolly that she had never looked more beautiful. Then they stood proudly by the door ready to greet their guests, and Joshua, Clem and George each sneaked a crafty bottle of beer whilst they waited for the party to begin. Nellie looked pretty in a new white blouse and grey skirt as she whisked between sink and table making sure that everything was neat and tidy.

Lily Cockhill and her husband, Frank, were the first to arrive, closely followed by May and Fred Sykes and then Hetty and Clifford Lumb. Drinks were served: beer for the men and Lily, and lemonade for the others. Dolly and Theo, their faces glowing, fielded congratulations and ribald comments, the chatter and laughter rising as everyone mingled. A knock at the door had Dolly rushing to answer it, and when Verity and Oliver walked in, a respectful hush descended on the kitchen.

Oh dear, thought Verity, *we have put a damper on things*.

She need not have worried. Clem came forward, hand outstretched. 'Welcome, Miss Lockwood. We've heard so much about you from our Dolly; it's a pleasure to meet thi.' He turned to Oliver. 'And you an' all, lad, though I've known thee from when tha wa' in britches.' Clem shook Oliver's hand.

'Here you are, sir.' George shoved a bottle of beer into Oliver's hand.

Dolly took Florence by the elbow. 'This is my mam, Miss Lockwood.' A smile passed between them. Verity shook Florence's hand. So, this was the mother who had taught her daughter to read and speak properly but had warned her not to rise above her station.

'Pleased to meet you, Mrs Armitage. You have a daughter to be proud of. She's been a great help to me.'

Florence's cheeks reddened with pride as she bobbed a little curtsey.

'And this is Theo,' Dolly said, tugging at his arm to introduce him to Verity and Oliver. Verity looked at the handsome, well-dressed boy. She could see why Dolly had fallen for him.

Theo came forward and introduced himself. 'Pleased to make your acquaintance.'

Verity was soon enjoying herself immensely. Oliver fell into conversation with Joshua, and as food and drink were consumed, Verity chatted with Florence and Dolly and the women from the weaving shed.

Clem rapped a spoon on the table and called for order.

'Now that everybody's been fed an' watered, I'd like to say a few words.' He cleared his throat noisily. 'Our Dolly has allus given me an' her mam cause to be proud. We couldn't have wished for a better daughter. And now she's found hersen a man as grand as she is so I ask you all to make a toast to...' Clem paused for effect, 'Dolly and Theo.'

'Dolly and Theo,' the guests echoed.

Dolly had cringed when her dad had started to speak, but now she found she had tears in her eyes. 'Thanks, Dad. That was lovely,' she said, her voice thick with emotion.

Theo added his thanks. 'Your kind words mean a lot. I'm honoured to be accepted into your family as Dolly's fiancé, and be assured, I'll take good care of her.'

This met with more cheers and the party continued merrily.

Lily began to warble 'Daisy Bell', helped out by Nellie and George when she forgot the words. Then everybody sang 'Little Brown Jug', and Joshua surprised them all by giving a beautiful tenor rendition of 'Love's Old Sweet Song'.

Dolly and Theo exchanged triumphant smiles.

Verity and Oliver left the party much later than they had anticipated. Verity had given Dolly and Theo an engagement present of a beautifully embroidered linen tablecloth and six matching napkins, and Oliver now remarked on it as they walked down Silver Street.

'That was a rather generous gift,' he said.

'Dolly's worth every penny,' Verity replied, her voice rich with sincerity and her heart full of a wonderful sense of belonging: that Dolly and her family were more than just friends. It was a marvellous feeling. Then, clinging on to Oliver's arm and feeling his strength and his warmth, she began musing on the prospect of making a family of her own.

21

'I've heard that the Unions are strongly agitating for a reduction of hours in the working day,' Verity said as she and Oliver dealt with the accounts at the start of the week before Christmas. 'It was all the talk yesterday at the Hartley's pre-Christmas get together. It caused quite an uproar. Brierley and Blamire were adamant that they wouldn't shorten the twelve-hour shifts down to ten, and most of the others were in agreement with them.'

At Verity's slightly contemptuous tone, Oliver raised his head. He was already cognisant with what the Unions had been demanding for some time now.

'I'm sure they were,' he said dryly, then lowered his gaze back to the column of figures he was totting up. He had an uneasy feeling where this was leading.

Verity's lip curled as she related the comments she'd heard the previous evening, the mill owners airing their opinions of the working classes and the Unions in the foulest terms. 'I suppose it's only to be expected,' she said.

Hearing Verity's barely concealed disparagement, Oliver gave her his full attention.

'And where do you stand on the matter?' he asked warily.

Verity rested her elbows on the desk, her chin propped on her fists and her frowning expression thoughtful. 'You have to acknowledge that twelve hours' physical labour is exacting, even with half-an-hour respite at breakfast and midday, so I'm inclined to side with the Unions.' She stood, her grey eyes the colour of honed steel and her stance regal as she added, 'In fact, I am so in agreement with the Unions that I intend to start the working day at seven instead six. We'll introduce it in the new year.' She gave Oliver a bright smile.

He returned it with a stern look, and not for the first time, he thought that Verity was getting too big for her boots, and that she no longer listened to his advice. 'You need to give that idea some serious thought before you do,' he said grimly. 'You don't have to be the one to lead the way. I advise you to wait until the other mills in the valley give their response to the demands. They stick together when it comes to deciding matters like this.'

'I'm aware of that, Oliver, but it doesn't mean I have to agree with them.'

Verity's icy retort caused his temper to rise.

'It won't make you popular. It will cause further dissent in a lot of the mills where the workers are dissatisfied. The Unions are breathing down their necks as it is without you capitulating before any decisions have been taken. As I've already said, they abide by their own rules and won't appreciate your breaking with tradition.'

'They can think and do as they like. This is my mill and I'll run it as I please,' Verity replied hotly. 'Furthermore, our workers will be the ones who appreciate it. Might I remind you, it's their efforts that have us in the happy position of making a profit.' She slapped her hand on the ledger that recorded proof of the mill's newfound prosperity.

Oliver sighed wearily. 'I don't disagree with your philanthropy. It's commendable, but it doesn't always pay to jump the gun. You already gave them a Christmas bonus, one that I might add does not sit well with some of our competitors, and you've provided a canteen. Causing aggravation by being overly generous can lead to trouble.'

'I don't see why it should. All the mills have different ways of managing their affairs; why not mine? Hargreaves's pays twopence less than we do for a finished piece but that doesn't mean that I have to follow suit.' She dropped her gaze, hiding the spark of defiance in her eyes but also masking the guilt she felt at mentioning Clarence Hargreaves.

Oliver bristled. The mere mention of that name made him seethe. Swallowing his anger and determined not to be riled, he said, 'Aye, and Brierley's pays twopence more. We're sitting comfortably in the middle and should stay there. I understand there's a need for change, that working conditions must be improved if we're to meet the Unions' demands but we have to tread carefully.' He forced a chuckle in an attempt to lighten the mood. 'Before you know it, they'll be asking for a two-day working week and a hundred pounds a day.'

Verity wasn't amused. 'I've had no complaints from the Union men who represent our weavers and spinners, or the dyers and the carders,' she said haughtily.

'That's because they are old men who don't have fire in their bellies like some Union members. The fair rates you pay along with the canteen and safe working conditions you provide are keeping them quiet for the time being but it won't last.' Oliver ran his fingers through his hair. 'The Unions need to be handled carefully,' he warned.

'They do, and that's why I encourage our women to attend meetings and voice their opinions. They need to break through the male hegemony that rules every aspect of society. After all, they have as much right as any man to decide their terms of employment.'

'And the men strenuously object to that and hold you responsible for the women's interference,' Oliver replied gently. 'Sometimes, my dear, your impetuosity leads you to run before you can walk. I agree that the women have a right to have their say but such intervention has to be carefully planned if it's to be successful.' He gave a half-smile that begged for her understanding. He received a look of cold disdain in return.

'Don't lecture me, Oliver. I will not sit idly back when I can bring about change.'

Oliver gave her a despairing look. The Unions were growing more powerful with each passing year and yet she chose to underestimate their powers and to ignore the practices that other mills in the district adhered to by common consent. He shared her ideals for better working conditions and improved earnings but these things had to be approached with caution. He'd admired and supported most of her actions so far, and had advised against those he thought unwise. Now he feared that she was getting too big for her boots, as his mother would say, and he felt the need to rein her in before it was her undoing. He blamed the social gatherings for Verity's inflated opinion of herself. She being a bit of novelty and they making game of her. But he'd heard rumours that out of her hearing, the mill owners scorned and belittled her. Although he resented their gossip, he chose not to share it with her. His heart ached for the lovely, kind-hearted girl he had fallen in love with; where had she gone? Now, he addressed her calmly enough but deep down, he was simmering with pent-up rage.

'All I'm saying is don't rock the boat by being too ambitious,

Verity. For the time being, be content with things the way they are.'

'I'm still going to reduce the working day by an hour in the new year,' she said, her stubborn glare defying contradiction.

'Oh, do what you damned well like,' Oliver snarled, his patience at an end. 'If you refuse to see reason, I'm done.' He leapt to his feet and stormed out of the office.

Verity stared at his empty chair, shocked by his anger. What had brought this on? They didn't quarrel; they reasoned things out, she told herself. *Or we used to,* she thought dismally. *This should be the happiest time of my life. Next week, we'll announce our engagement, let the world know we love one another – if we do.* Was Oliver having second thoughts? It didn't seem like it when they were alone, or when they went to concerts as they had done only two evenings before to listen to the Choral Society's annual performance of the 'Messiah'.

Perhaps we've been foolish in hiding our relationship for so long, she thought. *Nobody knows of our intentions to marry. We're not accepted as a couple in my social circle, and his family don't wholly approve of me.* The more she thought about these things and the spat they had just had – nay, it was more than a spat – the more anxious she felt.

Over the weekend, Verity and Oliver were uneasy in one another's company. Whenever they were together, they avoided talking about her decision to reduce the working day and it wasn't until late on Sunday evening as Oliver was putting on his overcoat ready to leave Far View House that he brought it up again. Calmly and reasonably, he reiterated his opinions.

'I know you mean well but I advise you to think twice before announcing it,' he said as Verity saw him out.

Verity gave a tight-lipped nod. 'I will,' she murmured as he dropped a kiss on her forehead then strode off into the night.

* * *

On Friday morning, the atmosphere in the office was tense. Verity closed the ledger she had been working on and stood up. Oliver raised his head, laid down his pen and looked at her from across the desk, his eyes dark and questioning.

'I'm going to the canteen,' Verity said through gritted teeth.

'As you will, Miss Lockwood.'

His mocking tones cut Verity to the quick and she dithered. Whenever he addressed her as such, she knew that he was angry.

He saw the hurt in her dove-grey eyes and had to steel himself from relenting. Her gaze imploring, his own did not waver. Then, her eyes flashing defiance, she marched to the office door, her back rigid.

'Stubbornness is not one of your best traits, Miss Lockwood,' he called after her.

The canteen buzzed with chatter and the air was ripe with the smell of raw wool, sweat, and tobacco smoke. Verity made her way through the fug to the front of the room, then clapped her hands together. A respectful hush fell and all eyes turned on her. She forced a smile that did not reach her eyes.

'As is now customary in Lockwood Mill, three days holiday will be granted to celebrate the season. The mill will close after the last shift on Friday and not reopen until Wednesday. I also intend...'

Verity's voice was drowned out as noisy comments bounced off the walls. One accusatory, raucous, male voice yelled above the rest, 'Aye, three days off an' on'y paid for two. You can stick that up your arse.'

'Aye, you gave us an extra day off last year but we on'y got paid half o' what we could have earned if we'd worked on.' This time, the disgruntled voice belonged to a woman. This was true, Oliver having advised that they could only afford to pay a covering allowance for the extra day.

'Have you forgotten we're paid piece rate? If we can't come in to work, we're losin' out,' another woman shouted. 'I can well do without havin' to tek a day off I don't bloody need.'

The heckling grew uglier. In the past, only Christmas Day and Boxing Day had been paid leave; the Unions had fixed that some time ago. Now, whilst they all liked the idea of an extra day, there were some who simply couldn't afford it.

'Do we get full pay for Christmas Eve?' The shout hung in the air.

Suddenly, as the angry shouts rang in her ears, Verity saw a side to her employees that she had not seen before. Shocked to the core, she swallowed the announcement she had been about to make: starting time would remain at six o'clock. With a sense of rising panic, she realised that Oliver was right. She had been too hasty, trying to do too much too soon and she should have given it more thought.

Her palms clammy with sweat, she clapped her hands to gain their attention. Taking a deep breath, she addressed the present problem. 'With full pay,' she said above the noise, but the thrill that she had anticipated in telling them that come the new year, their working day would start an hour later now evaded her. They would have their extra day's holiday but as she walked to the door, the disgruntled comments mixed with wishes for a 'Merry Christmas, Miss Lockwood' ringing in her ears, she took no pleasure from it.

'Three full days off again,' Nellie squealed, 'an' wi' full pay this time.'

'Miss Lockwood always has our best interests at heart. There's not another mill owner in the valley as kind and generous as she is,' Dolly said. 'But she didn't look happy, did she?'

'Can't say as I noticed,' Lily replied. 'An' anyway, what's she got to be miserable about? It's not as if she has any money worries. Her sort come an' go as they please. Every day's Christmas for the likes o' them.'

'Don't be mean, Lily. Miss Lockwood's worked as hard as we have to keep the mill going,' Dolly reprimanded. She would have continued to defend the woman she admired above all others, barring her mother, but the hooter signalled them back to work.

Back in the office, Verity sat alone mulling over what had just taken place. Out in the yard, the mill hands made their way back to work, their merry chatter reaching her ears. She should feel happy, she told herself, but in the pit of her stomach, she felt nothing but misery.

'You've given them something to cheer about,' Oliver remarked wryly as he came in.

'I made no mention of reducing the hours next year. I heeded your advice,' she asserted, her expression begging his understanding then hesitating as she gave him a rueful glance and muttered, 'However, I did agree to full pay for the extra day's holiday.'

Oliver groaned. A noisy, guttural sound that expressed his despairing feelings. He followed this with a dismissive shrug.

'Please, Oliver. Let's not quarrel about it,' Verity implored.

'I'm not arguing. It's done. You're the boss, and I'm needed in the dyehouse,' he said and picking up a sample of yarn and turning on his heel, he walked out.

At midday, Verity told him she was going out. 'I'm going to meet Millie and Henry in the George Hotel. It's my last chance to see her before she goes to spend Christmas and New Year in

Barnsley with her family. Why don't you come too?' she asked as she pinned on her hat, her smile hopeful.

'Too much to do here if we're to cover the cost of the extra day's holiday,' he said, his curtness sharp as a knife.

Verity sighed, but she didn't persist. Even so, as she travelled into the town, she couldn't shake off the niggling feeling that her relationship with Oliver seemed to be coming apart at the seams. The worry and fear that this caused had her feeling extremely out of sorts by the time she arrived at the hotel.

* * *

'I'm so glad you could come,' Millie said as Verity joined the Shawcrosses in the dining room at the George Hotel. 'You're such a busy working woman you make me quite ashamed of my lazy life.' Millie didn't look at all remorseful, and Verity thought her remark held more than a hint of mockery. She wondered if she was being over-sensitive. She was still feeling hurt and annoyed at Oliver's recalcitrance.

'Indeed, Miss Lockwood seems to spend an unconscionable amount of time at her mill encouraging all manner of things that go against the grain with some of us.'

This time, there was no mistaking Henry's barbed comment and Verity seethed. However, she sought to lighten the mood. 'I'm sure you're busy enough, Millie, preparing for the baby and all that entails,' she said warmly.

'Yes, her lazy days will soon be over once my son's born,' Henry brayed, his arrogance making Verity bristle.

'What makes you so sure the baby will be a boy?' she heard herself say rather more sharply than she intended.

Millie gave her a surprised look. 'If Henry says it's going to be a boy, it will be,' she said firmly. 'He always gets what he wants, don't you, darling?' She patted Henry's hand then turned to Verity. 'I'd like it to be a son and heir too.'

'My father would have liked nothing better,' Verity replied, a sinking feeling invading her stomach as she asked herself why she was behaving in such an ungracious manner? *Stop it*, an inner voice advised. But immediately ignoring the warning, she added, 'But he got me instead.' The bitter words hung like dead crows on a wire.

'But you've taken on his mill just as a son would do. He'd be proud of you.' Millie gabbled, attempting to take the heat out of the awkward conversation.

'I'm not entirely sure Jeb Lockwood would have agreed with you, Millie, my dear.'

Henry's snubbing remark shocked both his wife and Verity and they finished the meal in silence. Then they made their way into a large reception room where several of their acquaintances were already gathered. They were greeted noisily, and Verity found herself surrounded by people intent on making an early start on celebrating Christmas. Still stinging from Henry's cruel jibe, she felt increasingly uncomfortable and more than once, judging by certain hostile glances thrown her way, she suspected that she was the subject of unkind conversations between several of the mill owners. Millie, under Henry's watchful eye, seemed to be avoiding her. That Millie should choose to do this both hurt and angered Verity. Obviously, Millie's first duty was to her husband, but her unfriendly manner surprised Verity. She had believed they had a better understanding of one another. When she saw Millie deep in conversation with Clarence, she felt even more betrayed, and when Millie glanced in her direction with a mischievous glint in her eye, she suspected that something was afoot.

Not for the first time that day, Verity pondered on true

friendship and loyalty; first it had been the unpleasant furore in the canteen, and now Millie. A girl she had been only too glad to have as a friend. Her discomfort spiralled.

* * *

Meanwhile, Oliver mooched from one corner of the mill to another feeling utterly dejected. He still held fast to his argument against extra pay and a reduction in hours, but going against Verity did not sit well with him. He loved her, but she was too naïve, too generous for her own good. Yes, the mill was making a small profit and the order book full but Oliver had experienced how quickly things could change. Jeb had brought the mill to its knees by his profligacy. Now he was afraid that Verity's impetuous philanthropy could soon undo the success that they had fought so hard to achieve. Still, the fact that she ignored his advice did not make him love her any the less, and although it was too late to alter part of the situation, it wasn't too late to make amends. Hurrying to the office, he grabbed his hat and jacket. He'd go to the George. After all, tomorrow he was going to give her the sapphire ring he had bought and set a date for their marriage.

* * *

The hotel lounge was packed with merrymakers. Verity found a seat on the edge of a banquette on which sat the wives of the mill manufacturers she was acquainted with. They studiously ignored her and continued chattering to one another. Waiters in white shirts, black waistcoats and trousers flitted in and out of the tables delivering drinks, and the noise and the heat of so many bodies made Verity feel nauseous. She was still regretting the unfortunate conversation she'd had with Millie and Henry, but having been abandoned by them and ostracised by the women she was sitting beside, she decided it was time to leave. She got to her feet and was halfway to the door when who should bar her way but Clarence Hargreaves.

'My dear Verity,' he brayed drunkenly. 'Allow me to wish you the best of the season and steal a Christmas kiss.' He lunged, grasping her with both arms and pulling her into a tight embrace, his wet, blubbery lips feverishly seeking hers. Verity, caught completely off guard, endeavoured to free herself without causing a scene. Clarence tightened his grip, his lips finding hers in a disgusting, slobbery kiss.

Just then, Oliver walked into the lounge.

Mesmerised, and feeling as though he had been struck by lightning, he couldn't look away, couldn't even blink because once he moved, he knew that nothing in his life would ever be the same. Verity and Hargreaves...

A fury like he had never before felt surged through him. Pushing his way through the throng, his long stride took him swiftly across the room. Grabbing Clarence by the scruff of his neck, he yanked him away from Verity then smashed his fist into Clarence's shocked face. Bones crunched and blood spattered. Verity screamed.

'Oliver! No! No!'

Uproar ensued, some of the mill owners rushing to Clarence's aid and others, agog with excitement and curiosity, cheering the opponents on.

Oliver wiped his fist on his trousers then spinning on his heel, he bolted.

By the time Verity had gathered her wits and fled from the hotel out into St George's Square, Oliver was nowhere in sight.

22

Verity drove the trap back to the mill at breakneck speed. Oliver wasn't there. In a daze of embarrassment, shame and regret, she huddled in the office, awaiting his return. *Damn Clarence Hargreaves and the entire mill-owning fraternity,* she cursed inwardly. None of them mattered a jot. She didn't need them or their approval. But she did need Oliver – not to run her mill but to hold her, tell her he loved her and make her feel whole again.

The silence in the little office was oppressive and she sat listlessly in Oliver's chair, idly lifting his pens and picturing him there with his dark hair falling over his brow and his restless fingers combing it back as he looked up at her, his eyes filled with love.

Shadows lengthened, and still he didn't come. A bitter cold seeped into Verity's bones. Swaying unsteadily, she got to her feet and went and stood in the yard, her heart in her boots as the mill hooter gave its plaintive blast. Machinery rattled and hummed into a silence broken by the jolly shouts of the mill hands as they poured out of the sheds ready to begin their three day holiday. Clogs and boots thudded on the cobbles and cries of, 'Merry Christmas, Miss Lockwood' rang in Verity's ears as the mill hands hurried to the gate.

'I hope you have lovely Christmas, Miss Lockwood,' Dolly cried, her eyes shining and her flame-red hair springing free from her turban as she tugged it off and bounced up to Verity. Her sincere felicitations brought tears to Verity's eyes.

She blinked. 'Thank you, Dolly. The same to you. Give my regards to Theo and your parents,' she replied, swallowing the lump in her throat and pasting on a smile.

'Oy, come on, Dolly. We're all off to the Somerset Arms for pint,' George shouted. He grinned at Verity and said, 'Why don't you join us, Miss Lockwood?'

Verity forced another smile and shook her head. 'Things to do, George, but thank you for asking.'

'Well, you know where we'll be if you change your mind. Merry Christmas.' Nellie echoed his words and, tucking her arms into George's and Dolly's, the three of them headed off to the pub. Gradually, the stream of noisy workers dwindled to nothing.

The silence in the mill yard seemed to swell and grow, and Verity felt a moment of violent loneliness. There was still no sign of Oliver. Joe, the grizzled old gateman shuffled towards her. 'I've all locked up. Will tha be long, Miss Lockwood?' he asked, eager to be off and join the others in the Somerset Arms. He licked his lips at the thought of a pint.

'Just give me a minute, Joe,' she said, stepping back into the office and breathing in the faint tang of Oliver's cologne. She gazed at his empty chair. Where had he gone? And what was he thinking. She had to find him.

The office locked and the pony and trap at the gate, she wished Joe the best of the season. The mill gates clanked shut, the sound echoing on the frosty air like a death knell. Verity shuddered. Slowly, she drove to Oliver's home at the foot of Almondbury Bank.

'Good evening, Mrs Hardcastle. I'm here to see Oliver.'

'Oh dear, you've just missed him. Was it something to do with the mill you wanted him for?' Evelyn's voice was cold and her eyes stony.

'Where has he gone?' Even to her own ears, Verity knew she sounded pathetic.

Evelyn drew back her head, glancing round the door jamb into the parlour. 'It's a quarter past six so I'd say he'll be on his way to Ambleside by now. His train left at half-past five.' A smug little smile curved her lips when she saw Verity blanch.

'When will he be back?' Verity asked, her voice barely a whisper.

'He didn't say, but I don't think it will be any time soon. Goodbye, Miss Lockwood.' Evelyn stepped back, closing the door with a short, sharp slam.

Verity stared at the shiny black door. She felt faint, and before her legs could buckle under her, she tottered to the trap and drove homeward, engulfed in troubled thoughts that were as dark as the twilight shadows.

Her stomach curdled at the thought of being without him, and her mind reeled with all the things she needed to explain. But Oliver was gone. He'd left without giving her a chance to tell him that Clarence meant nothing to her, that she was in no way to blame for what had happened in the hotel. But was that true? The cold realisation that it was blatantly untrue made her shiver so violently that she yanked on the pony's reins and came to a sudden stop. Eventually, she reached the conclusion that it was her fault for spending so much time in Clarence's company, and although she hadn't encouraged him, she hadn't entirely dismissed his pursuit of her. She had been too enthralled by the attention she'd received from the mill-owning clique, and so full of her own importance that she had neglected Oliver. The reality of this made her feel like weeping but before her tears could fall, a spurt of rage flooded her veins. Surely Oliver should know her better than this? Hadn't she proved her love for him? He must know that she would never betray him. Yet he'd cast her aside like an old rag and gone off to Ambleside without a thought for her.

By the time she reached home, Verity's mood was blacker than the night sky.

* * *

'Eeh, Miss Verity, are you sure you don't need me to come in over Christmas?' Clara said, wringing her hands and shaking her head in disbelief when Verity told her to stay away until the day after Boxing Day.

'I'll manage perfectly, Mrs Medley,' Verity said bravely even though she was having difficulty holding herself together in front of the housekeeper. 'There's plenty of food in the larder, and I can feed myself as I choose. I don't need to be waited on, and I shall be out for much of the time,' she lied, thinking of the goose and the trimmings she had intended to share with Oliver on Boxing Day and her lips began to tremble.

Clara looked at her anxiously. 'Well... if you're sure... you will be all right, won't you?' She lifted her shawl and, her curiosity getting the better of her, she asked, 'Will Mr Hardcastle be calling on you?'

Verity gulped. It felt like swallowing stones. 'Mr Hardcastle has gone on holiday,' she croaked. 'Now, off you go and enjoy Christmas with your family. Give my regards to Bert.'

Clara let herself out of the back door and headed off into the night. *Summat's gone wrong, and it's to do wi' that manager.* She'd suspected for some time now that there was more going on between Verity and Oliver than just mill business, and now he'd let her down. Her kind heart ached for the poor, lonely girl but there was nothing she could do about it. Verity was the mistress and she gave the orders.

Alone in the kitchen, Verity gave way to her grief.

* * *

On Wednesday morning, Verity rose early, eager to go to the mill. The last three days had been a nightmare of weeping, toying with badly cooked food for which she had no appetite, and sleepless nights. She dressed carefully and applied make-up to her ravaged face just in case Oliver returned. Then hearing Clara rattling pans in the kitchen, she went downstairs.

Seeing her mistress dressed for outdoors, the housekeeper said, 'You'll take a bit o' breakfast afore you leave, Miss Verity.'

'I've already eaten, thank you, Mrs Medley.'

Verity's lie did not fool Clara. The untouched food in the larder also told its story. She looked at her mistress's haggard face and red-rimmed eyes. 'Is there owt I can do to help, lass?'

'Nothing,' Verity replied, her hollow voice tugging at Clara's heart.

'Medley has the trap ready for thi, Miss Verity,' said Clara. But what she really wanted to do was to take Verity in her arms and comfort her as she spilled out her misery, tell her that no man was worth the heartache and that a lovely girl like her would soon find someone else. Sadly, she watched her mistress leave.

The December morning was chill and snow had fallen during the night, a crisp, white layer blanketing the roads and fields. As Verity steered the trap down the steep incline, a great desolation swept over her, and she saw an empty wasteland stretching before her, her life as bare as the trees on the wayside. She passed by Aunt Martha's empty house, reflecting on how much she missed the old lady, and wondered how she was faring in Pateley Bridge.

When she arrived at the mill and entered the office, she knew that Oliver had not returned. Everything was as she had left it on Friday evening. She stared at his empty chair, his pens and a pair of armbands he had left on the desk. This was a place of too many memories. Every nook and cranny seemed to hold a happiness she now no longer felt. She hurried out into the yard.

Take control, pretend everything is as it should be, she told herself as she did her rounds of the mill, moving from the scouring and bleaching and carding then to the dyehouse and the spinning room: so many things to check on and her mind not really on any of them. On reaching the weaving shed, she walked down 'weaver's alley' and, arriving at Dolly's loom, she paused, her heart heavy.

Dolly greeted her with a big smile and above the roar of her thrashing loom, she mouthed, 'Good morning, Miss Lockwood.'

Verity returned the smile, although hers was wan and didn't reach her eyes. She had to suppress the urge to take Dolly on one side and express all that was troubling her. It would be salving to have a friend in whom she could confide the dreadful events of the past few days. Millie was still in Barnsley, and even if she had been at home, Verity was uncertain of her welcome. Henry would make sure of that. And was Millie's friendship as sincere as Verity had once thought it was? Verity didn't know what to think, and as she stood watching the shuttle fly back and forth on Dolly's loom, she dwelt on the fact that Dolly Armitage was the nearest thing she had to a real friend.

Her thoughts tumbling, Verity moved away and after exchanging a few words with the Mrs Weaver, she went back to the office. It was not yet half-past eight and the day, cold and bleak, stretched endlessly in front of her in a miserable haze.

* * *

Days crawled by in a pointless spiral. She felt numb, incapable of feeling anything, not even grief. She existed in a dream-like state where nothing seemed solid, not even the ground under her feet. Matters were not helped by the mill hands asking her where Mr Hardcastle was, and looks of disbelief were followed by speculative gossip that did not escape her ears when Verity tersely told them that he was taking a holiday.

Pride would not allow her to go back to the Hardcastle's house and ask Evelyn if she'd had any word of when Oliver might return. She had to learn to manage without him.

When Millie returned from Barnsley the week after New Year had been celebrated, she sent a note inviting Verity to her birthday party at the house in Lindley. Feeling the need to ease her aching loneliness in the evenings that had once been filled with Oliver's presence, and nursing a curious dread as to what had been said about her after the debacle in the George Hotel, Verity accepted. Maybe she could steal a moment of Millie's time to find out. She would have to face her mill-owning acquaintances sometime. She couldn't live in hiding for the unseeable future.

The night before Millie's party, Verity took the Friday evening reading class that now numbered twenty pupils. The classes were convivial affairs with those who were now able readers helping those who had recently joined. The laughter and chatter as the mill hands shared their knowledge should have been uplifting, but Verity took little pleasure from it, merely going through the motions and relying on Dolly to organise things.

At the end of the session, Dolly, aware of Verity's discontent and saddened to see that the spark for teaching had died, took matters into her own hands.

'Are the classes becoming too much for you, Miss Lockwood?' she asked once they were alone. 'You've a lot on now you're running the mill on your own.' When Verity didn't immediately answer, Dolly took a deep breath and said, 'You're missing Mr Hardcastle, aren't you?'

A stab of pain at the mention of his name pierced Verity's heart so sharply that she flinched, and the despair that suffused her face tugged at Dolly's sympathy.

'Do you want to talk about it?' she asked.

'I do miss him, Dolly. Mr Hardcastle was very much part of the mill,' said Verity, struggling for composure and failing miserably.

'And was he a part of your life outside the mill?' Dolly ventured. Her own love life was so perfect, she couldn't bear to think that her mistress's anguish was caused by something that involved Oliver Hardcastle. Casting caution to the wind and dearly hoping she wasn't being impertinent, she said, 'I've thought for a long time that you and Mr Hardcastle were more than just good friends. I could tell by the way you looked at one another. You made each other happy.' She paused, thinking that she'd said too much, then unwilling to leave it there, she asked, 'Have you fallen out? Is that why he's not here any more?'

Verity felt tears building behind her eyes and bit down on her lip to stop them from spilling over. After all, she was the mill mistress. But Dolly was her friend, and she knew that her concern was genuine. What was it they said? A trouble shared is a trouble halved.

'It's true that Oliver and I did have an understanding, Dolly,' she said evenly. 'But we quarrelled, then something dreadful happened to make things worse.'

'Tell me about it. It sometimes helps,' Dolly said gently.

In a low voice, Verity told Dolly how her love for Oliver and his for her had grown and that they had planned to get engaged on Christmas Eve then marry in the spring. And feeling utterly wretched, she went on to tell her about Clarence Hargreaves and the scene in the hotel. 'I've ruined everything, and I don't know how to make reparation,' she concluded dismally.

'Mr Hardcastle must love you very much if he felt hurt enough to punch Hargreaves and then leave his home and his job.'

Verity blinked. All this time, they had been standing facing one another. Now, Verity plumped down on the nearest bench, staggered by Dolly's sage deduction. It had not occurred to her that he had left because he was heartbroken. Angry, yes, but not hurt beyond bearing.

'Do you think so?' she asked, marvelling at the idea.

'Course I do. If what Hargreaves did to you had meant nothing to Mr Hardcastle, he wouldn't have given him a hiding. He was angry and hurt. He might be thinking that you and Mr Hargreaves are carrying on behind his back. That 'ud make any man mad. Mad enough to lash out then walk away from a job he's put his heart and soul into for years and years, and devastated to think that the woman he loved had betrayed him.'

Verity digested Dolly's words and saw the truth in them. 'But how can I let Oliver know that I love only him and detest Clarence Hargreaves? I don't even know where Oliver is.'

Verity's impassioned cry had Dolly taking her hand and giving it an encouraging squeeze.

'He'll come and find you. If he really loves you, he'll be back before long.'

Verity pulled her hand free and embraced Dolly with both arms. 'Thank you for listening, Dolly. You've given me hope.' She drew back and looked deeply into Dolly's face. 'You're a really good friend, and I want you to think of me as your friend. From now on, whenever we're not at work, I'd like you to call me Verity. And I'd like you and Theo to visit me at Far View, like friends do. Please say you will.'

'I've always thought of you as a friend, Miss Lo... Verity. But for the time being, I think we should keep this just between us.' Dolly laughed. 'Lily Cockhill 'ud have a field day if she thought I was being favoured, and she'd not be the only one.'

'Did anyone ever tell you that you're wise beyond your years, Dolly Armitage?'

'I'm not sure me mam would agree with that,' Dolly chirped.

* * *

The next evening, a hard frost on impacted snow made the roads like glass and Verity chose to forgo the journey to Millie's birthday party in the pony and trap and hired a hackney cab. As it trundled through the dark streets from Almondbury to Lindley, she anticipated the evening ahead. Millie's invitation must mean she had put the dreadful incident in the George Hotel to bed and wanted to continue their friendship. Verity dearly hoped so and was looking forward to meeting her again, but she quivered at the thought of being in the company of the other mill owners. They would be keen to know why Oliver had left Lockwood Mill. She was sure that this and the incident with

Clarence Hargreaves would be uppermost in the minds of the gossipmongers. Another thing of which she was fairly certain was that Clarence would not be there; if Millie was truly her kind, thoughtful friend, she would not subject her to being in the same room as him. With this in mind, her emotions see-sawed from optimism to dread, and as she arrived at the house her nerves were on edge.

From the upshot, the party was a disaster. Millie, rosy and blooming in her sixth month of pregnancy, was so busy entertaining her guests that Verity had no opportunity to speak with her at length. When she approached a small group of women whom she had thought of as friends, the air bristled with antagonism and, embarrassed, Verity hurried away to be by herself. As she stood disconsolately sipping a sweet sherry, she was cornered by two irate mill owners who accused her of breaking with tradition by granting her workers three days' holiday. Then two elderly matrons and their husbands sidled up to her, the women making sly remarks about her relationship with Clarence and the men asking all sorts of awkward questions about the mill and Oliver.

By now, the large drawing room thronged with people and, feeling hot and bothered, Verity went and stood by the French doors. Half-hidden by the heavy, velvet drapes, she gazed out at the garden, and her head swimming with the heat and the noise, she opened the door. She didn't see Clarence as he swaggered into the room – but he saw her.

Verity stepped out into the cool night air, and in a shaft of light from the open door, she wandered across the frosty lawn, heedless of the dampness soaking into her shoes. Clarence pushed his way through the throng, briefly acknowledging those who greeted him, then he darted to the French doors and ducked out, his excitement making him gasp for breath. Slowing his pace, he crept up on her, his footsteps muffled by the wet grass.

In the shadow of an ancient oak, Verity stopped to admire a snowberry bush. Tiny, white, waxy balls dangled in ghostly profusion from fragile, wiry stems like lanterns lighting up the blackness, and she was just thinking how beautiful the gifts of nature were when she was gripped from behind by a pair of strong arms. She yelped with fright but her body froze as though suddenly paralysed. Fumes of alcohol wafted in her nose as she was yanked round. Clarence's florid face leered into hers and she gave a little scream. He tightened his hold.

'Got you now, all to myself,' he slurred.

'Let go of me!'

Verity struggled to free herself but this only increased Clarence's ardour. He pushed against her until her back pressed against the oak tree's trunk, its bark biting through the soft fabric of her dress. She squirmed as Clarence, imprisoning her with his bulk, brushed his lips over her cheek and neck then began to burble endearments into her ear.

'I desire you with all my heart, my dear girl. I long to make you mine,' he babbled. 'Think of it, Verity. What a fruitful union ours would be. I'm offering you the opportunity to marry into one of the oldest, most prestigious families in the valley. Your mill united with mine.' His blubbery lips slid from her ear to her mouth.

Revulsion like she had never before felt rose in Verity's throat and for a moment, she was so overwhelmed by it that she ceased to struggle. Clarence relaxed his grip.

Verity saw her chance. Lashing out with hands and feet, she sent him sprawling and, towering over his prone body, she stared down at him with eyes as cold as honed steel. It was Clarence's lustful attack that had driven Oliver away; he was to blame for the stress she felt when things went wrong at her mill, and the reason why the other mill owners at the party had ostracised her. Her emotions spiralled into a frenzy of rage and disgust.

Barely aware of what she was doing, she brought her foot down hard on Clarence's neck.

His eyes bulged. A whimpering, choking sound escaped his lips. He looked very afraid.

'I wouldn't marry you if you were the last man on earth,' Verity snarled before slowly raising her foot and stepping away from him. 'Never approach me again.'

Clarence spluttered. 'You'll regret this, you bitch,' he croaked. 'I'll make you pay.'

Giving him one final glare of fury and hatred, Verity took flight, her shoe soles slipping on the wet grass as she ran round the side of the house to the front door. In the hallway, the maid's eyes boggled as she handed Verity her cape. Hysterical laughter bubbled in Verity's throat as she caught sight of her dishevelled appearance in the mirror. But she was past caring. *Damn them all.* The mill owners, their wives, and most of all, Clarence Hargreaves. From now on, she would plough her own furrow.

23

Verity had only a vague recollection of how she had got home, but the next morning, she woke with a newfound sense of determination. Work, she promised herself as she climbed out of bed. Work would be her salvation. There was plenty to organise, much to do, and today, she would see that it was done.

'Is this the order for Spellman's?' Verity asked as she inspected five bolts of worsted in the baling shed later that day. Bill Farrar told her that it was. She lifted one of the bolts, frowning as she felt its weight. She set it back down. Spellman's was a small garment factory in Bradford, and although the worsted came off the loom in lengths of two hundred-and-fifty yards, they preferred to have their cloth delivered in bolts measuring fifty yards.

'Who measured and cut these lengths?' she tersely asked Bill.

Bill stopped readying the large brown paper sheets that they used to wrap the bolts.

'Cyril,' he said, nodding his head in the direction of a thin, sallow-looking man who had recently come to work in the mill.

Cyril raised his gaze from the bale he was handling and glanced from Bill to Verity, his expression surly.

Verity's eyes narrowed.

'Measure that length, Bill,' she ordered. He did so, his face creasing and his neck reddening as he laid the last yard against the brass measuring ferule on the edge of the table.

'There's nobbut forty-seven yards i' this one,' he spluttered.

'Measure the rest,' said Verity, her cold eyes fixed accusingly on Cyril as she stood, arms folded and her foot tapping impatiently as Bill measured each of the bales.

'They're all short by two or three yards,' Bill said eventually and glared at Cyril before looking apologetically at Verity. 'He wa' measuring fine t'other day when I checked what he wa' doin'. I thought it wa' safe to let him get on wi' it.'

'Where's the missing yardage, Cyril? Twelve or fifteen yards of worsted doesn't just disappear into thin air.' Verity's steely gaze and icy voice made Cyril cringe.

'I... I don't bloody know,' he blustered, his expression ugly and his eyes shifty.

'Where does he keep his coat?' Verity asked Bill.

'Over here,' said Bill, hurrying to the corner of the shed with Verity hot on his heels.

Cyril let out a roar and bolted for the door. Bill whipped round, ready to give chase. Verity put a restraining hand on Bill's arm, her other hand holding a few yards of worsted that had been hidden inside Cyril's overcoat. 'Let him go; it saves sacking him,' she said wearily.

'Nay, he should be prosecuted, Miss Lockwood,' Bill protested. 'An' what about rest o' t'stuff he's pinched? There's no more than three yards there.' He gestured at the cloth in Verity's hands.

'He'll have already sold it on,' she said with a disconsolate smile. 'We're well rid of him, and don't blame yourself for his dishonesty, Bill.' She patted the arm of the man who had worked at Lockwood Mill all his working life. He was a good man. 'Just keep a sharper eye on the job in future, eh?'

'I will, Miss Lockwood, I will,' Bill promised. 'I'm shamed it happened.'

Verity gave him a reassuring smile, but as she walked out of the baling shed, she wondered if any of her other employees were taking advantage of her in Oliver's absence. Thieving was a punishable offence.

At midday, she went to the canteen and, calling for the attention of the mill hands tucking into hot soup or eating the snap they brought from home, she told them about the incident. 'I could have him arrested,' she said, her voice hardening as she added, 'and if I find anyone else stealing from my mill, I won't hesitate to call in the law.' She gave a sad smile. 'You see, if you steal from me, you are stealing from yourselves. This mill relies on keeping our customers satisfied. If we fail to fulfil their orders properly, it will result in us having no one willing to buy our cloth. Then the mill will have to close down and you will be out of work. I like to think we're all in this together, doing the best we can to make our mill a successful, happy place. I hope you feel the same.'

Her solemn speech delivered, she walked quickly from the canteen to a rumble of mutterings that grew to a roar as the mill hands cheered her on her way.

Feeling both exhilarated and exhausted at one and the same time, she went and sat in the office. The workers were on her side – for now. But where was Oliver?

* * *

One day ran into the next, but try as she might, things did not go as she wished. A carding machine, old and in need of replacement, broke down again. 'If Mr Hardcastle was here, he'd know how to fix it. He always did,' the gloomy operator told her. Verity too wished Oliver was there, not to mend the blasted carding machine but to take her in his arms and tell her she was doing a good job.

But I'm not. I'm barely coping, she told herself as one miserable day followed another.

A consignment of wool she had bought from a new supplier was substandard; the spinners complaining that the fibres were weak and the thread breaking on the looms, much to the weavers' annoyance. Each day brought some new disaster, and Verity realised just how much Oliver had contributed to the running of the mill, that daily, he had attended to matters of which she had little or no knowledge.

Six weeks without him and she felt crushed by the sheer weight of responsibility, as though she would snap under the strain. She dreaded each day, shafts of panic lancing through her as though she was in some strange, dark place from which there was no escape. Nowhere felt safe.

And the least safe place were the hours she spent alone each night.

She would have gladly given up her inheritance just to have him back. The mill's problems were trivial when she compared them with the loss of Oliver's smile, his gentle voice, and the feel of his strong arms as he held her close, kissed her and told her that he loved her. She, who had never been afraid of the dark, now feared night-time, the sleepless struggle to stifle her tears, the haunting dreams that suddenly wakened her, and the sinking feeling that came with each day that she had to face without him.

Then, just when she thought things couldn't be worse, she received a brief note from her aunt's niece, Cora, informing her that Martha had died peacefully in her sleep and that the funeral was on Friday. So, on a wet and windy day in March, she travelled to Pateley Bridge feeling guilty at not having made time to visit her aunt before her death. With a heavy heart, she watched as Martha was buried alongside her late husband, Joseph, in a bleak, windswept graveyard and came away not in the least surprised to learn that her aunt had bequeathed her property to Cora.

* * *

Time was making no difference at all. There were days and nights when she wanted Oliver back so badly that it made her feel sick. She slept restlessly, the shadows beneath her eyes purple and ugly lines etching her mouth. These did not escape Dolly's notice, and one day at dinnertime, she broached Verity in her office.

'Excuse me, Miss Lockwood,' she said on entering, 'but are you feeling unwell?'

Verity raised her gaze from the mound of paperwork cluttering the desk, and hollow-eyed, she stared at Dolly as if she had been wakened from a nightmare.

'We can't meet Hepworth's order on time and they're threatening to take their business elsewhere.' Verity's voice broke under the strain. She buried her head in her hands.

Dolly dithered. What could she say or do? Even though Verity was her friend and she desperately wanted to help her, was she in a position to tell her where she had gone wrong? She stood, deep in thought. Since Oliver Hardcastle's departure, she'd noticed a laxness in the weaving shed and in other parts of the mill, the workers taking advantage of Verity's distraction. They liked her well enough, but she was a woman. It was Oliver who had kept them in line.

Eventually, after voicing her thoughts, she said, 'I might have spoken out of turn... but they see you as a soft touch, Verity. They take your kindness and generosity for granted and it's making them careless and idle.' She gave Verity a look that asked if she'd overstepped the mark.

Verity nodded ruefully, aware that without Oliver there to curb her need to be seen as a fair boss, unlike her father, that what Dolly had just told her was true.

'What do you think I should do?'

'Well, you could still get Hepworth's order out on time if you tell the spinners and the weavers that they have work overtime all this week. Tell 'em the mill depends on it, and while you're at it...' Dolly sharpened her tone of voice, 'remind them of how good you've been to 'em in the past.'

'Overtime?' Verity's eyes widened. 'Why didn't I think of that?'

'Because your mind's on other things and seeing as it doesn't look as though Mr Hardcastle's coming back, it's up to you to crack the whip and show 'em who's boss.'

'It is, isn't it.' Verity got to her feet and, giving Dolly a brave smile, she hurried to the canteen.

Calling for the mill hands' attention, Verity outlined the need for them to work extra hours.

The room vibrated with muttering and grumbling and someone shouted, 'Have you squared this wi' t'Union?'

Verity overruled the heckler. Then, in carefully couched words, she spoke of teamwork, praising the workers for their efforts in the past, and steeling her voice, she reminded them that it was orders like the Hepworth's that paid their wages and that success had to be earned.

'If that means we have to work overtime then overtime it will be,' she concluded.

Heads nodded in agreement, and several voices called out, 'Right you are, Mrs Hardcastle,' and, 'We'll see that it gets done.'

'It was like buttering parsnips,' Dolly said as the workers left the canteen. 'You had 'em eating out of your hand by the time you finished.'

Verity, her cheeks blazing with exertion, laughed grimly. 'Thanks again, Dolly.'

* * *

In the next few weeks, some surprising changes took place in Lockwood Mill. Lengthy discussions at Fair View House with Dolly, and sometimes Theo, resulted in Dolly moving out of the weaving shed and into the mill office.

'I can't cope with invoices and all the other paperwork on my own – Oliver and I always did that together – and I'm in a muddle. I need someone who can read and write, and understands how the mill works,' Verity had sadly admitted as she gave Dolly a hopeful look. 'I can't think of anyone I'd rather have to help me out, so what do you say, Dolly?'

Dolly had been stunned and thrilled. Whilst she didn't dislike weaving, she had always dreamed of doing a job that challenged her brain rather than just her hands. She'd readily agreed to Verity's offer, and when George was promoted to oversee all the processes in the mill, which he gladly accepted along with an increase in his wages, their mother's heart had swelled with pride.

'We're going up in the world, Georgie boy,' Dolly said one

morning in March as they walked to the mill, Dolly wearing a smart grey skirt and white blouse under her coat rather than her overall.

'We are, Dolly, and I'm glad of it. I don't mind doing that bit extra, and the wages are more than welcome,' her brother replied, slowing his pace then pausing his stride to look at her. 'I'm thinking of asking Nellie to marry me later on in the year. What do you think?'

'Oh George! That's wonderful,' Dolly exclaimed, throwing her arms round him and giving him a big hug. 'You make a lovely couple, and Nellie will be over the moon.' They resumed walking and had only gone a few paces when Dolly pulled George to a stop. 'Hey, why don't you ask her now and we could have a double wedding, me and Theo and you and Nellie,' she cried, her eyes sparkling.

'Are you sure you'd want that?' George looked surprised.

'It 'ud make sense. Mam and Dad will only have to fork out for one wedding instead of two. If we all share the expense, it'll work out cheaper and we'll be saving money to put towards our new homes.' Dolly's excitement was mounting by the minute as she skipped along at George's side.

'That's true, and it 'ud be a grand celebration us getting wed on the same day,' said George, his enthusiasm now matching her own. 'I really do want to marry Nellie but...' he gave a deep sigh, 'we'll have to find somewhere to live first. I don't want to start married life with Mam and Dad, and I definitely don't want to live with the Haighs.'

Dolly grimaced at the mention of the overcrowded house in Tinker's Yard. 'Aye, you'd most likely end up having to share a bed with Pip and Nellie 'ud still be sleeping with Maggie and Dora.'

This made them both laugh, but George soon looked miserable again.

'Don't worry, George, you'll find somewhere,' Dolly said, giving his arm a squeeze. 'Just lately, luck seems to be on our side.'

'Lucky for you since Sir Arnold's granted Theo a cottage up at Thornton Hall.'

'Yes, it is, and I could hardly believe it,' she agreed, 'but as I just said, things seem to be in our favour what with you being the mill's overseer and me in the office. The future's bright, Georgie. Just wait and see.'

George sighed again. 'I suppose you're right, Dolly. We've a lot to be thankful for.'

By now, they'd reached the mill gate and as the gatekeeper saluted him, George's spirits rose. Miss Lockwood trusted him and the mill hands respected him. He was worrying unnecessarily.

'You're not too grand to speak to us then,' Lily scoffed when he and Dolly called out cheery greetings to their workmates as they walked into the mill yard.

Dolly and George laughed and chorused, 'Morning, Lily.' They were both so popular with their workmates that nobody begrudged them their new positions, although Dolly's promotion had been met with a derisory sniff from the Mrs Weaver, Gertie Spragg.

'Good morning, Miss Lockwood,' Dolly said as she entered the office. They had agreed that she should only address her as Verity when they were not at the mill.

'Good morning, Miss Armitage.' Verity's formal use of the title made them both grin.

They worked well together, and by the time Verity was due to do her rounds of the mill, Dolly had the invoices ready for posting.

'I'll nip to the post office to catch the first collection,' Dolly said, pulling on her coat.

They walked together out into the mill yard, Dolly to the gate and Verity to the dyehouse. George greeted her with a beaming smile. 'All's well this morning, Miss Lockwood. The new yarns are top quality and taking the dyes perfectly.' He gestured to the huge, steaming vats.

'I'm glad to hear it, and thank you, George.' She gave him a warm smile, knowing that he would have already done his rounds checking on machinery and deliveries. 'Have the two broken spinning mules been fixed, and has the raw wool been delivered?'

George assured her that they had and Verity continued her rounds, her step lighter.

Things were going well, and although she felt exhausted for much of the time, she clung to the belief that her efforts were not in vain. But no matter how successful the mill might be, it wasn't the same without Oliver by her side. She had given up all hope of him returning. As she made her way up to the spinning room, she felt such a deep sense of loss and emptiness that her head started to spin and she feared she might fall. Tears spilled down her cheeks. Leaned against the stair rail, she pressed her eyes shut and clamped her lips together to stem the tide, forcing herself to harden her heart. She didn't need a man in her life. She was the mill mistress, a businesswoman with no time for romantic notions. Love was for those who had nothing better to do. Over and again, as though she was donning a suit of armour, she dismissed all the reasons for wanting to be loved. Her composure regained, she mounted the stairs. She was afraid to feel. Numbness was far safer. It didn't hurt.

* * *

Dolly was just about to leave the post office when Evelyn Hardcastle walked in carrying a small parcel. 'Good morning, Mrs Hardcastle,' Dolly said cheerily, then cocking her head on one side, she asked, 'Any word from Mr Hardcastle? We do miss him at the mill.'

Oliver's mother had known Dolly from when she was a little girl. She'd heard about her promotion and how she was now working in the mill office with that woman who had driven her beloved son away from home. She glared into Dolly's enquiring, green eyes. 'My son is fine, thank you for asking,' she snapped, 'and you can tell that deceitful mistress of yours that he has no need of her, or her mill.'

Dolly's jaw dropped. She hadn't expected the vitriolic response. Then she saw that the older woman was close to tears. Aware that the postmaster was craning his neck and listening in, she took Evelyn by the elbow and ushered her outside. 'Oh, Mrs Hardcastle. I didn't mean to upset you. I am sorry. I was just asking, that's all. We all loved Mr Hardcastle.'

Evelyn sniffed. '*She didn't!* My lad gave his heart and soul to her, more fool him. And all the time, she was playing around behind his back with that Hargreaves fellow from Dogley Grange.' Evelyn seemed to shrink inside her coat, her shoulders sagging, the absence of her son too painful to bear. Then struggling to gain control of her emotions, she said, 'I warned my Oliver not to mix business with pleasure, but he wouldn't listen. I told him women of her class looked to their own sort for husbands, that she was only being nice to him so that he'd work his fingers to the bone running that mill of hers.' She shook her head angrily. 'And once it was back on its feet, she played him foul.'

'No! No, Mrs Hardcastle. It wasn't like that,' Dolly cried. 'It was all a dreadful misunderstanding. Verity loves Oliver. She was devastated when he went away – still is. Clarence Hargreaves had been after her for ages but she hates him. He wanted to marry her to get his hands on her mill but she would have nothing to do with him.' Dolly paused for breath, her eyes entreating Evelyn to believe her. 'When the drunken fool was foisting himself on her in the George Hotel, your Oliver saw it and didn't even wait for Verity to explain the truth of the matter.' Her cheeks on fire, Dolly looked at Evelyn, hopeful that she had done justice to Verity's side of the story.

'Is that what really happened?' Evelyn didn't sound entirely convinced.

'Absolutely! Verity loves Oliver with all her heart and...' Dolly hesitated – was she speaking out of turn, she wondered – 'and you'd do both of them and yourself a favour if you let Oliver know the truth of it the next time you write to him, Mrs Hardcastle.' Fearing she'd said too much, she patted Evelyn's arm and dashed back to the mill.

Back in the office, she made no mention of her meeting with Oliver's mother. Better to wait and see what transpired than to give Verity false hope.

* * *

George waited at the mill gates that evening for Nellie to come from the weaving shed. His heart was thumping; what if Nellie turned him down? Theirs was a romance that had grown out of mutual friendship and the need for company since Amy had betrayed him and Dolly spent all her free time with Theo. But they had never talked about marriage; they'd just had fun. And affectionate as Nellie was, she might not want him as a husband.

He twisted his large, dye-stained hands, his palms clammy at the thought of what he was about to ask.

Out she came, her mousy hair bouncing as she ran across the yard to the office to call for Dolly. They often walked home together. Dolly, still hugging her secret exchange with Mrs Hardcastle, bade Verity goodnight and stepped outside to where Nellie waited. When George joined them, his sister gave him a sly nod and an encouraging wink.

'Oh, there's Lily. I just want a word with her,' Dolly said, dashing on ahead to catch up with Lily before Nellie and George could respond.

George would have liked to make his proposal in a more romantic setting but, enthused by his earlier conversation with Dolly, he wanted to get it over and done with and know how he stood. Tucking Nellie's arm into his, he waited until they came to where she would leave him to go to Tinker's Yard and he to Silver Street. Close by was a short flight of ancient steps that led down to the towpath.

'Let's take a little walk, eh?' he said, leading Nellie down the steps then further along the path, away from the noise of the traffic. The river tumbled on its way to the sea, its white-crested waters swirling around boulders or slinking in and out of trailing reeds and its grassy banks dotted with early celandines. This was nicer than the pavement in George's opinion.

'Where are we going?' Nellie's confusion raised her voice an octave.

George got down on one knee. Nellie gaped at him. George cleared his throat.

'Nellie Haigh, will you do me the honour of becoming my wife?'

Nellie's mouth shaped a big, round O. Then giving something between a scream and a giggle, she flung herself at George, toppling them down the riverbank and almost into the water as she gasped, 'Oh, George! I thought you'd never ask.'

They teetered on the river's edge, clinging to one another for joy.

'I take it that that's a yes then,' said George before scrambling up to the towpath and pulling Nellie with him.

'Yes! Yes! Yes!' Nellie warbled as they brushed the dirt from their clothes. Then arm in arm, they clambered back up the steps to the road. On their way to Tinker's Yard to break the news to the Haighs, George told her of Dolly's suggestion.

'A double wedding! I can't think of anything I'd like more,' Nellie said, wiping happy tears from her cheeks. 'It's like a fairy tale, George, a fairy tale.'

24

Oliver Hardcastle leaned on his spade and gazed into the distance at Wasdale Pike. Low white clouds scudded across a blue sky threatening another April shower. He was digging ditches on his cousin's farm outside Ambleside, just one of the many manual jobs he had undertaken in the past three months in the hope of counteracting the misery he had felt ever since he had seen Verity in Clarence Hargreaves's arms. The violent anger that had driven him away from home, the mill and Verity had gradually died and now, at best, he felt deeply disappointed and at worst, he was heartbroken.

He found it hard to believe that Verity had never truly loved him. She had seemed so genuinely affectionate when they were alone. But was that the nub of it? Had he just been an exciting dalliance whilst she looked for a husband whose social standing matched her own? It didn't seem possible. She had appeared to be so innocent and kind-hearted. All the changes she had made in the mill had been for the benefit of the mill hands, and she had generously given her time with the reading and sewing classes to better their lives. Surely, they were not the actions of a devious schemer. He scuffed his boot in the loose soil, the memory of something she had once said invading his thoughts. Ah, yes. She had a Machiavellian streak; she manipulated people. Had she manipulated him? He looked up at the scudding clouds and cursed himself for a fool. He had allowed himself to dream, to believe, and it had all been a fantasy of his own making.

Don't get involved. His mother's words echoed like a distant warning.

But it was too late for that. He was already involved. He loved Verity Lockwood with every fibre of his being and he knew that life without her would...

The heavens opened, huge spots of rain spattering the crown of his head and his bare arms. Pulling the spade from the soil, he ran across the field to the stackyard and into the farmhouse. The delicious smell of frying bacon met him as he entered the warm, cosy kitchen. He hooked his foot under the rung of the nearest chair and, pulling it away from the table, he sat down.

Sylvia, his cousin's wife, smiled at him. 'You timed it well, Ollie. Got rained off, did you?' She tossed him a towel. 'I'm doing a fry. Do you want one egg or two?'

'Two,' Oliver replied, towelling his hair and arms. The good food and fresh air, along with the physical labour, had toned his muscles and tanned his skin and the already handsome man had acquired a virility that made him even more attractive.

'There's a letter for you on the mantelshelf.' Sylvia gestured with the fork she was using to turn the bacon. 'The postman told me Mrs Holt at the farm down the road got a letter telling her that her son has been killed in South Africa.' She slapped the fork on the range. 'The poor soul's demented,' she continued hotly. 'Them Dutch Boers have a lot to answer for, and our lads shouldn't be fighting a war that has nothing to do with us.'

Oliver wasn't listening. He was reading his mother's letter for the second time, a gamut of emotions flitting across his face and through his mind. He pushed back his chair.

'I'm leaving,' he said. 'I'll go and pack my things.'

Sylvia whirled round, shocked. 'Leaving! Why? What's up? Is it your mother?'

'No, she's fine.' Oliver hurried to the stairs, and with his bag packed, he was back in the kitchen, ready to leave when his cousin, Alf, walked in. Seeing Oliver in his coat and hat and the bulging bag in his hand, Alf gaped. 'Going somewhere?'

Oliver grinned. 'Back to Huddersfield to repair the damage I've caused. I've been a fool burying my head in the sand up here when I should have been man enough to face up to my problems and put them right. If I go now, I can get the train from Windermere,' he said, his energy and excitement sparking like electricity.

'Nay, have summat to eat afore you go,' Sylvia begged.

Her plea fell on deaf ears. Thanking them profusely for their hospitality, Oliver left and within the hour he was on the train, on his way back to Verity.

* * *

In Lockwood Mill, the weavers stood idly at their looms waiting for the power to be restored: something to do with the boilers. Isaac was warping Nellie's loom. As he looped the thread from the heddle to the foot, keeping the tension just right, he said, 'Rumour has it that Clarence Hargreaves 'as gone bust. His loom tuner told me that his creditors are hammerin' on the door every day now, and them that works for him have had their wages cut again.'

'I'm not surprised to hear that,' May Sykes said. 'His cloth wa' allus poor quality an' he treats his workers something shocking.'

'Aye, not a bit like Miss Lockwood,' Nellie agreed, her face creasing in sympathy as she added, 'She misses Mr Hardcastle, you know.'

'Eeh, did you hear that Amy Dickenson's back?' Lily butted in, the mention of Oliver's name bringing to mind what she'd heard the previous night. 'She's had the baby. It's a lad.'

This news led to various comments about unmarried mothers, and Amy in particular.

'Do you know who's the father?' Katie mouthed.

'I know she wa' knocking about wi' a chap what wore one o' them hats like Mr Hardcastle wears: you know, a soft hat wi' a floppy brim. I saw 'em more than once canoodling in that passage in our street. I allus thought it wa' him. In fact, I'm fairly sure it wa'.' The purveyor of this information lived close by Amy.

'Mr Hardcastle wouldn't bother wi' the likes of Amy Dickenson,' Nellie protested.

'He's a man like all the others. He'd not say no if she wa' givin' it away for nowt,' Lily scoffed, her eyes opening wide as she blurted, 'Eh! Do you think that's why he left all of sudden, like?'

This opened up a minefield of speculation.

Nellie lapped up the gossip, pleased to hear of Clarence Hargreaves's downfall but not sure what to make of the things the women were saying about Oliver. At breakfast time, she made a point of letting Dolly know what she'd heard. Dolly gave an exultant grin when Nellie told her about Hargreaves, but was seriously concerned to learn that some of the weavers were spreading malicious gossip about Oliver.

Dolly gave some thought as to how she would pass on all that Nellie had said; part of it would need careful handling, but she wasted no time in telling Verity about Clarence Hargreaves. 'It serves him right, Verity, after all the pain he's caused you.'

Verity gave a rueful smile. 'Oliver once told me that Clarence was only interested in me so that he could get his hands on my mill. I was foolish enough to be offended because I thought Oliver was saying that in his opinion, no man could be attracted to me just for myself. Now I know that he was right – just like he was about so many other things.' She shrugged. 'I don't have an iota of sympathy for Hargreaves but I do feel sorry for his workforce.'

'My Mam says you reap what you sow, and it looks as though he's due a bad harvest,' Dolly said. 'He must be spitting tacks knowing that he failed to get you to marry him and bail him out.'

'Clarence Hargreaves can go to hell for all I care. I wouldn't spit on him if he was on fire. He—'

A throaty cough had her looking towards the open office door. Gertie Spragg's bulk filled the opening. The expression on her box-like face was sour.

'Sorry to disturb you, Miss Lockwood,' she said, sounding not in the least contrite, 'but Isaac wants to know how many looms he's to set up wi' that new Jacquard pattern.'

Verity hurried out of the office. Dolly followed her, the opportunity to tell Verity what the women were saying about Oliver and Amy Dickenson lost. She didn't want her to hear it from another source, and whilst Verity was dealing with Isaac, Dolly prayed that she wouldn't overhear any careless chatter. But she would have to tell her sometime, and the sooner, the better.

A while later, when Verity and Dolly had returned to the office, Dolly broached the awkward subject of Oliver. 'There's something else I think you should know,' she began, then recounted the gossip about Oliver and Amy in a manner that let Verity know she didn't believe a word of it. Verity blanched as she listened.

'I thought it best if you heard it from me first,' Dolly said sadly.

'Oliver and Amy Dickenson!' Verity looked stunned. 'Wasn't Amy George's girlfriend... the one who was pregnant and tried to...?'

'Aye, the one who tried to get our George to marry her. She went away to have the baby. But now she's back, the little guttersnipe.' Dolly continued to vilify Amy and assure Verity that Oliver was innocent.

Verity, still reeling from what she had heard, was only half-listening. Maybe she didn't really know Oliver Hardcastle at all. His sister, Rose, had claimed he had an understanding with Lucy Whittaker. Now his name was linked to Amy Dickenson. Was he a ladies' man after all? Had he, like Clarence Hargreaves, been playing her along so that he could get his hands on her mill? It hurt to think that this might be true, but by now, she had recovered her composure and, her thoughts bitter and her voice icy, she said, 'Thank you for telling me, Dolly, but Oliver Hardcastle's affairs are no concern of mine.'

* * *

Clarence Hargreaves was slumped in a corner of the Pack Horse bar slugging whisky and nursing his grievances. It was all the fault of that bitch at Lockwood Mill. Had she accepted his proposal, he wouldn't be in this mess. Instead, she'd belittled him, made a fool of him in front of everyone in the George Hotel, and worst of all, she'd bested him in the Shawcross's garden. As his befuddled, black thoughts strayed to the incident, his fingers strayed to his bloated neck. It was no longer bruised from the pressure of her foot but the memory of the degrading experience still seethed in his mind. God, what would his friends say if they knew about that? He tossed back his whisky, the sharp spirit plummeting into his empty stomach. He'd get even with her if it was the last thing he did.

Calling for another bottle, he continued to drown his sorrows.

Sam Firth shuffled into the Pack Horse, hopeful that somebody would stand him a drink. His pockets were empty. Not since Verity Lockwood had sacked him had he had regular work, and he blamed her for his misfortune. He glanced round the bar looking for someone to sponge off and seeing Hargreaves in his cups, he sidled over and sat down.

'Tha looks miserable, Mister Hargreaves. As miserable as I've been since that rotten bitch that runs Lockwood's gi' me marchin' orders – an' all over nowt.'

Sam's obsequious manner appealed to Clarence, and his tongue loosened by the whisky, he too began denigrating Verity in the foulest terms.

Sam called for the bartender to bring him a glass then, helping himself to a large measure of whisky, he gleefully aided and abetted Clarence. And as Sam continued to play on the hapless mill owner's emotions and refill their glasses again and again, the sacked overseer and the mill owner vowed to seek revenge.

'My sister told me that she heard that Lockwood woman say she wouldn't spit on thee if tha wa' on fire,' Sam said spitefully.

Clarence grunted. 'Fire! Wouldn't spit on me if I was on fire,' he slurred and, swivelling round, he clutched at Sam's shirt, a malevolent gleam in his eye. 'Listen up,' he urged.

* * *

At the same time as Hargreaves and Firth commiserated with each other in the Pack Horse, Oliver was slowly making his way back to Huddersfield. The train from Windermere to Kendal had travelled at snail pace and a missed connection to Manchester had further prolonged the journey. Now, as he stood on the platform at Piccadilly station fuming over the delay and waiting for the next train to Huddersfield, he tried to concentrate on what he would say once he was back at Verity's side. He would not beg forgiveness but he would apologise for his impetuous departure, and he would let her know that he loved her above all else.

* * *

At Lockwood Mill, the hooter blasted, signalling the end of the working day. Verity looked up from the ledger on the desk in front of her and gave Dolly a tired smile. 'You get off with you, Dolly. I'm sure you have plenty of things to see to,' she said, her smile widening.

'Thanks, Miss Lockwood. We're going to look at a house on Carr Pitt this evening for Nellie and George to rent,' Dolly said, her eyes warm with gratitude as she put on her coat.

'I do hope this one meets their approval.' Dolly had made Verity aware of the difficulty they'd had in finding something suitable.

'So do I,' Dolly groaned. 'Every house we've looked at so far has either been rat infested or so damp and mouldy, you'd catch your death within a month, but we've been told this one on Carr Pitt is grand.' She made for the door, pausing to add, 'With only a week to go before the wedding, I was worried that they'd have to start married life living with Mam and Dad.' She pulled a face and giggled. 'Fancy having to spend your first night with your parents listening in on the other side of the bedroom wall.'

Verity chuckled at Dolly's inference as to what couples did when they made love, and fleetingly she wondered if would she ever know what it was like. 'Wish Nellie and George luck from me,' she said, waving Dolly off then turning her attention back to a column of figures.

Gradually, the mill yard fell silent. A short while later, a discreet cough at the office door let her know that Joe was standing there. 'Everywhere's locked up bar t'gate, Miss Lockwood, an' nightwatchman's here. He's in his hut.' He chose not to mention that the fellow was the worse for drink. The poor chap's wife had just run off with a travelling salesman and left him with five children to care for. 'Will you be long?' Joe asked, clunking the huge bunch of keys on the desk with finality.

'You go on, Joe. I'll lock up when I leave.'

'Right you are, Miss. I'll gerroff then.'

Verity continued working. After a while, the columns of figures blurred and she leaned back in her chair. Closing her eyes, she mused on her recent exchange with Dolly. Was there any truth in the gossip about Oliver and Amy? She found it hard to believe. He was so upright and honest in his dealings with everything and when they had been together, she had never doubted his love for her. Now, the very idea that the gossip could be true made her feel ill, and she told herself that she must do her utmost to put it out of her mind. She had too many problems already without adding that one to the list. She had a mill to run.

Even so, she couldn't help recalling Dolly's eager chatter about her wedding. *How exciting it must be to prepare for your wedding day*, she thought with more than a twinge of envy. Tears seeped from under her closed lids and giving a great, gulping sob, she said out loud, 'It could have been me.' With her head lolled back and tears trickling into her hairline, she fell asleep, worn out by the exertions of the day and the constant craving for Oliver.

25

The dark figure made his unsteady way to Lockwood Mill's gate, the cans he carried in either hand heavy and the liquid inside softly sloshing. To his surprise, the gate was ajar and he smiled; it made his job all the easier. Shouldering the gap wider, he slipped into the mill yard then paused and glanced round, his nerves on edge.

Stealthily, he approached the nightwatchman's hut and peered through the grimy window. Syd Cooper was slumped in his chair, head back, his mouth hanging open and his eyes tight shut as he snored peacefully. The intruder gave an ugly grin – another stroke of luck. He hadn't fancied having to bash him over the head. Syd was a big lad and a bit of a brawler.

The man leaned against the wall and tried to slow his thumping heart. *Where to next?* he asked himself muzzily.

Hargreaves had said to start in the baling room – or had he said the raw wool shed?

Sam Firth's befuddled brain was now playing him false. Panic tightened his chest.

Regret at downing one too many whiskies almost made him

turn tail, but the torn half of a five-pound note in his pocket reminded him that he'd only collect the other half when the job was done.

Like a fox preying on a rabbit, he crossed the cobbles and crept to the rear of the mill.

Outside the baling room, he set down the cans, and taking a jemmy from his overall pocket, he forced the door. The crack of splintering wood echoed in the stillness like gunshot. Sam hugged the wall, sweat coursing down his forehead. With trembling hands, he lifted the cans then shuffled inside. It was almost pitch black but Sam had worked too many years in Lockwood Mill to forget the layout of the room: bales of finished cloth to his right and shoddy blankets against the far wall.

He waited for his eyes to adjust to the darkness, his thoughts as black as his surroundings. That hoity-toity heiress was going to get what she deserved. She'd ruined his life. Now he was going to ruin her mill. Cackling throatily, he unscrewed the caps from the cans. Kerosene fumes swirled up into his nose.

Moving cautiously, he began dowsing the bales, the stringent vapour stinging his eyes and its pungent stink making him feel dizzy. Then, eager to get the job over and done with, Sam quickened his movements. Like a man possessed, he began flinging the kerosene with wild abandon, splashing his boots and soaking his jacket sleeves. In a haze of fumes, revenge and fear, he laughed demonically as he fumbled for the box of matches in his pocket.

* * *

Verity woke with a start. The crick in her neck and the ache in her buttocks against the hard chair let her know she wasn't in bed. Rubbing her eyes, she peered into the darkness. The office jumped into shape. How long had she been asleep? Searching her pocket for her fob watch, she was shocked to see its hands pointed at ten minutes past ten. She stood too quickly, her head swimming. Then gathering her wits, she put on her cape and opened the office door.

Out in the dark yard, the air smelled tainted. She looked towards the mill. Sparks like tiny fireflies twinkled in the night sky. 'Oh, my God!' she shrieked. Her mill was on fire.

* * *

Oliver had walked briskly from Huddersfield railway station and had reached Aspley Wharfe when he saw flames shooting up at the rear of Lockwood Mill. Two young men walking towards the town had also spotted the flames. They shouted and pointed to the mill.

'Get the fire brigade! Go, quick as you can,' Oliver yelled.

The men set off running up into the town and Oliver dashed towards the mill gates and into the yard. By now, fire was bursting through the roof of the baling shed and he ran to the rear of the mill. Dense smoke billowed out of the shed's open door, the smell of burning cloth thick on the air. Oliver skidded to a halt and peered into the oily, black clouds. His heart missed a beat.

Through the haze, he saw that Verity was beating at the flames of something burning on the ground. The something writhed and flailed as she lashed out with the large piece of cloth in her hands. Then she fell to her knees, using her cape to smother the flames.

Oliver charged forward, a choking cry erupting from his throat.

Verity was so intent on her task that she did not hear his

approach, and she continued smothering the flames licking at Sam's kerosene-soaked jacket and trousers, the putrid stink of singed flesh strong in her nose.

Suddenly, she was scooped up by a pair of strong arms that felt wonderfully familiar, as did the lips that brushed against her own. The last thing she heard just before she lost consciousness was the strident clanging of bells, the clatter of horses' hooves and the rattle of wheels. The fire engines had arrived.

* * *

Verity opened her eyes. The cream walls of the infirmary slowly came into focus. She felt her own hands being salved by gentle hands and heard a voice saying, 'Back with us are you, Miss Lockwood?'

Verity turned her head and looked into the kindly face of the young nurse who was applying an oily-smelling liquid to Verity's hands. 'It's lime water mixed with linseed,' the nurse said. 'It'll help stop the blistering.' She set the ointment aside and began swathing Verity's right hand in a bandage.

Transfixed, Verity watched the nurse's deft fingers lapping the strip of white gauze and tried not to flinch. The palms of her hands were stinging and her nose and throat were stuffed with the acrid smell of smoke, kerosene fumes and burned flesh. Then it all came rushing back to her in a deluge of terrifying recall. Her mill had been on fire. Again, she saw the horrified face of the burning man as he lurched from the inferno in the baling room, heard his screams and her own as she had beaten out the flames engulfing his flailing body. She began to weep, choking on sobs that wracked her own body. Sam Firth had set fire to her mill.

'Miss Lockwood! Miss Lockwood, please, be still.' The nurse

placed her hands on Verity's shoulders, pushing her back against the pillows and then waiting for her patient to calm down.

When the nurse went away, Verity cried until she was empty. She must have dozed and in her dream-like state, she remembered the feel of strong arms bearing her away from the flames, and the lips that had covered her own.

Another nurse bustled into the screened cubicle, her starched apron swishing with efficiency. 'There's a gentleman waiting to see you, Miss Lockwood. He's been here all night. Would you like me to tidy you up before I let him in?' She cocked her head to one side as she looked Verity up and down.

'Tidy me up?' Verity echoed the nurse's words and looked about her in confusion.

'I'll wash your face, Miss. It's black with soot and your hair's—'

'Is there a mirror?'

The nurse helped Verity out of bed and over to a mirror on the wall. Verity stared aghast at the dirty, bedraggled woman looking back at her. 'Oh, my goodness!' she gasped. 'Yes, please. Tidy me up by all means. I can't meet anyone in this state.' She presumed that the gentleman was a police constable investigating the burning of her mill. In her muddle-headed state, she had not registered the nurse saying that he had been waiting all night.

The nurse washed Verity's face and neck then brushed her tangled hair, leaving it to fall in soot-streaked, chestnut curtains to her shoulders. 'There, that's better,' she said then whisked out of the cubicle. Verity sat back on the edge of the bed and heard her say, 'She'll see you now, sir.'

Oliver walked into the cubicle, stopping uncertainly just

inside the screen. He gazed at Verity, his dark eyes filled with remorse and tenderness.

Verity gasped. 'Oliver.'

'Verity.'

The silence that followed was so deep that she felt she could almost touch it.

'This isn't how I had imagined coming back to you would be,' he said, making no move to come nearer.

'Nor I,' she said, amazed that she could sound so calm when her heart was thudding and the blood in her veins tingling fit to explode. He was here, and a pain like a knife piercing her innards shot through her when she thought of how she had yearned for his return. The misery of all the long lonely nights and days, the strain of running the mill on her own after his sudden departure and the fact that he had not trusted her enough to let her explain what had really happened. All this reared uppermost in her thoughts. Bitterness soured her mind and she turned on him, her eyes ablaze.

'Go away! I don't want to see you,' she said flatly.

Oliver dithered, then stepped forward. 'Please, Verity. Hear me out,' he begged.

'Nurse! Nurse!' Verity shouted as she lost control of her temper.

The nurse hurried in. She took one look at her patient's blazing cheeks, then turned to look at Oliver. He looked like a broken man.

'I do not wish to speak to this gentleman,' Verity told her. 'Please, send him away.'

'I think you'd better leave, sir. You're upsetting Miss Lockwood.'

Oliver gave a despairing shrug and swivelling on his heels, he left.

Verity burst into tears.

* * *

The next day, Verity travelled home to Fair View House in a hackney cab. As the cab rumbled through the streets of the town, she stared aimlessly out of the window, her bandaged hands useless in her lap. She wondered how she would wash or brush her hair. She could just about manage to lift a spoon to her mouth.

When the cab reached Aspley Wharfe, she peered through the window, craning her neck to look to where her mill stood on the riverbank, but they were travelling quickly and before she could ascertain the extent of the damage, the driver swung the cab into Somerset Road.

In Almondbury village, the apple and almond trees were in blossom, the pavements dotted with pale pink and white petals that glowed in the late afternoon sun. Verity thought of confetti. Dolly and Theo, and George and Nellie, were to be married this coming Saturday. What a beautiful time of year for a wedding. She felt tears building behind her eyes and bit down on her lip to stop from crying out loud. She mustn't indulge in such behaviour, she told herself firmly. The emptiness she felt was beyond tears.

For a second, her thoughts returned to the blazing baling room and Sam Firth's squirming body. She felt paralysed, couldn't breathe, the image too painful. Gradually, it faded and she shook her head to dispel the awfulness. Then sitting upright, her shoulders pressed back and her head high, she looked to the future, acknowledging that she had grown independent in Oliver's absence and she determined to be so in the weeks ahead. She had a mill to repair, and she would make it successful again.

With plans of how she would go about restoring the damaged mill crashing inside her head, she was startled when the hackney cab drew to a halt at her front door and the driver called out, 'We're here, Miss Lockwood.' He gave her an anxious look as he opened the cab door and saw her wild-eyed, almost demonic expression. 'Are you all right, Miss?'

Verity jolted back to reality, and giving him a distracted, watery smile, she accepted his assistance and stepped down onto the gravel. 'Thank you. I'll manage from here.'

She stood at the front door watching the cab drive away and suddenly realised that she couldn't turn the large brass knob to let herself in, and she wasn't going to risk trying to lift the heavy knocker. She kicked the base of the door instead.

A few minutes passed before the door flew open, Clara crying, 'Oh. Miss Verity, thank God tha's safe. We were that worried when we heard the mill had gone on fire an' we—' Her words were swallowed in a rush of choking sobs.

'Please, Mrs Medley. Don't cry. It's just my hands that are hurt. I couldn't open the door for myself,' she said, grimacing as she walked into the hallway.

'Eeh, an' look at the state o' thee! Your lovely hair an' your dress.' Clara bobbed round her, distressed by what she saw.

'My hair will wash and the dress is fit only for the rag bag.' Verity kicked out the singed hem, bits of burnt cloth flaking onto the hall floor. 'I need a bath but…' She gestured with her bandaged hands and gave a helpless shrug.

'Never you mind, Miss Verity. I'll see to it. I bathed thee often enough when tha wa' a little girl. I've not forgotten what to do.' Once more in control, Clara led the way upstairs.

* * *

The fire in Verity's bedroom burned brightly and she felt pleasantly weary as she knelt before the blaze. Clara drew the brush through Verity's hair in long, swift strokes, the heat from the fire drying it to a glossy, chestnut sheen. It felt good to be cosseted.

'There we are,' Clara said, setting the brush aside. 'Tha looks more like thi sen now.' She gave a nervous smile. 'I didn't say owt afore 'cos tha needed cleaning up, but Mr Hardcastle's downstairs wi' Bert. He's been here all day waiting to see thee an' I thought—'

'Mr Hardcastle! Here!?' Verity scrambled to her feet.

'Aye, like I said, he wants to see you but I thought tha'd feel better about seein' him if tha wa' more presentable.' Her flushed face said that she knew more than she was letting on. 'Tha will see him, won't thi?' she asked, her eyes pleading.

Verity didn't answer. She went over to the dressing table, in need of a few moments to decide how she felt, and to assess her appearance. Her heart told her that she should run to him but her legs refused to move. He had let her down, hadn't trusted her. Could she ever trust him again? And would he have faith in her? she asked herself. Oliver might have made mistakes, but she too had her faults. In the past, they had always resolved them by talking to each other, but now what would they do? *You'll never know the answer to that if you don't let him have his say,* her reflection told her.

'Show him into the drawing room, Mrs Medley. I'll see him there.'

'Right you are, lovey,' said Clara, her use of the old endearment letting Verity know that in Clara's opinion, it was the right thing to do. Clara scurried off, smiling. Verity looked long and hard at the woman in the mirror, then slowly made her way down to the drawing room.

Oliver was standing by the hearth staring into the fire, his hands clasped behind his back. Verity paused in the doorway, her gaze lingering on his broad shoulders and the loose, black curls at the nape of his neck. She loved this man but...

Sensing her presence, Oliver turned, his dark eyes drinking in the picture of her and his lips curving into a small sad smile. 'Verity,' he said softly.

She walked further into the room, the look on his handsome face and the sound of his gentle voice robbing her of speech. She began to tremble. What would her life be without him? How would she survive?

Oliver stepped forward, his arms reaching out for her.

'Don't touch me!' she murmured, afraid that if he did, she would break into a million pieces because in her heart, she wanted him to do exactly that. But...

Oliver let his arms drop to his sides.

'You left me,' she cried, 'ran away without a thought for my feelings and how much I needed you.' Tears brimmed her eyes. 'You said you loved me, wanted to marry me and...'

Oliver stayed where he was but leaned towards her, his hands held out in supplication and his eyes begging her forgiveness.

'I do love you... please... believe me... I want nothing more than to make you my wife,' he implored as he moved close enough for her to feel his hot breath on her cheeks.

'But what about Amy Dickenson? The girl that the mill hands are saying gave birth to your child? Did you go to be with her?'

Oliver looked absolutely dumbfounded. 'Who? I don't understand. I don't know the girl. I didn't go away for that reason.'

Verity's veins flooded with relief. She knew him well enough to know that he was telling the truth. 'Then why did you leave me? Why did you not trust me? I believed in you, Oliver.'

It was a cry from the heart. But he had shattered her faith in him. She shuddered, and choking on the words, she said, 'I don't need you in my life.' Then, as if she had found an inner strength that had turned her heart to steel, she snapped, 'Just go! Go, and don't come back.'

The icy command brought Oliver up sharp. He glared at her, then barked, 'What did you expect me to do? I'd heard the rumours about you and Hargreaves and tried to ignore them. Then when I came to the hotel, I found you in the arms of the bastard. What was I supposed to think?' A pulse in his temple throbbed and he looked so broken that Verity's rage suddenly melted.

'You could have asked me for the truth of it,' she said softly.

Oliver hung his head. He could not meet her gaze.

Shrouded in silence, they were each thinking the same thing: that although their devotion to each other had never waned, they had somehow stopped talking and listening to one another. Realising this and what they were about to lose if they continued in this way made them both tremble.

There was tension between them and a spark that had nothing to with the anger they had both felt. Oliver raised his head and looked deep into Verity's eyes but he didn't move. Verity's pulse was racing and her legs felt weak. He was standing so close that she could have reached out and touched his face, traced the line of his strong jaw or smoothed back the unruly lock of black hair that fell on his forehead as she had done so many times before. She gazed into his dark eyes and felt as though she was drowning.

'Oh, Oliver, what are we doing to one another?' The words came out in a deep sigh.

'Oh, my darling girl, my precious love,' he groaned, and taking her in his arms, he gently pulled her to his chest. They stayed that way for some time, lost in the moment. Verity felt safe, back where she belonged. Dizzy with relief, she heard her heart thumping with joy against the rapid beat of Oliver's and it was so heavenly, she thought that she might be dreaming. She held on to him, trembling at how close she had come to losing him, and feeling furious with herself that they had let others come between them. When she pulled away from him, they gazed into each other's faces, their expressions saying that never again would they let anything like this happen to them.

* * *

That night, Verity slept deeply and did not waken to sour dreams. Oliver was back and she felt whole again. When he arrived at Far View shortly before midday, her heart soared.

'I've been to the mill,' he said. 'I've also spoken with the police.'

Verity led the way into the drawing room and they sat on the couch, Oliver telling her what the police had told him. Sam Firth had confessed that Hargreaves paid him to set fire to the mill, and further enquiries had uncovered enough evidence for them to believe this to be true. 'Apparently, Hargreaves broke down when they interviewed him,' he concluded with a wry smile.

Verity returned the smile. It felt good that she wasn't having to deal with this all on her own and she cupped his face in her hands and kissed him. He kissed her back, and at the feel of her bandaged hands rough against his cheeks, he covered her hands with his, the fear of what could have happened creasing his face and thickening his voice as he said, 'Whatever were you thinking? You could have been killed.'

'Much as I hate Sam Firth, I couldn't stand by and watch him burn to death,' Verity replied. 'And now that I know he was a pawn in Clarence Hargreaves's evil plan, I'm glad I saved him.'

'Sam will never work again, and Hargreaves is ruined. The police have him under arrest and even if they don't find him guilty, he'll not be able to hold up his head in the valley if I know the other mill owners as I think I do. Firing a mill is tantamount to treason.'

'How much damage has been done?' Verity's voice shook and her desolate expression let Oliver know that she dreaded hearing what he was about to say. He lifted her chin, his thumb caressing the cleft and his eyes willing her to be brave.

'Not as much as you might think, my darling. Of course, the baling and the finishing rooms are completely destroyed and we've lost all our cloth, but the fire brigade stopped it from spreading further, thank God.' Oliver gave a little shrug. 'Unfortunately, there's some damage to the engine and the dynamo so we've neither water nor electricity to keep production going. The looms will be idle for some time.'

'My poor mill. What will we do about it?' Verity asked bleakly as she snuggled closer to Oliver, seeking comfort in his strength.

'We'll put it right. We saved it before and we can do it again.' His confidence was such that Verity didn't doubt him. Even so, she did see it as daunting and she worried that if they failed, their employees would be the first to suffer. Then she looked at Oliver.

'With you by my side, I can do anything,' she said, holding his hand to her cheek.

* * *

The bells of All Hallows Church peeled out a welcome to the wedding guests and the women and girls who spectated at every wedding. The sun was shining, the April sky a clean, blue sheet, and the beech, oak and ash trees in the churchyard flourishing the first show of leaves, the greenery a delightful backdrop to the medieval church. As Verity and Oliver walked past the assembled crowd, she resisted the temptation to rush wildly from one person to the next, passionately exclaiming, 'This man by my side loves me. Soon it will be our wedding day.' Even so, they had yet to make a public announcement.

Instead, she strolled by on Oliver's arm, and as they stepped out of the sunlight into the gloom and sanctity of the ancient church, she offered up a silent prayer thanking God for her deliverance from all the hurt and misery that had been hers for far too long.

Theo and George stood at the altar, two broad backs dressed in jackets made out of Lockwood's finest dark grey worsted and tailored by Ruddimans in response to an urgent request from Verity. A flurry of excitement at the door announced that the brides had arrived. All heads turned. The organ trumpeted. Dolly and Nellie walked sedately down the aisle followed by two of Nellie's younger sisters.

Dolly's red locks, crowned with a circlet of flowers intertwined with dark green ivy, streamed over her shoulders like a veil of fire, and her gauzy white gown made from butter muslin showed off her slender curves. Nellie looked sweetly demure in a gown made from the same stuff, but hers featured a full skirt with a ruffled hem and a pretty, heart-shaped neck. A little hat with a lacy veil covered her mouse-brown hair. Both girls a vision of loveliness, they took their places at the altar by the sides of their prospective husbands.

Theo gazed in awe at Dolly, love shining from his eyes. She gazed back, her green eyes twinkling wickedly as if to say, *We've overcome every obstacle and won. Nothing can stop us now.*

Nellie looked shyly up into George's face and saw love mixed with pride as he whispered, 'You are beautiful.'

Verity listened intently to the marriage service for soon she would be exchanging her own vows with Oliver. Silently, she made solemn promise to be a loving and faithful wife, that theirs would be a partnership not only at the mill but in every aspect of their lives. Then letting her imagination run riot, she pictured Oliver waiting for her at the altar, handsome in a dark suit, his jaw firm and his eyes looking into her own. She couldn't quite see herself but she knew for certain that she wouldn't look like a gawky, ugly girl. She would look beautiful because that was how Oliver made her feel, and that feeling was just wonderful.

The vicar seemed to be in a tizz. He'd never handled a double wedding before. *Most unusual,* he kept thinking, his pouched cheeks flushed with exertion as he repeated over and again the solemn words. At one point, Dolly took a fit of giggles. Theo suppressed his own mirth and gave her a dig with his elbow. Then, slipping the thin, gold band on her finger, he looked so deeply into her eyes that her heart flipped, and as she returned his gaze, Theo's heart felt as though it might burst.

George, sombrely nervous, and Nellie, shy and feeling as though she was dreaming, made their vows and when the vicar pronounced, 'I now declare you man and wife,' the congregation cheered. The strains of the wedding march thundered from the organ loft and the newlyweds walked back down the aisle bestowing radiant smiles on their friends and relatives.

Halfway towards the door, Dolly paused and, catching Verity's eye, she gave her a nod and a smile that seemed to say, *See, I was right. I told you Oliver would come back.* Verity's heart swelled with fondness for this girl who had shown her true friendship.

* * *

'How long do you think it'll be afore we're back to work?' Lily Cockhill asked Dolly when she met her a few days after the fire at the mill. 'I've bills to pay, an' wi nowt comin' in now, both me an' him are laid off, I'm at me wits' end.'

'Oliver's doing his best to get things up and running again, but he told me that the electrics were damaged and there's a lot of cleaning up to do before production can start again.' Dolly gave the woman she'd once worked alongside in the weaving shed before she married Theo a sympathetic smile.

Lily looked even more despondent. 'An' how's Miss Lockwood?'

'Her hands are healing nicely but her chest's still bothering her. She inhaled a lot of smoke, you know.'

'Brave lass. I'd have let that bugger, Sam Firth, burn to death after what he did,' Lily said, regaining some of her usual fiery spirit.

Dolly shuddered as she thought how close Verity had come to being seriously injured.

Then she said, 'Verity Lockwood always has other people's best interests at heart.' And all at once, that remark gave her an idea. When she put it to Lily, it met with her full approval.

Oliver could hardly believe his eyes when, the next morning, he met Dolly and a large group of laid-off mill hands at the mill gate. Looking askance at Dolly, he said, 'The mill's still closed, and what are you doing here?'

'We're here to help,' Dolly told him. 'We reckon that after all

Verity has done for us, it's the least we can do. She always treated us with respect and cared for our welfare. She made this mill a place where you were glad to work, so now we're returning that kindness.'

The mill hands cheered as they trooped through the gates to do whatever was asked of them.

When the mill resumed production far sooner than expected, and Verity was feeling well enough to return to work, she did so with a full heart. The smiling faces that greeted her as she did her rounds of the mill brought tears to her eyes and she felt humbled to be held in such high regard.

* * *

On a glorious day in June at half-past ten in the morning, almost the entire workforce gathered outside the closed gates of Lockwood Mill. There was no hum of machinery, no carts trundling up and down the yard, or men and women to-ing and fro-ing between the sheds. Lockwood Mill was closed.

It had been Dolly's idea for them to assemble there so that they could walk together to All Hallows Church in Almondbury, but seeing as she was elsewhere, it was Nellie who was doing the organising. Thrilled to be given such an important task, Nellie strutted among the crowd making sure that everyone was on their best behaviour. The mill hands, dressed in their best, buzzed with excitement. Today was a very special day.

'Right, everybody. Listen up,' Nellie shouted above the noise, and when the chatter died, she gave the weavers, spinners, carders and dyers, and all the other employees their orders. 'When we get to the church, we'll form lines either side of the road and the path leading up to the church door, and after the ceremony, we'll do the same to show our respect for Miss Lockwood and Mr Hardcastle.'

The mill hands cheered then set off walking at a brisk pace to make sure they arrived in time for the marriage service at 11 o'clock. They were looking forward to seeing their mill mistress and her manager get wed, not to mention the spread that awaited them in the mill canteen for afterwards.

In Far View House, Verity carefully fixed her long white veil over her glossy chestnut hair. *Leave your hair undone,* Oliver had tentatively suggested, and Verity knew that he meant for her to let it flow over her shoulders rather than dress it in the neat rolls she wore every day. She'd smiled when he'd said it. That Oliver thought she was beautiful and wanted her to look her best was still nothing short of a miracle. She had resigned herself to believing that she would never meet a man who considered her attractive enough to want to make her his wife. Her father had convinced her of that.

Smiling ruefully, she secured the veil with a final pin. Then standing back and gazing into the mirror, she softly said, 'Well, Jebediah Lockwood, your great gawky girl has found a fine, handsome man who wants to marry her. What do you think to that?'

Would he have baulked at her marrying his mill manager, a man without a fortune? she wondered as she went over to the bed and picked up the small satin purse containing her mother's prayer book. Or would he have been glad to get her off his hands, and celebrate by getting rip-roaring drunk? Most likely, she thought wryly, as footsteps on the stairs let her know that Dolly was on her way back from dealing with Verity's Aunt Flora, her husband and daughters who had arrived from Leeds earlier that morning.

'I've sent them on their way to the church,' Dolly said as she burst into the bedroom, her eyes glinting mischievously. 'The last thing you want is your Aunt Flora fussing over you and telling you how you should have done things.' Dolly tilted her nose and mockingly adopted an exaggerated refined manner of speech. 'Why only one bridesmaid? Magda had eight and Ivy six, and as for holding the reception in a mill canteen, I never heard the like of it. Why not the George or the Imperial hotel?'

Verity laughed out loud. 'Oh, Dolly, you are such an inspiration.' She had not seen her aunt since leaving Leeds although she had written to her on a couple of occasions. Flora had pleaded a cold and hadn't attended Jeb's funeral, but a wedding was a different matter and she had been agog to come and arrange it; after all, she didn't think her niece would have much idea. Then the conversation had gone something like this.

'You will of course be asking your cousins to be bridesmaids.'

'No Aunt, I will not. It's to be a simple affair.'

'Is that because of your difference in station? He works for you – you pay his wages.'

'I could never pay Oliver what he is truly worth.'

Flora had arrived that morning expecting to take over the proceedings, even at that late stage. Verity had made it quite plain that she required no assistance and sought sanctuary in her bedroom, leaving Dolly to fend off her relatives.

'Pamela's green with envy that you've made it to the altar before she has,' Dolly chirped as she adjusted Verity's veil.

'Serves her right,' said Verity, remembering the cruel jibes the youngest of Aunt Flora's daughters had often delivered. 'She used to taunt me something shocking about my height, and constantly remind me that she was far prettier.'

'Not now, she's not,' Dolly stoutly declared. 'She's a dumpy little baggage with a sour face. None of your cousins hold a candle to you, Verity.'

'Oh, Dolly, you say the nicest things.' Swallowing threatening tears and careful not to crease her gown, Verity gave Dolly a warm hug. 'I was feeling terribly nervous about today but you give me the confidence I so badly need. You always have done.'

'You don't need me to bolster your confidence. You're as brave as a lion,' Dolly praised. 'Look at the way you pulled the mill back from bankruptcy, and saved it from being burned to the ground. You're a woman to be reckoned with.' Dolly gave Verity a beaming smile. 'You made a difference to my life and the lives of all the women who work for you,' Dolly continued, 'and you deserve all the happiness in the world.' This time, it was she who delivered a fond embrace. 'Now, come on, the carriage is at the door and it's time we got you to the church. Mr Hardcastle's waiting for you.'

* * *

The carriage, pulled by a white horse with a plumed headdress, slowly made its way down Far View Hill and as it descended, Verity gazed up at Castle Hill and the recently completed tower. She hadn't attended the opening ceremony in March – it had somehow seemed wrong without Oliver being there. Now, built to commemorate Queen Victoria's Diamond Jubilee, at eighty feet tall, it dominated the landscape and was the pride of the Huddersfield Corporation. But to Verity, it seemed to symbolise her own meteoric rise to the happiness she was feeling right now.

When the carriage reached All Hallows Church, an almighty cheer went up from the men and women lining the paths, the men doffing their caps and the women waving the tails of their shawls. Verity gave a gasp of delight, and Dolly a satisfied smile. Nellie had followed her orders.

'Oh, my goodness! I never expected this.'

Verity's surprise made Dolly laugh.

'They're showing their respect for you, Verity.'

The coachman opened the carriage door and Dolly stepped down, as pretty as a picture in a green silk dress she and Verity had chosen in Rushworth's Bazaar. She held out her hand to Verity and teasingly asked, 'Now is Miss Lockwood ready to become Mrs Hardcastle?'

Verity took Dolly's hand and alighted from the carriage, her white satin gown shimmering in the bright sunshine as she walked towards the church gate, Dolly at her heels. Oohs and aahs erupted from the lips of the spectators when they saw the bride. The gown's sheathed skirt enhanced her height, and its high-necked, pointed collar and long, tight sleeves that also ended in points over the backs of her hands made Verity look as regal as an Arthurian queen. Tall and stately, she walked between the lines formed by her smiling employees, acknowledging them with smiles and nods of her own.

'My, my, if it isn't Queen Guinevere,' a literary chap in the crowd said out loud.

'Nay, it's not,' his neighbour told him, giving him a cock-eyed look. 'It's Verity Lockwood, her what inherited Jeb Lockwood's mill.'

Inside the church porch, Verity and Dolly stepped to one side to allow the workers to file in, and Dolly made a last-minute check on Verity's appearance. 'You look beautiful,' she said, adjusting the veil that flowed down Verity's back.

'I feel beautiful,' said Verity, a sad little smile flitting across her face. 'My father told me I was too big and ugly to ever be a man's bride, but I've proved him wrong.'

'Oh, Verity, he was wrong about a lot more than that,' Dolly said; her voice was rich with sincerity. 'You are a daughter he would be proud of if only he could see you now and know all that you've done for his mill.' She poked her head round the open door and told the church warden, 'Let the organist know we're ready,' and then turning back to Verity, she said, 'It's time to make Mr Hardcastle the happiest man in the world.'

The organ pealed, and Verity began walking down the aisle feeling as though all the love and the joy in life was hers.

Aunt Flora tutted; she really should have insisted that Verity let her uncle give her away, but Verity had told her in no uncertain terms that she wasn't a piece of property, and that she was quite happy to walk to the altar without him.

Oliver turned to watch her approach. Their eyes met. He gave her a look full of love and admiration. She returned the look with one of wonder, her dove-grey eyes pooling with tears. She blinked them away and went to stand beside the man who had made her life complete.

Then, their vows made and the register signed, Verity and Oliver went out into the sunlight to be met by a cheering crowd of mill workers showing their respect for the mill heiress and her manager. Verity's heart swelled. Their smiles and warm wishes seemed to say that they knew their livelihoods were safe in the hands of the newly married couple, that Lockwood Mill would continue to thrive and prosper.

And secure in Oliver's love for her, Verity knew that she would do the same.

* * *

MORE FROM CHRISSIE WALSH

Another heartbreaking historical saga from Chrissie Walsh, *The Workhouse Lass*, is available to order now here:
https://mybook.to/WorkhouseLassBackAd

ACKNOWLEDGEMENTS

Behind every book that reaches the shelves there is an army of dedicated agents, publishers, editors and marketers. Therefore, I'd like to give a massive thanks to my wonderful agent, Judith Murdoch, and the Boldwood team for their unstinting support.

In particular I must show my appreciation for Sarah Ritherdon, Boldwood's Publishing Director, and to my editors, Emily Ruston and Emily Reader. Their friendly, good-humoured and brilliant advice are priceless. Thanks also to Rose Fox for her superb proofreading and Claire Fenby and her marketeers who continue to provide fabulous covers and promote my work. Finally, thank you, Amanda Ridout, for heading-up the magnificent Boldwood team.

ABOUT THE AUTHOR

Chrissie Walsh was born and raised in West Yorkshire and is a retired schoolteacher with a passion for history. She has written several successful sagas documenting feisty women in challenging times.

Sign up to Chrissie Walsh's mailing list here for news, competitions and updates on future books.

Follow Chrissie on social media:

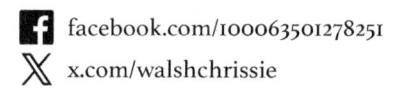

facebook.com/100063501278251
x.com/walshchrissie

ALSO BY CHRISSIE WALSH

The Weaver Street Series

Welcome to Weaver Street

Hard Times on Weaver Street

Weaver Street at War

The Lockwood Inheritance Series

A New Dawn for the Mill Girls

Standalone Novels

The Midwives' War

The Orphan's Heartbreak

The Workhouse Lass

Sixpence Stories

Introducing Sixpence Stories!

Discover page-turning historical novels from your favourite authors, meet new friends and be transported back in time.

Join our book club Facebook group

https://bit.ly/SixpenceGroup

Sign up to our newsletter

https://bit.ly/SixpenceNews

Boldwood

Boldwood Books is an award-winning fiction publishing company seeking out the best stories from around the world.

Find out more at www.boldwoodbooks.com

Join our reader community for brilliant books, competitions and offers!

Follow us

@BoldwoodBooks

@TheBoldBookClub

Sign up to our weekly deals newsletter

https://bit.ly/BoldwoodBNewsletter

Printed in Dunstable, United Kingdom